THE
TERMINAL
LIST

Center Point
Large Print

| Books are produced in the United States using U.S.-based materials | Books are printed using a revolutionary new process called THINKtech™ that lowers energy usage by 70% and increases overall quality | Books are durable and flexible because of Smyth-sewing | Paper is sourced using environmentally responsible foresting methods and the paper is acid-free |

This Large Print Book carries the Seal of Approval of N.A.V.H.

THE
TERMINAL
LIST

JACK CARR

CENTER POINT LARGE PRINT
THORNDIKE, MAINE

This Center Point Large Print edition
is published in the year 2018 by arrangement with
Atria Books, an imprint of Simon & Schuster, Inc.

The text of this Large Print edition is unabridged.
In other aspects, this book may vary
from the original edition.
Printed in the United States of America
on permanent paper.
Set in 16-point Times New Roman type.

ISBN: 978-1-68324-943-6

Library of Congress Cataloging-in-Publication Data

Names: Carr, Jack (Joint pseudonym) author.
Title: The terminal list / Jack Carr.
Description: Center Point Large Print edition. | Thorndike, Maine :
    Center Point Large Print, 2018.
Identifiers: LCCN 2018033696 | ISBN 9781683249436
    (hardcover : alk. paper)
Subjects: LCSH: United States. Navy. SEALs—Fiction. |
    Serial murders—Fiction. | Political corruption—Fiction. |
    Retribution—Fiction. | Large type books.
Classification: LCC PS3603.A774235 T4 2018b | DDC 813/.6—dc23
LC record available at https://lccn.loc.gov/2018033696

For the Soldiers, Sailors, Airmen, and Marines who didn't make it back, and for our children, who are not yet old enough to read this.

There's a Man Goin' Round Taking Names
—Author Unknown

THE
TERMINAL
LIST

PREFACE

This is a novel of revenge.

The Terminal List explores what could happen when an apex predator, a warrior at the top of his game, is thrown into a situation from which there is no return. It is about what could happen when societal norms, laws, regulations, morals, and ethics give way for a man of extraordinary capability, hardened by war, and set on a course of reckoning; a man who is, for all practical purposes, already dead.

This work would not exist without the efforts of my dear friend and writing partner, Keith Wood. Though his name does not appear on the book jacket, this book is as much his as it is mine. On a handshake at SHOT Show in Vegas, we decided to fulfill our shared lifelong dream of writing a novel. This is the result.

Due to the sensitive nature of the security clearances I held while in the military as a Navy SEAL, I am required to submit any written material intended for public release, including works of fiction, to the Department of Defense. In order to fulfill that obligation lawfully, this manuscript was submitted to the DOD Office of Prepublication and Security Review and was "cleared as amended" by that office. Throughout the writing process, I took great pains to ensure no tactics, techniques, or procedures were compromised. The last thing I want to do is give the enemy something that could possibly give them an advantage on the battlefield. The government review process exists for a reason, and having had the honor of defending this great nation at war, I am still bound by my former clearances to have my writing reviewed. The government's redactions are included as amended and are blacked out in the novel.

While this is a work of fiction, each scene draws from emotions that I experienced during real world events over twenty years in the military. Those emotions, coupled with time in combat, add an authenticity to the novel that we hope makes for a thrilling reading experience.

Though my time as a SEAL certainly influenced our choice of a protagonist, I am not James Reece. He is more skilled, witty, and intelligent than I could ever hope to be. Though I am not James Reece, I understand him. He has the experience, training, skill, and drive to administer justice on his terms.

This is also a book about control. The consolidation of power at the federal level in the guise of public safety is a national trend and should be guarded against at all costs. This erosion of rights, however incremental, is the slow death of freedom. We have reached a point where the power of the federal government is such that they can essentially target anyone of their choosing. Recent allegations that government agencies may have targeted political opponents should alarm all Americans, regardless of party affiliation. Revisionist views of the Constitution by opportunistic politicians and unelected judges with agendas that reinterpret the Bill of Rights to take power away from the people and consolidate it at the federal level threaten the core principles of the Republic. As a free people, keeping federal power in check is something that should be of concern to us all. The fundamental value of freedom is what sets us apart from the rest of the world. We are citizens, not subjects, and we must stay ever vigilant that we remain so.

Jack Carr
August 6, 2017
Park City, Utah

PROLOGUE

It didn't take a tactical genius to pick the spot. Humans are creatures of habit and some were more religious about it than others. Accountants, it seemed, were practically monastic in their routines. From June 1 to November 1 of every year, Marcus Boykin lived in his mountain house in Star Valley Ranch, Wyoming. Star Valley sounded far more appealing to the east and west coast real estate buyers than its previous name of Starvation Valley. It was an enclave of wealthy outsiders in otherwise rural western Wyoming, stuck into the mountainside like a well-manicured finger of civilization, full of multimillion-dollar homes in a part of the world otherwise populated by ranchers and cowboys.

Every Monday, Wednesday, and Friday, Boykin rose early and climbed into his silver Mercedes G550 SUV to drive the fifty miles to the relative metropolis of Jackson. With a summertime population of bankers and hedge fund managers that would rival the Hamptons, it was the only place within hours where he could eat a gourmet meal with an eight-hundred-dollar bottle of wine. In Jackson he could sip lattes and read the *Wall Street Journal* in the company of fellow seasonal residents from New York, Greenwich, Boston, and Los Angeles. Three days a week he could connect with real people in person instead of waiting impatiently for his friends to comment on his Facebook posts. Dinners at Rendezvous Bistro were far tastier and the conversation more stimulating than his usual meal alone on the deck, no matter how spectacular the view.

U.S. 89 runs north and south through the steep valley that straddles the line between Wyoming and Idaho. Irrigated hayfields near the roadway lie in the shadows of the rugged ten-thousand-foot peaks to the east and more gentle hills to the west. Just north of the tiny town of Alpine, the route to Jackson turns east along the Snake River and winds into the mountains of the Bridger-Teton National Forest. At this point in the journey, the jagged ridgelines of the Tetons run nearly to the roadside, like towering cruise ships moored alongside an asphalt pier. Ten feet from the well-maintained road was terrain as rugged as nearly anywhere in the Lower 48, the home of trophy mule deer and giant elk as well as plenty of black bears and the occasional moose. Having never touched a gun or hunted in his life, it would never occur to Boykin that September 15, the opening day of deer season in Wyoming's Region G, fell on a Monday that year.

James Reece had hiked in the previous afternoon from a trailhead on the opposite side of the mountain from the U.S. highway. The trail began near the road as the crow flies, but was many miles away by vehicle. The vistas of the highway were as close to the remote backcountry as most seasonal residents like Boykin ventured. Though it was only a few hours' hike from his truck, Reece may as well have walked in from a different world. He wore a light pack with a nylon rifle scabbard strapped to the side, high-performance digital camo hunting clothing from Sitka, and the Salomon hiking boots he had worn on countless operations around the world. Walking through the Wyoming backcountry in the traditional sniper's woolly ghille suit and heavyweight rifle, he would stick out like a man wandering the mountains in a tuxedo, but clad in the garb of a hunter, he was as invisible as a guy in a blue blazer at the airport. The anonymous tip that he'd called in about the moose poachers just south of Jackson would probably occupy every game department cop in the region, but in the unlikely event that he ran into someone of authority, the hunting license and deer tag in his pocket would verify him as just another hunter out looking for mulies on the busiest day of the year.

He could have hiked in at night with a head-lamp or brought along his night vision, but he wanted to get into his spot before dark. No sense twisting an ankle or worse in this rough country, and he was anxious to get started. He had studied the topography on maps and satellite imagery hundreds of times, but he'd still hiked the route two days earlier to ensure that it looked the same on the ground as it did from the air.

The country was steep and high. It didn't matter how well you were conditioned at sea level, eight thousand feet was still eight thousand feet. He stopped to catch his breath and guzzle water from the hose clipped to his shoulder strap. His legs burned and his lungs were starved for oxygen. His base layer was covered in sweat despite temperatures in the fifties, so he zipped his top down to let some of his body heat escape. He wasn't in a rush, but he moved with purpose. It certainly wasn't the first time he had pushed himself up a mountain to a target.

His perch was just as he'd left it, a small U-shaped slot eroded into the mountainside that could only be accessed from the front. There was very little chance of a hunter or game warden wandering up on his six while he was in position, and he'd have a clear view of anyone approaching from the front long before they reached his hide site. The spot overlooked a saddle of highway that ran between two steep hills. His position was near the top of the second hill if you were driving toward Jackson.

Like a cave without a roof, the spot would protect him from the prying eyes of hunters

18

glassing for deer the afternoon before the season opened and would keep him out of the wind as the temperature dropped into the low thirties overnight. He pulled his rifle out of the scabbard and laid his pack down just short of the mouth of the slot so his muzzle would not be visible from below. The rifle was an Echols Legend, built by a master in Utah whose handmade rifles sold for several months of his Navy salary. It was a gift from his father after his first post-9/11 deployment and was one of his most prized possessions. He had planned to hunt more after he retired and entered the private sector. The rifle was chambered in .300 Winchester Magnum and, despite weighing far less than the sniper rifles he'd used overseas, was even more accurate. Instead of a traditional hunting scope, he had installed a Nightforce NXS 2.5-10x32mm, the same glass he used at work. The pack supported the rifle's forend and a small beanbag steadied the butt. Lying prone, with the front and back of the rifle supported, he was able to hold the rifle as steady as any bench rest. As cars and trucks crested the hill to his west, he would dry-fire at the driver's position of the windshield to get the timing right. The vacationers and local residents traveling this mountain road in the fall afternoon had no idea that they were in the crosshairs of one of the nation's deadliest warriors.

Satisfied that his position was solid and that

he'd have the right angle on the target, he retreated to the back of his mountain cubby and fired up his backpacking stove to heat water for his freeze-dried dinner. When the sun dropped below the skyline and the temperature fell by double digits, he crawled into his sleeping bag. He thought about his little girl, all blond curls, tears welling up in her brave blue eyes as she saw daddy off on his last deployment. Six months away and he would be home for good, *promise*. He could still see her face, pressed up against the airport glass for one last look as he boarded the plane. The hardest parts of a deployment were the first couple of weeks when you'd just left home, and the last couple when you started anticipating your return. That it was his last trip overseas made the light at the end of the tunnel brighter. Finally the end of the train/deploy/train treadmill he and his SEAL brothers had been on for well over a decade.

Curled up in his sleeping bag underneath a light show of stars that a city dweller couldn't comprehend, he slept sounder than he had in weeks. No waking up to realize that the nightmare was real. No reaching across the bed for a wife who wasn't there. No hearing the soft cries of a daughter who would never again crawl into his bed for protection from the boogeyman.

He was already awake, staring at Orion, when his watch chirped at 0500. A swig from his water bottle and an energy bar would be his breakfast. He got into position behind his rifle and waited patiently for the sun to rise.

Marcus Boykin was an early riser, as was nearly everyone in the financial sector. You were either up and at the table in his line of work, or you were asleep and on the menu. He looked at the weather forecast on his iPhone before slipping on a pair of designer jeans and some tan Italian loafers. He wore a Patagonia fleece over his pink Lacoste polo and put on a Yankees cap to hide his bald spot from the twenty-something waitress he was currently trying to bed. To him, she wasn't Sarah with the degree in environmental engineering working to save up for her master's, she was "the waitress." He'd been unsuccessful in getting into her pants so far, but she was broke and he was rich. One night, sooner or later, she'd get drunk and slip up, and he'd be there to take advantage. Living this far out was part of the challenge, though he knew that to better his chances he might have to get a condo in town at some point to help seal the deal. He grabbed his keys from the marble kitchen counter and pressed the remote start. It was freezing, and Boykin wanted the SUV nice and toasty with the heater running and the seats warmed by the time he made his to-go coffee and headed out. He opened his giant oak front door and took out his phone to tweet a photo of the orange glow of sunrise making its way over the mountain before he lost Wi-Fi coverage; the cell service was crap until you got to Jackson. He didn't really care about the view. In his mind the sun would do the same thing tomorrow, but it would make his friends on both coasts jealous, a thought that he relished. As he climbed into the SUV and headed down the mountain road to U.S. 89, his mind turned to thoughts of what he'd say to the waitress when he saw her.

Combat is sensory overload, total chaos, especially if you're in command. The noise is deafening, both from the incoming and outgoing fire, while the overpressure of muzzle blasts and explosions rock your body down to its DNA. Men are yelling, not out of fear or panic, but to communicate above the roar. Tracers come in, rockets fly past, dust from explosions and bullet strikes shroud your immediate world in a tactile cloud of dust. Radio traffic in your ears adds to the storm and demands a conscious response, which means one's actions in the moment must be subconscious. Identifying targets, firing weapons, changing magazines: all must happen automatically, as seamless as steering, shifting gears, and working the gas pedal of a car while talking on a cell phone. As a leader, you must rise even further above the storm and look beyond your own survival. You must direct the fire and movement of the entire element and resist the instinct to become just another gun in the fight. The whole thing is one tachy-psyche blur of constant decision making.

This was the opposite of chaos. Reece's senses registered nothing unnatural, just the calm of aspens in the breeze and the relaxing melody of wildlife easing into another day to a beautiful mountain sunrise. There was no radio, no one to communicate with, just the occasional hum of a car or pickup on the asphalt of the highway. The range to the dip in the road was exactly 625 yards, which meant that the bullet would drop eighty-six inches in its path from his barrel to the target. The rifle's scope was zeroed for 100 yards, so he would have to compensate for the difference. He came up 14 clicks, 1.4 MILS, to make up for the drop. By dialing for the range, there would be no holdover. He could put the center of the reticle right on the target. *Fight with every advantage you can get.* The winds were light this early in the morning, which was a good thing. Wind calls were always tricky in the mountains, even for a pro. The Kestrel told him it was blowing two miles per hour from his left, a full-value wind that required six inches of hold. Since winds could shift at any moment, he used the MIL-DOT reticle to "hold off" for the 0.3 MILS.

He heard the hum of the tires even before

the blue halogen headlights haloed above the highway as the SUV climbed the rise. The silver Mercedes was unmistakably Boykin's; thank God this guy didn't drive an F-150. The vehicle was coming straight at him, which meant no lead was required, but it was still hauling ass. He didn't have much time to admire the success of his planning. He tracked the target as it came down the hill, just as he'd done with the two other vehicles that had passed earlier that morning. He took a full breath, briefly rested at its peak, then exhaled to find his natural respiratory pause when his lungs had expended their air, steadying and focusing him for the task at hand. Doing so caused the movement of the scope's reticle to slow from an orbit to a small tremor. Even with a solid rest, it was never as steady as in the movies. The Mercedes hit the flat spot and appeared to stop for a second as he lost the perspective of its forward progress. He couldn't see the driver, not at this range and certainly not in this light. Holding just right of the windshield's center, he slowly pressed the trigger.

His ears heard the shot but his brain barely registered the sound. His only sensation of recoil was the scope's image jolting into a blur as the rifle rocked skyward. Despite putting rounds into countless men in shitty corners of the world, his body still jolted into "fight or flight" mode, adrenaline surging into his body like a shot of heroin. He had killed plenty of men with his country's blessing in the past, but this time pressing the trigger meant breaking the most sacred bond of society; he'd just committed murder.

The monolithic bullet was a Barnes Triple Shock, made from solid copper and scored inside the tiny hollow point to split into four petals upon impact like a deadly flower. It was engineered to penetrate deeply on big game animals and worked so well that special operations troops adopted it for use during the Global War on Terror. When it hit the nearly vertical glass windshield of the Mercedes, the petals sheared off, leaving a cylinder of copper a third of an inch in diameter and still moving faster than most handgun rounds do at the muzzle. It struck Boykin on the bridge of his nose, and angled downward slightly as it smashed cartilage, brain, and bone into jelly. It severed the first vertebra and exited the back of his neck looking much like it did on the way in, before punching through the leather headrest and terminating its flight in the foam cushioning of the backseat.

The Mercedes's cruise control was set on sixty miles per hour when its driver's brain ceased sending command signals to his body. His limbs quivered and jerked the way most animals and humans do when shot in the central nervous system, but the Teutonic engineering of the SUV kept the wheels traveling straight up the rise of the highway as if nothing had happened. When it roared past Reece's position, he thought for a second that he'd missed. As the vehicle crested the rise, having accelerated to make up for the steep grade, Boykin's lifeless body shifted forward in his restraint and caused the wheel to turn sharply to the left. The forward momentum, downward slope, and the SUV's high center of gravity created a snowball effect and caused the Mercedes to roll forward on its right front wheel, cartwheeling off the pavement and into the steep shoulder. The sound of rubber and steel meeting asphalt and rock were deafeningly loud, but only one man could hear it.

Reece smiled for the first time in many months as he pulled a Ziploc bag from a pocket inside his jacket. Out of the bag came a folded-up crayon drawing with a list of names written on the back. With a tiny stub of a pencil, he crossed the first name off the list and returned it to its home against his chest.

PART ONE

THE
AMBUSH

CHAPTER I

Three months earlier
Khost Province, Afghanistan
0200 Local Time

Not one of the guys on the ground had liked this mission. Now, moving to within a klick of their target, they had pushed that distraction from their minds and were solely focused on the deadly challenge before them. Glancing at the GPS attached to the stock of his rifle and scanning the terrain ahead, Lieutenant Commander James Reece called a quick perimeter. Snipers were already moving up to the high ground as team leaders joined Reece for a last, quick update before the final push to the objective. Even with all the technology at their disposal, things could go wrong in a heartbeat. Their enemy was cunning and highly adaptive. After sixteen years at war, the Afghan saying, *"The Americans have all the watches, but we have all the time,"* rang a bit more true than it had in the early days.

"What do you think, Reece?" asked a huge beast of a man, looking like a creature from another world with his AOR1-patterned camouflage, body armor, and Ops Core half-shell helmet with NODs firmly in place.

Reece looked at his most seasoned troop chief. The light green glow of the NODs illuminated through the beard on the other man's face a slight smile that could not be mistaken for anything other than the confident look of a professional special operations soldier.

"It's just over that rise," Reece replied. "Predator shows nothing moving. No sentries. Nothing."

His troop chief nodded.

"All right, guys," he said to the other four men in the circle. "Let's do it."

They rose with resolve and moved with the poise of men who were comfortable in chaos, moving up the rocky ridgeline to get their Teams in place before approaching the target to make entry.

This is too easy. You are thinking too much again. It's just another mission. Then why this feeling? Maybe it's just the headaches.

The headaches had plagued Reece for the past several months, finally prompting a visit to Balboa Naval Medical Center before this deployment for a series of tests. Still no word back from the docs.

Maybe it's nothing. But maybe it's something.

Reece had learned a long time ago that if something didn't look right, then it probably wasn't. That judgment had kept him and his men alive on many a deployment.

Everything had lined up a little too easily for

this target: the intel, the offset infil, the current state of the objective area. And why the pressure from higher authority to go after this target? When was the last time a flag-level command injected itself into a tactical planning process? Something wasn't adding up. *Maybe everything's fine. Maybe it's the headaches. Maybe it's a bit of paranoia. Maybe I am getting too old for this. Focus, Reece.*

This wasn't the first time that they had approached a target they suspected was a possible ambush. At one point in the war, when intel had pointed to the high possibility of an ambush, corroborated by multiple sources both human and technical, Reece would have knocked on the door with a thermobaric AT-4 or a few 105mm rounds from an AC-130 gunship. This was the first time that actual tactics had been dictated from higher, from men who would not be on the ground. *Focus on the mission, Reece.*

One more check with the Tactical Operations Center, a forward-based command also called the TOC, and a look at the Predator feed. Nothing. Another check with the sniper teams. Nothing moving.

Reece glanced up at the military crest of the hill in front of him. Through his NODs he could see the assault teams set and ready to move. He couldn't see the snipers, which gave him cause for a thoughtful smile. *Best in the business.*

Reece keyed his radio and opened his mouth to give the order to move.

Then it all went black.

The explosion knocked Reece back ten yards and ripped his helmet from his head as the entire military crest of the hill in front of him erupted in a concussion of violence and death. Teammates, friends, husbands, and fathers who one moment earlier had represented the best special operations force the world had ever known were gone in less than a second.

Reece never realized that he was momentarily knocked unconscious. The pain in his head brought him back into the fight before the dust began to settle and the reverberations from the explosion had drifted from the hills.

The professional in him immediately ensured he still had his weapon. *Check.* Next was a mental rundown of his body. Everything appeared to still be in the same place and working.

They knew. How? Later, Reece. Always improve your fighting position.

His eyes darted around looking in vain for his helmet and communications headset, eyes adjusting to the dark, hands moving in a frantic search until finally coming across it in the dirt.

Yes. Wait, too heavy to be my helmet. That's because it's not your helmet. It's someone else's. And the head is still in it.

Even in the darkness it was clear to Reece that he was staring into the face of his longtime friend and Teammate, the big man with the huge beard and confident smile, and that his head was no longer attached to his body. Reece couldn't stop the tears from welling in his eyes but quickly brushed them aside. *Focus. No time to mourn. Exploit all technical and tactical advantages. Check.* Reece unsnapped the chinstrap, letting his friend's head fall to the ground, and quickly put the helmet on his own head. Miraculously, the NODs still worked. His radio operator was facedown, twenty yards away. Reece could tell from the contorted position of his body that he was dead. Moving quickly to his side, Reece turned him over, checked for breathing and a pulse, knowing that the shrapnel sticking through his right eye and out the side of his head had killed him instantly. Removing his radioman's helmet, Reece ripped off the MBITR radio and headset to reestablish communications with the supporting aircraft and his TOC.

Nothing moved on the hillside. It was as if the sword of death had swept over the entire force. Reece heard footsteps behind him and spun, weapon up, off safe, infrared laser activated, searching for threats. He immediately checked up his M4 5.56mm rifle as he recognized three of his operators running up to him from their rear security positions.

The temptation to run up the hillside was a strong one but another thought was at the forefront of all their minds: *win the fight.*

His rear security found new positions without saying a word, forming a tight perimeter around their leader.

Reece shut the carnage and death of the ambush from his mind. It was time to act.

"SPOOKY Four Seven, this is SPARTAN Zero One," said Reece into his radio while looking at the Gridded Reference Graphic attached to his arm. "Request fire mission on building D3. 105s. Level it." Worn in a similar fashion as a quarterback's wrist coach, the GRG was instead an aerial image of the target area that allowed him to coordinate and maneuver forces who all used the same graphic.

"Good copy, Zero One. Six mikes out." The AC-130 gunship had been loitering ten minutes away so as not to give away the coming assault in the still Afghan night.

"Break—RAZOR Two Four, RAZOR Two Four. Request QRF and medevac on my position, ECHO Three. Stay off the hillsides. We have multiple personnel wounded from buried IEDs." One never mentioned the dead in a radio transmission.

"Roger, Zero One. Headed in for a hot extract on grid ECHO Three. Ten mikes out." The QRF birds were two CH-47 helos packed with fifteen Rangers each.

"MAKO," Reece said into the headset, "anything on that Pred feed?"

"Nothing, Zero One. Nothing moving on target."

"Copy."

Reece turned his attention to his four remaining operators.

"Who do we have?" He asked.

"Hey, sir. It's Boozer. I have Jonesey and Mike with me. What the fuck happened?"

"Ambush. They knew we were coming. Bastards. We have an air strike about five minutes out and QRF en route."

"Sir, we fucking told *them* this was an ambush. What the *fuck!* Sure as hell didn't expect this, though. Anyone alive?"

"Not sure. Let's go find out."

"Roger, sir. But take it easy. There could be hundreds of IEDs or mines set up and buried up here."

"Jonesey, you and Mike stay here to bring in those birds. Boozer and I are going to go check for survivors. Boozer, stay about fifteen yards behind me. Step only where I step. We will work our way up there slowly. TOC says nothing is moving on the other side of that hill but stay alert."

"Got it, Reece."

"Let's go."

The pair moved together up the hillside, though

mountainside was a more apt term. Rocky and steep at altitude, and weighed down by forty pounds of body armor and gear makes for slow going, especially when moving through a suspected minefield.

"SPOOKY, we are moving up from GRG ECHO Three to ECHO Eight. Anything on the north side of the hill is fair game."

"Roger, Zero One, still nothing moving."

Strange.

"Good copy."

Reece and Boozer inched up the hill, the smell of cordite, blood, dust, and death heavy in the air. Movement to the left.

"B, I have movement. Don't rush up. Continue to follow me," Reece whispered into his radio. Boozer responded by keying his mike twice, signifying *good copy*.

Reece moved in the direction of the movement and what he now identified as moaning. Donny Mitchell, one of the youngest members of Reece's team, lay dying among the rocks of eastern Afghanistan. His body missing from the waist down, he reached for Reece.

"Did we get them, sir?" Donny said weakly. "I've still got my rifle."

"Yeah you do, buddy. Yeah you do. Air strike is coming in now. We'll get them." Reece sat down next to Donny and moved to cradle his head in his arms. As the first of the 105s began to hit the compound, Reece caught the hint of a smile on Donny's lips as he drifted off to Valhalla.

Reece looked up, watching Boozer slowly work his way among the boulder-strewn hillside. Behind Boozer, Reece first heard, then saw the blacked-out 47s begin their descent into the valley where Jonesey and Mike now guided them in.

We will pound the hell out of that compound with air and then move in with the Rangers to conduct battle damage assessment and sensitive site exploitation.

It was then that the gravity of what had just happened began to sink in.

I've lost my team. It is my responsibility.

Reece's eyes began to mist over for the second time that night. He had no idea how bad things were about to get.

CHAPTER 2

Bagram Air Base
Bagram, Afghanistan

Reece awoke on his back, his vision blurry, blinking to clear his eyes and soften the pounding in his head.

Where am I?

As he turned his head slowly to try to clear the cobwebs, his eyes came to focus on the tube sticking out of his arm and he became aware of something strapped over his mouth and nose.

IV. Oxygen mask. Hospital.

Reece attempted to lift himself to his elbows but was stopped short by a blinding pain in his head.

"Reece . . . Reece . . . easy, buddy. Easy."

Reece recognized the voice immediately. Boozer.

"Doc, he's getting up!" Boozer yelled down the hall.

This place was a far cry from the field hospital tents of the early days. If you didn't know you were still in Afghanistan, you'd think you were stateside at a naval medical center in Bethesda or Balboa. The only giveaway that it was in the middle of a war zone was the ubiquitous hum of the diesel generators providing 24/7 climate control year after year.

Fighting in a country for north of fifteen years can do that.

Reece pulled down his oxygen mask and looked toward his friend.

Boozer was still in his op cammies, dirty, smelly, with dried white salt deposits straining through the Afghan grime from all the sweat of the night's mission, but other than that, looking none the worse for wear. Boozer was just one of those guys who never got a scratch. His body armor and weapon were absent but Reece knew he would have a pistol concealed somewhere on his person.

"What happened? How did I get here?"

Boozer took a breath, trying not to let a look of utter sadness with an edge of pity cross his face, but failing miserably.

"Reece, NCIS is already here. They asked me not to tell you shit. Fuck them, though. Of course I'm going to tell you."

NCIS?

"It's bad, Reece," Boozer continued. "What's the last thing you remember?"

Reece's eyes tightened as he searched his memory banks.

"We were on the crest of the hill, air strikes inbound, QRF and CASEVAC coming in . . ." He trailed off. "Holding, Donny."

"Yeah," Boozer confirmed. "That's right. Then the whole valley exploded. They baited us in, Reece. More elaborate than anything we've seen to date. They knew exactly what we would do after the hillside went up. They knew we would level that compound and bring in the cavalry for our wounded and dead. The entire floor of that valley, our exact position in the set point, was wired to blow. They knew when those helos were landing and they cooked it off. Dash-one dropped its Rangers, took off, and when dash-two came in they set it off. That second helo and all the Rangers, sir. They got them all."

Reece's eyes stayed focused on Boozer.

"Jonesey and Mike?" Reece asked, already knowing the answer.

Boozer shook his head. "Sorry, Reece. I wanted to make sure you knew before those NCIS guys got in here. I got a bad feeling from those clowns. What's weird is that their questions weren't about the mission. They were about *you*."

A confused look crossed Reece's face, which he quickly put aside. *"Me?"*

"I think they are looking for somebody to hang. Just my take, Reece. Stay strong, sir. You didn't do anything wrong. Higher forced us on that mission. They dictated the tactics. Those are the fuckers that should be investigated. They dictated tactics from the safety of HQ. Fuck those guys."

Boozer always had a way with words. Not one

to ever sugarcoat anything, he always gave his honest assessment. As a leader, that was what Reece expected. It is what he owed his troops and his chain of command. *Always give your honest assessment.* That was how one built trust as a combat leader. Without trust, there was nothing.

Your men trusted you, Reece. And now they are dead. Focus. Something is not right. Something is just not right.

CHAPTER 3

"Lieutenant Commander Reece," interrupted a voice from the hallway with more of a statement than a question.

Boozer looked at Reece with an expression that told his commander, *this is the asshole I was talking about.*

"That's me," replied Reece, pushing himself up in his hospital bed.

"Hi, I'm Special Agent Robert Bridger with NCIS," he said, entering the room and nodding at Boozer while at the same time displaying his credentials to Reece.

These guys love to show their creds, thought Reece to himself. He wondered if they knew the rest of the military thought they were all just guys who couldn't get into the FBI or CIA but didn't have the balls to be street cops, instead choosing to hide out in NCIS for a career of busting eighteen-year-old kids who pop positive on the monthly Navy drug tests.

Even their name was deceptive. Despite leading with an *N* for Naval, NCIS was not even a part of the Navy. Rather, it was a federal law enforcement agency staffed with civilian special agents focused on investigating naval personnel. No one liked them much.

Boozer stood and, though talking to Reece, stared directly into Agent Bridger's eyes and said, "See you later, sir. I'll be close if you need me," before departing the room, leaving it to the federal cop and his boss.

Reece swung his legs over the side of the bed, slowly getting his balance. Looking at his arm, he yanked out the IV and then rose to his feet before extending his hand to the shorter man. Agent Bridger seemed nice enough and for all Reece knew he was just doing his job. Bridger smiled and took the outstretched hand.

Good cop, Reece thought.

Bridger was dressed in the "uniform" of those not in actual uniform in a war zone, pressed tan pants with the requisite olive green button-up safari-style shirt complete with epaulets along with clean beige combat boots. Reece always wondered what the epaulets were for. His .40 SIG Sauer P229 was displayed prominently on his belt in a scuffed-up black leather holster, probably the result of getting in and out of his desk chair for coffee multiple times a day.

"If you feel up for it, Commander, we have a few questions about the mission. I'm sure you understand. We just want to get this wrapped up as soon as possible and get you back to your men."

Or what's left of them, thought Reece.

"Little quick, isn't it?" asked Reece, looking around the hospital room.

"Well, it's a big deal, sir. We need to get some questions answered for D.C. as soon as possible."

Reece nodded, resigned to take the blame he knew was his. He had always believed that as a leader you shared in the successes but owned the failure, and when successful you always pushed the credit down to the guys. They deserved it most. This was an unmitigated failure. His failure.

"Mind if I change?" Reece asked.

"No problem, Commander. I'll be outside."

Reece took a deep breath and surveyed his room. It wasn't what one would expect to find in Afghanistan. Modern and sterile, it stood in stark contrast to the world beyond its doors. Alone with his thoughts, Reece took another breath and located his clothes, op cammies covered in sweat and blood. He picked up his camo Crye Pro top and rubbed the blood-soaked material between his fingers, wondering which of his men the blood belonged to.

Reece knew that if anything were really wrong with him they would have put him in the ER, which was in a different wing of the hospital, behind another set of doors and always ready for the inevitable next mass causality event, which had become an all-too-frequent occurrence in the counterinsurgency fight. His weapons and body armor were gone. Boozer would have taken care of them.

"Ready," Reece said, exiting the room.

"Okay," the NCIS man answered.

This time he was not alone. Instead he was flanked by a large but portly uniformed Navy chief master-at-arms carrying a Beretta 92F pistol in a clean nylon holster. How the Italian gunmaker's awkward 9mm handgun had replaced the Colt 1911A1 .45 to become the official sidearm of the U.S. armed forces, Reece could only guess.

Great, more fake cops, he thought.

Reece fell into step with Agent Bridger as they made their way down the hallway toward the exit. The duo could not have been more different. Bridger stood about five inches shorter than Reece's six feet. His clean cargo pants and offset shirt were not stained by sweat, dirt, dust, grime, and blood like Reece's. His clean-shaven, pale face was a stark contrast to the taller man's stubble poking through the tough tanned skin of someone who had spent most of his life beyond the confines of an office.

Reece and his entourage pushed through the two sets of double doors separating the medical world from the Afghan dust, which, no matter how much gravel the U.S. military continued to lay down, got into everything. Emerging into the blazing sun, Reece squinted his eyes and shielded them with his hand, realizing he hadn't had time to glance at his watch and for some reason thought it was still night. Reece almost stumbled as a headache worse than any to date almost crippled him. Almost before he could react, it was gone again. *What were these things?* As Reece's eyes adjusted to the light, Bridger motioned to a parked side-by-side quad, a military-looking version of a golf cart. Bridger climbed into the driver's seat while Reece took the front passenger side. Their silent master-at arms "security" got in the back and they moved off toward what Reece assumed would be the base NCIS office.

They blended in with the normal buzz of daily activity at Bagram Air Base, soldiers moving to vehicles getting ready for a mounted patrol with their Afghan partner force, airmen switching shifts at the airfield, a line of military and civilian contractors forming at the chow hall. Just another Wednesday afternoon in a war zone.

As they cruised down Disney Drive, Reece couldn't help but shake his head at the officers who had to return salutes about every five paces as they passed junior soldiers. Even in a combat zone, some brass felt it was important to maintain this piece of military decorum. It made him appreciate the sterile uniform he wore; no rank, which meant he didn't need to return fifty salutes on his way to the PX or gym.

Bridger slowed the vehicle and pulled up in front of a structure left over from the time the Russians invaded Afghanistan in 1979. The outside was chipped with bullet holes—whether from the Russian occupation or the current conflict, it was impossible to tell. Funny, to Reece it looked like the old Russian brig. *Fitting.*

Bridger left the Navy chief outside and led the way into the building and down a hallway lined with offices, each with a similarly dressed agent typing away, sifting through papers or mumbling on the phone. Reece took it all in, noting which way the doors opened, which offices had windows, which agents were armed, until Bridger stopped at the last door at the end of the hallway.

"Please wait here, sir," he said before slipping inside.

Reece was left alone, assuming he was probably being watched by a small video camera surveying the hall. He looked at the BOLO, or Be On the Look-Out, printouts on the wall. Most were former Afghan workers who did the jobs too lowly for Americans, namely emptying the port-a-potties that baked day after day in the heat of the Afghan summer. Reece had always thought they were some of the best sources of intel for the insurgency, having paced out every corner of the base multiple times to ensure correct schematics for incoming mortars and rockets.

The door opened again and Agent Bridger nodded at Reece to come inside. It wasn't a big room, though Reece noticed immediately that there were no windows and no other points of entry. Seated at a rectangular folding table was a man who didn't offer his hand but introduced himself as Special Agent Dan Stubbs while holding out his badge and ID card. *Bad cop.*

Reece took a seat across from Agent Stubbs while Bridger joined the man who was quite obviously his superior. Stubbs made a show of organizing some papers before sliding his thin reading glasses down the bridge of his nose to address the SEAL he had summoned in an obvious power play.

It was much darker in this room than in the hall or adjoining offices. Reece's eyes adjusted once again while casually continuing to scan the room. A large stack of papers sat in front of Agent Stubbs and a microcassette recorder lay next to that. A video camera was set up in one corner on a tripod but appeared to not be recording.

Agent Stubbs was one of those guys who could be forty or sixty. His hair was buzzed so it was hard to tell its exact color. His double chin was pronounced enough to notice and, though he did not stand, it was obvious he had a belly not accustomed to daily PT. He wore a black polo shirt under a cheap-looking dark suit coat. Something about his demeanor suggested past military experience, though Reece was skeptical as to the type.

"Commander Reece," he began in an official-sounding voice while pushing a piece of paper across the table, "before we begin, please acknowledge your rights and sign below."

Reece knew better than to ever sign anything for a federal agent without an attorney present. He also knew that his men were dead and that it was his responsibility. He signed the paper and pushed it back across.

"We are not video-recording this interview, Commander."

First lie, thought Reece as he nodded in acknowledgment. Reece knew that the inoperable video camera in the corner was a prop, as was the microcassette recorder on the table. The entire interview was being audio- and video-recorded by a microphone and camera hidden somewhere in the room. The prop camera was to put the subject psychologically at ease while the microcassette recorder would be used at certain times to go "off the record," a provision that, of course, did not exist.

"I am going to start this recorder for my notes, if you don't mind," continued the fat man. Reece nodded again, more to acknowledge the theatrics of the scenario than to specifically give his consent for the record.

Stubbs made a show of starting the recorder and placing it back on the table. "This is Special Agent Daniel Stubbs of the Naval Criminal Investigative Service. Time," looking at his off-brand analog watch, "12:56 p.m., Wednesday,

June fourteenth, 2017. I am here with Special Agent Robert Bridger to interview Lieutenant Commander James Reece, Troop Commander, SEAL Team Seven, concerning mission number 644: Odin's Sword. Commander Reece, take us through the events surrounding Odin's Sword."

Reece started from the receipt of mission and went through the planning process. It had been a TST, or time-sensitive target, meaning it was a fleeting opportunity that needed to be acted upon immediately. The intelligence had come from a single source, which would normally disqualify it from consideration until it was more fully developed. Reece always validated intelligence across disassociated sources: two HUMINT sources coupled with SIGINT. Traditional and technical methods overlapping to ensure the target was viable and not an entity using America to settle a personal or political grudge. When Reece had pushed back to his next-echelon command he had been told in no uncertain terms that this was national-level intelligence, which was code for he was not authorized to know where it came from. Reece was cleared for Top Secret/Sensitive Compartmented Information, which meant he could be read into Special Access Programs on a need-to-know basis. Taking your men into battle was definitely need-to-know in Reece's book.

Reece's troop had been operating out of an out-station in Khost, bordering Pakistan's Federally Administered Tribal Areas near the town of Miram Shah, a hotbed of insurgent activity as well as a safe haven for terrorists and their enablers. Ever since the high-profile killing of Osama bin Laden in Pakistan, cross-border operations were a rarity, and the enemy knew it. Setting up in Khost, developing an indigenous intelligence network, working with host nation partner forces, and kinetically hitting the ratlines that moved people, weapons, and drugs between Afghanistan and Pakistan were the order of the day on this deployment. That is why the alarm bells started ringing when the TST came down the pike; no one knew that area as well as Reece and his Team. They had been working it for the past five months. None of their human networks or technical intelligence pointed to a Taliban compound in their area of operations. The Taliban were too smart for that. Their senior people could live and direct operations with impunity from the Pakistan side of the border. Something was off.

Reece didn't mention his call to Lieutenant Colonel Duke Bray, the Army Special Forces commander of the Special Operations Task Force of which Reece's unit was a part. Duke Bray was a Special Forces legend and the best soldier one could ever hope to meet. He had been one of the first into Afghanistan after September 11, 2001, part of Fifth Group's famed Triple Nickel, riding horses in support of the Northern Alliance offensive that retook Kabul in days rather than the months predicted by the talking heads at home. He had crossed paths with Reece many times over the years and both men had the utmost respect for one another. Over their private secure video teleconference, Reece could be as blunt as he wanted with the man he considered both a friend and a mentor.

"What the *fuck*, sir?" Reece had asked when he knew both were behind closed doors and in front of their computers.

"I know, Reece. This is shit. I've never seen this, well, not in a long time. I told CJSOTF to fuck off and that we were not doing it. What's crazy is that it wasn't their intel people pushing it. It's national-level intel and you know what that means."

Reece knew that meant CIA and it meant strategic-level intelligence, not the tactical kind they developed on the ground. This had to be important to come down so quickly from that high up.

"Reece, I called in a couple favors at Langley to see if I could get some color on this. Nobody's heard of it. How does the target package look to you?"

"It looks great. That's why I'm questioning it. I've never seen anything this thorough from that high up. And we've never even heard of this targeted individual, but there is sure a lot of intel to back up that he's a serious player with connections to Pakistani ISI," Reece said, referring to Pakistan's intelligence service.

"What did Stevens have to say?" Reece asked, referring to the colonel commanding the CJSOTF one level above Bray.

"You know Stevens, he's a good enough officer. Wants to do the right thing but he's a career guy. He said he had the personal guarantee from Tampa that this was a high-priority mission that has to go tonight."

Tampa was the headquarters of both Central Command, in charge of U.S. military operations in the Middle East, and the Special Operations Command, which has the lead on all special operations worldwide.

"Wonder who guaranteed them?" Reece wondered aloud.

"I don't like it, Reece," Bray continued, shaking his head. "Wish I was down there with you, Commander, but I'll make sure you have all assets of the Task Force at your disposal tonight. Your op will be the only game in town."

"Thanks, sir. A dedicated AC-130 and a Pred with Hellfires would be nice."

"My staff already has them dedicated to your mission."

"Good copy, sir. We better get to work. Thanks for the support."

"Godspeed, Commander."

To Reece's surprise, Agent Stubbs did not dig into any of the oddities of where the intelligence originated. It was almost as if that were not even an issue.

Interesting.

As hard as it was, Reece recounted the events once on the ground. The offset infiltration. The reports of nothing moving on target. The explosions. The death.

When he was finished, Stubbs's first question was not even about the mission. Instead he removed a paper from the stack in front of him and pushed it across the table to Reece.

"Is this from your email, Commander?" he asked.

Reece made no attempt to disguise the anger in his eyes as he looked back up at Agent Stubbs and then over to a nervous-looking Agent Bridger.

"Maybe a better question is, what the fuck are you doing reading my personal emails?"

"I will ask it again, Commander: is this from your email?"

One of the first rules in an interrogation is to always know the answer to the questions before you even ask, and this was most definitely not an interview; it was an interrogation.

"This is private email correspondence between me and my wife."

"Not only with your wife, Commander, but with members of academic institutions about ongoing military operations in Afghanistan."

Reece almost couldn't control his eye roll. "You mean Dr. Anna Scott at Naval Postgraduate School and Dr. David Elliot at Johns Hopkins? Subject matter experts in insurgencies and international relations?"

"What did you mean by this highlighted sentence here?" Stubbs asked, ignoring Reece's questions and pointing to a section of the printed email now in front of Reece. "It says, 'I question whether the tactical goals even support our national strategic vision.'"

"It means exactly what it says."

"And how about this one here?" Agent Stubbs asked again. "Well, let me read it for you, you wrote to Anna Scott on April ninth and I quote, 'I couldn't launch a mission today to apprehend a jaywalker with the same amount and quality of intelligence with which we invaded Iraq.' End quote."

"Well, Stibbs," Reece began, intentionally mispronouncing his interrogator's name, "Anna Scott is a dear friend and one of the world's leading authorities on insurgencies and counterinsurgencies. She's spent much of her life in the field immersed in the complexities of revolution, unlike those actually dictating policy."

Stubbs's hand reached for the microcassette

recorder and pressed the stop button. Reece knew immediately what was coming. "Commander Reece, off the record, what is your relationship with Dr. Scott?"

Unbelievable.

"Strictly professional, Stibbs. You should know that from reading all my personal emails."

"I see," pressing record on the recorder again, "and how do you explain actively promoting assassinations as an active-duty naval officer?"

"What are you talking about?" Reece asked incredulously.

"Back in 2014 you emailed Dr. David Elliot and suggested targeted assassinations as a viable government policy in your capacity as an officer, which is a violation of the Uniform Code of Military Justice."

Reece looked back and forth between the two NCIS agents across from him. It would almost have been comical had it not been so serious.

Reece had had many discussions with subject matter experts in the field of warfare. He felt it was his duty as an officer to constantly study his profession, resist groupthink, question assumptions, and seek out the most knowledge-able people he could across the industry to ensure he was going into combat as prepared and well equipped as possible. That was what he owed the men under his command. It is what he owed their families, the mission, and the country.

"I'm done talking with you two idiots. Am I free to go?"

"Don't make plans to go home just yet," Stubbs said, leaning back in his chair and exposing his well-nourished midsection. "It is going to take us a while to sort through this mess. You are officially under investigation for subversive activities, disclosure of sensitive information, and violation of Article 13: conduct unbecoming an officer." Stubbs voiced all this without much emotion, as if running on autopilot.

Reece stood slowly. Bridger looked like he wanted to be anywhere except for right where he was. Stubbs put the emails back into the stack. As he stood, Reece's hand instinctively went to the back right section of his hip, where he always carried his issued SIG P226 9mm pistol. He couldn't help but think that had it been about 150 years earlier, the government would be looking for two new federal agents.

CHAPTER 4

Dr. Peter O'Halloran exuded the confidence of a man at the top of his profession. In the weeks following September 11, 2001, Dr. O'Halloran turned the reins of his highly successful spine surgery center over to his team of surgeons and joined the Army to do what he felt was his duty.

As one of the best spine surgeons in the country, Peter had performed procedures on everyone from professional athletes at the height of their careers to aging politicians looking for a reprieve from constant nerve pain. He knew that men would be gravely wounded in this fight and he wanted to put his ample skills to work to keep those men alive. A waiver was quickly granted to bypass the age restrictions and, much to the dismay of his wife and children, Dr. Peter O'Halloran soon found himself Lieutenant Colonel O'Halloran of the U.S. Army Reserve, spending more time in uniform in Iraq and Afghanistan than in his spine clinic in La Jolla, California.

It had only been two days since the ambush and subsequent interrogation but physically, Reece was ready to leave the hospital. He had been asked to stop in and see Dr. O'Halloran before he left for good, and upon his discharge, the nurse in charge of the shift walked him to the surgeon's office. O'Halloran greeted Reece warmly and invited him to sit. The doctor swiveled his chair to face a desktop computer and selected a file before rotating the screen so that Reece would have a better view of it. He then pulled up an image on the screen that was clearly a brain scan. It immediately reminded Reece of the black-and-white forward-looking infrared (FIR) imagery they used on the battlefield, with its glowing white highlights showing three-dimensional relief on a black background. The doctor used his mouse to put a curser over a white blob on the image.

"Two of your men came in here wounded. We fought as hard as we could to save them but their injuries were just too severe. As part of our initial assessment, we did scans to determine the extent of their brain trauma and, besides a significant amount of shrapnel, we found this. This is the CT scan we took of Petty Officer Morales's brain. You see this?" He pointed to a white blob on the screen. "This is an abnormal mass that is not consistent with a traumatic injury. The pathologist who did the autopsy believes that the mass is an oligodendroglioma, a rare and malignant brain tumor. The lab will confirm or deny that suspicion but he knows his stuff and I agree with his assessment based on the imaging."

He clicked the mouse and a second image was displayed on the screen. "This is Lieutenant Pritchard's brain. As you can see here, he has a slightly smaller but similar tumor. The pathologist and I believe that it is the same type." A third image came up. "This is your brain, James. Now, we have no way of knowing for sure, but the mass on your brain appears to be similar in size and shape to that of your men. If we were in the States I would bring you in for a biopsy but we can't do that here."

Reece's mouth went dry and he suddenly had an overwhelming desire to be with his wife and daughter.

"I don't want you to panic, James. This could be a variety of things, and a malignancy is just one of them."

"What?" Reece stammered. "How . . . how rare is that, Doc? It seems crazy to me that three guys our age would have brain tumors."

"Extremely rare, James. The incidence of this type of tumor is roughly 0.3 per one hundred thousand. Only about two percent of all brain tumors are of this type. Let's assume that yours is something different, since we can't confirm it here. But for two men on the same team, both in their twenties, to have this same type of tumor . . ." O'Halloran shook his head. "The odds are astronomical. Have you and your men been exposed to any chemical or biological agents?

Been in any nuclear facilities, anything like that?"

"No, not that I'm aware of. I mean, when we first invaded Iraq there were a bunch of chem/bio scares but Pritchard was probably in high school at the time. And as far as I know they were just that, scares. A team was hit with a mustard gas agent of some sort but nowhere near where I was operating. As far as these two guys being together, nothing out of the ordinary."

"Hmm, well, keep thinking about it and let me know if you come up with anything. This is incredibly unusual. Like I said, we can't do any more here, but when you get back stateside you need to get checked out, just to be sure. I'm almost done with this deployment. It's been a long year but I'll be back at my California clinic early next month. I want you to come up to La Jolla and see me. There are some colleagues of mine who specialize in brain research that I'd like for you to meet. You haven't had any blurred vision, headaches, anything like that, have you?"

"No, sir," Reece lied, needing time to think.

"How about Petty Officer Morales or Lieutenant Pritchard: did they or any of your men mention any unusual headaches?"

"No, but that wouldn't be out of the ordinary with this crew. The Teams aren't really a culture where people complain about those sorts of things. They think it might take them out of the fight."

"I see," the doctor said thoughtfully. "I'm sorry about your men. I know that probably doesn't mean much but I really am. Get yourself home safely, hug your family, bury your men, and make an appointment with my office for when I get back. Take care, James."

Reece walked out of the medical facility a man adrift. Truly, he was already gone, occupied with the thoughts of the families of sons, husbands, and fathers whose bodies, or what was left of them, were being put into bags, then into flag-draped coffins for their final trip home.

CHAPTER 5

Naval Special Warfare Command
Coronado, California

The aide knocked before entering Admiral Pilsner's office. "Sir, the SECDEF's office is on the line."

"Tell Howard to get in here and then put them through," the admiral responded harshly.

"Yes, sir." The aide scampered back out the door.

The admiral's JAG, Captain Leonard Howard, entered without knocking less than thirty seconds later.

The phone on the admiral's desk rang and he pressed the button to put it on speaker.

"This is Admiral Pilsner, standing by for the secretary."

"Thank you, Admiral," an unidentified voice responded. "Secretary Hartley will be with you momentarily."

After close to five minutes of waiting, the line sparked to life.

"Good afternoon, Madam Secretary, what can I do for you?" the admiral said cheerfully in greeting.

"What the *fuck* happened over there, Admiral?" a furious Lorraine Hartley asked.

"Ma'am, we did our best to manage the situation but obviously we didn't fully achieve our mission."

"Your best? You're the goddamn WARCOM admiral and this is 'your best'?"

"Madame Secretary, we are doing everything we can to clean this up as soon as possible."

"I'm losing confidence in your ability to do that. First of all, I want the survivors tied up in the investigation over there as long as possible. I don't want the American public falling in love with these guys during the media storm around the funerals. I want them out of sight, out of mind, and I want the responsibility hung on their shoulders. I want that troop commander to be a modern-day Custer. I want charges brought against him yesterday."

Leonard Howard spoke up. "Madame Secretary, this is Captain Leonard Howard. We would have a difficult time charging Commander Reece with anything under the UCMJ until a full investigation has been completed."

"Get your head out of your ass, Howard! You find something to charge him with. We have so many federal crimes on the books the Department of Justice can't even count them all, and you're telling me you can't come up with something? Haven't you ever heard the phrase 'show me the man, I'll show you the crime'? Charge him with as much as you can but don't lock him up;

we need him to be a free man for this to end appropriately. Clean up this mess, gentlemen, or you'll wish you'd never met me." Both men heard a click and the line went dead.

Pilsner looked at his JAG. "Call Horn ASAP. We need a plan in place before those men are back on the ground stateside. And tell the NCIS guys to turn up the heat on Reece."

CHAPTER 6

Bagram Air Base
Bagram, Afghanistan

The days passed slowly while Reece was confined to Bagram. His men were being laid to rest in front of their devastated families while Reece was stuck halfway around the world, unable to look their wives, children, and parents in the eyes and assure them that he would find out what had led them into such a devastating ambush. He knew that he'd be crucified by WARCOM, and as far as he was concerned, he deserved it. He'd gotten all of his men killed, the cardinal sin of a combat leader. *And for what? Some target they didn't know shit about?* Add in the stress of a probable rare brain tumor and Reece's head was spinning. He was recalled almost daily to answer further questions from the NCIS goons and continued to answer all inquiries about the mission while refusing to answer the ones about his personal emails. The questions from NCIS had the smell of people with an agenda. Single sentences from emails going back over fifteen years were extracted to support a preconceived narrative. It was obvious to Reece that NCIS was not interested in what actually happened in the lead-up to and execution of the mission. They were there to put the blame on Reece and Reece alone. It had been brutal but he had taken it.

After a cruel two weeks of sleepless nights thinking about the brain tumors and of circular interrogations from NCIS, Reece was finally cleared to go home. He leaned back in his seat on the C-5 as it gathered speed down the runway, nose up, banking tightly to quickly gain altitude and get outside the range of enemy small arms and RPGs, leaving Bagram in the background. Reece's thoughts turned to what had happened at home in his absence. The command had mobilized. Casualty assistance officers and teams had been dispatched to try to beat the twenty-four-hour news cycle to the front doors of families scattered across the country: mothers and fathers, wives and children who would get the news every military family dreads, the unexpected knock on the door, the chaplain, an officer, a friend. The unthinkable. The screaming. The tears. The kids. The funerals. The blame. *The blame. It was my fault. I was the senior man on the ground. Responsibility lies with me. And I couldn't even be there to deliver the news in person, to do my duty.*

The flight would be a good way to get his thoughts in order.

He would call his wife from Germany, where he would have a few hours to decompress while the pilots had their mandated crew rest.

How can I go home and face my family when twenty-eight Rangers, four aircrew, and thirty-six SEALs of my Task Unit are going home in boxes?

That's war, Reece.

No. The enemy was good. But they were not that good.

This ambush was too well conceived and too effective. It was months, if not a year in planning. The explosives. What were they and how were they detonated? Why didn't any insurgents spill out of that compound with the detonation of the first explosives? Was there anyone in there at all? How did they know exactly where the helos would land? Why were they forced to go on this mission? Why was NCIS so pointed in their questioning so soon after the mission? What am I missing?

CHAPTER 7

Capstone Capital Corporate Offices
Los Angeles, California

Steve Horn was not accustomed to waiting for anything. First his tasty little assistant had made him wait five minutes for his beloved green tea, and now his most loyal lieutenant was running late, something he would not tolerate. The six-foot-four former Stanford quarterback sat behind a desk of polished walnut that he now visually inspected for any sign of dust or grime. He wore a finely tailored suit of charcoal cashmere that cost more than most families brought home in a month, cut not for comfort but to display his muscular physique. His tan neck was framed by a rigid spread collar and a violet Hermès necktie bound with a massive Windsor knot. A casual visitor would have thought that *Fortune* was arriving any minute to shoot him for the cover, but his staff knew better; this was Horn's everyday attire. Horn was the very image of vanity personified.

If Horn had ever consulted a mental health professional, he would likely be diagnosed with an "antisocial personality disorder." He felt absolutely no empathy for his fellow man and actually relished the discomfort of others. A counselor might explore whether this detachment resulted from the disinterest of his socialite parents during his upbringing or the harsh punishments dispensed by some of his many nannies. Maybe it was his failure to bond with a caretaker or perhaps he was born a sociopath; he would never know because he would never think to question what to him was as natural as breathing. To Horn, being ruthless was a competitive advantage.

An email on the twenty-seven-inch screen of his iMac indicated the arrival of the tardy lieutenant. Phone calls or door knocks from his receptionist were not acceptable. Despite his strong desire to hear what the man had to say, Horn made him wait ten excruciating minutes in the lavishly decorated reception area. With Horn, everything was about power, and he spared no opportunity to remind everyone that he was in charge, a fact that no one but him questioned. The touch of a key on the desk phone indicated to the receptionist that he was ready to receive his appointment, and she quickly and sympathetically ushered Saul Agnon through the thick oak doors and into Horn's office.

If Horn's appearance signaled power, strength, and grace, Agnon's did the opposite. He was slight of build, with small features, pallid skin, and a generally disheveled manner. His suit was

70

cheap and off the rack, fitting him accordingly. His shoes were worn and unpolished. His fingernails were soft from nervous biting; his hair, thinning and greasy. Horn observed him with disgust as he passed through the doorway, defeated and hopeless, with the posture of a man headed to his own execution. Horn had always suspected Saul of being a homosexual but couldn't fathom a gay man with such a hopeless lack of style. Saul Agnon brought two things to the table, though, that made him indispensable: cunning intelligence and unwavering loyalty. Agnon worshipped Horn the way an abused animal serves its cruel master, doing anything for a hint of approval or sign of pleasure.

"Not only are you late, Saul, but you come in here looking like a fucking rat. I thought Sears went out of business. Where did you get that suit? Don't sit down, this won't take long. What do you have for me?"

"Sir, I'm sorry for being late, there's no excuse, it's just that—"

"You're right, there is no excuse. Stop wasting my time with your contrition."

"Sir, the ambush went as planned. You've seen the media reports."

"As planned? I'm reading that there were survivors; that was *not* the plan. The admiral called. Hartley is pissed. She wants this thing handled before it gets out of control."

"Sir, I'm working the issue, and we will deal with it. This was always a possibility. There's another problem, though." Agnon paused to gain the courage to continue. "A doctor in Bagram discovered the tumors and was asking too many questions, but he'll be out of the picture soon. We'll use what they call a 'Green on Blue' since they are common enough not to raise suspicion. Our team on the ground found an Afghan military officer with a sick child. We promised to get the child medical care in the United States in exchange for one of his troops taking out the doc. Done deal."

"So now we have to arrange care for some sick kid from a third-world shithole?"

"No, sir, we have no intention of making good on that promise." Saul glanced down at his small spiral notebook. "Next item: As you know, Lieutenant Commander Reece survived the mission, as did one of his men. Reece is in the air now and will land in Coronado later this morning. Holder is headed to the other man's apartment as we speak."

"What's your plan for Commander Reece?"

"That situation is fluid, sir. The other events may have put him on guard, and we could have a problem on our hands. We don't have adequate personnel in the area to handle someone of his capability without the element of surprise."

"Saul, he's been put through the wringer by the

investigators and has flown halfway around the world. He'll be jet-lagged and exhausted. All he's gonna want to do is give his kids a hug, bang his wife, and forget about Afghanistan."

" 'Kid,' sir, singular. He has one daughter."

"Whatever. Get some gangbangers from L.A. or Mexico to take him out. Make it look like a home invasion robbery. Just make sure it gets done. We have cops on the payroll that can arrange it but don't let them know he's a SEAL. I don't want them going 'sentimental patriot' on us. Now get out of here, I have bigger matters to deal with."

CHAPTER 8

Coronado, California

The mammoth C-5 Galaxy touched down at Naval Air Station North Island and taxied slowly toward the small World War II–era terminal building. Upstairs in the barely occupied passenger area, James Reece stood and stretched, trying to shake the exhaustion and jet lag. He had long since shed his uniform for jeans and a T-shirt, the only connection to his combat load being the AOR 1–patterned pack and the hiking boots he wore nearly every day of his life. This pair was almost ready for the dumpster, he thought as he waited for the signal to deplane. He looked down at his right boot and smiled as he saw the unmistakable evidence that his three-year-old daughter had decorated it with a Magic Marker. The other boot, covered with the blood of his dying teammates, quickly wiped the smile away.

He'd taken an Ambien to try to force himself to sleep on the long flight but it wore off after three hours and he spent the rest of the trip in a surreal state of exhaustion, grief, and drug-induced fog. He'd replayed the events leading up to the op over and over in his head, trying to find an answer to what had led them into the ambush—some clue that he'd missed, some shred of evidence that would explain what happened. He found no answers, only a blinding headache like the ones he'd had leading up to the ill-fated mission. He scrolled through pictures of his daughter on his iPhone, his eyes misting over from the pain of his months-long absence from fatherhood. He couldn't get home soon enough.

Down in the massive cargo area, he steered clear of the pallets of gear and brushed past some Air Force ground crew personnel who were already preparing to offload what looked like enough crates and boxes to fill a Wal-Mart. He grabbed his oversize gear bag and weapons case and headed toward the ramp. The rest of his gear, along with that of his troop, had been palletized and sent back with Boozer on an earlier flight while Reece was spending quality time with the assholes from NCIS. He set down his heavy bag and pulled his sunglasses over his eyes before walking down the ramp and into the blazing Southern California sunshine. Love it or hate it here, the weather was always good.

There would be no one to meet him, no running hug with the wife and daughter, or Navy band playing "God Bless America," just a Navy base going about its business on a stateside Monday morning. There was always enough back-and-forth traffic that he figured he could bum a ride to his truck at Team Seven from someone headed to the Amphibious Base. He was about to set down the unwieldy weapons case to open the door to the terminal building when it opened as if on cue and was held wide by a heavily tattooed arm belonging to a short, muscular figure holding a giant cup of Starbucks.

The bearded man's face turned into a beaming smile behind a white-framed pair of surf shop sunglasses. The face was that of Ben Edwards, Reece's closest friend and former Teammate. Reece and Ben had gone through BUD/S together, deployed together as enlisted SEALs, and maintained a close friendship even after Reece became an officer and Ben migrated into the black side of Naval Special Warfare. Ben had since left the Navy for the nebulous world of the nation's intelligence agencies, though the lines between the two had grown increasingly blurred in the years following 9/11.

· "Welcome home, bro," said Edwards as he offered his hand.

"For a second, I thought you were a homeless guy," answered Reece as he grabbed the shorter man for a bear hug.

"I figured you might need a ride. Let me get your gear bag."

"Where's my coffee?" Reece asked with a smile.

Despite being identical in age, the two men walked through the small terminal building looking like complete opposites. The tall, clean-cut figure of James Reece and the stocky, ink-covered Edwards dressed in shorts and battered flip-flops: they were almost a caricature of the stereotypical differences between officers and enlisted SEALs. As they headed into the parking lot, Edwards fished into the pocket of his black hooded sweatshirt and the rear hatch of a black Chevrolet Tahoe began to arc toward the sky.

"Does Hertz have a fleet of rental Suburbans and Tahoes just for spooks?" chided Reece as he lifted the heavy black weapons case into the cargo area of the SUV.

"Yeah, but they're not up-armored, so don't drive us through any shit neighborhoods."

"Oh yeah, tons of slums here in Coronado," joked Reece.

"My truck is at the Team," Reece said as they climbed into the cab of the Tahoe. "This thing is plush. What is this, velvet?" he asked, rubbing his hand across the leather armrest.

"Anything is plush, compared to that shitbox you roll around in, man. When are you gonna get rid of that thing?" ·

"Ha! I'm driving the Cruiser until it dies. That's the whole point of having one. Us officers don't get those fat reenlistment bonuses."

Ben laughed. "You were enlisted once, too, remember? All that tax-free reenlistment money could have been yours."

He put the SUV in gear, slammed what was left of his coffee, and in a long, practiced motion that had obviously become second nature packed a can of Copenhagen that appeared out of nowhere with his right index finger before pinching a huge dip into his lower lip.

"How's quitting treating you?" Reece asked mischievously.

"Nobody likes a quitter, buddy." Ben smiled back, maneuvering the vehicle out of the parking lot and toward the gate.

"So I'm guessing you didn't tell Lauren you were coming home because you figured the plane would never get here on time?"

"Yeah man, you know how those C-5s are, always breaking down, usually in Hawaii when the aircrew decides they need to spend four days in paradise waiting for a part to show up. Always cool to surprise her and Lucy, anyway."

"I went by the house to check on them when I heard about the op. I knew from Boozer you weren't hurt bad and I wanted to make sure they didn't get bad info."

"Appreciate it, brother."

The inside of the SUV was dead quiet as they rolled through the gate of the air station. Clearly the small talk was over.

"I know what you're thinking, man," Reece said angrily without looking over. "My troop got wiped out, what in the fuck happened out there?

It was a shit op from the beginning; none of us wanted to go in the first place. It's my fault. I should have pushed back . . . I should have refused. Instead I said 'aye-aye, sir!' like some dumb-ass ensign and got all my guys killed."

"I'm sure you did what you could, Reece. Everyone in the community has heard it was a shit op. What the fuck were they thinking, anyway? When was the last time they pushed a target down to you instead of you guys coming up with your own?"

"That's what was crazy, Ben! You know it's never like that. If anything, they're telling you what targets you can't hit, not which ones you have to. Now they're gonna fry my ass for their bad intel, and I deserve it for letting my guys go out."

"You don't deserve shit, Reece. You're as solid as it gets, and everybody knows that."

"Yeah? I hope you told that to all of my guys' wives and kids at their funerals. Sorry, man, not trying to put this on you. What are you doing on the west coast anyway?"

"Looking for talent, man. Workload is crazy these days with the conventional stuff winding down. We're constantly needing new guys. You ready to come work with me yet?"

"I'm sure as hell gonna need a job but I think I've had enough of this shit. When they throw me out of the Navy, I'll open a sandwich shop or something."

"You'd have to touch mayo," Ben said, shaking his head. "That would never work."

"Yeah, well, I'll have to think of something else then." Reece's hatred of condiments was well known throughout the Naval Special Warfare community.

As they passed the Hotel Del Coronado and turned right toward the Silver Strand, they passed Miguel's Cocina, where they'd eaten with their wives dozens of times over the years. Well, with Reece's wife and each of Ben's three former brides.

"Too early for a margarita?" Ben joked.

"Never too early for a margarita. Just don't take me to Rick's. Don't think I could show my face in there right now," said Reece, referring to a hole-in-the-wall SEAL hangout bar in downtown Coronado. Operators would return from deployments and toast their fallen comrades in blackout sessions that often turned ugly. Rick's was a safe haven where they could blow off some steam without ending their careers, and there was always a steady supply of willing women looking to be a SEAL wife for the night.

"Ah yes, Rick's Palm Bar and Grill, home of the world-famous 'Slamburger.' I think I met wife number two in there?"

"Ha! I think you did," Reece said, remembering happier times.

"I'm actually banging this little spinner of a bartender in there now."

"Yeah? How old is he?" Reece asked, grinning.

"Fuck you. Heather, I think her name is. A bit of a Frog Hog but she does this amazing thing with her tongue. . . ."

"Okay, okay. Stop," said Reece, holding up his hands in mock defeat. "I don't want to know."

They passed through the gate to the Amphibious Base after showing their IDs and steered around a group of exhausted and soaking-wet BUD/S candidates running down the road with an inflatable boat balanced on their heads. "Shit, must be Hell Week. Poor bastards," Ben commented without a touch of sympathy for the aspiring frogmen.

"I'd trade a hundred Hell Weeks for the week I've had," Reece said, mostly to himself.

Ben spotted Reece's white 1988 FJ62 Toyota Land Cruiser in the parking lot of the Team building and pulled into the empty spot behind it. Both men were quiet as they transferred Reece's gear into the truck. When they were finished, the two friends faced one another and Ben Edwards extended his arm for a handshake.

"Call me if that piece of shit doesn't start."

"Thanks for the ride, man."

Reece needed to check in at the Team before heading home to surprise his wife and daughter. He walked across the parking lot and up the sidewalk of what looked more like a small office building than a den of amphibious commandos.

81

He wondered how the guys would look at him as he took a deep breath and opened the door to what had always been a safe haven. He'd barely made it through the entrance when a chief from one of the other platoons went running by him with panic on his face. He knew immediately that something was wrong.

"What's going on, Chief?" Reece pled. The forty-something chief spun around and faced Reece as he slowed his pace to a backward jog.

"Cops are at Boozer's, you need to get your ass over there," was all he said before turning and running out the front door of the building. Reece sprinted after him and covered the distance to his Cruiser in seconds.

CHAPTER 9

San Diego, California

Boozer was a bachelor and lived in a cookie-cutter apartment complex just off Interstate 5 near UCSD. It was the kind of place you'd find in every suburban city in the country, except the rent was probably double or triple what you'd pay in Middle America. Identical clusters of buildings and parking lots where young professionals and grad students lived among one another in anonymity, their lives separated by metal studs and cheap Chinese drywall. There was no traffic this late in the morning, and Reece drove like a man possessed. Boozer was a stud who could certainly handle himself, but Reece had a gnawing feeling that this was not going to end well.

Reece had been to Boozer's place only once before and he couldn't remember which building was his in the maze of two-story garden-style apartments. He took a guess and turned right as he passed the leasing office and blew by the first turn when he caught a cluster of emergency vehicles to his left. He slammed on the brakes and threw the truck into reverse before cutting the wheel hard and stomping on the accelerator.

When he reached the police cars, he quickly pulled into an empty space, slammed the shift lever into park, and raced toward the apartment. He ignored the police officer commanding him to stop and bounded up the stairwell. Brushing past an EMT, he tried to make it through the open front door of Boozer's apartment but was grabbed by two burly cops in uniform.

"He's one of my guys! I need to get in there!" Reece begged as he struggled against the two men who had pinned him to the doorjamb.

"You don't want to see this, sir!" the older of the two officers said as they loosened their grip.

Reece broke free and stumbled into the living room of the apartment as the too-familiar smell of blood and death filled his nostrils. Two detectives in civilian clothes with handguns on their hips were standing in front of a light brown futon couch, one of them holding a large DSLR camera with a flash sticking upward. They turned toward the commotion, and when they did, Reece could see Boozer's lifeless body sitting in boxers and a white T-shirt, his legs extended toward the two detectives. His usually pasty-white legs were deep purple in color and his face wore a mask of shock. A gaping exit wound was visible just above his left ear and a massive amount of blood, brain, and skull were splattered across the couch and onto the lampshade sitting on the end table. A SIG Sauer P226 was lying in an awkward position on his lap, the hammer cocked and ready to fire. Reece stood in shock, unable to move or speak. The two uniformed officers who had restrained him took him gently by the shoulders and steered him with care through the door of the apartment and into the hallway. Both had served combat tours in Iraq as reservists and knew the familiar look of a grief-stricken comrade. Reece sat down on the steps and put his head in his hands. What in the hell was going on? How could so many bad things happen at once? Various officers and NCOs from Team Seven had arrived at the scene and the chief that Reece had seen in the hallway guided him toward the parking lot, making him sit on the tailgate of an ambulance.

Reece's boss, the commander of SEAL Team Seven, appeared minutes later along with his command master chief, the senior enlisted SEAL in the command. Commander Cox was a good leader, a fair guy, and a legit warrior. He'd obviously had other plans for today, as he and the master chief were both in their full dress uniforms, something you didn't see often in the Teams. He had probably been dealing with family members of the men killed downrange. The two men quietly conferred with the other officers and NCOs on the scene as well as the detective in charge of the investigation. One of the enlisted SEALs pointed toward Reece, the commander turning to walk toward his grieving subordinate.

Still seated with his head in his hands, Reece did not see his boss approach until he was a few feet away. He started to rise to greet him but Cox pushed him downward with a firm but kind hand on the shoulder.

"Rough week, Reece, I know. I'm sorry about your Troop and I'm sorry about Boozer. There will be plenty of time later to point fingers, but for now I need to worry about you. I can't stand by while another life is wasted like Boozer's. Dan is taking you to Balboa. I want you cleared by the docs before you take another step. Does Lauren know that you're back?"

"No, sir. I was going to drive home after I checked in at the Team. Then I came straight here."

"Get cleared at Balboa and then head home. Take the rest of the week off, and on Monday we need to sit down and talk about the op."

CHAPTER 10

By the time the docs at Balboa Naval Medical Center had cleared Reece to go home, it was after 6:00 p.m. Dan Harvey, a lieutenant from the operations shop, had driven him to Balboa and babysat him all day as the doctors did their thing. He drove Reece back to the Team to get his truck and was kind enough not to say a word during the trip. After telling the shrinks what they needed to hear to be sure he wasn't going to eat a bullet or chase a handful of pills with a bottle of Jameson, the last thing Reece needed was some well-meaning new guy trying to cheer him up. His wife and daughter would be somewhere in the dinner-bath-book bedtime ritual, and he'd arrive just in time to see his little princess before she went to bed.

Reece thought he knew what love was when he met his beautiful wife, Lauren, but he'd never known complete, unconditional love until his daughter, Lucy, was born. She was her mother's spitting image, with enormous blue eyes and blond curls. Reece had killed insurgents on multiple continents, gone through the most rigorous military training in the world, and had stood his ground in confrontations with both admirals and master chief petty officers, but he was helpless in resisting the will of his three-year-old baby girl. When she said "sit," he sat. When she yelled "Daddy!" he dropped everything and bowed to her wishes. She had him wrapped around her tiny little finger, and they both loved every minute of it. After six long months, he was going to see her face in person in the next few minutes. He couldn't wait to scoop her up in his arms and hug her for as long as she would put up with it.

He thanked Dan for the ride and hopped into his Cruiser that one of the chiefs had driven back to the team, leaving the door unlocked and the key in the visor. It wasn't like anyone was going to steal his truck from the Team Seven parking lot. The chief obviously didn't know the weapons case was in the back. With all the turmoil of the day, Reece had never gotten a chance to turn it into the arms room. He was always wary about driving around with a box of weapons from work in his personal truck, given California's crazy gun laws, but under the circumstances he decided to risk it. He would bring the weapon's case home and run by the Team to turn it in late tomorrow morning after he caught up on some desperately needed sleep.

It was a ten-minute drive from Team Seven to the small house that his family had rented on the island for the past three years. He couldn't wait to get home. Homecomings from a war zone are difficult to describe to those who have not experienced them firsthand. They are exceedingly powerful experiences, made all the more remarkable when children are part of the picture. Emotional floodgates that have been held at bay month after month are finally opened, allowing those feelings of love and devotion to pour through all at once. Homecomings made the deployments almost worth it, *almost*. Those pent-up feelings, forced to take a six-month back seat to the mission of defending the nation, were now free to be expressed. For the Reece family, this one would be even more special; this would be their last. Reece had reached a rank where he would be precluded from leading men into combat, which is what he had joined the SEAL Teams to do in the first place. That it coincided with Lucy getting to an age where she needed him around made it a natural transition point for a man who had spent his entire adult life at war. It was time for a change and he knew it. It was time to focus on his family.

Reece thought back to his last homecoming, when Lauren had kept Lucy up way past her bedtime in anticipation of Reece's return, but not telling her why, just in case there was a delay, as happened so often with military transportation. The strains that such delayed returns placed on families could be significant; most guys would not tell their families exactly when they were coming home, lest they disappoint them with the inevitable delay. Delays of a day seemed like a week while a delay of a week felt like a month.

Reece remembered an entire Army brigade that was at the airport in Baghdad, ready to go home after a year in country, only to be turned around to fight for another four months. Some were even already safely back in the States and had to return to the quagmire that was Iraq. The sting of the deaths during those extended months must have been exceptionally hard to bear. Reece tried not to think of how the families of servicemen killed in action felt about the present-day struggle in the cradle of civilization.

On that last return, Reece had a taxi let him off at the end of the block so as not to ruin the surprise for Lucy, doing his best not to sprint down the sidewalk to his house. He had texted Lauren that he was almost home as he crept up past the front gate in the darkness. Before knocking he peered through the stained-glass section of the door to see Lucy curled up with Lauren on the couch watching what was inevitably a Disney movie. He had paused and let his eyes mist over with emotion, looking through the colored glass at the two people he loved more than anything else in this world: his family.

Lauren was stroking Lucy's hair and had looked toward the door, catching her husband's eye and smiling the most beautiful smile he had ever seen. God, she was gorgeous. Then he watched as she had whispered something in Lucy's ear and pointed at the door. Lucy had bolted from the couch with eyes as wide as saucers and a smile that would melt a glacier, rushing toward the door as fast as her young legs would carry her, her stuffed green frog clutched tightly in her small hand. Throwing open the door, Reece had taken a knee, Lucy running full speed into his outstretched arms and holding him with the strength only children hugging their parents possess, all the while repeating, "Dada, dada" over and over again like it was the only word she knew. Reece recognized that strength for what it was: a child's unconditional love. Standing with Lucy in his arms, Reece had moved into the house and met his stunning wife halfway across the living room floor, the three of them holding each other tight, the tears of joy flowing freely. "Welcome home, my love," Lauren had whispered. "We missed you."

Later that night, Reece read Lucy her favorite story, *Where the Wild Things Are*, acting out the goofy dances of the wild things so as to ensure it wasn't too scary for his daughter, and sang her favorite lullaby, "Hush Little Baby." As he concluded with "you'll still be the sweetest little baby in town" Lucy's eyes had closed, drifting off into the innocent slumber of youth. Reece had tucked the covers around her, smiling down at his little angel and kissing her forehead. He then made sure the night-light was plugged in before carefully and silently closing the door behind him and tiptoeing down the hall to join Lauren in the kitchen for a long-overdue glass of wine before whisking her upstairs to bed.

Turning off the main road and into his neighborhood, Reece was jolted out of his reverie, his heart sinking into his chest, the faint reflection of emergency lights on the treetops making the hair on the back of his neck stand up. The lights got brighter as he approached his turn and when the Cruiser made the left, his blood ran cold. Instead of the picturesque suburban scene he'd dreamed about during his entire deployment, his eyes were met by the violent flashing of red and blue lights coming from what appeared to be every police car, fire truck, and ambulance in Coronado. The emergency vehicles were scattered haphazardly in front of his home and a uniformed officer was stringing yellow "police line" tape around the perimeter of his well-manicured yard to keep the gathering of neighbors from trampling the scene. The rational center of his brain knew exactly what that meant but his emotions forced him into immediate denial. His family had to be okay; they were all he had left.

Leaving the Cruiser running in the middle of the street, Reece sprinted toward the front door of his home. He made it about halfway across his lawn when the officers spotted him and began yelling for him to stop. The first to reach him was a zit-faced patrol officer who looked younger than the kids showing up for BUD/S. He stood as if the badge on his chest alone would stop the speed and momentum of the larger man. Panic set into his eyes as Reece lowered his shoulder and sent him flying over a hedge. A second officer drew his handgun but wasn't prepared to use it and quickly found it out of his grasp. An unseen detective grabbed Reece from behind in a bear hug and got a broken collarbone for his troubles when his shoulder hit the sidewalk. More and more officers piled into the melee and soon all of Reece's adrenaline and rage-fueled skill was overcome by the sheer mass of bodies. As officers struggled to get control of his hands, someone sprayed his face with a full blast of pepper spray that set his senses afire. The handcuffs were already locked tightly around his wrists when the youngest officer, who had caught his wind and climbed his way out from the landscaping, got his revenge, kicking Reece's prone body in the face with his black combat-style boots.

A lieutenant grabbed the younger officer and four patrolmen dragged Reece toward the street and into the backseat of an idling Crown Victoria. Beaten, pepper sprayed, and prevented from knowing the fate of his wife and daughter,

Reece was suddenly overcome by the events of the past week. He'd lost the SEAL brothers he had sworn to lead, was kept from their funerals, scapegoated by a bureaucracy who helped seal their fates, lost another Teammate to a supposed suicide, and now faced the possibility that the two people he loved most in the world were gone, too. Lying on his side with his hands cuffed behind his back, he began to sob uncontrollably. The overwhelming emotions combined with the effects of the pepper spray turned the hardened warrior into a quivering mess. His body shook, he hyperventilated, and tears and mucus ran down his face and onto the seat of the patrol car. He had nothing left to give and nothing left to lose.

CHAPTER 11

Unlike the manipulative interrogation he'd faced at the hands of the NCIS investigators in Bagram, the questions posed by the local detectives were nonaccusatory. This physical evidence made it clear that this was not the act of a jealous husband or a guy looking to rid himself of the responsibilities that life had heaped upon him. The full-auto gunfire reported by the neighbors made the timeline for the home invasion and subsequent murders clear, and his alibi at Balboa was rock solid. The investigators had spoken to his CO before they'd even questioned him and were already familiar with how Reece had spent the day.

Reece sat emotionless as the detectives described to him the horrific crimes that would shock his serene community. Three to four men, undoubtedly armed with AKMs, judging by the steel 7.62x39mm cases that littered the scene, began firing into the home as they approached the front door. They kicked it in and continued firing as they worked their way through the rooms of the home, spraying rounds indiscriminately as they went. His wife was found facedown in the bedroom closet, shielding little Lucy's body with her own as she took her last breaths. It appeared

95

as if she'd wounded at least one of the shooters with the handgun she'd hastily grabbed from a small gun safe close to the bed. There was 9mm brass inside the closet and a blood trail that led out of the house. Lauren's wounds indicated that she was hit in the hands and arms while defending herself before she moved to cover her daughter and was killed by close-range rifle shots that took both of their lives. An entire thirty-round magazine appeared to have been emptied into Lauren at point-blank range. Death would have been more or less instantaneous from the multiple hits to her vital organs.

Lucy was still clinging to life when the ambulance arrived, but her badly broken body could fight no longer, and she died on the way to the hospital. The paramedics fought like lions to save her, but the trauma was too great. There was no indication of sexual battery on either body or any sign of theft, probably due to Lauren's brave resistance that wounded one of the shooters.

Neighbors saw the men flee the scene in a black Cadillac sedan. The detectives' working hypothesis was that this was the work of a crew of gang members from across the bay in Barrio Logan. They'd been increasingly suspected in "taggings" and property crimes in otherwise crime-free Coronado and had obviously upped the ante in committing such a brutal home invasion.

Reece listened to their narrative, knowing full well that this was no random act of violence by a crew of gangbangers, but neither was it the work of trained professionals. There was one last thing, the detectives told him, almost hesitatingly: Lauren had been pregnant. The little boy had been conceived just before Reece's deployment, according to how far along she was. Lauren had kept it a secret, a surprise to make his final homecoming especially memorable. He thought the pain couldn't have been any greater, but the news drove him deeper into despair.

While Reece met with the investigators, the crime scene team continued to process evidence at his home. Phillip Dubin had wanted to be a police detective as long as he could remember. He came from a long line of Boston cops and, much to his mother's chagrin, had never changed course. She had a momentary glimmer of hope when he had enlisted in the Navy, hoping he would use his GI Bill to become a doctor or a lawyer, but instead, Phil used his GI Bill to attend John Jay College of Criminal Justice in New York City, graduating at the top of his class. As upset as his mother was that he chose the family profession, she was even more dismayed that he decided to settle down across the country in San Diego, where he had spent the majority of his Navy time. He had caught the tail end of the First Gulf

War, spending most of that time in the bowels of a minesweeper, which did nothing to encourage him to pursue a career at sea. Stationed on the west coast, he fell in love with the weather, the beaches, and the laid-back atmosphere, which were all in stark contrast to his upbringing on the streets of Boston. He met his wife while she was working in the district attorney's office; she now ran their household full-time. After twenty years on the San Diego Police Department, he had attained the rank of lieutenant in the Homicide Division. Happily married and with three kids of their own, Phil could not imagine a more ideal life. He had a job he loved and a family he loved even more.

Detective Dubin had a tough time separating the cop in him from the husband and father as he slowly made his way through Reece's front yard. He had been called to the beautiful resort town that was Coronado on a few occasions for work, once for a brutal murder-suicide and another time for a questionable suicide by hanging. Coronado had detectives to handle such investigations but when there was a link to the city across the bay they would reach out for assistance from the SDPD.

After checking in and nodding to a few familiar faces, Phil climbed the front steps, knowing that the grislier parts of the crime scene awaited him. He had seen a lot in his career as a cop, but no father could ever get used to something like this. The nights he spent on murder investigations where young lives had been taken always caused him to pause and appreciate his own kids just a bit more when he got home.

"Hey, Phil."

"Hey, Chuck," Phil responded to the local detective. "How bad is it?"

"This one is rough. We don't get a lot of this over here, as you know. Thanks for coming."

"No problem. What do you have?"

"Looks like a home invasion, though we've never seen anything like this before out here. Hard to believe it's random. I just don't know why a bunch of gangbangers would want to hit a small house in Coronado."

Phil nodded and looked past the small town detective, who continued to fill him in.

The carpet was soaked in blood and the room was littered with shell casings marked by numbered yellow markers. Watching the medical examiner bag up a dead body was something Phil never got used to, and seeing the lifeless form of what had only hours before been a vibrant and beautiful woman caused the Boston native to look away.

"That was Lauren Reece. She was Signal Seven when the first units arrived on the scene. They found her daughter under her, still alive. The paramedics rushed her to the hospital but she didn't make it: multiple bullet wounds. Looks like the mom got a few rounds off with a Glock. We found a 19 and some spent brass close to her body, some blood in the hallway, and some more by the front door. The mom and daughter were shot in here, so we think she hit at least one of them."

"Any chance this was the husband?" Phil asked. He had seen his share of domestic problems turn violent.

"Surprisingly not. A neighbor gave us a good vehicle description and multiple perps. The husband is a Navy guy and was at Balboa Hospital all afternoon. We are interviewing him now but it looks unlikely."

"Thanks, Chuck. I'm just going to look around a bit. Our gang task force guys will be here soon."

"Okay. Let me know if you figure anything out."

Phil began to explore the home, trying to get a sense of what this family was like when they were alive. He wanted to understand them so he could make assessments and attempt to decipher what had caused their lives to end so violently in this normally safe section of San Diego. He entered a room off the bedroom that looked to be the home office.

Why would a gang hit this particular home?

When Phil had started in police work he would

always go straight to the family photo albums. More than once the story he gleaned from those family memories helped connect certain dots and allowed the young police officer to break a case. These days, hardly anyone kept family albums. Photos were spread out over different computers and hard drives and online accounts, making it exceedingly difficult to use them the way he had back in the 1990s. Now he used the photos on the walls and desks and dressers instead.

Phil took in the room methodically. Not messy but not particularly clean; "lived-in" would be the more apt term. Things looked organized but not remarkably so. At first glance, it looked like a typical home office, but it quickly became apparent that there was something different about this family.

Phil's eyes were immediately drawn to a wall containing three tomahawks of varying sizes. *You don't see that every day in San Diego.* Though he knew next to nothing about the weapons mounted to the office wall, he thought one reminded him of something out of the movie *Last of the Mohicans*. A more modern-looking one was attached to a plaque above a group photo of men in full military battle gear standing around a bombed-out building. *Operators.* Two of the men held a black flag with Arabic writing. All looked like serious people you'd want on your side in a fight. The plaque read, "To Lieutenant

James Reece from the men of Alpha Platoon." A skeleton of a frog was engraved under that with the warning, "Don't Fuck With Us," above a list of close to thirty names.

Phil stepped back and took in the remainder of the room. *Who is this guy?*

What Phil recognized as a samurai sword rested under glass in a presentation frame on the opposite wall. It looked old, not like the imitation ones Phil had seen for sale in shops downtown. A small brass plate was glued inside the glass under the sword. Phil bent forward to look more closely:

LTJG THOMAS REECE
SCOUTS AND RAIDERS
1945

Not a normal house and not a normal guy, Phil thought, moving to the desk and picking up a family photograph, James and Lauren Reece looking back at him. Even in the picture, he could tell these were special people. Both were beaming with joy, James holding his young daughter in his arms, Lauren's arm around him with her head on his shoulder. It must have been before some sort of formal event since James was wearing his dress blues, the unmistakable SEAL Trident gleaming off his chest. Phil pulled the photo closer. Was that a Silver Star? And next to that a Bronze Star with *V* adorned with two stars on either side? Though Phil had only served four years in the Navy, he knew the Trident well. His time on the minesweeper was spent with a few guys who had tried the famed SEAL training program and failed out for various reasons along the way. Phil looked back to the medals on Reece's chest and then back around the room, noting that none of the medal citations were displayed on the wall. *Humble guy,* Phil thought admiringly.

Opening a desk drawer, Phil rummaged through the contents: pens, some random business cards, and a few nice knives. As he was about to shut the drawer, Phil stopped and reached inside, a worn silver lighter catching his eye. Turning it over in his hand Phil looked at an enameled emblem of a beret-clad skull hovering over the letters "MACV-SOG" and the year "1967." The initials "T.S.R. III" were engraved beneath the image. Phil assumed that the lighter had belonged to Reece's father, based on the date and the last initial. Though he would have to do some research, he seemed to recall that MACV-SOG was some sort of covert action or special operations unit in the Vietnam War. Flipping it over, he was surprised to see an engraving of what appeared to be a strange-looking chicken with the words *Phung Hoàng* above it. *Odd.*

Returning the old Zippo to the drawer, Phil turned his attention to the bookshelves.

This guy sure likes to read.

Books, or lack thereof, often gave him an insight into the mind of a suspect. Phil had been in a lot of houses over the years, but he couldn't remember many like this. This guy was a student of war. The books seemed to be arranged loosely by topic and period. Titles such as *The Accidental Guerrilla, War of the Flea, Counterinsurgency, The Sling and the Stone, Counter-Guerrilla Operations,* and *A Savage War of Peace* jumped out at the detective. Right next to Machiavelli, Epictetus, and Marcus Aurelius were books on the Boer War, the Rhodesian Selous Scouts, and various other conflicts spanning both recent and ancient history. Phil pulled a book titled *The Book of Five Rings*, by Miyamoto Musashi, and cracked the cover. It was obviously well read, as the binding showed signs of wear, but what was most interesting to the detective were the page numbers written inside the front cover. Flipping through the book, Phil noted that these page numbers corresponded with highlighting and underlining, the margins filled with notes. Flipping randomly to one, Phil read a note that made him shiver.

Deliberately closing the book, Detective Phil Dubin returned it to its home on the shelf with respect. Looking back at the menacing-looking tomahawks on the wall, Phil had a thought he had never had on a crime scene before: *God help whoever did this.*

When his kids woke up in the morning, Phil would be there to hug them even tighter than usual.

The events of the next few days were a blur. Reece was in too much shock to even help with the funeral arrangements. Lauren's family lived in Southern California and her sister, a prominent L.A. attorney, handled all the details.

As it is when young people are taken before their time, hundreds attended the memorial service. Both caskets were closed, due to the severity of their brutal wounds. Reece was numb. The pastor, in whose church Lauren had grown up, gave the eulogy. It seemed like just yesterday that he was conducting their wedding ceremony. He did a good job of immortalizing the wonderful human being who Lauren was, and he tried his best to reconcile Lucy's death as part of "God's plan." Reece appreciated the kind words heaped upon him by well-meaning friends and relatives, but the "they are in a better place" comments nearly sent him into a rage.

The graveside ceremony was a private affair, but the SEALs from the other platoons at Team Seven showed up anyway. They were family. They all knew and loved Lauren and Lucy. She was the kind of SEAL wife who was always there for the other wives and girlfriends when times were tough and the guys were overseas.

Lucy was Reece's constant companion between deployments and every man had melted at least once before her angelic smile. Lucy's tiny casket flanked that of her mother's, her beloved stuffed frog tucked inside at Reece's request.

As the pastor concluded his short remarks, Special Warfare Operator Master Chief Petty Officer Ben Edwards approached Lucy's casket and stood at rigid attention in his immaculate dress blue uniform. He removed the golden Trident badge from his left breast and placed it on top of the casket's lid. He pressed downward, forcing the brass pins on the back of the badge into the highly polished walnut veneer until it sat flush. He then executed a hand salute with tears in his eyes and moved swiftly away. The scene was repeated by every SEAL present at the ceremony, until the entire lids of Lucy's and Lauren's caskets were clad in golden Tridents. These hardened warriors, most of them husbands and fathers themselves, had honored Lauren and little Lucy with a tradition reserved for SEALs slain in combat. As far as they were concerned, Lauren and Lucy had died in battle.

CHAPTER 12

Reece did not move for more than an hour. When he did, he knelt at the graves of his wife and daughter, head bowed, tears streaming. It was a knowing hand on his shoulder that revived him from his trance. Reece turned his head and looked up into the eyes of a short, almost scrawny man of Mexican heritage. The man helped Reece to his feet and embraced him.

Reece looked into the face of his friend but didn't change his expression. With considerable effort, Marco del Toro turned Reece from the graves of his family and slowly walked him to the waiting new Mercedes S-Class Maybach sedan. A driver, looking suspiciously more like a prison guard than a chauffer, opened the door for them and Marco helped Reece inside before moving around the big car to the opposite side door. "*La casa,*" Marco told the driver, who put the car in drive and headed back to Coronado.

"Tequila?" Marco asked.

Reece slowly shook his head.

Marco reached into the seatback, pulled out a bottle of Cuervo's best 1800 Colección, and pulled a swig.

"I am sorry I missed the funeral, my friend. I

was in Mexico City on business and could not get home in time."

Marco del Toro was one of Reece's closest friends. At first glance, one would think them an odd pairing: the naval commando and the Mexican businessman. But with further investigation it was evident that they connected around the ties of family. Marco's daughter Antonia was the same age as Lucy. They attended the same preschool and loved their playdates at the beach. Marco's wife, Olivia, and Lauren had bonded over tennis, which they both played with vigor. Try as they might to get their husbands on the courts, Reece and Marco chose to spend their time on the mat and in the ring, training in Brazilian jiujitsu and boxing. Marco was by far the better jiujitsu practitioner, besting Reece at every turn. How such a small man harnessed so much strength and determination was astounding. Reece could never quite figure out how to beat him. His technique was flawless. In the boxing ring Reece came close, but the one time he bested Marco he was fairly certain the smaller man had let him win.

Both men also enjoyed a shared love of custom motorcycles. Two years before, Reece and Lauren had joined Marco and Olivia on a trip to Sturgis for bike week. Marco had flown them all out on his corporate G550 jet and, with beautiful new Harleys waiting on them when they landed, they enjoyed a few days exploring the Black Hills of South Dakota and the spectacle that is the Sturgis motorcycle rally. Reece loved his adventures with his friend, but it was Marco's love and dedication to family that Reece admired most.

Reece knew that Marco was a wealthy man. His multiple homes in Coronado and what seemed to Reece to be an almost unending supply of new high-end vehicles made that abundantly evident, but it was not until Reece and his family joined Marco at one of his family villas in Mexico that Reece fully understood the extent of Marco's affluence. Reece had twice accompanied Marco down to estates in Mexico, hunting birds in areas not usually accommodating to foreigners, but those hunting estates were nothing compared to the villa. It was what most would consider a private resort and was located just south of the bustling beaches of Puerto Vallarta. A full staff waited on their every need while Antonia and Lucy played in the waves under the watchful eye of nearby private security contractors. Vast real estate holdings, a telecommunications company, and Mexico's largest insurance firm fell under Marco's portfolio, making him extremely prosperous. This also made him and his family prime targets for Mexico's kidnap-and-ransom industry.

After a close call in Mexico City a few years earlier, Marco decided to move his family to San Diego, choosing the resort community of

Coronado for its safety and proximity to his businesses across the border. As of the past year, Marco and his family were dual citizens, an honor for which Marco was exceedingly grateful. That America had welcomed him and his family with open arms, offering them a refuge from the violence and uncertainty of Mexico, was something he did not take lightly.

"It's okay, Marco. Thank you for coming. How long was I standing there?"

"Not sure, my friend," Marco said with compassion. "I arrived to see you standing alone. I waited for an hour. When I saw you hit your knees I knew it was time to lend a hand."

They sat in silence as the car made its way along the coastline, inching closer to home. Marco was a devout Catholic, and nothing was more important to him than religion and family. When Marco spoke again it was both with reverence and sealed resolve. "But for the grace of God, that is my daughter, my wife. Those that did this are scum, lowlife gangbangers. They violated an agreement. I will take care of the bosses regardless of whether they knew or not. And I will help you, my friend. I know what you need to do."

CHAPTER 13

Coronado, California

Reece sat alone in the darkness of his living room. His senses had been bombarded by too much; he just needed to see and hear nothing. The headaches had gotten even worse. Reece was sure that his tumor was killing him. Seeing his home looking like the aftermath of a firefight on a target overseas only intensified the blinding pain. The interior walls had been shredded by gunfire and the front door had been replaced by a four-by-eight foot sheet of plywood screwed into the frame. The blood-soaked carpet in his bedroom had been torn out by the cleanup crew and much of the furniture had been either shot up or smashed. For reasons unknown to him, the violence that he'd fought to keep overseas had come to his living room and taken his family.

What if he had come straight home from the airfield instead of going to the Team first? What if he hadn't gone to Boozer's? What if he had refused to go to Balboa Medical Center and driven directly home to his family? *What if . . . ?*

Could he have defended his family from a gang of heavily armed home invaders? Would his skill with a handgun have been enough? Could he have fought his way to his rifle or shotgun?

Reece knew the answer to any of those questions was that he would probably be dead alongside his wife and daughter. He had to believe that he was spared for a reason: to find out what happened and punish those responsible.

Reece thought he knew something about survivor's guilt, having seen some of the strongest special operators in the world fall prey to its ravages after losing Teammates in battle. The events of the past few days made him realize that he really didn't know the first thing about it.

I should have been here. I should have died with them, Reece thought, his gaze shifting to the space on the sofa next to him, where his young daughter had loved to curl up for a story, where his wife would snuggle beside him with a glass of wine to watch a movie after putting Lucy to bed. That space would never know that joy again. Now it was empty, a void never to be filled. Well, not quite empty. Now that spot was occupied by the cold dark metal and composite frame of his Glock 9mm handgun.

Would death make the pain go away? Should he just end it all and join Lauren and Lucy? More than anything, that was what he wanted. His hand reached for the Glock and slowly wrapped around it. It felt comfortable. It felt natural, an extension of his body. It felt right. Reece set it on his lap, his eyes moving to the family photo he had on the coffee table in front of him.

"I love you, Lauren," he whispered, moving the pistol under his chin and sliding his finger onto the trigger.

You've never taken the easy route, Reece.

This was too easy. *Fuck easy.*

Reece's eyes narrowed and he took a breath.

Let these feelings turn, Reece. Let them turn. . . .

Reece leaned forward, smoothly tucking the pistol into the holster behind his right hip and then turning the photo of his family over so that it was facedown on the table.

It was time to start figuring this out.

As much as he tried to clear his head of all of the noise, he just couldn't do it. Facts that didn't fit flashed in his thoughts like a slide show of evidence: the strange and urgent mission that left his men slaughtered, the tumors, the questions from NCIS, Boozer's "suicide," and an act of unspeakable violence brought upon his family on this quiet little street. These kinds of things didn't happen randomly, not in this kind of proximity to one another.

He started with the things that he knew for certain; Boozer's death was no suicide. First of all, Boozer wasn't the kind of guy to quit on anything, especially life, and he sure as hell wouldn't have abandoned Reece in the middle of all this, PTSD or not. The most telling fact, however, was something Reece had not shared with the police investigators. It was something you had to know about Boozer to understand; he would never have shot himself with a 9mm. An outsider trying to make it look like a SEAL suicide would find it convenient to use the same type of handgun that SEALs were issued. What they couldn't know was that Boozer was a real gun guy who'd grown up shooting competitively before he ever even thought about joining the Navy to become a Frogman. Boozer had a love affair with custom 1911s chambered in .45 ACP, which most people just would not understand. Boozer hated the "9 mil," and even though he had a SIG P226 in his personal collection to commemorate the pistol all SEALs had carried into combat since 9/11, his disdain of the smaller round was part of his identity.

But who in the hell would want to kill Boozer and go to the trouble of making it look like something it was not? The same people who would send an entire troop into an ambush and then kill a family in their home and blame it on gang violence. Whoever did this had some serious resources at their disposal, possibly even someone in the Naval Special Warfare chain of command, though Reece could not bring himself to make that jump yet. He did not buy in to government conspiracies, but he'd seen enough shady and unexplainable things go down overseas that he wasn't naïve enough to rule anything out, either. But what was the connection? The ambush, Boozer, his family, the tumors, they all had one common denominator: Reece. The tumors were the outlier. This had to be connected to the tumors. His head throbbed and he momentarily lost his train of thought. He needed a fresh set of eyes on this, but who, if he couldn't trust his own chain of command, could he trust?

Reece burst from the couch and ran down the hallway, flinging open the door to the garage. He grabbed his pack from a hook on the wall and reached in for the sleeve that held his laptop. Pulling out the MacBook Air, he opened the screen and a business card fluttered to the floor. He started to dial the number on his iPhone but stopped himself, hitting the END button before the call connected.

He looked at his watch: 10:36 p.m., probably not too late. He walked out the back door of his house and crossed the lawn to his neighbor's front door. He knocked quietly, trying to attract his neighbor's attention without waking his sleeping kids. He knocked progressively louder until his neighbor, who had obviously been sleeping, opened the front door shirtless and in his boxers.

"Hey, James, what's up? What can I do for you?"

His neighbor was a good guy, some kind of civilian software geek who was always polite and showed evidence of a slight man crush on his commando neighbor. When he saw that Reece customarily backed his truck in the driveway, he started doing the same. Next thing you know, he was wearing the same sunglasses as Reece and driving an old Toyota Land Cruiser. The guy was harmless, and maybe even useful. Reece could never remember his first name.

"Hey, man, my battery is dead and I really need to make a call. Can I use your phone?" Reece asked in his most neighborly tone.

"Of course, James . . . I mean, Reece . . . come on in and use the one in my office." The neighbor led Reece into a small home office, where a landline sat next to a panel of three computer monitors. He stood by the door and looked at Reece for a moment until he got the message and quickly left the room, shutting the door behind him.

"This is Katie," she said, picking up on the first ring.

"Katie, I'm sorry to call you so late. This is James Reece. We met in Afghanistan a couple of weeks ago."

"James, of course, oh my gosh. I read about what happened to your family and wanted to reach out. I'm so sorry."

"I appreciate that. It's actually what I'm calling about. This whole thing just doesn't make sense and I need to run it by a fresh set of eyes. I read the series you did on Benghazi. It was really impressive. Any chance you would be willing to sit down with me?"

"Absolutely, can you meet me in L.A. or do you want me to drive down there?"

"No, no, L.A. is fine. Can you meet tomorrow?"

"I can. Is eight too early? There's a Starbucks downstairs from my condo. It's at Fifth and Fig, downtown."

"Eight is fine. I don't sleep anyway. I'll see you in the morning."

"I understand," said Katie sympathetically. "How could you? See you in the morning."

"See you then, and Katie . . ."

"Yeah, James?"

"Thanks."

CHAPTER 14

Los Angeles, California

The drive up Interstate 5 to L.A. helped clear Reece's head a bit. Sleep hadn't come the night before, but strong Black Rifle Coffee, tempered with some honey and cream, and driving with the windows down made him feel halfway human. It was pitch dark when he left the house. If he was going to make it to downtown L.A. in time to meet Katie, he was going to have to do his best to beat some of the planet's worst traffic. Contrary to what civilians might think, not everyone in the military gets up before dawn, and Reece was definitely not a morning person.

Ordinarily he'd use an app on his phone to help navigate the L.A. traffic, but he'd purposely left his phone on his nightstand when he left the house. The joke in the Teams was that smartphones were "surveillance devices that also made phone calls," and he wasn't sure exactly who was watching him at this point. He took I-5 all the way to I-10 and then onto the I-110 simply because that was the way he knew best. Traveling to a monstrous city like Los Angeles wasn't something that he relished or did very often. Parking in L.A. could be a nightmare, but he knew from a shopping trip with Lauren that there was a garage near the Seventh and Fig shopping area downtown that would have plenty of space this early.

It wouldn't take much to have followed him, especially if any satellite or drone assets were involved, so Reece didn't play any counter-surveillance tricks to try to lose anyone. The parking lot was deserted and the three-block walk from Eighth to Fifth was uneventful but for the solicitations of a few of L.A.'s massive homeless population. Something about Reece's demeanor told the panhandlers not to be too aggressive with their requests, though most were too hungover to give it much effort. Reece had to chuckle when he saw a man facedown on the sidewalk with a length of rope tied around his neck and the other end tied around the neck of a bottle of cheap vodka.

He'd planned to hit the Starbucks before Katie arrived so that he could pick their seats without raising any eyebrows by asking her to move, but she'd beaten him to the punch. As soon as he walked through the door he spotted her in the far corner, seated with her back to the wall. She'd stolen his spot. Despite being a well-respected investigative reporter, Katie Buranek was quite young and undeniably attractive in a way that obviously required very little effort on her part. She was dressed in workout clothes: black yoga pants, and a tight-fitting bright orange zippered top. She wore little, if any, makeup and her dirty-blonde hair was pulled back into a ponytail. She wore black rectangular glasses, probably more for effect than to enhance her vision, Reece thought. Though she was a print journalist, she certainly had the looks and brains to put her on one of the cable news networks. Reece was in his late thirties, and he assumed her to be at least ten years younger than he, if not fifteen.

The last time they'd met had been at Bagram. Reece had just been discharged from medical when she tracked him down in a Green Beans Coffee, of all places. Bagram had turned into a mini-USA over the years and the Green Beans was similar to going to a Starbucks, with gourmet coffee, free Wi-Fi, and plenty of places to sit and enjoy your latte. To Reece, the more they tried to make Afghanistan like home, the more alien and out of place it became. Despite his civilian clothes, she knew exactly who Reece was when she sat down across the table from him. She had slid her business card across the table and simply said, "Commander Reece, I'm sorry about your men. I know that now is not the time, but if you want to talk about it, you know how to get a hold of me."

A reporter who had the good taste not to smear herself in the blood of his men was a rare bird, and her intel was obviously strong. Reece was a bit of a news junkie and he'd remembered her name from a series that she wrote exposing the lies and cover-ups that followed the Benghazi fiasco. He had known both of the SEALs killed that night in Benghazi, Libya, during a thirteen-hour gun battle in September 2012, so he had taken a personal interest in Katie's coverage and investigation of the attack.

She stood with a slight smile and extended her hand.

"Nice to see you again, James." Her face showed genuine sadness when she followed it with "I'm so sorry about all that you've been through and I'll do anything that I can to help. Thanks for making the trip up here."

She had the slightest hint of an accent, though most people would not have noticed. Eastern European, he suspected by her last name.

"Not a problem. I appreciate the kind words and your being able to meet on such short notice. Let me grab a coffee and we can talk."

Reece stood uncomfortably in the growing pre-workday coffee line as Katie pecked away at her laptop. She caught him glancing her way and flashed a polite and knowing smile. He finally got his coffee and sat down across from her at the small table.

Usually Reece would be very hesitant to talk about the events of the past few days in such a public setting, but the music in the coffee shop was loud enough that anyone's attempt to overhear their conversation, either in person or electronically, would have been a failure. As it was, Reece and Katie had to lean toward one another across the table to talk. He was relieved when she closed her laptop and pulled out a long spiral notebook to take notes; he wasn't dying to have this information on someone's computer.

"Start from the beginning and don't leave anything out. I promise I am not going to write about this without your permission."

Reece started the story with a week before the operation that wiped out most of his unit, to add a bit of context. He didn't disclose anything remotely classified, but he did convey how unusual it was for a target to come down from higher headquarters with this much specificity and urgency. She took scribbled notes that no one but a team of archeologists could decipher. Her head snapped up when he told her about the tumors found in his men's brains, and she asked questions that indicated she knew more than a little bit about the medical field.

He walked her through the bizarre questioning by the NCIS agents and the inconsistencies in Boozer's supposed suicide, and eventually got to the murder of his family. She stopped him at various points in the story, asking him to clarify details or expand on certain conversations. Stress, grief, and exhaustion clouded his memory in certain areas but he was fairly sure that he told her everything that was relevant.

When he finished the story she put away her notebook and took off her glasses. She locked eyes with Reece across the table and her voice took on a quieter and more serious tone.

"Look, James, I know what you do for a living and I probably don't have to tell you this, but you need to be careful. We both do. Whoever is behind this thing isn't playing games. It doesn't make any sense for them to have done all of this and left you alive, which means they probably intended to kill you along with your family. If I were you, I wouldn't trust anyone, including the Navy brass. When my Benghazi series broke, you wouldn't believe the intimidation tactics they used against me. They hacked my email; I had two huge guys that were obviously feds block me from going down the stairwell in my building; I was audited by the IRS; they even tried to sabotage my deal when I bought my condo. They were all about letting me know they could get to me and weren't the least bit afraid of me printing something about it. They own the big media outlets, dangle access to interviews, and exert their influence to manipulate the story while intimidating the press corps. It's not as bad as what my family endured in Czechoslovakia in the eighties, but it's getting there. I want to help you and I want this story, but I don't want either of us to get killed. We need to be very careful about how we communicate."

Reece nodded in understanding.

"You don't have to tell me about what they're willing to do. The last thing I want to do is get you hurt. I called you from my neighbor's landline last night, and my cell phone is back in Coronado. They probably don't know that we connected overseas so they won't be onto you unless I lead them to you, which I promise I won't do. Find yourself a used iPhone, maybe from Craigslist, where you have no relationship with the seller. Pay cash for it, toss the SIM card, and restore it to factory settings. You'll need to set up a burner email to get an anonymous iTunes account. Do that from a library computer or one not associated with you. You getting all this? I know it's kind of a lot."

"I've got it," said Katie, not looking up as she took detailed notes.

"Use cash to buy an iTunes gift card so you can download Signal. It's a private messaging service from the app store. Make this your username."

Reece took a napkin from the table and wrote down a series of random letters and numbers. He copied the same characters at the bottom of the napkin and tore the paper in half, sticking one half in his shirt pocket. He slid the top half across the table to Katie.

"It's basically a texting app. You'll need cell

service to get Signal, so just use a prepaid SIM bought with cash. After that, don't use cell again. Only use it over public Wi-Fi. Also download a VPN from Private Internet Access. Pay for it with a gift card you buy with cash. Keep Wi-Fi turned off when you are not actively using it. In fact, keep the phone turned off when you are not using it. Try to check it at least once a day. They can still get to you if they are specifically targeting you, but this will make it more difficult."

Katie looked up from her notes, "I'm guessing you've done this before?"

"We do a lot more than just swim around and shoot bad guys these days. Plus, all Team guys are paranoid about communication and social media. A lot of us use little tricks like this to keep Big Brother at bay. We've seen the capability we have to track our targets overseas using their phones and we don't want anyone doing that to us. If it weren't for cell phones, most of the HVIs we've hit would still be alive."

"Okay, so how do I get a hold of you?"

"I'll contact you later tonight. You'll know it's me."

"Sounds good."

"Are you sure you want to do this, Katie? I don't have anywhere else to turn, but I don't want to see anyone else get killed that doesn't need to be."

"Yeah, I'm one hundred percent sure. I can take

care of myself," she said, wondering what he meant by his "doesn't need to be" comment.

"I bet you can. Thanks again for listening."

"James, if I might, you should get that tumor checked out. Don't just assume the worst."

"You sound like Lauren."

Katie tilted her head sympathetically as Reece rose from his seat. "What are you going to do now?"

"I'm going to work."

Reece turned and walked toward the door, subconsciously scanning faces in the room. His meeting with Katie had shaken him out of his funk and put him back into operator mode.

CHAPTER 15

Riviera Country Club
Los Angeles, California

No one knew what Steve Horn looked like as a kid. Most just assumed that he appeared out of nowhere in a custom suit or golf clothes. Though he owned homes around the country, he rarely spent much time in them. If he was not in his office, Horn could be found on the golf course. He didn't love the game as some would expect. Rather, it was an outlet, and Horn was after the elusive perfect swing.

His real love was power, and money brought that power. He didn't want to be the president of the United States. He wanted to control the president of the United States. To him that was a much more formidable position. To control the most powerful person on earth made him the de facto king of the world. His hunger to be near the throne would have made him an ideal fit for Washington, but he couldn't stand the climate or the personalities. He liked to be around exciting and attractive people, and on that front the D.C. elite couldn't compete with L.A. To his way of thinking, the most beautiful people in the world had been moving to L.A. for more than a century. That was five generations of breeding encapsulated along the California coast. Why would one live anywhere else?

Horn was on the driving range when his cell phone rang. Paying no mind to the daggers thrown his way through the glares of those members on the line, he looked down at the caller ID and decided to take the call. Putting his earbuds in, he turned and walked toward his cart, stepping past a "no cell phone use" sign as he spoke.

"This is Horn."

"Steve, it's J.D."

"Congressman, what can I do for you this fine day?" asked Horn, already knowing he was going to have to exercise a bit of damage control.

"Steve, this thing with 'the Project' is getting messy. I've tried getting in touch with Tedesco but my calls keep going to voice mail, which is unusual. Is the group up to speed on where things stand and where we are going?"

"Are you calling on behalf of you or your wife?"

"Dammit, Horn, I'm calling because Lorraine and I don't want to watch this thing go south on the evening news. What is your plan to get this mess tidied up?"

Horn suppressed a laugh. Who watched the evening news anymore? And if J. D Hartley did tune in, he certainly wasn't viewing it with his wife.

"J.D., these things sometimes do not go as planned. You understand. What is important is that we keep our heads and adapt. Do you want to know why I am so successful?" Not waiting for an answer, Horn continued: "It is because I see opportunity in chaos and I adapt to it quicker than anyone else. Yes, our straggler is still alive and that is a problem. Due to media interest in the story we are going to need to explore activating one of your assets. It's time. And it will play right into the media firestorm surrounding the ambush and the home invasion. It will wrap things up nicely, and we will be home free."

"Horn, you shouldn't even know about those assets, and the only one who can authorize it is my wife. But I see your point. It would close the loop nicely. Are you sure it's the only way?"

"J.D., it is 'a' way, and in this circumstance, the 'best' way."

"All right. I'll call her now."

Congressman Hartley sounded more despondent about having to talk with his wife than he did about their current state of affairs.

"It will all be worth it in the end, J.D. Please give Lorraine my best."

Horn hit the END button.

Tossing the phone on the seat of his golf cart, he walked back up to his stack of balls and carefully placed his feet to address the tee.

CHAPTER 16

Coronado, California

Katie was right. He needed to get checked out. The headaches might be nothing, or they could be a mass in his brain. At least he would know for sure. Reece couldn't trust the naval medical system at this point, but he had another option.

When Reece got home he dug Dr. O'Halloran's card out of his deployment backpack, sat down on his couch, and dialed the number for the office in La Jolla.

"Head and Spine Associates, how may I help you?" a friendly female voice answered.

"Hi, my name is James Reece. Dr. O'Halloran saw me in Afghanistan and told me to call his office when I got back to the States. I know he's still overseas but I wanted to see if I could set up an appointment for when he gets back."

"Um, hold, uh, hold please," the voice stammered, clearly beginning to strain with emotion.

That's odd, Reece thought, a sinking feeling beginning to well up inside him.

After a solid two minutes a male voice with a thick Spanish accent picked up the line.

"Mr. Reece, this is Dr. German. I am a colleague of Dr. O'Halloran's; *was* a colleague, I should say. I regret to inform you that there was an incident in Afghanistan, devastating to all of us. Dr. O'Halloran was killed. It just recently hit the news. Someone we thought was an Afghan ally, I'm afraid. Such terrible business."

Damnit, this thing is for real.

"I'm so sorry, sir. I've been a little distracted since I got back. I had no idea. I didn't know Dr. O'Halloran well, but he sure seemed like a great man," Reece said sincerely, his mind already connecting the dots. *Could that really be a coincidence?* The doctor who discovered the tumors suddenly dead. Reece's family dead. Boozer dead. The ambush. *Green-on-blue incidents are not uncommon these days,* Reece thought. Good people die in war. Still, this is not adding up, or rather, it was adding up to something horrifying.

"That he was, Mr. Reece. An incredible man, a world-class mind, and a better person than most, I dare say. He did share your case with me over email, and I have been hoping you would reach out. I am very interested in getting to the bottom of this. Dr. O'Halloran asked me to help you if you called. I handle the neurosurgery here at the clinic and would be the one performing your biopsy. I am happy to do it; in fact, I insist. I consider it the last request of my late friend. Stay on the line and one of the ladies will schedule you an appointment. It is not a big deal, I promise you. And there will be no charge, on this I also insist. Hold, please."

Reece made an appointment for later in the week and was given instructions on how to prepare for the procedure. They made it sound so routine, though Reece couldn't envision a way in which they were going to get a tissue sample from inside his skull that he considered "routine."

Five minutes later, as Reece was contemplating the procedure, the phone rang. It was Commander Cox's command master chief, a SEAL named Dave, with a thick New York accent that, along with the ever-present toothpick in his mouth, made some words almost indiscernible over the phone. He had a long family history in the New York Fire Department and had lost his brother and an uncle when the towers came down on 9/11. Dave had worn their Ladder 55 patch on his shoulder each time he had pulled the trigger in combat ever since.

Dave got right down to business. "Reece, I'm not sure what this is about. Cox is out of the country so I took the call. You're to report to WARCOM at 1400 today. Admiral Pilsner wants you in his office."

The hits just keep on coming.

"Roger that, Dave, I don't think I can take any more good news. So much for taking the rest of the week off."

"Not our show, Reece. And Reece? Um, I'm

really sorry about your family. I don't have the words except to say that I'm sorry. Keep your chin up, you'll get through this. Let me know if there is anything I can do."

"Thanks, Dave, I really appreciate it."

Reece leaned back on the couch, wondering if he had a uniform clean enough for WARCOM.

CHAPTER 17

Naval Special Warfare Command
Coronado, California

Reece drove as if on autopilot. He was behind the wheel, but it felt like the Land Cruiser was driving itself and he was just a passenger, his movements dictated by something outside himself, as if in a dream. The numbness had given way to anger, which he knew had clouded his judgment. As he drove he couldn't help but think of his family, the pain in his soul pushing him toward the edge of that proverbial cliff of despair. Once over, it would be hard to return.

He pulled off the Silver Strand Highway as he had done innumerable times over the past eighteen years and pulled up to the gate. The young gate guard recognized the Land Cruiser immediately. Something about the guy driving it had always seemed special to him. In a world filled with egos, thousand-yard stares, and rank elitism, this officer gave off a different air, almost akin to a cool college professor. Never at a loss for a smile and a brief encouraging word, he stood out, especially because this was the same gate the admiral had to use to get to the Naval Special Warfare Command, more commonly referred to as WARCOM, from which all the SEAL Teams were administratively managed. To the gate guard, WARCOM had the aura of a death star, with the Admiral as Darth Vader, or even worse, Darth Vader's master, *what was his name?* The line of cars moving through the gate each morning filled with staff officers headed for their doom. . . .

"Morning, sir."

"Morning, Ken."

No officers called Ken by his name except for Commander Reece. In fact they barely acknowledged his existence, just a nuisance before finding a parking spot and starting their days.

Reece showed his military ID and Ken saluted, as was protocol for officers.

"How's your build coming?" They had talked cars once, and Reece knew that Ken was rebuilding an old '69 Mustang.

Jeez, even with what happened to his family, he still asks about my car.

"Good, sir. And, sir? Um, I'm so sorry."

Everyone knew.

"Thanks, Ken. You take it easy."

"I will, sir." Ken stepped back, and even though he didn't need to do it again, he straightened up and snapped his sharpest salute as Reece slowly moved through the gate.

The view of the Pacific Ocean through the sand berms in front of him was spectacular. Slow rollers were hitting the beach, the cacophony of the sound reminding all that within the beauty was a power that should not be underestimated. Reece couldn't help but think of their journey from Antarctica to their terminus here in Southern California.

Reaching a stop sign, Reece began to swing the wheel to the left but then paused. To the left were his beloved SEAL Teams, where he had spent the majority of his time in the Navy. He caught himself and remembered where he was going today. To the right. To WARCOM. Everybody hated going to WARCOM. The uniforms, the brass, the protocol. WARCOM was the antithesis of everything that drew guys to the SEAL Teams. WARCOM was where the senseless directives came from. Delivered down the chain from people so far removed from the tactical application of said directives that they became the definition of bureaucracy. *Politicians in uniform.* Reluctantly, Reece swung the wheel back to the right. WARCOM was where the admiral reigned supreme.

Reece pulled through yet another set of gates and began to look for a parking place. The SEAL Teams had expanded considerably in the years following 9/11: new commands, more SEALs, additional support personnel. What had been neglected was the parking to accommodate those additional bodies. *Typical military planning,*

Reece thought. He scanned the lot, immediately noticing a dark blue Bentley parked in the admiral's visitor spot. *Odd.*

Finding a place by the fence, Reece put his truck in park, leaned back in his seat, and took a deep breath. *Fuck.* None of this was making any sense.

The excruciating pain hit Reece like a lightning bolt out of the blue. *These headaches! Breathe through it, Reece. It's okay. Breathe. You can do this. Breathe.*

The pain dissipated almost as quickly as it had begun.

Reece took one more deep breath and exited the vehicle. He straightened his uniform, noting for the thousandth time that he was not armed. He never understood military base policies that prohibited those in uniform from carrying personal weapons on base or even keeping them in their cars. Reece could check out fully automatic machine guns and grenades from the same base upon which he was not allowed to carry his 9mm pistol. Policies created by bureaucrats in uniform essentially disarmed some of the most highly trained and competent warriors on earth. It was only a matter of time until the enemy took advantage.

Checking in at WARCOM was never fun. The air was different in there even though it was just a few hundred yards from the Teams. The poor quarterdeck watch had the look of a prisoner awaiting execution and did his job with as much enthusiasm. Encased behind thick plastic glass, as they were, they always looked as happy as gas station attendants stuck behind similar barriers in bad neighborhoods.

Reece turned in his ID for a visitor's badge and was buzzed inside the labyrinth that was WARCOM. He had been there a few times for briefings and had hated it every time. Haircuts and strict adherence to uniform standards were the measures of success this far from the battlefield. Reece did his best to hide his contempt. Most of the people in the building were too senior to fight when September 11 hit. When they did venture "downrange" it was usually to the safety of a Tactical Operations Center hidden on a sprawling base; an oasis in the heart of bad guy territory.

Admiral Gerald Pilsner was a short man. Not out of shape, but not someone who immediately commanded respect. He was the quintessential officer in the most derogatory sense of the word. He commanded respect due to his rank, in stark contrast to a guy like Reece, who earned the respect of his men through word and deed. In the world of special operations, your reputation was your currency, and in that sense Admiral Pilsner was a very poor man. He had never commanded men in battle; yet he let everyone out of "the know," both in the military and out, assume that he did. Behind his back the men referred to him as Lord Fobbit, a wartime take on hobbits from *The Lord of the Rings*. Fobbits were people who never went outside the safety of the FOB. The admiral was King of the Fobbits. How he had risen through the ranks to become an admiral was beyond Reece's comprehension, though truth be told, Reece never really spent much time thinking about it. He was too focused on his troops and the mission to pay attention to the politics of senior officers. Reece was built to fight. The admiral was built to administer and take care of his career. While Reece was a professional, the admiral was a careerist, a Massengale in the truest sense.

In recent years a series of very critical articles had surfaced in the *New York Times* and *Washington Post* bringing to light multiple investigations into Admiral Pilsner's conduct and vindictive behavior when dealing with subordinates. Two members of Congress with stellar military backgrounds had taken personal interest in replacing the leaf-eating admiral with someone more befitting leadership of one of the country's premier special operations forces, one even going to the floor of the United States Senate to expose the admiral's nefarious behavior. If any other officer in the SEAL Teams had anything close to what was written about the admiral appear in print, they would have been removed from their post and summarily "retired." Reece's guess was that the admiral's liberal political leanings under a far-left Democratic president had a lot to do with his ability to remain in his position. The admiral was clearly more concerned with force diversity and the push to open the SEAL Teams to females than he was with crushing America's enemies. Whatever got him his next star. Even so, Reece couldn't believe this guy could remain in the Navy for much longer, regardless of whom he knew in Washington's corridors of power.

Reece made his way to the reception room, where the admiral's aide sat obediently at his desk in neatly pressed khakis with a gold braided rope around his shoulder signifying his position as a flag aide.

"Here to see the admiral," Reece said, noticing the shut door to the senior officer's office.

"You're early, sir," the aide said in a tone that managed to seem both respectful and condescending at the same time.

"Well, I just couldn't wait," Reece responded in a voice that intentionally signified the opposite.

"Please take a seat, sir. The admiral is just finishing a meeting and will be with you shortly."

Reece looked around the room and took a seat in an overstuffed leather chair, briefly glancing at a coffee table adorned with a few horrible Navy-produced magazines. He took the time to relax and organize his thoughts.

Why does the admiral want to see you? Has to be the op in Afghanistan. Though usually the admiral would wait until all investigations were finished and his CO had talked with him first. Why so soon after the death and funeral of his wife and child? Was it about the tumors? Or to pay his condolences? To make sure Reece wasn't going to suck-start a pistol? Reece knew his thoughts were clouded by the trauma of recent events, made all the worse by the headaches. *Think, Reece. Something is not right.*

The door to the office swung open and out strolled a man who looked like he'd walked off the set of a Hollywood movie. His quick look at Reece betrayed a familiarity not shared by the commando before he moved off a little too hastily.

Interesting. Wonder who that was?

Captain Howard sat quietly and anxiously as the admiral stared out the panel of windows at the Pacific Ocean. He appeared deep in thought with a pair of horn-rimmed half glasses in one hand, the temple of which rested on his lips. After an extended pause, Admiral Pilsner rotated his chair to face his JAG and placed the glasses on the desk in front of him. "What's your read on Tedesco? Is he going to stay on the reservation?"

"I think you sold him, sir. To a guy like that, being part of your team is a big deal. These guys all want to touch the SEAL magic, and you just made him feel like he was your best operator."

"Let's hope so. We need him to stick with the plan. He's the one I'm worried about, but he's also our best link to the Hartleys, and without them, we have jack shit. This thing has gotten out of control. I have worked my entire career to build an impeccable reputation as a commander. Under my leadership, the Naval Special Warfare profile has risen above what anyone before me could have imagined. Why so many have tried to keep this organization's capabilities below the radar is beyond me. When Washington thinks of special operations, they think of *me*. I *am* the SEAL Teams, as far as the public is concerned. I cannot have my reputation or the reputation of WARCOM destroyed by James Reece."

Not wanting to mention the sore subject of the *New York Times* and *Washington Post* articles critical of the admiral's leadership, Leonard Howard leaned forward, his voice hardly above a whisper. "He will be here any minute, sir. Do you have a plan? Should we have him arrested?"

"No. We'll threaten to charge him with everything under the sun, of course, but we don't want him in custody, where he's protected. We want him out there, adrift. You will be my witness that he's a loose cannon, that he's gone apeshit and is capable of anything. I am going to make him lose his cool so that everyone in this command sees it on his face when he walks out of this office. After that, no one will question what happens next."

"How are you going to make this guy lose it, sir? I don't get the impression that James Reece is easily rattled."

"It will not be a problem, believe me. Reece may be a combat leader but he's got to be a ball of raw nerves at this point and I'll touch every one of them."

"Yes, sir, I'm sure you're right about that."

Pilsner looked at Howard's facial expression and frowned. "You're not going soft on me, too, are you?"

"No, sir, not at all. Just want to make sure we have all the legal angles covered."

"Good. I need everyone focused on getting this thing back on track. Let's get Reece in here. I'll do the talking."

"Yes, sir." Howard smiled.

An excruciatingly long fifteen minutes passed before the door opened again. This time it was Captain Leonard Howard, the admiral's judge advocate. He was slight of frame and, from reputation, slight of character. The admiral certainly surrounded himself with like-minded bureaucrats.

Not offering a handshake or greeting, he said, "Lieutenant Commander Reece, the admiral will see you now."

Wonderful.

Admiral Pilsner's office was almost exactly as Reece expected it to be. A large desk positioned opposite huge windows facing the Pacific Ocean. A million-dollar view, though Reece was sure the facility had cost the taxpayers considerably more than that. Scanning the admiral's office, Reece noticed the walls were not adorned with the usual trappings of a life spent in the armed forces; rather there were pictures of the admiral in uniform at various functions with the who's-who of Washington's political and military elite: higher-ranking flag officers, what looked to be a few well-dressed civilians that Reece didn't recognize, and even the secretary of defense. The pictures all seemed to be the receiving-line variety, each from a military-specific charity event set up with backgrounds denoting their cause. The admiral sure seemed to be having a good time while soldiers, sailors, airmen, and Marines fought and died on foreign soil. On a credenza in the corner sat a UFC championship belt given to the admiral as a gift in exchange for a tour of the BUD/S compound that he arranged for an MMA welterweight fighter. To its left was a Seattle Seahawks football helmet, the admiral's home team, signed by the players and coaching staff, another gift for a motivational tour before they played the Chargers. Apparently the BUD/S compound had gotten very popular in recent years. Quid pro quo.

On the desk, Reece noticed a Ka-Bar knife sitting in a presentation stand, obviously never used and presented to the admiral as a gift for a staff job at some point. It was rumored he liked to pick it up to intimidate his non-Trident-wearing staff.

Was the Admiral's desk on a platform? What on earth? Yes, it was. It was subtle but it was still a platform. Reece remembered reading something once about J. Edger Hoover having an office desk built on a platform so he could look down on those who entered his office. It was all about power.

"Sir." Reece nodded toward the admiral.

The admiral continued to write something down without looking up at his guest. Reece glanced from the admiral to Captain Howard, back to the admiral, and then out the window. He was not offered a seat.

"What the hell happened in Afghanistan, Commander?" the smaller man finally spat out.

"Uh, sir?" replied Reece.

"You know," said the admiral, finally looking up. "Your tremendous fuckup."

Reece shifted his gaze to the JAG, whose face remained unchanged.

"Sir, I take full res—"

"You are damn right you'll take full responsibility. This is a huge black eye for our community. Those men are dead, and you tarnished the hard-earned reputation of this brand!"

Brand? What the fuck is this guy talking about?

"Sir, there is no one to blame here but me. I was the ground force commander. The responsibility lies with me."

"We've already established that, Commander. What we haven't established is why."

Why?

This obviously was not a condolence call about Reece's wife and daughter.

What is this about?

Why? That is a damn fine question. Why? It suddenly clicked. The admiral wanted to test Reece to see if he was going to open up about the mission and tactics being pushed from higher. It had not been clear at the time exactly who "higher" was. Now Reece knew.

Reece's eyes didn't leave the admiral's, but they changed from merely serious to ice in less than a second. Reece thought he could see the admiral visibly shrink back in his seat.

"Sir, that mission came from higher authority," Reece said slowly in a voice devoid of emotion.

"No, it did not, Commander Reece. Do not shirk your responsibility. You were in charge and you failed. You failed your men and this nation." The admiral stood, finally hitting his stride.

146

"NCIS will finish their investigation shortly. They will find you negligent, and I intend to see you court-martialed. In the meantime I am ordering Captain Howard to pull your security clearance and start Trident removal procedures." Reece stood stone-faced, looking straight through the fuming one-star in front of him. "The list of charges against you is a long one, Commander, and I am going to ensure that when the military justice system is done with you there will be absolutely nothing left!" Sweat began to bead up on the admiral's forehead and upper lip, spit escaping as he almost shouted, "And, while we are going down this path . . ." The Admiral continued, standing and moving to the side of his desk, the platform putting him more or less on the same plane as Reece. "You couldn't protect your men, you couldn't protect your family, and it is high time you paid a price, not just for your failures but for the tarnished legacy your father left on the Teams."

Reece's jab caught the admiral off guard, his nose exploding in an eruption of blood as the bone and cartilage broke beneath Reece's left fist. Before the admiral could react Reece had already dropped his weight, pivoted his hips, and delivered a right cross to the already broken nose with such devastating power Howard thought the admiral might be dead on his feet. Reece practiced restraint, but one wouldn't know that from the left hook that caught the admiral's jaw and dropped him to the ground with a heavy thud.

Howard had never in all his life seen such a transformation as the one he had just witnessed. He watched in horror, his back pressed against the office wall, hoping it would envelop him and protect him from what appeared to be the very incarnation of pure rage.

Reece took a step toward Howard and stopped.

Leave him, Reece.

This is what the enemy must feel like when these guys come hunting them, Howard thought.

The look in Reece's eyes left no doubt in Howard's mind that Reece would have no qualms about killing him and leaving him dead on the office floor. His eyes were cold, and the JAG could only think of one word: *death*. Although it was warm and Howard was perspiring profusely, his body inadvertently shivered.

"Add that to the list," Reece hissed, moving to the door and closing it calmly behind him.

Howard slumped to the floor in disbelief, thankful to have escaped Reece's wrath and unable to take his eyes off the body of the unmoving admiral.

Back in the Land Cruiser, Reece took a deep breath. It had taken all his discipline to look as natural as possible as he hurried down the WARCOM stairs, turned in his visitor's badge, and made his way across the parking lot to his vehicle. *What next?* None of this was making any sense. No mention of the tumors. *Did they really not know?*

Reece knew the admiral was a spiteful politician, only concerned with his next rank. The articles in the *Washington Post* were a testament to that vindictiveness and the man's true character. The question was, how would someone with such a weak inner constitution react to being knocked out in his own office? Would he use the power of that position to throw the book at his subordinate commander, or would he be so embarrassed to such an affront to this authority that he would keep it quiet and try to attack indirectly? Reece assumed the latter but he wanted to be ready for the former. Regardless, his security clearance would be gone as soon as Howard could pull himself together and get to a phone, which meant he would no longer have access to any Naval Special Warfare facility. Reece glanced at his watch. It would take the admiral and his guard dog JAG a little time to recover and come up with their game plan, or so Reece hoped.

Reece put the Cruiser in drive and headed for Team Seven.

CHAPTER 18

Admiral Pilsner leaned forward in his chair, elbows on his desk, with one hand holding his head and the other pressing an ice pack to the right side of his face. With tissues stuffed into his nostrils and blood staining the front of what had been an immaculate uniform, he shut his eyes and tried to concentrate. The events of the past hour had left him shaken and humiliated. *At least Howard was the only one to see it,* he thought.

Sitting in the comfortable leather chair in front of the admiral's desk, Leonard Howard was anything but comfortable. Continually squirming and looking anywhere except directly at his defeated boss, the captain was relieved only by the fact that Reece had directed no physical violence toward him.

Against his better judgment, he broke the silence. "Sir, it is over for Reece. Assaulting a flag-level officer is beyond the pale, even in this community. I will have him in shackles and up for court-martial by the end of the day. We will keelhaul him, sir! He will not get away with this! We will strip him of his rank, revoke his security clearance, remove his cherished Trident, and have him before a judge within weeks. He will spend the next decade in Leavenworth breaking big rocks into small rocks."

If it hadn't hurt to talk so much, Pilsner would have cut his JAG off sooner. He knew his nose was broken and was thankful his jaw had escaped the same fate. Both eyes had swollen and would soon blacken. He had instructed Howard to have his aide cancel all appointments for the remainder of the week. He would have to come up with a believable excuse for the broken nose and bruised face that would allow him to escape with some dignity.

"Captain Howard," Pilsner began in a nasally tone, unbecoming of his station, "we will do no such thing."

"But, sir, he assaulted you in your office in front of a witness! He needs to be brought up on charges immediately!"

"Leonard, I am telling you no! Do you realize what will happen to my reputation if word gets out that I was beaten up by an O-4?" the admiral asked, referring to Reece's pay grade.

"Sir, we can't let him get away with this."

"Let me remind you, Leonard, that I am the admiral and you are the captain. Remember that, when we are in this building."

"Yes, sir," Howard muttered, looking at the floor.

"We are going to document this but will take no formal action. You know what happens if Reece is taken into custody. We have discussed this; it would make it harder to get to him. We have to stick to the plan; we are going to let him walk. I want you to fill out a witness statement that you'll keep to yourself until such time that we need to create a paper trail. I also want you to take photos of my face, in case we need them later. This evidence will fit into a pattern of behavior displayed by Reece that will leave no doubt regarding his guilt. I have a permanent solution for James Reece, and this fits right into it."

CHAPTER 19

SEAL Team SEVEN
Coronado, California

Reece's troop high bay was a gigantic room fitted floor to ceiling with rows of racks to hold the enormous amount of gear it took to remain one of the world's leading special operations units. Today it was empty, as Reece knew it would be. Putting his code into the cipher lock, he turned the knob and stepped inside into complete darkness, the door shutting and locking behind him with an audible click. Not only was it the depository of all the troop gear; it was also the epicenter of all things to an operator in a SEAL Team. The troop space was a clubhouse of sorts, though more exclusive than any fraternity on earth.

Gone were the confident voices that had once filled this room, voices of men who were the best in their field. No one was there to shout a greeting, make a joke, or ask a question. No one was busily adjusting gear or packing for the next training trip. *Empty*. All that was left above the roar of crashing surf was the hum of the air conditioners that never seemed to work properly. Reece stood in silent respect, eyes closed, imagining it as it used to be, filled with life and the unique camaraderie that drew and kept so many warriors in the Teams. The smell of dust and dirt accumulated from training venues across the country and combat deployments around the world were deposited back in this single space in Coronado, California. When mixed with the sweat and added humidity from being so close to the ocean, it gave off a distinctive odor that those who had prepared for war there would never forget.

His reflection over, Reece reached over and flipped the light switch, immediately illuminating the bay in a fluorescent white glow. Boozer had supervised getting the troop's gear back to the high bay and it was a mess. It took a few minutes for Reece to find his bags and a few more for him to separate them from the others, take inventory of it all, and then load them into his Land Cruiser outside.

Before leaving, Reece opened a small lockbox mounted on the wall. It was filled with keys. Reece ran his fingers through the semi-organized keys hanging inside until he found the set marked "Donny" and stashed them in his pocket. After one last look back at his troop space, he shut the door and headed for the armory.

"Hey, sir. How's it going? I mean, how are you? Uh, I uh . . ."

"It's okay, Carl," Reece said with a warm smile.

"I'll be okay." Though he didn't really believe that himself.

"It's just that I didn't expect to see you this soon after, well, after you know . . ."

Carl was the SEAL Team Seven armorer, not a SEAL but a gunner's mate senior chief from the fleet assigned to Naval Special Warfare. He had been on a deployment to Iraq with Reece a few years back when Reece was leading sniper teams into Ramadi at the height of the war.

"It's been rough, Carl. I won't lie. I'm a bit lost and confused right now. Just need to take some time and get a little perspective on things."

Carl was a religious man and looked up to the SEAL officer in front of him. In Ramadi, Carl had seen Reece off on more missions than he could remember. He also remembered the great respect Reece garnered from not only the men under his command but the more senior officers in theater as well.

"Carl, I'm going out to Niland for a couple days. Need to be with the boys right now."

Niland was the Navy SEAL playland just outside El Centro, California, up against the Chocolate Mountains, a place where platoons and troops could shoot and blow things up to their hearts' content while training to go downrange.

"Niland?" Carl questioned. "I mean, shouldn't you go to . . . um, anywhere . . . um, anywhere else . . . you know . . . because . . ."

"It's okay, Carl. Just want to get out with the guys and away from all this for a few days. Need to get behind a Mk 48 and throw a few rounds downrange."

Now he was speaking Carl's language.

"Understood, sir. And, sir? Um, my wife and I are praying for you every night."

"Thanks, Carl. That means a lot."

"I guess you want to take a couple of toys out there with you?" Carl said, changing the tone of the conversation.

"Absolutely!" Reece replied with a smile. "Can you grab me two thousand rounds of 7.62 link and a case of the 77-grain Black Hills while I get my weapons?"

"No problem, sir."

Well, at least it didn't look like the admiral had put an APB out on him yet.

Reece approached a machine on the wall of the armory and inserted his Team Seven ID. This would be the real test. He punched in his personal code, pressed his thumb against a pad on the wall, and looked into an iris scanner. NSW armory security procedures had come a long way over Reece's career. He could remember a time when there weren't any security measures in place other than a master lock on a cage full of weapons. *The good ol' days,* Reece thought. The machine beeped and blinked green, opening both the door to the armory and the internal door that housed all of Reece's troop weapons.

Reece grabbed a wheeled dolly for moving heavy items and made his way down the hallway, passing the other troop weapons cages until he arrived at the one he was looking for. He still had his personal weapons from deployment that he had never turned in, but still wanted to upgrade his stash for what was coming. *Be prepared.*

Reece gazed around the large cage, mentally taking inventory. Though it was called a cage it was really a room-size partition filled with instruments of death. Before Reece were rows and rows of rifles, pistols, shotguns, sniper weapon systems, extra NODs, AT-4s, LAW rockets, Mk 48 and Mk 46 machine guns, claymores, boxes of C-4 blocks, and data sheet for breaching; it was a gun nut's wet dream. Reece finished taking stock and began loading the dolly with the tools of his trade.

CHAPTER 20

Shady Canyon Estates
Orange County, California

"Mike. Mike. *Mike?*"

"Uh, what? Uh, sorry, honey . . ." Mike Tedesco responded, dropping his cell phone and reaching for the pacifier on the counter toward which his wife was not so subtly gesturing, then quickly looked back into his uneaten cereal bowl as if the answers to some unanswered question floated among the Cheerios.

Janet Tedesco looked at her husband and sighed. He had been more detached than usual over the preceding months. Maybe the back-and-forth trips to D.C. were getting to him? Maybe it was his almost daily commute up to L.A., though he never complained about it. She knew he lived in Orange County only because she had grown up there and loved it. Her friends were there, and her parents lived just thirty minutes away. Her mom and dad could look after their three children so Janet could attend many of the never-ending stream of lavish political fundraisers and charity events that were Mike's domain. Mike was always thanked and toasted for being the piece of the puzzle that linked all the others. This made her immensely proud.

Mike Tedesco was technically a business consultant but everyone who knew him referred to him as a "fixer." He was connected in some way to just about everyone who mattered in Southern California, from studio executives to key political figures. His friends called him "1D" since he appeared to be one degree of separation from just about anyone you'd want to meet. Tedesco was one of those people who are good at everything. He was the guy you hated in school because he never had to study and would beat you at golf on his worst day. His good looks and Ivy League education, combined with his athletic talents, gained him great favor with both sexes, but he was a surprisingly devoted husband and father.

From the outside looking in, he had the perfect life: a home on the golf course in Shady Canyon, Orange County's most exclusive private community; an incredible condo in Maui; and a mountainside ski retreat in Deer Valley. An always-new Range Rover for his wife and Bentley for himself completed the Southern California twist on a Norman Rockwell painting. Unlike many of those with whom he associated, he would have been just as happy, if not happier, as a river guide or ski instructor. He just happened to be good with people, and the truth was, he sincerely liked helping them.

His challenge was juggling all his competing

demands and making it all work. He lived in a constant state of guilt, probably from the two years he had spent in Catholic school early in life. His conscience ate away at him every time he was called to a meeting in D.C. or was stuck in traffic on the way to and from L.A. It was time spent away from his beautiful wife and children. He wanted out of the fast-paced life to which they had become accustomed.

Mike also had a plan. He had a dollar amount in mind, and when he hit that number he would retire. He could spend time with his family and travel on their schedule, not someone else's. Strangely, he did not feel the need to continue to accumulate wealth and prestige like so many others in his circle of "friends." Once he hit his number, he would fade away.

Two years ago, connecting the players in the business plan that Steve Horn had outlined seemed harmless enough, even commendable. Mike would get to build the team that would purchase, clinically test, and market a drug that would block the effects of PTSD before it even took hold. A neuro pathway beta-blocker that would revolutionize the medical treatment of future veterans, preventing the destruction caused by the psychological toll of war; a mental prehab for warriors. Mike had gone to enough military and veteran group fundraisers over the years to have seen and heard the stories of those whose lives were completely altered by what they had done in combat, and this was a way for him to contribute more than financially. Mike's involvement in "the Project" was not purely altruistic. Success in this endeavor would put him well above his number and allow him an escape from the trappings of his current life.

Fund-raising and supporting these foundations was a way for Mike to atone for the guilt he felt for not joining the military himself. If he was honest, it was because he was ashamed. Those nuns in Catholic school had certainly done their work. He had left his job as a congressional aide and was working in the Manhattan financial sector on a beautiful Tuesday morning in September when the first plane hit the World Trade Center. Rather than rush to help, Mike ran the other way. When others headed for recruiting stations in the wake of 9/11, Mike found refuge at the USC Marshall School of Business. It was there that he discovered his real talent lay not in the analytics, nor the leadership of business, but rather in the art of relationships and the nurturing of those relationships until they could be monetized.

One of his closest mentors was a former California congressman who had failed in his own bid for the presidency a decade ago when one of his many affairs hit the media. At the time, Tedesco thought that his best horse had fallen but it looked as if he was about to get a second shot at the title: that same congressman's wife was the current secretary of defense and a shoo-in for the Democratic presidential nomination next time around.

That he was a trusted confidant of one of the most powerful couples in Washington only bolstered his standing in both the financial and political communities. Mike was the bridge between big money and big power.

Unfortunately, the outcome of this particular bridge-building project had gone horribly wrong, and the actions of his partners had chilled him to the depths of his soul. What started out as something that could both save lives and help Mike reach his number had turned into a nightmare. To Mike it felt as if he had ordered the killing of the SEAL Team himself, though he did not become aware of the connection of the Project to the highly publicized ambush in Afghanistan until Admiral Pilsner and his JAG had briefed him yesterday, no doubt at the suggestion of Steve Horn. Perhaps Steve knew Mike was the weak link and had to be kept in line. Psychologically, having Mike read in by the SEAL admiral with whom he had sat at many a Naval Special Warfare Foundation charity event carried more weight than hearing it from Steve himself. The message was clear: if SEALs were willing to kill other SEALs to keep this project alive, it must be for the greater good.

But to walk out of Pilsner's office and actually see the face of one of the men Mike had a part in destroying was almost too much to take. There sat the true hero, a cancerous tumor growing in his brain, his troop and family dead, oblivious to the array of forces lining up to further dismantle his life and ultimately destroy him.

Mike was the weakest of the group. He knew it. And he knew that if he showed any signs of that weakness, the others would not hesitate to feed him to the wolves. This wasn't checkers, nor was it chess. It was three-dimensional poker, and Mike was going to have to play it out while bluffing if he was going to finish the game. Wait, not finish the game, but survive the game. His goal now was to make it through this disaster with his life and the lives of his wife and children. If he could just keep his head down he could deliver both his family and reach his number. Then he would be done with Steve Horn and his ilk for good.

He would atone for his sins in this life or the next, of that he was certain. God would punish him. The burden of his involvement he would carry alone, all the way to the grave and whichever way he was headed beyond it.

CHAPTER 21

Balboa Naval Medical Center
San Diego, California

Dr. Paul Russell finished his regular shift at Balboa Naval Medical Center and waved his goodbyes to the floor staff. He contemplated stopping at the gym on the way home but he'd been on his feet all day and just couldn't find the motivation. At forty-eight, his lack of drive was catching up to him, and he could feel his belly tugging against his loose-fitting scrubs. He walked through the maze of corridors that left visitors perpetually lost and headed for the staff section of the parking garage. He put the key into the door of his aging Volvo station wagon and climbed inside. His black nylon briefcase, swag from a medical conference, sat on his lap as he reached for the door to swing it shut.

As Dr. Russell slammed the door closed, an unseen hand grabbed a handful of his hair and slammed his head back into the head restraint. The muzzle of a handgun pressed tightly into his neck under his jaw, gagging him.

"Look in the rearview mirror," the voice said from behind him. "Do you remember me?"

Russell hesitated and then glanced toward

the mirror without trying to move his head. He immediately recognized the face of James Reece.

"Yes, I know who you are."

"Why did you tell me I was clear when you knew about the tumor?" Reece asked calmly.

"I don't know anything about a tumor," Russell stammered, trying to maintain some semblance of control and failing miserably. "Your labs and scans aren't even back yet. All they told me was to clear you no matter what was wrong with you. They were gonna kill my family."

"Who are 'they'?"

"It was a DOD security guy of some kind. I have his card in my bag, I'll gladly give it to you. Please don't hurt my kids."

"Reach slowly into the bag and get me the card. Anything but a card comes out of that fucking bag and you'll bleed out before they can get you into the ER." Reece shifted the muzzle of the Glock 19 slightly and pressed it firmly against Russell's carotid artery.

Russell's hands shook as he rifled through the unorganized bag, looking for the card.

"Here it is. I found it."

"Put it on the armrest to your right." Russell did as he was told. "What exactly did this guy tell you?"

"He knew everything. He knew I was having an affair with one of the nurses here at the hospital. He told me that he'd kill my wife and kids and

165

make it look like I did it to get them out of the way so I could be with her. I don't even *want* to be with her!" Russell said in desperation. "He said that you'd be coming through here on the way back from overseas and that I was to clear you ASAP no matter what your condition was. I haven't heard from him since."

Dr. Russell closed his eyes tight, wincing. Suddenly the hand released his hair, the back door clicked, and the gun was off his neck. He felt the weight of the Volvo shift and heard the rear door slam shut. He glanced at the armrest; the card was gone. He shifted his bag to the passenger seat and realized that his scrubs were soaking wet. He had pissed himself. He sat in the car for twenty minutes, trying to stop shaking, before starting it up and speeding home to his wife and children.

Reece was starving as he drove away from Balboa and realized that he hadn't had anything other than coffee in more than twenty-four hours. He headed for an old-school Italian sandwich shop that he'd been to a couple of times over the years. It was a family business and the kind of place with no surveillance cameras and no one asking questions. When he pulled into the vintage strip mall, he found the parking lot mostly empty. The grocery store that had anchored the building had long since moved to a newer location and left a series of independent businesses in its wake, each trying to take advantage of the relatively inexpensive rent.

It was the pre-dinner lull and Reece was the only customer in the small restaurant. He ordered a sandwich, no mayo, and a glass of ice water, paid cash, and sat at the table closest to the glass doors at the entrance in an attempt to get a Wi-Fi signal from a nearby business. He had run home after his meeting with Katie and grabbed an old iPhone out of his overseas gear. He'd bought it used in Korea during a training mission a few years earlier. He turned it on and found a weak signal from the nail salon two doors down. With the VPN running, he pulled a business card out of his pocket.

H. JOSHUA HOLDER

SPECIAL AGENT

DEFENSE CRIMINAL

INVESTIGATIVE SERVICE

The card listed an address and phone number in Mission Viejo, California, as well as an email address. A cell number was handwritten in ballpoint pen on the back of the card, which he assumed was Holder's.

DCIS? Reece had only ever heard of those guys in the context of procurement fraud and couldn't figure out why they were involved in this investigation. *And why would this agent leave his card? Maybe because he was certain I was going to be killed in a home invasion.* Reece put Holder's name into the search engine and got hits for a bunch of Facebook pages, none of which appeared to belong to a DCIS agent based in Southern California. He scrolled down until he found a LinkedIn page for "Josh Holder—Department of Defense." Bingo. He took a screenshot of the page and opened up the Signal app, putting in his password.

He pulled the napkin out of his shirt pocket and typed the list of characters that he'd given Katie into the search bar. Her account was up and running so he added her as a "friend" and sent her a message.

it's your friend from green beans coffee, this guy fits in somehow, he typed, referencing their initial meeting at Bagram for authentication before attaching the screenshot of Josh Holder's account.

He deleted the search history, turned the phone off, and put it into his pocket as his sandwich arrived. Ten minutes later, his Cruiser was pulling out of the parking lot, headed toward Coronado.

ambush in Afghanistan, I 'suicide' the only other survivor, and then a random home invasion takes out his family. Don't you think it would be just a little bit suspicious if he suddenly turns up dead at this point? Can we give the cops and the press a little bit of credit?"

Agnon started to speak but stopped himself, looking to Tedesco for backup.

The taller man finally spoke. He too was intimidated by Holder, but his relationship with their common mentor gave him a measure of courage. "Josh, Horn spoke to J.D. and he offered to help. I followed up with him and he has a solution for us."

"Solution?"

"He offered us the use of a 'sleeper asset.' He said that you would know what he meant."

"J.D. told you that?" Holder's disposition softened at the mention of his rainmaker.

"Yes, he said that it was the best way to take Reece out without raising suspicion. With all the publicity from the Afghanistan fiasco and then the home invasion, Horn thinks this particular sleeper agent won't arouse that kind of suspicion. There is a lot at stake here, Josh."

"Hmm . . . If that option is on the table, I agree that we should move forward with it. If J.D. has offered it up, I'll make it happen." Holder took another sip of coffee before staring directly at Tedesco. "You holding up?"

"What do you mean?"

"I mean, this kind of thing isn't your deal. You gonna be able to keep your shit together or do I need to keep an eye on you, too?"

"Me? I'm fine, Josh. Don't worry about me."

"Just don't get weak on us, Tedesco, we need everyone on the bus. How's that pretty wife of yours doing?"

"She's fine. I'm good . . . seriously."

"Good. Now, if you'll excuse us, Mr. Agnon and I have a couple of things that we need to discuss."

"Um, okay. Let me know what you need from me." Tedesco rose from the booth and walked nervously toward the door, wondering what it was that they couldn't say in front of him.

Coronado, California

Reece slept better that night than he had since before the last operation overseas. He awoke, without an alarm, at 6:45 a.m., splashed some cold water on his face, and looked in the mirror over the sink. Eighteen years of jumping out of planes and helicopters along with lifting weights and practicing combatives on the mats had taken a toll. He looked tired. Not quite forty, he was surprised his thick dark hair still didn't show signs of gray, though he did notice specks of it beginning to take hold in the beard that was coming in. All in all, he felt very fortunate to have escaped the ravages of combat relatively unscathed when so many other service members had returned from theater broken in body, mind, and spirit. Reece shuffled stiffly into the kitchen and found the coffeepot empty. Lauren was an early riser and always had the coffee made. He knew that little reminders like this would dredge up the grief of her death for the rest of his life and there was nothing that he could do about it. Nothing but kill everyone responsible. He skipped the coffee and put on his running gear.

Each combat deployment as a SEAL was prefaced by a training period where team members physically and mentally prepared for the dangerous tasks that lay ahead. Small errors in combat can lead to men coming home in body bags, and skills such as shooting, demolitions, using communications equipment, and employing first aid are perishable. Reece knew he had a fight of a different kind ahead of him, and ensuring that his body and mind were ready for it was the first step in his own personal work-up.

Preparing for his early morning run, Reece went though a series of active stretches before looking down at the iPod shuffle in his hand. He hesitated for a second before hitting the PLAY button and closing his eyes. It was Lauren's shuffle. He knew the music would take him right back to her. He wanted her to be with him, but he also knew that when it came time to do the business, he would not want the distraction. Right now, however, it would fuel him. Pressing play and clipping the device to his shirtsleeve, he was rewarded with "I Will Wait," one of Lauren's favorite songs by Mumford & Sons. He remembered listening to it with her, wrapped in a blanket on the lawn section at a late fall concert, sneaking sips of whiskey that Lauren had smuggled into the venue in her boot. When they first met in college, Reece couldn't stand Lauren's taste in folk rock. He much preferred a more hard-core sound, but she soon had him converted and they enjoyed many a night to the sounds of harmonicas, drums, fiddles, and guitars from bands around the world, with a few songs by Hank, Waylon, Haggard, and Cash thrown in for good measure. With Lauren's playlist vibrating through his earbuds, he began a run that would take him on a seven-mile loop around the island.

He took the first mile at a slow and even pace and then began intervals of two minutes each: running at a hard, almost sprinting anaerobic pace and then alternating to a normal jog. For the final mile of the run, he left the sidewalk for the white sand of the beach, the same sand that he'd run on during BUD/S nearly two decades earlier. His legs screamed as he fought to propel his body forward in the soft sand, pushing the pace as hard as he could. He sprinted across his self-imposed finish line at the rear of the famed Hotel Del Coronado, joining the line of vacationers coming in from carefree walks on the beach heading toward the cluster of structures said to have inspired the Emerald City in L. Frank Baum's classic *The Wizard of Oz*. Being a sweaty guy in workout clothes made you virtually invisible in most parts of the United States, especially hotels. He made his way to the nineteenth-century lobby and accessed the free Wi-Fi.

There was a message from Katie waiting for him.

> *I've found some stuff that you need to see. When can we meet?*

Reece responded, *i don't have a job anymore so i'm good whenever, tell me where you'll be.*

Reece stood for a second staring at the screen and hoping that she was logged in and would respond immediately. She did.

> *I have a rehearsal dinner tonight for a college friend who's getting married. I'll be staying at the Hyatt on Huntington Beach. Can you be there between 4 and 6?*

i can. i'll find you, Reece typed, turning off the device and descending the steps out the front entrance of the hotel to grab breakfast on his walk home.

CHAPTER 23

Huntington Beach, California

Reece wheeled the Cruiser into a spot on the beach parking lot and made his way across the pedestrian bridge to the Hyatt. He was dressed in khaki pants, an oxford blue button-down shirt, and a blue blazer. He would pass equally well as a salesman or a guy headed to a rehearsal dinner, urban camo at its finest. He walked past a lawn area where party planners were putting the final touches on what he assumed would be the event Katie was attending. Judging by the elaborate setup and decorations, he was fairly sure the groom's father wasn't operating on a Navy salary.

He wanted to avoid the lobby, if at all possible, but assumed that all of the beach-facing doors required room keys to access; he was right. He pulled out his phone and held it up to his ear as if in conversation. When he saw a sunburned vacationing couple about his age walking in from a day spent drinking by the pool, he said, "Okay, bye," to his imaginary caller and followed through the doors behind them. He walked down the main hallway toward the elevators and found a house phone on a small table. He picked up the handset and immediately heard ringing.

"Guest services, how may I help you?"

"Can you connect me to Miss Buranek, please? B-U-R-A-N-E-K."

"One moment, please."

"Hello?"

"Katie, it's me. I'm here. What room are you in?"

"Twenty-two thirty-one. Second floor, east side of the building. Great view of nothing."

"See you in a minute."

Reece walked past the elevators and took the stairs to the second floor. He wandered the halls in a direction that he assumed to be east until he saw a sign directing him to the numerical collection of rooms that included hers and knocked on the door.

It opened immediately and his jaw nearly hit the floor. Katie was obviously dressed for the rehearsal dinner. She was wearing a tight-fitting black cocktail dress that showed off her slim, toned physique. Her hair was down and she glowed with just the right amount of makeup. She wasn't wearing shoes, making her almost a full foot shorter than Reece.

"Jeez, how tall are you? Six two?" she asked, popping up onto her tiptoes for effect.

People always thought Reece was taller than he actually was.

She surprised Reece by giving him a big hug, and he stiffened up uncomfortably. Unsure of how to respond, he patted her on the back as if he were hugging his grandmother.

God, she smells good, he thought with more than a little guilt.

"I'm sorry, I'm a hugger," Katie said, as Reece stood speechless. She looked him up and down. "You clean up well. Come sit down. I have a ton of stuff I want to show you."

She pulled a manila folder out of what looked like a beach bag and spread a series of photos on a small table near the room's balcony. She sat down in one of the chairs and Reece took the other. The photos were printed on regular printer paper, so the resolution wasn't great, but they were still decipherable.

"I pulled all of this stuff up using the database at Fox. I freelance for them so they give me office space when I need it and access to their systems for research. They have an extremely sophisticated database and the ability to search using facial recognition technology. I don't have my own username or anything so it would take some work to figure out that I'm the one who pulled it up."

She held up the first photo, which was an enlarged version of the head shot from the DCIS agent's LinkedIn profile. The man depicted in the photo was likely in his early forties, fit, with a hairstyle that made him look more like a TV anchorman than a federal agent. "This, as you know, is Josh Holder. He apparently was an Army CID investigator before hiring on with DOD. DCIS agents do a lot of contract fraud cases, but their powers are fairly broad. From what I can determine, he's from Northern Virginia and moved out here relatively recently."

As she pulled out the next photo, Reece couldn't contain his shock. It was one of those file photos that are taken by pool photographers outside of congressional hearings. It depicted the secretary of defense walking through the Longworth House Office Building, surrounded by what looked like a rugby scrum of aides. Walking closest to the secretary was none other than Josh Holder.

"What's he doing with the SECDEF?" Reece asked.

"That's a really good question. What is a midlevel DOD law enforcement agent doing walking alongside the secretary of defense, and likely next president, Lorraine Hartley? Best as I can tell, he's never been employed in a security capacity and nothing lists him as being part of her staff."

The third photo that Katie produced was a screenshot from a society magazine in L.A. and showed a tuxedo-clad Holder standing among a group of partygoers at a swanky charity event.

"Who is this guy?" Reece wondered aloud.

"According to the magazine, that is Saul

Agnon. I ran a search on him, and he's an employee of this man," Katie said, pointing to a tall man in the center of the photo. "Steve Horn. Big in finance. He runs Capstone Capital, which is a private equity fund. They do a lot of international work. The other guy in the photo is Mike Tedesco, Capstone affiliated and a well-known fundraiser for the Hartleys."

"That Mike guy was leaving the admiral's office the day I was called on the carpet."

"Well, that is not a coincidence. Somehow these guys are all connected, James, and I'm betting that whatever they're up to involves a lot of money and a lot of important people. I couldn't find out much more. Other than LinkedIn, Holder does very little on social media, and public records searches didn't turn up much of any substance. The only way I even found these photos was using facial recognition software."

"I can't thank you enough for this, Katie. It gives me something to go on. I really appreciate your help. Go enjoy your party."

"Happy to help and I'm not going to ask what you're going to do with this information because I'm pretty sure I don't want to know. Just be careful."

"Will do. Can I have these?" Reece asked, pointing to the photos.

"They're yours." Katie tucked them back into the folder and handed it to Reece.

"Got an appointment for tomorrow to get my head checked out. I'll let you know how it goes." He extended his hand, and she slapped it out of the way, coming in close for a hug.

"I told you. I'm a hugger."

CHAPTER 24

Head and Spine Associates
La Jolla, California

Reece was supposed to be at the clinic to get prepped at 6:30 a.m., but he couldn't sleep, so getting up in time for the appointment was not challenging in the least. He wouldn't have admitted it, but he was more than a little nervous about the biopsy. Not only did he know they were going to stick something into his brain, but the results could confirm that he was, in fact, dying. Added on to the events of the past weeks, it was all a bit overwhelming but also freeing in a strange sense.

The next world was calling, the one with his wife and daughter. He was certain he did not want to die in bed after an excruciating battle with a brain tumor. Knowing his death was imminent and assured made what he had to do all the more clear. There was nothing holding him back. In fact, death propelled him forward. He would die avenging his troop and his family. It would be a good death: a warrior's death.

The staff of the clinic could not have treated Reece any better, or gone any further to put him at ease. The recent publicity of SEALs and their daring missions had given the public a glimpse into what guys like Reece had been doing for decades. People went out of their way to be helpful when they found out what Reece did for a living and, while he appreciated all of it, he found the attention somewhat uncomfortable. He didn't feel that the American public owed him anything in return for his service. He felt lucky to have had a job that he loved for so many years, working among some of the finest soldiers in the world.

The clinic was an architectural marvel: concrete and glass with wood accents that made it appear warm and natural. Designed and purpose built as a world-class spine and neurosurgery clinic, it clearly catered to those with concierge medical service plans. There was no waiting and no other patients in the building as far as Reece could tell. It was quite simply the best care that money could buy.

After filling out some paperwork and answering a battery of questions asked by one of the nurses, he was taken into a room where they performed a CT scan with a device attached to his head. He was then led to an examination room where, after less than ten minutes of waiting, a balding man in his late sixties entered the room.

"Commander Reece, I am Dr. German, thank you for coming."

Despite the name, the man's accent and heritage were clearly Latin American.

Reece stood to shake the man's hand. "Thank you for seeing me, sir, I really appreciate it. Your staff has been wonderful."

"It is nothing, Commander. Let me tell you what we are going to do today," he continued, getting down to business. "We are going to take a biopsy of the mass in your brain to see what it is. The procedure we will use is called a stereotactic biopsy. We have the exact location of the intracranial lesion from the CT scan. We actually use coordinates, probably similar to the way you do when navigating. The computer gives us a map and tells us where to enter the skull. We will set up what's called the stereotactic frame on your head, which will guide the needle to the right spot. We are going to shave a very small portion of your scalp and give you a local; you will be awake for the entire procedure."

Reece's eyes widened even though he had been briefed and had researched the procedure ahead of time.

"I know this probably sounds scary, Commander, but it is very routine. You have faced far worse in your career, I am sure. I will make a very small incision, and we will use a drill to enter the skull. Again, I do not want you to be concerned, but I want you to know what we are up to back there when we are working. We will insert the needle into your cranium at that point and take a few samples from different areas of the lesion so that they can be analyzed by the lab. Then I will sew you up, and you can rest here for as long as you'd like. When you feel up to it, you can go home. There is no need to stay overnight so long as everything goes as planned, and I am here to see that everything goes as planned. Do you have any questions for me, Commander?"

"Yes, sir, well, you see a bunch of these, I assume?"

"Yes, Commander, every day."

"Does this one look bad? From the scan, I mean."

"I am just the mechanic, Commander Reece. My job is to go in and grab some tissue. I wouldn't know a good spot from a bad one. Any other questions?"

"Ah, yes, one more. How long would I have to live if this biopsy comes back as cancerous?"

"That is hard to say, Commander. There are too many factors to weigh and consider. If that is the case we will ensure you have the best in the field evaluate the results and discuss options and outlook. I know that is not a very concrete answer and for that I apologize. Let us not concern ourselves with that now. Let's first find out what we are dealing with. Then we will plan the way ahead. Sound good?"

"Yes, sir. Let's do it."

"Again, try not to worry. I promise we'll put everything back where it belongs. My staff will get you ready, and I will see you shortly."

"Thanks, Doc."

"You are most welcome. Thank you for your service to this country."

Reece asked his questions not because he was worried about dying, but because he was worried he might die before he could figure out why his troop and family had been killed and before he could deal with those responsible.

The procedure wasn't really painful. It was an odd feeling knowing that someone was cutting a hole in your brain; hearing the drill was the most unnerving part. Reece rested at the clinic for a couple of hours under observation of the medical staff before being discharged.

They sent him home with a couple of prescriptions that he filled on his way back to Coronado. It felt strange to be driving after just having his skull drilled open, but there really wasn't anyone to call for a ride. He took the prescriptions as directed and climbed gently into bed, spending the rest of the afternoon and evening sleeping intermittently and thinking about his next move.

CHAPTER 25

Naval Amphibious Base
Coronado, California

Admiral Pilsner stood in the front yard of his taxpayer-funded home on Naval Amphibious Base Coronado overlooking San Diego Bay. The waterfront house on Rendova Circle was huge, even by flag-level standards, and blocked the views and bay access of the lower-ranking captains and one or two commanders lucky enough to have filled an empty housing slot.

On-base housing was often filled with the type of officers who thought living in proximity to their bosses might help them with advancement. This created an environment fraught with envy and jealousy for their wives, some of whom wielded their husbands' ranks with a toxic disregard for basic decencies, with no official rules and for which few spouses were prepared. No one placed as much emphasis on their husband's rank as Mrs. Admiral Pilsner. She ran the "wives club" in much the same way her husband ran WARCOM, making her even less popular with the SEAL wives than her husband was among his men.

They had met on Admiral Pilsner's first

deployment to the Philippines. He had never had much luck with women back home. His status as a SEAL officer got him many first dates but his inflated sense of self ensured that things rarely progressed further. When Lieutenant Junior Grade Pilsner met a friendly local Filipino girl who gave him the time of day, he decided she was "the one." For her part, the future Mrs. Pilsner saw the American officer as her family's meal ticket, steady income in a poor nation with few opportunities, and she wasn't about to let this catch get away. Within a few months, Larissa Catacutan became Larissa Pilsner and was eventually granted U.S. citizenship.

Assimilation was not a problem for the new bride; she took charge of her husband's bank account and became adept at maxing out his credit cards. Though it caused the admiral great financial stress, he felt compelled to provide her with a steady stream of new black Mercedeses, her car of choice. Mrs. Pilsner loved nothing more than to park it in the flag officer reserved parking at the base commissary or PX, flaunting her jewelry and, by extension, her status to the primarily Filipino grocery baggers. The couple had never had children, not because they couldn't, but because they were both too selfish to give what is required in parenthood.

Today, even the admiral needed a break from her incessant talking, nagging, and gossiping.

As she Skyped away with a relative back in the Philippines, Admiral Pilsner took his leave and made his way out to the front yard to make a call on a cell phone he used for only one contact.

His first call went to a full voice mail box, which Admiral Pilsner knew was kept full by design. His second call to the same contact went to his assistant.

"Capstone Capital. Steve Horn's office. This is Kelsie."

"It's Gerald Pilsner for Steve Horn."

"One moment please. Let me see if he is available."

Two minutes later Horn picked up the line.

"Gerald, how's the nose?"

How the hell did he know about that?

"It's fine, Steve. It was all part of my plan to build support for the story that Commander Reece is unstable and capable of anything," he lied.

"Well done, Admiral. We appreciate your sacrifice. How did Tedesco take the news in your office?"

"He didn't look great. I think he's having trouble with this. We always knew he would be the weak one. He's great as a fundraiser but gets wobbly in the knees when things get tough."

"We needed him for the Hartley connection. Keep him cool until this blows over. What's the latest on your man Reece?"

"This is an unsecure line, Horn."

"You worried about them monitoring your calls? You're king of the SEALs, for God sakes!"

"They monitor everyone's calls, Horn, everyone's."

"Okay, let's just say that a plan is in motion, Admiral. Our problem will be solved in a week. Our friend who is in town from Virginia is setting it up now. Wish I could tell you more—*need to know* and all that. And don't worry, the drama with his wife and daughter play right into it. All loose ends tied up so we can finish the new set of trials. The drug is fixed, Gerald. It works and it's going to make us a lot of money. You might finally be able to afford to keep that wife of yours."

The line went dead before the admiral could respond.

CHAPTER 26

San Diego, California

Knowing where Holder worked was a huge advantage. At some point he would stop by his office, and it would be easy to trail him from there. The hard part was not getting spotted; Reece's Cruiser wasn't exactly a "gray man" car. There was a huge subculture of Land Cruiser aficionados built around the iconic vehicles and more often than one would expect he would be stopped in a parking lot by an admiring fan to talk shop, something that had annoyed Lauren to no end. Reece needed another vehicle.

Though it was sitting right there in the driveway where she had last parked it, he couldn't bring himself to use Lauren's old char-gold Jeep Grand Cherokee. She had loved that old car, and though Reece had often offered to upgrade her to something newer, she had shrugged it off. Her Jeep worked just fine. They would upgrade when more children entered the picture, she had said, and Reece knew better than to surprise her with a minivan. Lauren was not about to be a minivan mom, of that he was sure, regardless of how practical the things might be.

Leaving the car parked in front of their home

somehow created the illusion that Lauren was still there with him, and at any moment would appear with a Lululemon bag over her shoulder while leading Lucy toward the Jeep for tumbling class, giggling together like coconspirators in a joke known only to themselves. Her car would stay where it was.

Reece knew that he was a likely target for whoever was behind this conspiracy and that he should be hiding out somewhere, but he just couldn't bring himself to leave. Being in the house kept him connected to Lauren and Lucy, something that was more important to him than the threat of death. Besides, as far as he was concerned, he was already dead.

He spent the weekend getting the house back in order, planning for the next phase of his operation, and working out to keep his head straight. He went through the stack of condolence cards and letters and did his best to respond to all of the texts and emails from friends around the world who'd heard about Lauren and Lucy.

Late Sunday evening Reece took a long run. He wanted to ensure everything in his skull was still where it was supposed to be after the biopsy and he had something he needed to pick up on base. Running had always helped him clear his head and keep him focused. After a quick warm-up he moved off at a brisk clip, weaving his way past the golf course and across the main drag to the public beach, where he headed south. He passed the Shores Condominiums, seventeen stories of the worst architecture the 1970s could produce, and which was now a permanent fixture on the coastal skyline and marked the southern end of Coronado's private property. Reece paused to flash his military ID at a bored sentry situated in a small makeshift guardhouse on the beach before continuing his run past WARCOM, BUD/S, and the SEAL Teams, sprinting up and over a berm and onto the SEAL obstacle course.

As it was always a good test to ensure he was in top shape, Reece loved hitting the obstacle course. In BUD/S, they would line the class up according to their previous times to keep things running smoothly. Reece was never the fastest in the class but he was always in the top three. In a group of hungry alpha males, that was a world-class time. After BUD/S, Reece and his teammates would run the course in body armor to ensure they could move effectively in the gear they would wear downrange. The workouts were a good test of physical strength, stamina, endurance, and agility while at the same time bonding Reece's SEALs together as they pushed through it as a Team. This evening it was all his and he attacked it with everything he had: parallel bars, tires, low wall, high rope wall, cargo net, balance logs, rope transfers, the dirty name, the weaver, Burma bridge, slide for life, rope swing, monkey bars, incline wall, spider wall, vaults, and a final sprint to the end. Thankfully, everything in his head seemed to still be in place. Though breathing heavily, he felt good. He felt ready.

Reece jogged back toward the Team and scanned the parking lot until he found it. Donny Mitchell's Nissan Sentra, its original green faded almost gray, was still in the Team Seven parking lot where he'd left it just before their deployment. He had been one of the single guys on the Team who'd been KIA, so no one had figured out the logistics of getting the car to his next of kin. When guys left their cars in the parking lot long-term, their keys were left in the troop space in case the cars had to be moved in an emergency due to flooding or facility maintenance.

The car cranked over easily, and Reece's ears were shocked at the immediate blast of hip-hop music blaring from the speakers. He quickly found the button to turn the radio off and reached down to move the seat back; Donny had been quite a bit shorter than Reece. Quarter tank of gas. Reece would have to remember to fill up before he started to surveil Josh Holder in the morning. Putting the car in drive, Reece drove out the front gate and headed for home.

The DCIS office was just off I-5 in a busy area near a hospital. The office building's parking lot

194

was adjacent to a Chili's restaurant, which made staking the place out without being suspicious a piece of cake. Reece didn't know what kind of car Holder drove, but he knew where he worked and what he looked like, which was a good start. He parked Donny's Nissan in the shade of a large palm tree in the corner of the lot, rolled the windows down, moved to the passenger seat to attract less attention, and set in for a long day. He figured that the DCIS guys probably used the Chili's like a cafeteria out of mere convenience, and around lunchtime he wasn't shocked to see a trio of guys who looked the part walk out of the office building and across the parking lot to grab a bite at the popular chain.

As Reece waited hours for Holder to show, he ran through everything he knew about the events of the past few weeks. Why did these people want him and his troop dead so badly? It had to be related to the tumors. Why else would they want the entire detachment wiped out and then kill the doctor in Bagram who had discovered them? They had to be connected. But what could cause tumors like that? He considered the communications gear they were using; maybe it created some type of harmful radiation? That didn't make sense, though, because virtually every unit in Naval Special Warfare used the same comms gear. Most Army and Marine Corps units used similar equipment as well. If it had something to do with the radios, the problem would go far beyond Reece's element.

His train of thought was broken by a black Cadillac Escalade pulling into the office parking lot. A man climbed out of the SUV wearing a dark gray suit with a white shirt and no tie. Even with sunglasses shielding part of his face, Reece recognized Special Agent Josh Holder. Holder scanned the parking lot as he closed the door, his head on a swivel as he walked toward the office building. This guy wasn't walking around with his head in the clouds or staring at his phone. Holder was a wolf.

Reece looked down at his Resco UDT dive watch and took note of the time: 11:24 a.m. He couldn't risk taking a photo of Holder but snapped a few of his car after he entered the building to capture the license plate and details for future planning. Reece was using an old Nikon D90 he and Lauren had purchased in hopes of taking better-quality baby photos when Lucy was born. It did the job but he wished he had some assistance from his friends down at Special Reconnaissance Team One. That Team specialized in this kind of work and had an assortment of tracking devices that would have been extremely useful to the current problem set, but with what Reece had planned, he didn't want to bring any other active-duty guys into the fold. He was on his own.

He assumed that Holder would be in the office for at least a few hours, so this was his chance to take a quick break and rid himself of some coffee. Surveillance was not Reece's forte. He had some rudimentary training but it was not something he considered his main skill set, which is why he now found himself desperately needing to use the restroom after just having sighted his prey. He thought of urinating in Donny's car but that just didn't seem right, so he swiftly walked across the parking lot to use the Chili's bathroom.

The restaurant was starting to fill with the prelunch crowd so Reece attracted no attention as he skirted the hostesses and went down the hall to hit the head at the other end of the building. He washed his hands and was walking quickly back to assume his surveillance duties when he passed a young hostess carrying a stack of menus. He stepped aside to let her pass as four men in suits turned the corner behind her. He grabbed a menu from the bin mounted to the wall and quickly looked down to obscure his face. The first man clearly saw him but didn't take notice. The second and third men trailed along behind the hostess and never looked up, clearly more interested in her tight black jeans than their surroundings. The last man looked him up and down but couldn't see his face. That man was Josh Holder.

Once the men had passed, Reece ditched the

menu and walked directly out of the front door of the restaurant, thinking that he desperately needed a surveillance skills tune-up. His heart was racing as he moved across the parking lot and hit the button to unlock the small sedan. Reece was carrying his Glock 19 and could defend himself if they made a move on him, but shooting it out with four federal agents in broad daylight would have immediately compromised the rest of his mission. He also couldn't maintain his surveillance position any longer. A guy like Holder would notice the Nissan sitting in the same spot and possibly recognize him. Hopefully the DCIS boys would grab a few beers and let their guard down, but he couldn't count on that.

Reece started the Nissan, looking for a new spot to continue his surveillance. The next-best option was a nearby Montessori school, but an adult male sitting outside a preschool was a sure way to attract suspicion, not to mention that it would probably be letting out soon, and he could easily get stuck behind a line of soccer moms in minivans picking up their kids.

Across a small side street from the backside of the DCIS office there was a Botox and Beauty Boutique.

Only in California, Reece thought.

If there was any place where the clientele were too self-involved to notice a guy sitting in an economy car, this was it. He pulled into a spot where he had a view of Plaza Road, which was the only way that Holder could exit the office. He couldn't see Holder's Escalade from where he sat, but he would most likely be able to see him leave.

Reece didn't have to wait long. Holder must have stopped by the office just to have lunch with the guys before heading back out. The car made a right out of the parking lot onto Plaza and then made an immediate right toward the intersection with Crown Valley Parkway, which was the main thoroughfare that connected with the interstate less than a half mile away.

Reece assumed that Holder would head for I-5, so he went in the opposite direction on Plaza, turned left onto Los Altos, and stopped in the right-turn lane, preparing to turn as Holder passed his intersection. Instead he saw the black vehicle cross Crown Valley farther east and pass out of sight. Cars started to line up behind him as he was cleared to turn right with no way to get left without going the wrong way across eight lanes of traffic. Stomping on the accelerator, he made a right turn onto the parkway. If he'd been in his Cruiser he could have jumped the median and done a U-turn, but Donny's sensible commuter car would probably high-center on the curb. Reece sped west until he hit the next intersection and steered into the extreme left-turn lane. He caught a green light just as he approached the intersection and made a quick U-turn, failing to yield to the four lanes of oncoming traffic. He pinned the gas pedal and immediately wished that Donny had driven something with a lot more power. He steered into the right lane and quickly made up the distance back to the street where he had last seen Holder's Escalade. He made a right and immediately realized that he'd gotten lucky; this wasn't a street at all, but an entrance to an apartment complex. He drove up toward the simple wooden arm gate and saw his target vehicle parked in front of one of the buildings to his right. *Bingo*. Now he knew where Holder slept.

Reece turned around in the cul-de-sac in front of the gate and drove back out toward the main road. He made a left and then a right into a bank parking lot. He wanted to make sure that Holder hadn't pulled into the complex simply to ditch him, which was highly unlikely, since Holder had access to the gate and it would have been difficult for him to have spotted the Nissan. He watched the parkway for nearly an hour, then left his vehicle on foot, not wanting to risk burning his car in a second drive-by, and walked back toward the apartments. He walked in via the access road until he caught sight of Holder's car. The vehicle hadn't moved. He made his way back to his car and headed for San Diego. He had accomplished his recon objective and was reasonably sure he hadn't been compromised.

It made sense that Holder would live that close to work. A guy coming out to the west coast from the D.C. area without a family would do one of two things: get a place as close to the beach as possible or get one very close to the office. Holder didn't strike Reece as a guy who took long walks on the beach, so parking himself within walking distance of work was probably it. Deciding not to return Donny's car to the Team, Reece headed for home to make plans for the next phase of his reconnaissance.

CHAPTER 27

The next morning, Reece headed out the door well before dawn, dressed in khaki pants, a white button-up shirt Lauren had bought for him, and a pair of brown loafers. He tossed his blue blazer into the backseat of Donny's Nissan and climbed into the driver's seat. He'd done an aerial recon using Google Maps and determined that another, ungated apartment complex just to the northeast of Holder's place offered a view of Bellogente Circle, the access road that led to the DCIS man's gate. Reece didn't think that a government employee who lived two minutes from his office would leave home too early, but you never knew.

He found a spot with an unobstructed view of Bellogente through the oaks and waited for the sun to rise. When there was enough light to see, Reece pulled out the legal pad that he'd been making notes on and went back over all the facts. Katie had to be right; this was surely some kind of money deal. DCIS involvement suggested some type of procurement scam, but there wasn't a contract in the special operations community big enough to get this many people killed. It just didn't make sense. Besides, he couldn't imagine a contract deal that could give people cancer.

At 8:25 a.m., the black SUV pulled out of the

complex and crossed the parkway for the one-minute commute. Holder must report to the office at 8:30. He wasn't exactly kicking the rooster in the ass to get there early. Reece waited until 9:15 a.m. and then pulled out of the parking lot. He drove up to the gate and pressed zero on the keypad.

"Can I help you?"

"Yes, ma'am, I'm looking for the leasing office."

"Come on in." He heard dial tones and the white gate arm swung upward. He drove through the gate and pulled into one of the spots marked "Future Resident." He grabbed his legal pad, put on his blazer, and walked up to the leasing office with a smile on his face.

"Hi, I'm Carmen," said a middle-aged woman wearing a tan suit, too much makeup, and an overly healthy dousing of pungent perfume as she extended her hand. She wore gold rings on each of her fingers and had bright red nails that looked as fake as they were.

"Hey there, Carmen, I'm Roy Boehm."

"How did you hear about us, Roy?"

"I'm in medical sales and make quite a few calls in this area. I noticed this complex a few weeks ago. It looks like a great place to live."

"It's a wonderful community. We have luxury apartments, and the amenities are fantastic. We have a pool, a fitness center, and a community room that you can reserve for parties or events."

"How many bedrooms do they have?"

"We have two- and three-bedroom models. Would you like to see one?"

"I'd love to. A two-bedroom is fine. My wife and I don't have any children."

"Let me grab my keys, and we can take a look." The model apartment was in the closest building to the leasing office and Reece followed Carmen down the sidewalk at a painfully slow pace thanks to a pair of high-heeled shoes that she hadn't quite mastered. "Isn't this place just gorgeous? Can you see yourself living here?"

"It's really nice. The main attraction for me is the location. It would cut down my drive time every day."

"Oh yes, we get a lot of that."

As they approached the unit, Reece pulled a small digital camera from his pocket.

"Carmen, do you mind if I take a video to show my wife? She's away on business this week."

"Of course, whatever you need to do. All of the two bedrooms are identical to this one."

As Carmen fumbled with a large ring of keys, Reece pressed a button to begin recording, being sure to zoom in closely on the door locks. She found the correct key, put it into the well-worn dead bolt, and opened the exterior door. Reece took a tour of the decorated model apartment, pacing off dimensions and writing them on his legal pad as well as filming the locations of light switches, power outlets, and the circuit breaker. He asked questions about utility rates, opened kitchen cabinets, and went through all the painful motions of someone looking for a place to live. "I notice there's no security system. Do any of the units have them?"

"No, there are no alarm systems. Our lease agreement does not allow you to do any wiring or install any permanent systems. We are a gated community, though, in a safe area so it's never been an issue."

"Well, that's comforting. I was just curious. How much is the rent?"

"It's twenty-nine hundred per month, and we offer both twelve- and twenty-four-month leasing agreements."

"Oh, wow, that's really more than we were looking to pay. You see, we bought our house back in Las Vegas at the height of the real estate market and we're underwater on it. It's really stretching our budget. I thought these would be more like fifteen hundred a month."

"Oh Roy, I'm sorry, we don't have anything in that price range. Maybe if your wife falls in love with it you can make it work?"

"I'm so sorry. We just can't swing it. I hate that I've wasted your time. I don't want to take up any more of it," Reece said, heading for the door.

"Please, let me take down your information

and I can speak to the owner," Carmen pled, desperate to make a deal.

"I'm sorry, ma'am, I really better go. I'm so embarrassed." Reece picked up the pace as Carmen stumbled along behind him in her heels.

Reece started the car and waved out the open window to her as he backed out of the parking spot and steered toward the automatic exit gate.

Having completed his close target reconnaissance he was ready to move to the next phase of mission planning.

CHAPTER 28

By late afternoon Reece had reviewed the video and his notes and had created a floor plan of the apartment on a large piece of poster board. On a second sheet he had drawn a sketch of the apartment complex and adjoining area and had pinned both to his bedroom wall. He would have preferred to have done it in the living room, but it would have been difficult to explain what he was up to if a friend or neighbor had dropped by to check on him. He'd purchased the same brand and model dead bolt that the apartments used and installed it on his bedroom door. It had been years since he'd messed around with lock picks, and it would take some practice to get his skills back up to par. He'd pick the lock, then stand and stare at the floor plan and sketch, making notes on the legal pad on his bed. He'd use the picks to relock the door and then do it all over again. He ordered a pizza and kept at it until midnight, when he finally had the plan developed to his satisfaction.

His idea was based on some assumptions. Since whatever conspiracy Holder was involved in spanned at least two countries and probably both coasts, there was most likely some email or other message traffic going on among the players. He would not risk putting that kind of information on a DOD-issued computer, where it would be subject to scrutiny. Whoever was behind this wasn't inept enough to get caught by a nosy reporter filing a FOIA request. His second assumption was that Holder did not carry the non-DOD computer with him to work. Doing so would arouse suspicion that he was either up to no good or doing personal business on government time. He also wasn't carrying a computer when Reece saw him in the parking lot or in the restaurant. It was most likely stashed in either his vehicle or his apartment. Reece was banking on the latter.

War had become extremely technical over the past decade and even door kickers like Reece had to learn to exploit electronic avenues to defeat the enemy. He'd been sent to several schools to learn how to harvest and decipher data from cell phones and computer networks, and though he was far from an expert in the field, he knew enough to get the job done.

Equipment existed that would have allowed him to access Holder's computer remotely, but he left that kind of thing up to the technical guys, and trying to obtain that equipment in his current situation could leave a clue as to his intentions. Reece did have a less sophisticated device that he'd secured from his gear locker, one that required him to physically access the computer in question. As much as he wanted to simply kick the front door down, shoot Josh Holder in the face, and grab the computer, that didn't exactly fit into the overall plan, at least not yet. Reece needed the information on Holder's computer to map out the enemy network so he could destroy it piece by piece.

Knowing that Holder wasn't likely to leave his apartment too early, Reece pulled into the parking lot of the medical office building adjacent to the complex at 7:00 a.m. The only separation between the parking lot and Holder's building was a strip of grass and trees along a four-foot aluminum fence. At 8:15 a.m. he got out of the small Nissan and stood by an oak tree near the fence line, going through the motions of the world's longest stretching routine.

He wasn't sure which unit was Holder's, so he put himself in a position where he'd be able to watch him walk out of any door on that side of the structure. The Escalade had been parked on that side all three times that Reece had seen it over the preceding days. He was dressed in running clothes: shorts, a lightweight gray windbreaker, a cap pulled low, and sunglasses. He hadn't shaven since his trip to Katie's hotel, and his dark and increasingly gray beard was starting to change the appearance of his face.

Holder walked out of his apartment seven minutes later and locked the door behind him. He scanned the area as he walked but took no notice of the jogger stretching on the other side of the fence. Reece waited for the big Cadillac to pull out of the complex and pass through the gate before vaulting over the fence and casually walking toward Holder's apartment door. Putting on gloves, he unzipped his windbreaker, exposing a nylon Hill People Gear runner's chest pouch that held the equipment he would need. It took him about ten seconds to open the deadbolt. He didn't worry about any "telltales" left at the door to betray his intrusion, since he had watched Holder swiftly exit the unit. If Holder had installed any type of security system on his own, Reece was about to find out.

He locked the door behind him and found an apartment almost completely devoid of furnishings, making it seem larger than the model unit. The living room had a flat-screen television sitting in the built-in entertainment center, a cheap black faux leather couch, and a small coffee table where Holder probably also took his meals. The area where you'd expect to find a dining table was empty. There was no sign of an alarm system or any type of surveillance device, though you could hide a camera anywhere these days.

Reece went for the smaller of the two bedrooms first, assuming that Holder would be using it as an office. He was right. He found a small computer desk and office chair common to big-box office retail stores. A black neoprene zippered case was lying on top of the desk. Reece opened it and extracted a black laptop computer. Taking a silver aluminum device out of his pouch that was slightly larger than a smartphone, he connected it to the computer's USB port. A red light on the unit began flashing, indicating that the contents of the hard drive were being downloaded.

It would take several minutes to download the information so Reece took a knee in the corner of the room and drew the Glock from his runner's pouch to cover the doorway. If Holder realized that he'd forgotten something and returned home, it was going to get loud. After ten minutes that seemed like an eternity, the blinking light turned green. Reece holstered his handgun and retrieved the device, putting Holder's laptop back in the case exactly as he'd found it.

He did a quick recon of the remainder of the apartment, particularly of the bedroom. Holder's sleeping quarters were slightly less Spartan than the rest of the apartment, but not by much. He obviously wasn't planning on spending much time in the area. Reece resisted the temptation to do something unmentionable with Holder's toothbrush, but instead peered through the peephole before exiting the apartment, spraying the hinges with a small can of WD-40 as he shut and locked the door behind him. Closing the chest pouch, Reece zipped up his windbreaker and jogged back to his car.

CHAPTER 29

Hartley Family Foundation Offices
New York City, New York

J. D. Hartley was in his Manhattan office when the call came in on his secure line. It was the best encryption that NSA could provide. Nobody but the president had anything close. The call was from his wife, Lorraine, to whom he rarely spoke about anything other than business.

"Lorraine, what do you need?"

"What are you doing, J.D.?"

"Reviewing a foundation event speech. Is everything okay?"

"Have you been under a rock, J.D.? Everything is not okay. We need to close the loop on this drug thing. Tedesco is your man, J.D. This is your show. I need this Reece guy dead and I need it to happen now. I am not going to let one of your get-rich-quick schemes take down my political career. I've given them access to all kinds of classified assets. They better not fuck this up."

"I know, I know. This guy has proven to be hard to kill. It's not like we're trying to take out a mess cook. What do you want me to do? Another attempt on him in his house would definitely raise some eyebrows."

"I want you to get on a plane and make those clowns understand that this needs to end now or we're out and the deal is off. I don't care how much money is on the table or what disease this thing is going to cure. I should have never let you talk me into this in the first place."

"Lorraine, I can't go to L.A. I've got meetings here in New York."

"Jesus, J.D., isn't there a skirt you can chase in California? I know damn well that your 'meeting' involves you and some blonde young enough to be your daughter. When are you going to grow up? You let your dick ruin your chances of becoming president. I'm sure as hell not going to let it ruin mine."

"Fine, Lorraine, fine. I surrender. I'll get on a plane and get it handled."

"You'd better. I don't want to hear any more about this. If anyone on the Hill even gets a sniff of what we're up to, we'll be dragged into hearings for the next two years."

"I agree. I'll handle it."

CHAPTER 30

Coronado, California

Reece had been to enough specialized schools to handle the basics of electronic eavesdropping and on-site exploitation of data, but he was an operator, not a hacker. A guy like Holder would no doubt have information of this magnitude encrypted and firewalled, and that was outside Reece's lane. At work, he'd simply hand the cloned hard drive over to the technical guys, who would take it from there, but he didn't exactly have that luxury now. As much as he wanted to do this completely alone, the reality was that he was going to have to rely on some friends to execute his plan. There was only one guy whom he could really trust who had enough computer knowledge to get it done. It was time to bring Ben Edwards into the fold.

Ben was still in Southern California, doing whatever spook work he did, and had checked in on Reece daily via text or phone call. He'd continually asked Reece if he wanted to get dinner or drinks, but Reece maintained that he wasn't ready for company. He now sent Ben a text message asking if he could drop by later for some beers. Ben wrote back right away in the affirmative. Ben had been over to Reece's house dozens of times, so their meeting would be as routine as it got and shouldn't cast any suspicion onto Ben as a conspirator in things to come.

Ben Edwards knocked on the back door at 8:00 p.m. carrying an armload of Arrogant Bastard Ale and a pizza. You couldn't show up at someone's house in San Diego these days without some of the best local microbrews available. They made small talk about the condition of the house as they ate and drank until it was time to get down to business. Reece turned on the TV and raised the volume almost as high as it would go. He pointed to his pants pocket and mouthed "phone?" as he cocked his head to one side.

"No, man, it's in the car. I'm clean," Ben responded, immediately understanding what Reece was asking.

Reece turned down the TV volume to a level where they could speak, but didn't turn it all the way off.

"Remember after the funeral when you told me to holler if I needed you, no matter what?"

"Yeah, I meant it, you know that."

"I know you did, and I've got a favor to ask. It's a big one, though, and it could get you in a pile of trouble if anyone ever knew you were involved."

"I was bound to get in a pile of trouble at some point. Might as well be for helping you," Ben quipped with a smile. "What do you need?"

Reece told him most of what he knew about Josh Holder and his potential involvement in what could only be some type of conspiracy. He left out some key details, including any mention of Katie Buranek. Ben was understanding and didn't ask too many probing questions.

"Like I said, I did a download of Holder's laptop, but you know I'm not a tech guy. I need your help in breaking through the encryption and sorting through the data to find something relevant."

"Easy day, bro, but I don't have the hardware to mess with it here. If you give me the hard drive, I'll take it in tomorrow and get it done. Assuming I can find something, I'll come by tomorrow night and show you what we've got. I know what you've gotta do, man, and I'm with you, no matter what. And, just so you know, I've already got assets working on finding the gangbanger fucks who did this." Ben motioned to the shattered drywall and plywood-covered front door.

"Appreciate it, brother, I really do. I don't want to involve anyone more than I have to, but I need the information on that drive to help unravel this thing. Just know that when the time comes, I'm handling the wet work."

"Well, with talk like that," Ben said, breaking out a pen and notepad, "I want you to check this folder in a shared SpiderOak room from time to time. Ever use it?"

"No," Reece replied, "but it sounds familiar."

"Probably because it gained some popularity when Edward Snowden used it in his escapades."

"That's it. I must have heard about it in the debates about government surveillance programs."

"Yeah, that fucker did incalculable damage to national security by leaking that NSA information," Ben said with disgust.

"Probably so, but he also made us all a bit more cautious about how we communicate and who may be listening."

"We are always listening, bro," Ben added with a smile. "If I need to pass you anything sensitive I'll leave it in this shared room on SpiderOak," he continued, writing down a username and a random number/letter/symbol set of twenty-six characters. "Use this to get in. It's like a very secure version of Dropbox where not even the Company can get access to the file. It drives the NSA nuts. Use a VPN that you buy with a gift card purchased with cash from Wal-Mart or Starbucks or something and it's about as secure as we can get off the shelf."

"You're a lot brighter than you look, you know."

"Ha! Thanks. Just know I'm here if you need me, brother."

"I know, Ben. It means a lot."

Ben Edwards finished his beer and stood to leave. He and Reece locked thumbs in an upward handshake and then gave each other a backslapping hug.

"Remember, my cabin back east is always available if you need a place to go to get away from all this," Ben offered sincerely.

"Thanks, Ben. I appreciate that."

"Absolutely. Later, buddy," Ben said over his shoulder as he departed out the back door.

Reece collected his thoughts and then walked into the garage to start organizing the weapons, ammunition, and equipment that he'd taken from his cage and the armory. He looked like a man preparing for war, which is exactly what he was. Whoever these people were, they had taken everything from him. Everything but his will to fight. For that, they would pay dearly.

Ben returned the following evening wearing a small backpack and carrying a six-pack of Ballast Point Sculpin IPA, a perennial San Diego favorite, this time supplemented with Thai takeout.

They exchanged greetings and Ben removed a small device from his pack, making small talk with Reece as he walked around the living room. He was sweeping the room for listening devices, his level of caution indicating that he'd found something meaningful on the hard drive. The device showed no sign of a bug, but Reece turned the TV on anyway and pumped the volume up higher than normal.

"Aside from the disturbing amount of 'baby-sitter porn,' I found a bunch of shit that you're gonna want to see, Reece. I had to get one of the tech nerds to help me decrypt the data but don't worry, he didn't have any idea what he was looking at." Edwards removed a file folder from his pack and placed it on the coffee table.

"Let's see it," Reece said, as he took a seat on the couch next to Ben.

"Mainly, we have emails, traffic between Holder and a guy named Saul Agnon. Also some between Holder and another cat named Marcus Boykin. Some email chains with all three guys on them. Those names mean anything to you?"

"Yeah, I think Agnon works for Capstone Capital, some kind of private equity fund. Haven't heard of Boykin."

"That's about right. Agnon seems to be doing the legwork on this thing for someone named Horn, and Boykin appears to be an outside advisor. They keep referencing 'the Project' and 'RD4895.' Whatever that is, it looks like it's the basis of this entire thing. Check this one out." Ben handed a printout of an email to Reece.

From: MBokyin
To: Agnon
Subject: re: our last
Recommend eliminating all evidence of adverse events- manner of death should, if

possible, prevent discovery of abnormalities.
Leverage IPs to clean the slate and start over.
—MB

Ben took a sip of his beer and handed Reece a second sheet.

From: Agnon
To: MBoykin
Subject: re: re: our last
Got it. Coordinating with frog to take out test subjects while overseas. Will handle any cleanup from our end. Please advise timetable for RD4895-C, boss is impatient.

Reece didn't have any idea what "RD4895" was, but he was now sure that it had caused the tumors in his men and gotten a lot of good people killed, including Lauren and Lucy. He wasn't confident of much at this point, but he was sure that more people were going to die before this was over, but this time they weren't going to be innocent.

PART TWO

THE LIST

CHAPTER 31

San Diego, California

Humza Kamir heard the bell and instantly dropped his gloves to his sides, his arms and shoulders exhausted from hitting the heavy bag. Most of the fighters mingled cordially at the end of the workout, but Humza kept to himself. He didn't share a common culture with any of the other members of the gym; their only bond was a love of boxing and a willingness to suffer. Sure, there were some other men who called themselves Muslims. All were black men who converted during stints in the state prison system, but they treated the religion more like a gang membership than a true belief. Kamir's beliefs were pure. He did not chase women, he did not drink alcohol, and he read the Qu'ran daily.

The gym's locker room would be considered dingy by U.S. standards, but to a man who grew up in the slums of Lahore, Pakistan, it was perfectly comfortable. Despite his feelings toward the sins of Westerners, he felt fortunate to live in California, where he and his family could at least be safe. He showered quickly and changed back into his street clothes, a pair of Levi's and a Manchester United football jersey.

He walked through the metal door of the gym without talking to or making eye contact with anyone and climbed into his workplace, his refuge, a yellow taxicab. He pulled his cell phone out of his pants pocket to call his dispatcher and saw that he had a text message. The message was not from one of his contacts, but from a number that he didn't recognize. When he read it, the blood in his veins ran hot, and his neck flushed.

Your mother is sick and needs you to call her.

Kamir's mother had died twenty-six years ago, during his birth. He was raised by his maternal grandparents and a stable of aunts and uncles, abandoned by a father that he never knew. Uneducated and resentful of the excesses of American culture, he was a prime target for radicalization, which took place for the most part online. As far as he was concerned, his father was the Prophet and the text message was from one of his father's messengers. The message was from a man whom he'd never met but prayed to hear from each day. His calling in life was not to drive people to the airport and bring drunks home from bars; it was to carry out the word of Allah. The messenger was to help his life meet its purpose. He put the Crown Victoria into drive and headed east.

The U-SHIP store was in a strip mall in a middle-class neighborhood in the San Diego suburbs. He'd come here often, ever since being given the key, and had spent many hours sitting in his cab in the parking lot wondering what his calling might one day be. When his brothers had risen up in the Levant and toppled their puppet governments, he knew his time was near. Soon sleeper cells in the West composed of men like Kamir would do their duty and pave the way for a worldwide caliphate. His moment of glory would soon be upon him.

He watched the storefront for nearly twenty minutes, until three different patrons walked through the doors with objects to ship. He didn't want to have to answer any questions and he assumed that the busier the store's employees were, the better. He left the Ford unlocked and strode quickly toward the shopping center, looking around nervously for any sign of law enforcement, knowing full well that he'd never be able to spot the FBI agents if they were on to him.

Only one employee appeared to be working, and she paid him no mind when he entered. She was busy helping an elderly woman pack what looked like children's gifts into a shipping box as other customers in line rushed her along with their glaring eyes. The post office boxes occupied the portion of the store closest to the entrance and could be partitioned off by a sliding metal gate so that the boxes could be accessed after normal store hours.

He scanned the boxes and quickly located 2102, the number he'd been made to memorize. Choosing the only unused key from his key ring, he slid the key into the lock and opened the windowed brass door. A brown cardboard box, slightly larger than a cigar box, sat inside the rectangular opening at an angle. Kamir reached inside and slid it outward, surprised at its weight.

He closed and locked the box and turned toward the front of the store. What he saw there froze him in his tracks: a uniformed policeman was opening the glass entrance door, looking directly at him.

Panic set in. He wasn't sure whether to attack the officer and try to get his gun, or run past the counter and hope for a back exit. If he got a hold of the gun, he could at least kill the officer and the other customers in the store before he was martyred. It wasn't how he'd dreamed of it, but it was better than spending the rest of his life in a small cell, thinking about how he'd failed Allah.

As he stood for a moment, trying to make up his mind, the officer spoke. Kamir's ears were rushing with blood, like the sound of the ocean, and he couldn't make out what the man was saying. Finally the officer stood outside the opened door and gestured for Kamir to pass; the policeman was smiling. A feeling of total relief washed over him. He forced a smile and bowed his head at the officer as he passed by into the parking lot.

He hurried back to the security of his cab and thanked Allah for his helping hand. Quickly starting the car, he drove around the back of the strip mall, where dumpsters sat askew along a battered chain link fence. Putting the car into park, he took a cheap Chinese-made pocketknife from the center console. He cut through the tape surrounding the box and carefully opened the flaps, peering curiously inside. Whatever his future held, he would find it here. The box contained two envelopes: a legal-size white one and a larger manila one. He fished the smaller envelope out and cut it open with the small knife.

The envelope contained three folded sheets of paper, which he opened and examined carefully. The first page was a letter from his handler, telling him what he must do. He was to kill a man, a man who had brought about the deaths of scores, perhaps hundreds, of his Muslim brothers. His handler would help guide him, but Kamir was to have the honor of avenging those lives. He was to wait for a text message that would direct him to his objective. The second page was a description of the target: a home address, a list of places he was known to frequent, and a description of his vehicle. On the third page was printed a series of photos: one that looked like a mug shot of a man in a military uniform, another full-body candid shot of what appeared to be the same man, a photo of a small but well-kept suburban home, and a photograph of a white Toyota Land Cruiser similar to those prevalent throughout the Middle East.

After rereading the letter on the first page, Kamir reached into the box and took out the larger manila envelope. He tore open the sealed top and found a heavy black handgun inside along with a spare loaded magazine. He'd never shot a gun before but he'd seen it done a million times in movies. As a Middle Eastern–looking man, he stayed away from the local gun ranges so as not to arouse suspicion. America was a tolerant and diverse place, something that warriors of Islam could exploit. Still, it was better to be safe and keep one's distance from flight schools and gun ranges.

He felt a mixture of fear and power as he wrapped his fingers around the grip of the handgun. It felt massive. He studied the lettering on the side of the steel slide: PIETRO BERETTA—MADE IN ITALY. Kamir recognized the weapon as a common one, though this particular gun lacked the prominent safety lever or exposed hammer. Clutching the grip with his right hand, he pulled back on the slide with his left hand and was so surprised when a loaded 9mm cartridge ejected from the gun and flew into the backseat that he nearly dropped the pistol. Embarrassed by his fumbling, he stashed the handgun under his seat, put the cab into drive, and headed toward the San Diego–Coronado Bridge.

CHAPTER 32

Coronado, California

After Ben had left, Reece stayed up all night, drinking coffee and sorting through the pages and pages of documents, emails, spreadsheets, and notes that had been retrieved from Holder's hard drive. Ben had done everything he could to convince Reece to get out of his house and hole up someplace safe, but in the end, Reece would have none of it. He wanted to be close to the memories of his family, and if whoever was behind this came to call, all the better as far as Reece was concerned. He would be waiting.

Reece sat on the couch in the living room with hundreds of pages of documents collated into stacks on the coffee table, love seat, and floor. He began to put some of the pieces in place, but the players were fairly careful with what they put in writing. Like pieces of a giant four-dimensional jigsaw puzzle, bits of information that meant nothing on their own made more sense in context with events of the past month.

Reece's enlisted rate, or military occupational specialty, prior to going to Officer Candidate School was Intelligence Specialist, which sounded far more interesting than it actually was.

Still, that training, along with close to two decades of experience studying obscure information to develop target packages, was helpful. At roughly 4:00 a.m. he'd gathered enough information to start the planning phase. He stood and walked into the kitchen, standing in front of the refrigerator. He pulled a piece of paper held by a magnet from the front of the fridge and held it in both hands as if it were a sacred document. On the paper was a crayon drawing of three figures standing on green grass with a sun in the sky and a rainbow arcing downward. Above the heads of the three figures, in his wife's handwriting, were "Daddy," "Mommy," and "Lucy." With the drawing in hand, Reece returned to the couch and flipped the paper over. He took a pencil from the coffee table and began carefully writing a list of names on the back:

Josh Holder
Marcus Boykin
Saul Agnon
Steve Horn

CHAPTER 33

Reece managed a few hours of sleep before he awoke with the sun shining into his eyes through a slit in the curtains. He put a cup of last night's coffee in the microwave and changed into his running clothes. He ran for an hour, pushing himself hard during two-minute interval sprints and slowing to a measured jogging pace for a minute in-between. He spent half of the run on the beach, staying in the soft dry sand instead of the easier track at the tide line. Finishing his run, he blended into the vacationers at the Del and steered for the main lobby. He connected to the Wi-Fi signal and logged in to his Signal app. No messages from Katie, but he had one from his friend Elizabeth Riley. He touched the screen to decrypt the message.

Reece, here on wings if you need me. Thinking about y'all,
—Liz

Liz Riley was one of the toughest human beings Reece had ever met and as loyal a friend as one could have. He could definitely use her help on what was to come. He typed a response:

231

thanks for the kind words, Liz. i may take you up on that. how flexible is your schedule these days?

He tapped the screen to get to his contacts and chose Katie Buranek's name.

lots to tell you. we should meet, somewhere secure, I can come to L.A.

He walked to a coffee station in the lobby and filled a paper cup from the urn. He was trying to kill a few minutes, hoping that Katie would respond. The good news was, these days, staring intently at the device in your hand was about as innocuous an activity as you could find. No word from Katie, but a message from Liz Riley appeared.

Boss is out of the country, sitting on my thumb with gas to burn. You say when and where and I'll be there.
—Liz

Reece set the coffee down and typed a response:

thanks. will keep you posted, won't be this week.

Eighteen years as both an officer and enlisted man in Naval Special Warfare had forged some extremely loyal friendships for Reece, and his actions throughout multiple combat deployments put more than a few of his colleagues into his debt. Perhaps no one was more loyal to James Reece or had more in his debt column than Elizabeth Riley, though Reece never would have thought of it in those terms. Liz Riley was an Army aviator who'd grown up beneath the shadows of passing Blackhawk and Apache helicopters in South Alabama, just outside the gates of Fort Rucker.

Every Army helicopter pilot in the country learned to fly over the planted pines and peanut fields of the Wiregrass region, and while most residents ignored the noisy machines overhead, Riley spent her childhood looking skyward. Her mother left when she was young, leaving her to be raised by a tough but loving former Marine NCO father and a genuinely kind stepmother. Her teachers laughed when she told them that she'd fly one of those helicopters one day, but she was undeterred. By the time she was old enough to enter the Warrant Officer Flight Program, the Army had begun accepting female applicants. The tomboy turned cheerleader's proudest moment came when her father pinned her wings to her uniform.

Riley was flying a close air support mission over Najaf, Iraq, when her OH-58D Kiowa Warrior was hit by an RPG round. The resulting crash killed her copilot and severely injured Riley's lower back. A group of Shiite insurgents surrounded the crash site within minutes, determined to capture and torture any survivors. Despite her wounds, she killed half a dozen men with her M4 before escaping into the urban maze of the ancient city. Facing unmentionable torture and degradation if captured, she was determined that she would not be taken alive.

Reece and his four-man sniper team were holed up in an overwatch position of a heavily IED'd street corner when they saw the helo go down a few blocks away. Reece had radioed back his intention to move to the crash site to check for survivors but had been ordered to remain in overwatch while an assault force mobilized a response. When information came back that the assault force was two hours out, Reece ordered his men to prepare to move. Hearing Liz's M4 start to mix with the cracks of the insurgent's AKs, Reece and his Team moved toward the sound of the guns.

Muqtada al-Sadr's Mahdi Militia controlled most of the city at that time and Reece's team faced extraordinary danger by going in as a four-man element. They took over a house closer to the crash site and herded the family into a bedroom to keep them quiet. Reece found the keys to the family's battered old minivan while one of his snipers took position on the top floor inside a small bathroom. The other watched the front door and kept an eye on the family.

Figuring out where Liz had found refuge was not difficult. Reece and the two other snipers in the second floor of the home watched as eight black-clad Mahdi Militia members converged on one particular building across from the crash site.

Reece and his snipers dropped all eight with suppressed shots from their Mk11 7.62 sniper weapons systems. Then, leaving one sniper in overwatch and the other still watching the entrance and the family, Reece and Boozer borrowed the sequestered family's minivan and parked in an alley adjacent to what they suspected to be Liz's position. Reece left Boozer in the driver's seat under the watchful eye of his team's best sniper, surveying their movement from the home down the block.

More Mahdi Militia were converging on the scene as Reece made entry into the target building, forcing him to run through a wall of PKM machine gun fire to reach Riley's location.

The adrenaline from the crash had worn off, and her back injury was so severe at this point that she was unable to walk. Reece put his own body armor and Kevlar helmet on Liz before gently hoisting her onto his shoulders and running his way back through the .30-caliber hornet's nest under the suppressive fire of his sniper to Boozer's minivan, parked just behind the cover of a thick wall in the nearby alley. An enemy round ricocheting off the street felt like a baseball bat when it passed through Reece's calf, but he was able to stay on his feet long enough to get Riley into the alley where Boozer was waiting with the van. Reece placed Liz onto the floor of the vehicle as carefully as if he were putting a baby into a crib before Boozer sped back toward the house where the other half of the sniper team was waiting.

They all exfiltrated via the "borrowed" van back to base, where Riley was airlifted to Balad for emergency surgery before being flown to Landstuhl Regional Medical Center in Germany for more advanced care.

Reece was called on the carpet for insubordination for failing to obey the order to stay put even though his decision to move saved the Army pilot's life. Things calmed down when Riley's commanding officer called to express his sincere thanks to Reece's entire chain of command for taking such decisive and courageous action. He followed up by forwarding Army Commendation Medals with Valor to Reece's sniper team.

Liz Riley's spine injuries ended her military career but didn't sap her desire to fly. She worked herself to exhaustion during months of brutal rehabilitation, which paid off when she regained full range of motion and functionality in her back. Medically retired, she found a great gig as a private pilot for a Texas oil tycoon. He spent most of his time jetting around the world with two other pilots in his Global Express jet, but when he wanted to fly into small backcountry airstrips to fly fish or elk hunt, Liz flew him there in his single-engine turboprop Pilatus.

In Liz's mind, she owed Reece her life, and she had built a lasting friendship with him and Lauren over the ensuing years. She was single and, with no children of her own, had treated little Lucy like a favorite niece. Their deaths hit her hard.

Reece strolled out of the lobby and back toward the beach for his walk home. His mind began racing as he started to formulate the specifics of his plan. He was so preoccupied with his thoughts as he stepped off the curb to cross Orange Avenue that he was nearly hit by a yellow Crown Victoria taxicab. He jumped backward as the driver blew his horn, turning heads from the bustling crowd of pedestrian shoppers. Reece quickly realized that he was going to get himself killed if he didn't get his head back in the game. Whoever was pulling the strings on this no doubt still wanted him dead, and if they were willing to wipe out an entire element of special operators and an innocent woman and child, they'd sure as hell take Reece out on the streets of Southern California.

Reece knew of a sandwich shop up ahead with free Wi-Fi. He sat on the bench in front of the shop, this time with his head on a swivel. He connected to the Wi-Fi and logged back into the app on his iPhone. There was a message from Katie:

Can you meet for lunch? Great Wall Chinese on Broadway in Chinatown. Super old school, no one even speaks English. Can you be there by 1?

Reece looked around for a few seconds before responding.

see you then.

CHAPTER 34

Los Angeles, California

It might take two hours to get to L.A. this time of day, or it might take four. You never knew about the traffic. Reece ran home to shower and change so that he wouldn't be late. He pulled on a pair of semi-clean jeans, a dark T-shirt, and his Salomon shoes. Before leaving his bedroom he opened the drawer of his nightstand and picked up his Glock 19 handgun. He used his left hand to pull the slide back just enough to confirm that there was still a round in the chamber, a technique called a "press-check." It was loaded with sixteen rounds of 77-grain ammo from DoubleTap. The solid copper hollow-points were designed to work at near rifle velocities and would do extensive damage while minimizing the risk of overpenetration. He secured the Glock into a BlackPoint Tactical mini-wing inside the waistband holster and slipped the holstered handgun between his boxers and jeans. The holster had two small clips that folded over the top of his pants and secured the rig to his belt. He slipped a spare magazine into his back pocket and clipped a small knife to the inside of his right. Reece had an extensive collection of knives but preferred to carry the cheaper ones for his daily carry so that he wouldn't have a heart attack if he lost one.

Overseas, he didn't go to the port-a-potty without a firearm, but California was a different story. Even a SEAL had to jump through hoops every other year to get a concealed carry permit. It was a pain in the ass dealing with the local sheriff, but Reece hadn't been about to let something happen to his family because he was too lazy to get a permit. Now that he'd failed to protect them, all he could do was keep himself alive long enough to exact vengeance upon those responsible for their deaths. He grabbed a Padres visor from a hook in his closet and headed out the door.

Traffic going north was relatively light and Reece made it to L.A. in just over two hours. Katie was smart to choose a spot like this one, where there weren't surveillance cameras on every corner and where the locals knew how to keep their mouths shut. The unwillingness to get involved that had plagued Reece and his Teammates' efforts to fight terrorism and insurgencies among populations across the globe would now be to his advantage as he worked to avoid whoever it was that wanted him dead.

Reece had fifteen minutes to kill before his meeting with Katie and he spent it putting his best counterintelligence skills to work, making a series of random turns while looking for any familiar cars in his rearview mirror. With no signs that he was being followed, Reece parked several blocks from their meeting spot and walked a circuitous route to the restaurant, stopping several times to pretend to talk on the phone or to look into store windows, using the reflection to study passersby. Despite his best efforts, he could not spot anything out of the ordinary. Of course, if they were using drones or other sophisticated means of tracking him, he'd never know it until it was too late.

Reece arrived at the restaurant and was somewhat surprised when he walked in the door, as doing so was like crossing onto another continent. The sound of dozens of voices across the dining room speaking rapid-fire Mandarin was overwhelming. China's cigarette culture was in full swing. Despite state law, virtually every patron was smoking. The interior was dimly lit, with candles in red glass jars illuminating each table and combining with the haze of grayish-blue smoke to create a surreal show of light. He scanned the chaotic scene, but there was no sign of Katie.

He approached the hostess and motioned toward the dining room, holding up two fingers to indicate the size of his party, unsure whether she spoke English. She nodded and turned to a shelf where she looked under and between stacks of paper, looking for an English language menu, Reece correctly guessed; obviously they weren't needed very often. She found them and motioned for Reece to follow her, weaving her way across the dining room and inviting him to sit in a red pleather booth near the back corner of the restaurant. He sat facing the door and gave the room a more thorough look for potential threats or signs that he was being watched. Despite the fact that he was a fish totally out of water, the other patrons seemed to pay him no mind whatsoever.

He saw Katie's silhouette come through the front door and caught himself smiling. The hostess pointed to where Reece was seated and Katie made her way across the room to Reece's booth. He stood to greet her and, this time, was prepared for the hug when it came. He hoped he'd reacted less awkwardly this time around. She was dressed in jeans, high-heeled ankle boots, and a tight tank top with an olive green cotton blazer over it. Her hair was pulled back into a ponytail and she was wearing the same small black-rimmed glasses that he'd seen at the Starbucks. For some reason, her appearance matched Reece's idea of exactly what a young female journalist should look like. She slid into the booth across from him as he sat back down, looked both ways, and leaned forward across the table as if she were about to tell a secret.

"Isn't this place insane?" she said with a smile. "It's like you're in China. The smoke is terrible but there's no way anyone here is going to overhear what we're talking about."

"Perfect spot, and you're right, it's definitely loud enough. Thanks again for coming, I feel guilty every time I involve you in this."

"Don't be silly, Reece, you know that I'm all in. I know a good story when I see one." She grinned again, as they both knew she wasn't sticking her neck out this far for purely journalistic reasons.

"So I've got a ton of information to give you. Don't ask me where it came from, just trust me that it's all credible." Reece slid a fat manila folder across the table that contained photocopies of all the relevant documents that he and Ben Edwards had recovered from Josh Holder's computer and gave Katie the executive summary.

"It involves the players that you found in those photos: Agnon, Holder, and another guy named Boykin. They don't specifically mention Steve Horn by name but he's obviously Agnon's boss and is referenced plenty. Here's the short version: I think they were using me and my guys as guinea pigs for some kind of new drug. When they found out that it was giving us brain tumors, they had us all killed. They somehow arranged for the ambush overseas, and when that didn't finish the job, they went after us back home.

"What? That's crazy! Why would they test

drugs on SEALs? They can't do that without your permission and an IRB would never approve something like that. Even if the drug worked, they could never use the study to gain approval."

"You obviously know more about this stuff than I do. What's an IRB?"

"Oh, it's an Institutional Review Board. Basically it's a committee that reviews bio-medical and behavioral research when humans are involved in the testing. They were a response to what amounted to human rights violations by both the government and private institutions during the Cold War. You've probably heard of the Stanford Prison Experiment from the early seventies?"

"Rings a bell. That was the one about the psychology of imprisonment, right? Got out of control, as I remember, with some of the guards really losing it."

"That's right. Did you also know that it was funded by the Office of Naval Research?"

"Really? I had no idea."

"Yep. That study along with the Tuskegee syphilis experiment, Nazi physician experiments highlighted at Nuremburg, and classified CIA mind control studies brought to light by the Church Committee in 1975 unearthed a web of relationships between financial institutions, the military, the CIA, pharmaceutical companies, hospitals, and universities, with the unwitting subjects being prisoners, college students, and, you guessed it, members of the armed forces."

"Unbelievable," Reece said, shaking his head. "And that wasn't really that long ago."

"No, it wasn't. IRBs were put in place to ensure that that type of research and abuse never happened again."

"Well, somebody didn't get the memo, and it's clear from the documents here that that's what they were up to. I don't have a clue as to why they did it the way they did it. I just know that they did it."

A waiter approached and Katie ordered tea for both of them, surprising Reece by doing so in Chinese. Clearly she was the kind of girl who wasn't afraid to take charge. The waiter retreated, and she turned back to Reece.

"My Mandarin is horrible, but I know enough to get by. Benefits of a semester abroad in college." Katie smiled.

"Wow. Impressive," Reece said earnestly.

"None of this makes sense, Reece," Katie said, getting back to business. "A private equity firm running a clinical trial on a group of commandos without their consent and then having them killed to hide the side effects? There's more to this story."

"I'm sure you're right and I can promise you that I'm going to find out, no matter what it takes."

"Reece, I understand that you've got to do some things that I don't want to know about. First of all, I can't blame you. I can't fathom how much pain you're in after all that's been taken from you. I want you to know that I'm with you on this. No matter what you do, no matter what, I'm in."

"Why? I don't get it. I appreciate it, trust me I do, but I don't understand your loyalty to someone that you barely know."

The hot tea arrived and Katie made a big production of squeezing the lemon and stirring in the sugar. Satisfied that she'd sufficiently doctored it up, she took a sip and put the cup back on the small saucer, looking Reece directly in the eyes.

"In the eighties, there was a young army doctor living in Czechoslovakia. He loved his country, but he hated what the oppressive government was doing to its people. As he rose in the ranks, he saw the hypocrisy of the leaders close-up and was determined to help make a change. He started giving information to the Americans, little things at first, but he ended up being one of their most important assets in the country. As a military physician, he had access to the medical records of most of the party elite and knew things about their physical and mental health that were of great importance to the CIA. He gave them everything that they wanted and he asked nothing in return; he was doing it for his country, not for himself. It went on like this for a few years before the secret police caught on to what he was doing. He, his wife, and their baby boy went into hiding, but not before getting a message to his handler at the Agency. Apparently the folks back in D.C. were willing to let him hang but his case officer had made him a promise that he'd get him and his family to safety or die trying if something ever went wrong. He risked his career and his life getting the doctor and his family out of Czechoslovakia and eventually to the United States, where they grew their family and still live today." Katie paused. "Reece, that doctor was my dad and the case officer was your father, Thomas Reece."

Chills ran through Reece's body. He had thought that he was dead inside and unable to feel emotion, but he was completely overcome by the bomb that Katie had just dropped.

"How did you know it was my dad? I didn't even know he worked in Czechoslovakia. It must have been when we were living in Germany when I was a kid."

"Your father was like a god in my house growing up, Reece. All my dad ever talks about are Thomas Reece and Ronald Reagan, his two American heroes. I got curious about him later in life and did some homework. I saw your name as a survivor in his obituary, and when I heard about your team getting ambushed, I put two and two together. I emailed my dad, and he confirmed that you were Tom's son. They stayed in touch through the years. Your dad was so proud of his son the SEAL that he told my dad all about it."

"No way! What a small world. My dad was a SEAL before he was Agency. I worshipped him growing up. He did two tours in Vietnam with Team Two before going to work for the CIA. I was born in Virginia when he was still going through his intelligence training. Of course, I didn't know any of this until way later. He always had some cover job at State. I spent a lot of time with my mom and my grandparents while he was running around Europe and South America fighting the Cold War."

"I actually met your father as a little girl. He came to our house to visit my parents, and they treated him like absolute royalty."

"I can't believe it, wait, actually I can, knowing my dad. He was a mystery wrapped in an enigma. He touched a lot of people during his time in this world. People might have a hard time believing what a gentle soul he was, knowing what he did for a living, but he really was a great guy."

Katie reached across the table and put her hand on Reece's. He didn't pull it away. "I was so sorry to hear about his death. I would have loved to have spent time with him as an adult. He was the kind of person they write books about."

"Thanks, Katie, I really appreciate it. After all he lived through, I still can't believe he's gone."

"I can only imagine."

"He was a great man and a better father."

"I know he was, James, and that's partially why I'm helping you. My family owes yours a debt of gratitude, and life has put me in a position to help pay that debt."

"You don't owe me anything, Katie, but I'm glad to have your help. I will not let you get hurt because of this. I'm not going to let these assholes hurt anyone else that I care about."

Reece was embarrassed as soon as the words came out of his mouth, his face flushed, trying in vain to hide in his menu. Mercifully, the waiter approached at about that time to take their order, and Katie took care of it for both of them. She was obviously better versed in the ins and outs of real Chinese food than Reece, who was happy to let her handle it.

Kamir had been sitting in the taxi waiting line at Lindbergh Field when he received the text from his handler. His instructions were to head north to Los Angeles as fast as possible and await further instructions. Adrenaline surged through his body at the thought that finally his time had come. He pulled out of line and headed for Interstate 5. It was late morning and at this time of day he could take it all the way to L.A.

He was passing through Anaheim when he received an updated text message providing him with the location of an intersection where, *Inshallah,* he would find his target. Five minutes later, they sent him the name of a restaurant. His journey took him into the heart of L.A.'s Chinatown, which, due to its crowded hustle and bustle, reminded him of his home in Pakistan. He found a curbside parking spot that afforded him a good view of the restaurant's entrance and shut off the engine.

He looked at the photo of his family that sat on his dash and was overwhelmed with sadness, knowing that he would probably never see them again in this life. He would kill his target and as many infidels as Allah would allow. Now was not the time to be weak, though; now was the time to be strong. His service to the Prophet would fill his family with pride. He would meet them again in paradise.

Their food arrived and Reece and Katie spent the rest of the meal talking about life: where they grew up, where they went to school, places they'd traveled, normal topics in a most abnormal set of circumstances. The conversation put Reece at ease and helped him escape his pain, if only for a short while. The lunch reminded him of some of his early dates with Lauren, which brought the agony of her death back into his conscious thoughts.

When they finished lunch, Reece realized that they'd spent more than two hours sitting at the table talking. The dining room was nearly deserted as Reece paid the bill in cash before heading for the door.

"Where are you parked? I'll walk you to your car."

"I'm a big girl, Reece, you don't have to do that."

"I'm not asking you, I'm telling you. Remember when I said I wasn't going to let anything happen to you? I meant it."

"Okay, tough guy, I'm a block over, let's go."

There had been a steady stream of people filtering in and out of the restaurant all afternoon. Kamir tensed every time he saw the door open, but, to his dismay, everyone who exited the building over the next hour was Chinese. He began to grow impatient, checking the time on his phone constantly and wondering whether he was in the wrong spot. He rechecked the text message over and over and was sure that he was indeed at the correct location. He retrieved the handgun from under the seat and examined it. He had found a YouTube video describing its operation but still wished he had taken the time to test-fire it. Allah would guide his hand.

Finally, just after 3:00 p.m., the door opened and a blonde woman exited, followed by a tall

Caucasian male. Unlike the man in the photos that he'd studied, this one had a thick dark beard, but he still met the description. Something about the way he walked told Kamir that he was the target; he looked like a predator. When the man turned to scan the area, Kamir got a good view of his face and was sure he was looking at James Reece.

Reece and his female companion were moving down the sidewalk away from where he was parked, so he started the cab to follow them as they walked. He would intercept them at the next block, get as close as possible, and then start shooting.

"Did you ever get that biopsy?" Katie asked with genuine concern.

"I did. After we talked, I made the appointment and did it. I won't lie, it was a bit unnerving to have someone drill into your head, but I survived." Reece smiled. "I haven't heard back with the results yet. I guess it takes a few weeks. With the headaches that I've been having, I'm just going on the assumption that I'm terminal. It makes what I'm going to have to do that much easier. I'm certainly not afraid that somebody's going to kill me. I just can't let them get to me until it's done."

Reece discerned a mixture of concern and sorrow in Katie's face and quickly turned his head away to avoid her gaze and scan the street. That turn probably saved their lives.

Reece's eye caught movement, looking left, past Katie, to where a yellow taxicab was parked in the street with its driver's-side door open. His body went into autopilot even before he saw the handgun, his left hand roughly shoving Katie down onto the sidewalk as his right hand went to the Glock inside his waistband. The man had the drop on him and already had his gun raised by the time Reece's brain registered the threat and began the process of reacting.

Observe. Orient. Decide. Act. The whole world went into slow motion. His handgun was already clearing the holster and rotating toward the target before Katie hit the ground. He saw muzzle flash and the blast of the assailant's handgun but he felt no pain or any indication of being hit. His body had pivoted left to face the gunman, and he fired three quick rounds as soon as he indexed the handgun at the outside edge of his pectoral muscle. Two of the jacketed hollow-point rounds entered the gunman's chest and the third struck the outstretched hand that was gripping the pistol, severing a finger. Reece's left hand slid across his chest and formed a two-handed grip as he pushed the gun forward until his elbows almost locked out, taking up the slack of the trigger as he drove the Glock toward his target. The G19 barked two more times at the instant that the front sight met his eyes. Both rounds found their mark on the gunman's face and gravity sent him straight to the ground in a bloody heap.

Reece did a 360-degree scan of the area, looking for other threats to engage. Seeing none, he diverted his attention to Katie, who had curled herself into a ball on the sidewalk at his feet. He dropped to one knee beside her and grabbed her upper arm with his left hand, pointing the muzzle of his Glock skyward.

"You okay? You hit anywhere?"

"No, no, I, I don't think so. Who was that?" Katie asked, visibly shaken and wide-eyed.

"No idea."

Reece rose and inserted a fresh magazine into his Glock, placing the partially spent one in his back pocket. He continued to scan the area as he covered the ten or so yards to where the man's lifeless body lay on the street in a rapidly expanding pool of blood. His senses became aware of screaming bystanders running for cover as he kicked his would-be assassin's handgun away and removed the wallet from the dead shooter's back pocket, tucking it into his own. Beginning to rush back to Katie, he stopped and turned toward the taxi, approaching it purposefully, yet cautiously, weapon ready for more work. Reece swiftly cleared the vehicle through its windows to ensure there were no other threats and confirmed it was empty. Though there were no dangers of the human variety, what he did see confirmed his worst fears. Lying on the passenger seat was a paper with a series of four photos, one of them Reece's official Navy photograph, the one commands make SEALs take before deployment to ensure they have an appropriate death photo in case they don't make it home. He quickly opened the passenger-side door and grabbed it before hurrying back to Katie's position.

"C'mon, we gotta move. Let me have your keys," Reece said, pulling her upright as he began, half dragging, half pushing her toward her parked car a block down. He opened her door and gently helped her into the driver's seat of her silver 4Runner. "Look, that wasn't a random act of violence. Check this out," he continued, showing her his Navy file photo from the front seat of the taxi. "They're onto us, or at least me. You can't go back to your place. Is there somewhere else safe you can go?" His voice was calm and his speech was methodical.

Katie was all but calm and struggled to process what he was asking. "Um, yeah, my brother is a cop in Angels Camp. It's a tiny town in the Sierras."

"That works. Get there. Don't go home. I'll be in touch."

Reece turned to walk away and then stopped. "Wait." He reached into Katie's SUV and put his

Glock on the floorboard under her seat. "Don't shoot anybody unless you can't drive away. Don't forget that this truck can be a weapon. The Glock is loaded, and there's no safety. Just point it and pull the trigger until they go down. Take a couple of deep breaths. You're gonna be okay. Now it's time to go. Stay alert and be safe."

Reece shut the door and watched her compose herself through the window. As she hit the starter and looked up toward the rearview mirror, Reece turned and began making his way back toward his own vehicle. With sirens blaring in the distance, he took a route to the interstate that did not take him back past the scene of the gunfight.

CHAPTER 35

Reece made it home without incident. The first thing he did was retrieve a replacement Glock from his safe and load it. *Two is one, one is none.* He favored the Glock 19 over the SIG he used at work due to its reliability, durability, and size. Just change out the factory sights with aftermarket night sights and you were good to go. He put the handgun into the empty holster inside his waistband and topped off the magazine in his pocket with fresh ammo. He then checked the phone he left on his dresser and found the usual texts and emails from friends and family. This was the phone tied to him by name, number, address, and credit card, which was easily tracked and targeted. There was nothing to indicate that anyone knew he'd just killed a man in broad daylight on the streets of Los Angeles. Setting the phone back down, he opened his laptop and checked a few L.A.-area news sites. One had a short blurb about a shooting in Chinatown, but it was little more than a headline with no relevant facts.

The shooting was clearly justified as self-defense, but leaving the scene was surely a crime of some sort. Reece had made the decision that the risk of waiting for the police to arrive and being publicly involved in a shooting incident would have an adverse effect on his current mission. There was very little to put him at the scene other than a physical description that matched thousands of white males in Southern California. If someone did tie Reece to the shooting, it would probably be too late anyway.

Reece had studied the evidence collected from the taxicab on his drive home. The shooter's name was Humza Kamir, according to his driver's license. Who was he and why did he want Reece dead? And how did he get pictures of Reece, one his official Navy photo, and of Reece's home and vehicle? It looked like there had been another page or pages attached but only a portion was left clinging to the staple that had held them to the page of photographs. He would have to ask Katie to look into Kamir and any possible links to Reece or Naval Special Warfare. The attempt on his and Katie's lives had to be connected to the killings of his family, his troop, Boozer, and the tumors, but how did they find him in Chinatown?

You can plan forever but at some point you have to execute. It was time for Reece to do what he did best. It was time to start killing. He had only four targets on his list at this point but as he started taking them down, he would generate further actionable intelligence and more names would emerge. It reminded him of the hot-and-heavy days at the height of Iraq's insurgency.

They would hit a house, roll up some bad guys, and exploit the intel gained from the site. Within the hour, they'd be hitting another house down the road based on the information they'd gleaned. It would go on and on like that, house after house, night after night as they dismantled the enemy's network.

Based on the intel from Holder's hard drive, he had developed a basic sequence of how he'd implement the plan. This group had the resources to scatter if they knew he was onto them, so timing was crucial, as was the importance of making each hit look as little as possible like the targeted assassination it actually was.

It was also time to move. The L.A. shooting had cemented beyond a shadow of a doubt that someone or something had targeted him, just as they had his family and his SEAL troop. Reece used SpiderOak to leave Ben a message asking for access to a safe house. Ben responded immediately saying he would be right over, but against his better judgment, Reece wanted to spend one more night in his home, with the memories of his wife and daughter. Ben sent the address and urged Reece to get over there as soon as he could.

Reece spent the rest of the night looking over emails, maps, and images on Google Earth, cross-referencing dates, times, and places. By 3:00 a.m. he had built target packages on his four targets: "high-value individuals," Reece would have called them at work. He checked the news sites again for any updates on the Chinatown shooting and, satisfied that they knew very little, rigged explosive charges to the front and back doors before passing out on his couch for some much-needed sleep in his body armor, his M4 close at hand.

CHAPTER 36

San Diego, California

The place was called the "Landing Strip," a classic trashy double-entendre related to its location near the airport. This was no "gentleman's club" with dress codes and top-shelf liquor. This was a down-and-dirty strip club straight out of the 1980s, and Reece was fairly confident that he'd hear Mötley Crüe playing when he opened the door. He had been in his share of adult establishments as a Navy man, especially in his enlisted days, but he never really got the point of throwing money at women who were among the least likely on earth to go home with you. He always thought it much like a restaurant where you paid to look at the menu and smell the food but couldn't actually eat dinner. He paid the five-dollar cover charge to a heavily tattooed bouncer with a shaved head, the kind of guy who likely relied on size and intimidating looks rather than actual fighting skill to keep the clientele in line.

It was just after 5:00 p.m. and the place was almost empty, a few sad-sack middle-aged or older men feeding dollar bills to the dancers in exchange for conversation with women who wouldn't otherwise give them the time of day. The place was exceedingly dark. Reece doubted anyone would sit down if the lights were on. What little illumination there was came from a few neon and black lights placed in several spots on the ceiling. The black lights were flattering to the blemished skin of the dancers, but gave the whites of their eyes and teeth an odd, almost alien green glow.

A DJ in an elevated booth looked over the scene like a prison guard surveying a cellblock from behind bulletproof glass, pumping out music that was far too new and loud for any of the patrons to appreciate. Reece took a seat at a small round table in the corner, as far away from the stage as possible. He smiled to himself recalling how he and his Teammates used to describe the front row of seats as "Pervert's Row." There was always one guy who insisted on posting himself there as if he'd never seen a naked woman before. A cocktail waitress, who appeared to be more attractive than any of the girls onstage, approached Reece's table to take his drink order. He ordered a beer, which was delivered swiftly. He paid for it in cash, leaving a nice tip but not enough to be remembered.

Each girl would mount the long stage and do a two-song routine as they disrobed and performed acrobatic feats on the rotating brass pole while wearing obscenely high heels. After their dance, each stripper would make her way around the room, asking the men to "tip her dance" while sizing each customer up for a private show in the secluded section of the club where the real money was made. The girl who was onstage when Reece sat down was way too attractive to be working in a place like this. Who knew what motivated her to work in such a shithole. You wouldn't get the real story if you asked anyway and he had enough problems of his own without trying to save every twenty-two-year-old stripper in San Diego. More than one young SEAL had been led astray by the legendary stripper with a heart of gold. He nodded politely and tucked a dollar bill into her garter when she came by his table asking for a tip. The next girl up to the stage was overweight, possibly even pregnant, and stomped awkwardly across the stage in heels that made her look that much more ridiculous. It would have been amusing had it not been so sad.

A hand on his shoulder pulled his attention from the stage. Reece looked up at a tall, gaunt figure standing over him. She asked in his ear if she could sit. He motioned to the seat next to him but instead she sat sidesaddle across his lap. She was wearing a black nightie and G-string bottoms with the stripper-standard clear high-heeled shoes. She had a gold hoop in her nose, and the majority of her body was covered in tattoos. Her hair was dyed jet-black, which contrasted with her pale skin like the keys of a piano. She was exactly what Reece was looking for.

"I'm Raven," she announced, her hands on his shoulders.

"Your parents must have predicted your career path at a young age," was Reece's pithy response over the blare of the music.

She either ignored the joke or was too much on autopilot to notice. "You're too cute to be in here. What's your story?"

"Just looking to have a good time."

"Isn't everybody? Care to buy me a drink?"

Reece knew the scam; you buy the dancer a drink and she splits the cost of the overpriced champagne or, worse, fruit juice with the house.

"Sure," he answered.

Raven waved to the cocktail waitress, who brought over some sparkling liquid in a champagne glass, and Reece threw a twenty down on the table. "Keep the change if there is any." He earned a knowing grin from the cocktail waitress.

"You're pretty fit," Raven opined as she patted him on the chest. "You don't look military, and you're too old to be a baseball player; construction?"

"Something like that."

"You want to go for a private dance? I'll take real good care of you."

"How about we sit here and talk for a minute? I'll make it worth your time."

"I love to talk, baby. Not like
else in here for me to talk to, anyw

"I'm guessing you like to party?"

Her eyes lit up at the dog-whistl
use. "Oh yeah, I *love* to party. You
a party guy."

"You never know, do you? You h

"I can be, what are you look
playful demeanor turned all bu
ditched her dancer hat for that of a
drug dealer.

"Something for my back: Lo
Percs, whatever you've got."

"I think the DJ has some 'dor
You're not a cop, are you?"

"I am most definitely not a cop.

"Let me ask him." She strode
the elevated DJ booth and disap
steps. She came back two minutes
narrowed as she grinned mischie
back down on Reece's lap, this t
him. "He's got four; he'll sell then
each. I'm not making anything, I'
you up."

Sure you are, Reece thought
aloud. Based on his research he l
was highway robbery, but he did
He reached into his pocket and ha
one-hundred-dollar bills. Raven tu
the front of her panties and retr

of fo
pock
have

"T
and l
lap a

Back
glove
of pi
the p
to tre
use v
meth
thera
dose
is als
use n
due t
articl
overc
studie
exam
U.S.
by wl

Ree
small
of th
and s
medic

from the same, tucking it in Reece's shirt
. He was somewhat relieved that he didn't
) touch it with his hands.
nks, baby," Raven said as she leaned in
ssed him on the cheek. She climbed off his
1 he headed for the door.

at home, Reece put on a pair of nitrile
 and retrieved the foil-wrapped package
s that he'd bought from Raven. Despite
rception of methadone as a therapy used
t heroin addicts, the compound's primary
1s as a pain reliever. Reece had learned that
done is very tricky to prescribe since its
eutic dose overlaps with a potentially lethal
1nd, as a long-acting opioid, its half-life
) very long. Nonetheless, many providers
ethadone for the treatment of chronic pain
 its low cost. He'd read a series of news
s about Medicaid patients accidentally
)sing on their methadone prescriptions and
1 a slide deck from a conference of medical
1ers on the prevalence of adult males in the
ying of prescription drug overdoses, mostly
1t they referred to as "polypharmacy."
e placed two large methadone tablets in a
plastic Baggie along with two tablets each
 alprazolam that he was given at Balboa
me carisoprodol that he found in his own
ne cabinet, leftover from a neck injury he'd

sustained a couple of years earlier playing rugby with some British counterparts during an exchange program. He dropped the Baggie inside a larger Ziploc bag and laid it on the kitchen counter. Using a small hammer, he pounded the tablets until they were reduced to a fine powder. He put the Baggie into one of the pockets of his small nylon pack and dumped all of the remaining pills down the toilet. He then collected the prescription bottles and gloves into a brown paper grocery bag to burn.

All of his gear was laid out on the floor of his home's one-car garage: weapons and the assorted kit that one accumulated over the years in the profession of special operations. He cleaned and lubricated weapons, loaded magazines, and prepared demolition charges. He did it the same way that he had for countless training and real-world missions over the past eighteen years, only this time he wasn't doing it alongside his teammates, though he hoped that they were watching from above.

Each item was checked off a list as it went into the various kit bags and equipment cases that lined the closed garage door. Despite his desire to stay at home surrounded by what was left of his previous life, he was clearly too exposed. Reece would take along everything that he needed to complete his mission and set up his base of operations in Ben's "employer's" condo.

At 6:00 a.m. the next day, after another night sleeping in body armor, Reece's white Land Cruiser was loaded down and heading east on Interstate 8. Reece sipped coffee from a Yeti Rambler travel mug and felt a slight relief from the tension that had wrenched his body for weeks. His mind was clear and there were no signs of a headache. He reached over and turned on the stereo, heard a familiar guitar riff from one of his favorite bands, and managed a confident smile as he pulled out of the driveway to AC/DC's "Highway to Hell."

CHAPTER 37

Capstone Capital Corporate Offices
Los Angeles, California

This thing was starting to turn to shit. James Reece had a decidedly bad habit of not getting killed, and it was beginning to cause serious problems among the interested parties. J. D. Hartley had demanded an in-person meeting and his assistant called Mike Tedesco to let it be known that he was on his way to L.A. His jet would be landing at Santa Monica in an hour, and he'd be at the Capstone offices shortly thereafter. Saul Agnon scrambled to arrange the impromptu meeting between J. D., Horn, Howard, and Tedesco. The latter three were waiting impatiently in Horn's conference room when they received word that the congressman was in the building. The entire success of RD4895 was contingent upon the Hartleys' continued support.

The consummate politician, no one could recall ever seeing J. D. Hartley with so much as a hair out of place. With a commanding height of six three, a thick head of salt-and-pepper hair, and a 365-day-per-year suntan, you knew Hartley was *somebody* even if you didn't know who. He walked into the frosted-glass conference room and sat at the massive black marble table without greeting anyone or shaking hands.

"Tell me you have a plan, gentlemen."

Horn spoke first, "Congressman Hartley, it's great to see you as usual, though we all wish it were under better circumstances. As you know, efforts to remove Commander Reece from the situation have been problematic."

"*Problematic?* Is that what you call it when my wife gives you the keys to the intelligence kingdom and you fuck it up? First you send a bunch of wetbacks in to do the job when the bastard isn't even home and then you blow it when we put a damn jihadi ready to martyr himself right into your lap?"

"Sir, Agent Holder was handling the sleeper asset," Captain Howard interjected.

"Don't you fucking blame this mess on Holder. He's more competent than all of you in this room put together. What are you going to do now? Do you even have a plan to take this guy out?"

"Sir, if I may," Horn spoke up, attempting to regain control of the meeting. "As you know, Capstone has a security element of very experienced individuals. Our men have all been working overseas, thanks to the DOD contract that you and the secretary have so generously allowed us, but I've called a team back to the States. These men will hunt down James Reece and finish the job at all costs."

"No, they won't. I'm not going to have a bunch of private military contractors with ties to my wife getting in goddamn gun battles in the suburbs. You keep those men on a leash until I tell you otherwise."

"Yes, sir, I understand," Horn replied.

"I don't know that you do understand, Mr. Horn. If the damn media gets ahold of this they will turn it into a tabloid show full of every bullshit conspiracy theory that floats down the creek. I cannot afford to have my wife exposed to any bad press on this. We have worked for a decade to rebrand the Hartley family name and we are not going to have it thrown in the garbage over a favor that we've offered you people."

"Sir, we are preparing charges against Commander Reece. I could have him arrested on my order at any moment. You just say the word," an eager Leonard Howard offered.

"Great idea, counselor, put him in custody where he's impossible to kill and some Navy doctor who we can't control can diagnose his tumor. Thanks, but no thanks. Gentlemen, you get this shit handled or you won't be able to count on the support of the secretary whether this pipe dream comes to fruition or not. Keep Agent Holder in the loop, if you please. Now I have other business to attend to while I'm in town."

Everyone in the room knew that the congressman's "other business" meant something young, blonde, and silicone enhanced. J. D. Hartley rose from the table, buttoned his coat, and turned his back before anyone could so much as offer a handshake.

CHAPTER 38

Arizona Desert

East of Yuma, Arizona, Reece found a road on the map that looked like it headed south into relatively empty desert. A trail cut east that showed no signs of recent traffic. He took it for several miles until he found its terminus, then made a U-turn and returned to a spot he'd seen roughly halfway down. He drove off-road slowly, being careful to avoid the largest of the rocks that were strewn on the ground to the horizon.

He put the Cruiser in park and cut the engine, taking an empty cardboard box from the passenger seat before he walked around to the rear to open the hatch. He moved a suitcase and two smaller duffels, pulling away a blanket to uncover the large plastic case underneath. Unclasping the latches, he reached into the foam interior and pulled out a laser range finder, which went into his jacket pocket. Using a staple gun from one of the duffel bags, he attached a large piece of paper printed with a grid pattern to the side of the cardboard box. The blanket that had been covering his cargo was spread on the ground with the leading edge in line with the rear bumper. Reece carried the box out into the desert a distance before removing the range finder from his pocket and aiming it back toward his truck. He picked up the box and took several large steps backward before taking another reading with the range finder. Satisfied, he placed the box on the ground with the paper side oriented toward the truck. He then put a rock the size of a soccer ball into the box and closed the lid.

Reece returned to the Cruiser and opened the back passenger door, taking a soft rifle case from the floorboard and placing it on the blanket. He moved to the back of the truck and retrieved two sand-filled shooting rests, positioning them at the front and middle of the blanket before removing a set of electronic earmuffs and a plastic ammunition box from one of the bags. Pulling the earmuffs over his hat, he knelt on the blanket and unzipped the padded canvas rifle case to reveal a hand-built hunting rifle. The man who built these only made ten or so per year because he spent so many hours getting them as close to perfect as his abundant skill and patience allowed. Reece would be traveling very near the spot where this rifle was created; too bad he wouldn't be able to pay its maker a visit.

Reece opened the bolt and arranged the rifle so that it was balanced on the two shooting rests, one on the forend, one at the butt. He moved himself into a prone position behind the rifle and opened the translucent blue plastic ammo box. Fifty copper projectiles gleamed in the morning sun, each looking as if it could rocket to the moon. He smiled as he thought of his father, carefully loading each of them by hand at his bench. He took a cartridge from the box and inspected his father's handiwork; the brass cases had been annealed at the neck and carefully polished. *Things of beauty*. The case mouths had been chamfered, the primers seated to consistent depth, the powder charges weighed carefully, and the bullets seated to sit at a specified distance from the leade of the barrel's rifling. His father had presented him with the rifle and these fifty rounds of hand-loaded ammunition back in Coronado almost fifteen years ago. It was the last time Reece had seen his father alive. A small piece of paper, cut perfectly to size, was taped inside the lid of the box. Printed on it were the details of the load, down to the smallest detail. The muzzle velocity was listed, as was the drop of the bullet at specified distances. At the bottom, written in blue ballpoint pen, was a note from his father:

James——Precision with a rifle requires precision in thought. Don't miss, Son. Love, Dad.

Reece didn't plan on missing. He loaded a round into the magazine, pressing the cartridge downward until it clicked under the frame rails of the action. The bolt went forward and down like silk, a testament to the many hours its designer spent fitting and polishing the parts. Reece found the target in the scope and raised his head from the comb to take note of the wind. There was very little of it this morning, which certainly made his life easier. He settled back into position, holding the rifle firmly but without exerting any undue force. His right handhold was on the grip of the stock, and his left hand on the bag supporting it. He carefully shifted the rifle and bags until the rifle pointed at the center of the target without him commanding it there, assuming what is called the "natural point of aim." Reece held just above center to account for the distance, slowing his breathing, and the scope's reticle aligned with the vertical and horizontal lines of the target's grid. He filled his lungs with air and carefully exhaled as his finger moved toward the trigger and began applying pressure. At the natural respiratory pause between breaths, Reece continued the trigger press until the sear was released, sending the firing pin toward the primer under spring pressure and setting off a chain of events that sent the bullet spiraling forward across the desert floor.

The rifle's recoil was significant, but not painful due to the design of the fiberglass stock. Reece recovered from the muzzle rise and put the scope back on the target to find a .30-caliber hole placed perfectly at the target's center. His current location was just above sea level and his target would be at a much higher elevation, but knowing his zero was a necessity. He could make adjustments when he knew the precise density altitude at the target site. He pulled the bolt to the rear and the empty case flipped onto the blanket. He loaded three more rounds into the magazine and closed the bolt, moving the safety lever to its center position. Reece pulled a pair of Swarovski binoculars from one of the bags and found a distinctive-looking boulder several football field lengths away. Setting down the Austrian binoculars, he checked the distance using his range finder: 735 yards. He consulted his data card and made the appropriate elevation changes using the dial on top of his scope. The wind had picked up a touch, a half-value breeze from his right that was somewhere between three to five miles per hour. Settling back into position, he held for the wind using the scope's reticle and repeated the careful process of sending a precision shot downrange. The second shot once again sent his image of the target into a blur of recoil as the bullet left the muzzle. He was able to get the scope back on the boulder in time to see the bullet's vapor trail descend into the center of the target: hit. He found two other targets at different ranges and made two more solid hits. Satisfied, he dialed the elevation back to zero and placed the rifle back into its case. The empty brass was returned to the vacant slots in his father's box of hand loads and both the rifle and ammunition were placed on the floorboard behind the front seat.

Reece could have tested his Echols Legend hunting rifle on most any public rifle range but the next two weapons would attract far too much attention. He was sure he was breaking half a dozen federal laws as well as various sections of the Uniform Code of Military Justice by failing to turn in his weapons case and a few more by liberating the gear, heavy weapons, and explosives from the armory, but those charges would pale in comparison to the crimes that he was about to commit. He pulled his 10.5-inch barreled M4 assault rifle from inside the hard-sided Pelican case and inserted a thirty-round PMAG into the mag well. Essentially a shorter version of the weapon that most U.S. troops used in combat, Reece's rifle had been spray-painted in a tan and brown camouflage pattern. The railed forend of the rifle held an ATPIAL infrared laser that was only visible through night-vision devices, but it also had a visible-laser setting that Reece selected. A Surefire Scout Light was mounted at an angle on the weapon's right side between two rails for easy access from the vertical foregrip. On the flat top of the rifle's receiver, an EOTech holographic weapon sight was mounted with a 3x magnifier sitting directly behind it. The sight worked much like the head-up display on a fighter jet, allowing the shooter to keep both eyes open and use the reticle image reflected onto the sight's "windshield" as an aiming point. By looking through the magnifier, the illuminated image of the reticle was still visible, but the target appeared three times closer, allowing for a greater effective range. In a close-quarter battle situation, the shooter could quickly flip the magnifier out of the way, or remove it completely, for faster target acquisition.

Reece resumed his supported prone position and fired a round at the box target as carefully as he did with his .300 Win Mag. The assault rifle's trigger was nowhere near as light or as clean as the one on his Legend, but recoil was far lighter, almost nonexistent with the suppressor attached. Contrary to popular belief, the suppressor did not "silence" the report of the rifle or the supersonic crack of the bullet, but it did make it more difficult to determine the shooter's position and lowered the noise level just as a car's muffler does the sound of an engine. As usual, technology had outpaced the military's outdated acquisition process, resulting in U.S. servicemen and women going into combat without the best gear and weaponry available. Reece would have loved to be running a suppressor from SilencerCo, but bureaucrats who would never see combat ensured that he only had access to decades-old accessories, as part of political haggling that had nothing to do with putting the best gear into the hands of America's warriors.

Reece fired two additional rounds, which gave him a three-round group on the two-hundred-yard target. The tiny .224-inch holes on the target were too small to see with only 3x magnification, so Reece traded the rifle for his binoculars. The three-shot group was about the size of a fist and was centered on the target. Thousands of miles of air travel had not caused his zero to shift but you never knew unless you checked. Reece rose to a kneeling position and pressed the pressure switch to activate the visible laser, firing at and shattering a rock fifty yards from his position.

Reece moved the selector switch to SAFE and cleared the weapon before pressing the two takedown pins on the port side of the rifle's receiver. He pulled the pins until they locked open and removed the 10.5-inch barreled upper receiver from the weapon's lower. He then retrieved a second upper from the Pelican case and attached it to the same lower receiver. The second upper wore a longer 14.5-inch barrel with a 40mm grenade launcher attached underneath. A Trijicon ACOG sight was mounted to its top, along with another ATPIAL laser aiming device. He removed the Knight's Armament suppressor from the shorter upper and placed it on the longer barrel before confirming that both the ACOG and the laser were zeroed correctly. He reassembled the rifle with the short barrel and suppressor and placed everything back into the case.

The last weapon was one that, as an officer, he hadn't used in quite some time. The Mk 48 MOD 1 was a compact, belt-fed light machine gun that basically served as an improved version of the old Vietnam-era M-60. Like his far more compact assault rifle, the Mk 48 that he'd checked out of the armory was painted camouflage and fitted with both a laser aiming device and an EOTech sight. Reece set the weapon down on its bipod and lifted the feed cover. He placed a five-round belt of 7.62x51mm ammunition into the top of the feed tray, closed the cover, and pulled the bolt to the rear, where it locked into place; true machine guns fire from an open-bolt position. Unlike the rifles, which he controlled with minimal muscle tension, he bore down hard on the Mk 48 to control the weapon. Reece found the box in the sight and pressed the trigger, which fired two rounds before he could release it. He reacquired the target and fired the remainder of the belt. The binoculars showed at least four .30-caliber holes in the target in addition to the one he'd fired from his Legend. As far as he was concerned, that was damn good for a belt-fed machine gun. He repacked all of his gear into the back of the

Cruiser and concealed the weapons cases and ammo cans under the blanket before stacking his luggage on top. His business concluded, he climbed back into the driver's seat and made his way back to the interstate.

Flagstaff, Arizona

As Reece headed east and then north, he steered toward Flagstaff, where he had one last important stop to make. He pulled into the Mount Elden Assisted Living and Nursing Center and walked through the main entrance. He asked for directions to Judy Reece's room and signed himself in as "Jim Watson" before heading down the hallway. When he opened the door to the small but immaculately kept room, he saw his mother sitting upright in a recliner. She wore a white sweater and khaki pants, hair perfectly coiffed and her makeup a bit smeared. Despite her condition, and with the help of the understanding staff, she'd maintained her outward dignity as a southern lady.

She seemed to take no notice of him as he walked in the door and shut it behind him. He gave her a hug and a kiss on the cheek, taking a seat on the couch directly across from her. He'd been in high school when she had her first stroke, and though she recovered physically, she was never the same again. Her dad used to joke lovingly, "She didn't play the piano before and isn't going to start playing now." Not surprisingly, she began showing signs of dementia in her late sixties and after his father's death she went downhill quickly. It took every dime that his father had left behind to put her in a place that would take good care of her, and she had quickly become a staff favorite. Reece made it to Flagstaff as often as he could, though never as often as he intended, sitting with his mother and reading to her from her favorite books. In reality, much of the mother he knew was already gone. Still, he had to say goodbye to what was left.

His mother rarely spoke these days and when she did, it never made much sense. On a good day, she would ask you what time it was every thirty seconds. She seemed to listen, though, and she stared past Reece toward the window as he told her the whole story. If she were lucid, he would have spared her the pain of knowing that her beloved daughter-in-law and only granddaughter had been slain in their home, guilty only by association. Under the circumstances, he was pretty sure that she didn't understand and he needed to get it off his chest. Growing up, he could always tell his mother anything. When he finished telling her of the tragic events that had transformed his life, her face remained unchanged. Then, without breaking her gaze from the window, she spoke softly but clearly.

"In Judges, Gideon asks God how to choose his men for battle. The Lord told Gideon to take his men down to the river and drink. The men who flopped down on their bellies and drank like dogs were no good to him. Gideon watched as some of his men knelt down and drank with their heads watching the horizon, spears in hand. Though they were few, they were the men he needed. You've always been one of the few, James. Keep watching the horizon." Chills shot over Reece's body. She looked into Reece's eyes and, for a second, he knew that she was there and that she understood.

"I love you, Mama," Reece said as he kissed her on the forehead and headed for the door, tears in his eyes.

CHAPTER 39

Oak Tree Gun Club
Newhall, California

"Pull!" Horn shouted, raising his over/under shotgun and tracking the rapidly moving targets. As he fired, a pair of bright orange clay discs exploded in quick succession over the green shrubs in front of his barrel. He broke the gun open, allowing the spent shells to eject onto the shooting position's elevated wooden deck.

"Well done, Steve," a slightly annoyed Josh Holder commented as he moved forward to take his shooting position. This was his first time on the course and he was visibly impressed by the first-class operation. The Oak Tree's owner had made more money in tech than he would be able to spend in one lifetime and didn't seem to mind that his gun club didn't make any money. For him, the real value was in knowing how uncomfortable its existence made the Los Angeles liberals.

Horn was shooting a Krieghoff K-80 Crown Grade Sporting model 12-gauge shotgun. He had purchased it at one of the special operations fundraisers he had attended with Tedesco and Admiral Pilsner. It had cost more than the average

American's car and had come at an even steeper price because some other asshole had tried to outbid him on it. The glossy stock of Turkish walnut, the Germanic deep-relief engraving, and the precision fit and finish of the world-class competition shotgun were lost on Horn. All he knew was that it was the type of gun that others would envy. The bidding package even included a trip to Germany to tour the factory and have dinner with Dieter Krieghoff himself, though Horn never made the journey. He did take the tax write-off for supporting the charity, of course.

His assistant booked him two lessons a week with the best shotgun instructor in Southern California, who trained Horn until he could outshoot nearly anyone with whom he might walk a sporting clays course. Never one for a fair fight, he always made sure to shoot with partners who couldn't match his skill level. Holder was one of the few people who intimidated Horn and he wanted this meeting in his comfort zone, not Josh's.

"Pull," Josh Holder ordered, swinging his rented Remington 1100 toward the crossing pair, clipping the first target and missing the second. Sporting clays was not his game.

"You have to swing through both clays, Josh. These aren't rifles."

"Thanks for the tip, Horn," Holder said without the requisite enthusiasm.

Agnon recorded both men's scores as they walked to the golf cart that would carry them to the next station.

"What are we going to do about Reece?" Holder cut to the point of their outing.

"Well, Josh, your wannabe jihadi asset couldn't manage to kill him even when guided in with a drone to his exact location. That would have been perfect! It would have looked like some crazy ISIS type had been radicalized online and was trying to get laid by his seventy-five virgins."

"Um, seventy-two, sir," Saul Agnon said, speaking up from the backseat for the first time since leaving the gun club's pro shop.

"What was that, Saul?" asked Horn without turning his head to look at his lieutenant.

"I believe it's seventy-two virgins."

"Whatever," Horn continued. "The bottom line is that was our best shot at him without raising too many red flags. The evidence would have pointed to some crazy lone-wolf terrorist who had seen Reece in the paper with the coverage of the Afghanistan debacle and then from the additional coverage of his family's funerals and decided to martyr himself for the cause. Case closed."

"First off, that was the Hartley's classified asset," Holder corrected. "It still boggles my mind that you even know about it. Secondly, I just ran the agent, gave him the instructions. I didn't train him up."

"It's still your fuckup, Josh. Don't worry, the Hartleys don't blame you, but they are done helping. We need you to handle this."

"Let me remind you that you guys were supposed to take him out overseas. I've more than pulled my weight on this."

"You're the right man for the job, Josh."

"I work for J.D., not you."

"What do you want?"

"I want points on this thing."

"Fine. We can't afford to dilute this thing much further but you can have a piece."

"I want ten percent."

"Horseshit, I'll give you two. Two percent of this is enough to set up your unborn grandkids."

"Five percent or Reece is your problem."

Horn stared ahead silently as he steered the cart.

"Five it is, but you get jack shit unless you take him out."

"Fine. Any preference on how I do it?"

"Can't you just 'suicide' him like you did his little buddy? You know, make it look like he is so distraught by what happened in Afghanistan and to his family that he just couldn't take it and decided to eat a bullet. No one would question that. How many veterans kill themselves everyday anyway?"

"Sir, estimates run from one-point-five to twenty-two," Agnon offered.

"That was rhetorical, Saul. Stop interrupting."

"Yes, sir."

"That's easier said than done, Horn. Reece is on alert now. He knows he's being hunted. He's probably using prepaid phones and I'd be surprised if he goes home again. Without DOD's drone assets and access to national intelligence databases, it will be tougher to find him. Not impossible, just tougher."

"If he drove a newer car we could just hack its GPS system, get his location, and send my contractors to kill him. He'd be no match for the fifteen battle-hardened mercenaries we pulled back from overseas to handle this. Too bad he drives that ancient piece-of-shit Land Cruiser."

"Horn, do not send those Neanderthals to kill him. They are tied to you and the Hartleys through your military contracts. Plus, they are the hammer. We need a scalpel."

"Can you get it done or not?"

"I said I'd get it done, Horn. I just need to find him again. We might not be able to track his old truck but we can find his reporter friend's car."

"Good. I will consider this in your hands now." Horn stopped the cart behind the pro shop and stepped out. "Let me know when you finish it. I need to get back to L.A. Enjoy the rest of the course. You need the practice."

"You drive. I need to make a call," Horn said as they approached his Aston Martin Vanquish S, its silver color cleverly called Skyfall by the marketers at the British car company. Horn couldn't bring himself to buy a Tesla, the car that most of his competitors in the California finance world seemed to prefer, chalking up their concern for the environment to a moral vanity he simply could not stand. No matter how fast, an electric car could never muster up the mixed feelings of admiration and jealousy that his twelve-cylinder Aston Martin did when he dropped it with a valet.

After ensuring that Agnon had carefully slid the Krieghoff into its leather case and set it in the backseat, Horn lowered himself into the passenger side and pulled out his phone. He disconnected it from the car's Bluetooth and stared impatiently at the screen, though he knew that the canyons surrounding Oak Tree blocked all cell service.

Saul cautiously maneuvered the sports car down toward the freeway, expecting every turn to draw criticism.

Once back in cell range, Horn made a call.

"It's Horn. I need you to get creative on dealing with James Reece." Without waiting for an answer, Horn terminated the connection.

"Who was that?" Agnon asked his boss.

"That, Saul, was the final option. Now, keep your eyes on the road and let me get some work done."

Agnon did as he was told.

CHAPTER 40

Wyoming Backcountry

The biggest adjustment for Reece, when it came to targeting individuals on his own personal crusade, was the lack of intelligence support. Overseas, an entire contingent of support personnel, not to mention the massive U.S. intelligence apparatus, was on hand to help guys like Reece find, fix, finish, and exploit the enemy. On this mission, not only did Reece lack that support, but he had to do it all without creating a trail of evidence. It wasn't that he was afraid of getting arrested, since no punishment from the state could match what he'd already endured. He had to elude the law and postpone the death he knew was coming. It just couldn't happen until his mission was complete. The longer Reece could keep the other side, and the law, in the dark, the better.

Knowing that he was already dead from a tumor growing in his brain was nothing short of liberating. His sole focus was on bringing justice to those who had taken everything from him. He felt no restraint, no moral conflict. He was clear in his purpose and vision. Understanding the violence he was about to bring to those who had killed his wife, daughter, unborn son, and Teammates gave him an odd sense of peace.

Reece had set aside a week for surveillance, only to discover that his target readily broadcast his every movement to the world via social media. It was as if he were saying, "Here I am, come and kill me." Having lived low-profile for his entire professional life, this mind-set was baffling to Reece. Boykin's movements were routine and predictable, and the terrain and timing were ideal for what Reece had envisioned back in Coronado.

He hadn't been in the mountains since the op went bad in Afghanistan, but hiking the Wyoming backcountry with nothing but lightweight clothes and a small pack in the daylight felt a lot different than patrolling hostile territory in total darkness, burdened with the heavy tools of war. He assumed that he'd see a few hunters scouting this close to the season opener, but he never came across another soul as he followed the ridgeline that paralleled the highway.

He actually walked right past the area that he eventually chose, only spotting it as he glassed back toward the country he'd just crossed. The U-shaped notch in the mountainside offered an unobstructed view down the length of the highway without being exposed in any direction other than from above. The only thing above him today were clear blue skies, so the chances of being spotted by anything but a helicopter were slim.

Reece took out a small notebook and his laser range finder, making a careful sketch of the area and noting the range to various terrain features. As cars and trucks made their way up the northbound road, he envisioned the timing of taking a shot at each. The best spot seemed to be a dip in the road 625 yards away, and the configuration of the road and elevation matched his "accident" theory. It was as close to perfect as he could hope for. He marked the site on both his map and GPS and headed out in search of the most direct path back to his vehicle.

With two days to kill, Reece spent some time exploring the area. Parked in front of the Soda Springs, Idaho, public library, he turned on his secondhand iPhone and checked in with the world via the free Wi-Fi. He had a message on Signal from Katie's alias.

It's me. I made it safely to my brother's. You saved my life. Be safe.

He prayed that Katie would be careful. He couldn't stand the thought of her getting hurt or killed trying to help him. No time to focus on that now. He then logged into SpiderOak, ensuring his VPN was engaged, and opened the folder he shared with Ben Edwards.

*Hey bro, got some info on the gangbangers—
meet you at your new home when you get
back.*

Even though it was supposedly secure, Reece
and Ben still kept their comms as innocuous as
possible. He didn't have a way to make a secure
voice call to Ben without the potential of leading
someone to his location. It would be obvious to
anyone at that point that he was after Boykin,
so the information on the gangbangers would
have to wait. He drove back east to the spot
he'd picked to camp; just another guy in a truck
getting away from town to spend time in the
outdoors, and spent the next twenty-four hours
going over the maps and imagery and readying
his gear for his patrol to the hide site.

The night before his planned hit he built a small
fire. There was something primal about fires. Since
the early Stone Age fires had quite literally sustained
human life. They offered warmth and allowed the
heat-treating of hard woods and eventually metals,
turning them into weapons for hunting and war.
They permitted cooking and early pottery, were
natural gathering places, could signal, and were
almost always a part of ceremonial tradition. Fires
were sacred, but more than anything else, fires
offered hope. Reece pondered the paradox; there
was no hope for Marcus Boykin, just as there was
no hope for James Reece.

Staring into the burning embers of the small campfire, Reece started to remember. It had been just before his last deployment. He had taken Lauren and Lucy on a predeployment camping trip to Big Sur. Nestled into the Northern California coast just south of Carmel was a stretch of land that Reece considered to be one of the most beautiful on earth: the sea and the mountains, Reece's favorites.

Lauren had retired for the night into the tent, leaving Reece and Lucy to connect by the fire, knowing that six long months of separation lay ahead. Years before, Lauren had confided to Reece that every time he left the house, whether to deploy or train, she knew that he might never be coming back. She had accepted his chosen profession and would not be the kind of wife and mother who was always worried about her husband. She was immensely proud of what he did, but she had a daughter to raise, and she wasn't about to let that child see her in a constant state of worry. When Reece left, they would get on with their lives: exploring, learning, and growing. In hindsight, she must have also been tired; tired from supporting the life that grew inside her. Reece assumed that she had wrestled with whether to tell him and had decided to let it be a surprise when he returned. Lauren had always loved surprises and there were so few joyful ones left in life. This was a gift she could give to him. He also knew that she would want him focused on the job overseas, not distracted thinking about his pregnant wife. That was something she could give the families of the men under Reece's command. They needed Reece focused on the task of leading SEALs into combat. To do it right would require his full measure of devotion.

Reece had watched his daughter inch the marshmallow, skewered on the end of a straightened wire hanger, closer to the fire.

"Wait a little bit longer, sweetie," Reece had cautioned. "Wait for the embers so you can get it a nice golden brown."

Lucy just smiled and moved it closer and closer to the fire until it burst into flames and she burst into giggles as Reece leaned forward and blew out what was now a charred mess.

They had hiked into a desolate stretch of shoreline to avoid the more populated areas of Big Sur State Park and set up camp on the beach. In a state that had laws governing almost all aspects of daily life, it was surprising and refreshing to be allowed to still enjoy driftwood fires along the coast.

Reece and Lucy were bundled up, cuddled together against the crisp cold of the Pacific twilight in a lightweight backpacker's chair behind the fire and looking out over the rocky shore, the waves, and the distant horizon. Reece

would remember that sunset every day while overseas, would remember holding his little angel, wrapped in a poncho and lightweight blanket, listening to the cadence of the surf as the sky transitioned into night, constellation after constellation breaking through the darkness, much to Lucy's wonderment.

"What's that bright one?" she had asked, pointing skyward.

Though not an astronomer by any stretch of the imagination, Reece had a rudimentary knowledge of the constellations. It was the by-product of a life spent outdoors. He smiled, remembering when he asked his father the same question all those years ago under the same night sky.

"That's Orion. See those stars there?" Reece asked, pointing skyward. "That's Orion's belt. Makes him easy to spot up there, doesn't it?" Lucy nodded in agreement. "If you look hard enough you can see his shield and club. He was a hunter."

"How'd he get up there?" asked a quizzical Lucy.

"Well, if I remember correctly," Reece continued, struggling to recall his mythology, "he was stung by a scorpion, which now occupies a spot on the other side of the sky, so they never see each other."

"That's weird," Lucy commented. "Were they friends?"

"Not exactly," Reece replied, hoping she didn't ask too many more specific questions as to what had led Orion and the Scorpion to their ultimate positions in the cosmos.

Thankfully she switched topics, to one Reece knew was coming.

"Daddy, why do you have to go away on a big trip?"

Reece and Lauren had called shorter training trips "little trips" and referred to the upcoming deployment as a "big trip." Easier for a young mind to grasp and come to terms with.

"Well, sometimes daddies have to go away on big trips."

In their circle of friends, "daddies" were always leaving on "big trips." Reece felt lucky that Lucy didn't quite realize, sometimes those daddies didn't come home.

"This is my last big trip, sweetheart. Then I'm not going away again. I'm going to stay home with you and Mommy. I can't wait."

"I can't wait either, Dada!" she said, as much to herself as to him. "Do you go away because of the bad people?"

Reece paused. He and Lauren had shielded her as much as possible from some of the harsher realities of growing up as a military child in a country on constant war footing. This was her time to be innocent. Obviously she had picked up more than they thought.

"Sometimes daddies need to fight the bad guys far away so we don't have to do it here in our country. We do it to keep us free. You and your mom are a big part of it. The three of us are a team. We all make sacrifices to keep our country free."

"When I grow up, I want to fight bad guys, too."

Reece swallowed, a lump rising in his throat.

"My hope is you won't have to, sweetheart. I love you, angel."

"I love you too, Daddy."

She nestled her head into her father's shoulder and cuddled up against him. Reece would not have wanted to be anyplace else on earth right then. It was that memory to which he would return throughout deployment. When he was back from a mission, dirty and tired, just before lying down to rest, he would return to that beach, to the waves, the fire, the marshmallows and Orion. It was to that memory he returned now, hoping nothing more than for one more chance to hold his daughter safely in his arms, rocking her to sleep on a distant beach. To him, that was heaven.

"See you soon, baby girl," he whispered into the dying embers of the fire as he drifted off to sleep.

CHAPTER 41

The sheriff of Lincoln County, Wyoming, arrived on the scene an hour after the call went out. His office was down in Afton and the crashed Mercedes SUV was at the extreme north end of his jurisdiction. Two highway patrolmen, two of his deputies, and a state Game & Fish officer were on-site along with the detective from his office. An ambulance had pulled in but the paramedic and driver were still inside since there was not much they could do for the man in the silver Mercedes. One of the trooper's cars was parked to block a lane of the highway as he stood in the road to direct the occasional driver around what had become a crime scene. A tow truck driver stood staring down at the shredded vehicle, obviously trying to figure out how he was going to remove it from the steep ditch.

The sheriff approached the gaggle of law enforcement officers gathered on the road's shoulder above the vehicle.

"All right, what do we have?" he asked, glancing at his watch before peering down the ravine.

The detective spoke up, "Sheriff, as you know the Highway Patrol discovered this vehicle just after nine a.m. this morning. They saw the skid marks on the highway and pulled over to investigate. EMS arrived and discovered what appears to be a bullet wound at the center of the driver's face and an exit wound at the back of his skull. Based on the trauma to his head, I'd say it was a rifle round, maybe a thirty-caliber or so, just looking at the entry." The detective motioned toward the fresh black marks on the roadway. "Our theory at this point is that the driver gets shot while heading this way and the speed and abrupt turn of the wheel cause the vehicle to flip over and down the embankment."

"That certainly makes sense, except the part about the oh-six round to the face. Who shot this guy and why?"

"It's opening day for deer in this unit, Sheriff," the Game & Fish officer offered. "Some guy with a tag in his pocket, probably an out-of-stater, takes a shot at a skylined buck from the road. It's illegal, but we know it happens. He misses, shoots over the top of the deer, and the bullet's trajectory takes it over this rise. Gravity drops the bullet down into that dip in the road just as this poor bastard is coming the other way. I'd say this guy's number was up."

"I'll buy it. I've seen stranger things. Who is he?"

The detective answered, "DL says he's Marcus Boykin. He's driving on a New York license, but we have a listing for a Marcus Boykin at Star Valley Ranch. Typical summer resident."

Satisfied that his men were conducting a thorough and proper investigation, the sheriff nodded and turned back toward his government-supplied Ford Expedition. He was the featured speaker at a Chamber of Commerce lunch at noon and he didn't intend to be late.

CHAPTER 42

Bird Rock, California

Invigorated by the shot of adrenaline the morning's success had brought, Reece drove straight through to Southern California, stopping only for food and fuel at hole-in-the-wall gas stations, all paid for in cash. He arrived at Ben's place at midnight, backing down the driveway and into the garage, where he unloaded his gear. Even at night he could tell it was a beautiful place, a contemporary condo in the trendy Bird Rock neighborhood of San Diego, nestled between La Jolla and Pacific Beach. The design was open, incorporating light natural woods with industrial steel finishes. Huge floor-to-ceiling windows led seamlessly to a deck that overlooked the dark ocean. Even though it was a few houses back from the cliffs, Reece could still hear the surf breaking on the rocks below. He took a shower and checked his SpiderOak folder, sending Edwards a message that said only, *at your place, bring breakfast,* before hitting the sack.

Seven hours later he heard someone pounding on the door and realized that he'd slept like a rock. He grabbed the Glock from his bedside table and looked through the crack in the bedroom blinds to find Ben's rental car parked below him in the driveway. Still half-asleep, he tossed his handgun onto the bed and opened the back door wearing boxers and a T-shirt.

"Holy shit, did I wake you up? I can come back at noon if you want. You think you're back in college, frat boy? You need a haircut and a shave. You're starting to look like the bad guys. I brought your favorite, Night and Day Cafe."

Reece gave Ben the one-finger salute as he walked into the condo's small kitchen to make coffee while Ben unpacked the short order to-go food on the counter.

Taking a huge bite of his breakfast burrito, Reece gestured to the surrounding condo with its sweeping view of the Pacific. "Nice place."

"Yeah, my employer has a few of these scattered across the country. We use them for debriefings and meets that require an off-site due to sensitivity issues. This one is pretty nice and hardly ever gets used."

"Our tax dollars at work, huh? This place must have cost you hundreds."

"Good ol' Uncle Sugar," Ben said and smiled. He finished his breakfast and packed a dip of tobacco into his lower lip before pulling a file folder out of a nylon backpack he'd hung on the back of his chair.

"All right, bro, it turns out that the shitheads who did this weren't local gangbangers. They were legit bad hombres from Mexico. DEA watches these guys very closely, as you know, and actually have them coming and going the night of the attack. I don't have specific IDs on the shooters, but we know they are Cártel Jalisco Nueva Generación, 'CJNG' or 'New Generation,' and we know where they live." Edwards slid a series of photos across the kitchen table, each depicting a different angle of the same three-story concrete block structure with caged balconies and barred windows, a cluster of satellite TV dishes mounted to the roof. "They live and work out of this house in Tijuana. Typical shithole. You can expect a dozen or so, equipped with small arms along with some women and even kids hanging around. Call it a gang clubhouse. These aren't high-level dudes; they're foot soldiers."

Reece looked at the photos carefully, taking note of various features on the house's exterior.

"Any idea on the interior layout?"

"Negative, DEA doesn't have eyes inside."

"How about the neighborhood? How quick can they summon the cavalry if something goes down?"

"CJNG is just starting to get a foothold in Tijuana, so they're pretty exposed. This is like an outpost for them. They're trying to increase their reach into the city and they're running it from this place. Kinda like when we'd set up a combat outpost during a 'clear, hold, build.' The Tijuana and Sinaloa cartels don't want them there; so it's a fight. I wouldn't want to hang around that neighborhood very long, but it's not like they have a hundred reinforcements across the street."

"Check. Where is this place in the city?"

"That's the challenge; it's in La Sánchez Taboada. Here." Edwards pointed to a spot on an aerial photograph of the city. "Real bad neighborhood. It would be tough to get on target without some local help. It would be one thing to roll up with a couple of Strykers or Bradleys, but I wouldn't want to be wandering around there solo at three in the morning looking for a place to park. You want me to find you some help? I bet the Sinaloa guys would be happy to assist you in taking out their competition."

"Negative. This is my show. I'll handle it. Besides, the last thing I need is to roll into a gunfight in a third-world slum with a bunch of criminals I can't trust."

"Gotcha. Let me know if I can support with anything else. This stuff is all yours to keep. The best intel we have is in there. If you change your mind about having help, let me know. You know I'll roll down there with you if you need me."

"Thanks, Ben. You've helped more than you know. I don't need you getting more involved in this than you already have."

"Happy to help. I'm headed out. Gotta go to work. Trying to poach some talent from Team Five. Be safe."

"Thanks, buddy, you too."

Reece spent the next few hours looking at the target info on the house in Tijuana. As much as he wanted to exact immediate vengeance on the monsters who murdered his wife and daughter, he knew that now was not the time to act on emotion. If he was going to come out of Mexico alive, it would take some planning to pull off. He also assumed that they were most likely hired guns, and if he was going to figure out who hired them and why, he was going to have to stick to his plan.

He had one shot at pulling off the next phase of the operation before his current intel went stale. According to email traffic between Josh Holder and Saul Agnon, Agnon would be at a resort in Palm Springs for a conference in two days. Agnon, who appeared to be the hub of this conspiratorial wheel, was Reece's best chance to put the pieces of this puzzle together.

Hard lessons learned in Iraq and Afghanistan had taught Reece that going after the head of the snake could be counterproductive. Killing or capturing a senior Al-Qaeda leader always led to another one taking his place, now smarter, having learned from his senior's mistakes. After some amount of studying and bringing in civilian anthropologists and counterinsurgency experts from academia, some commanders began to use crosscut targeting as a way to more effectively take out the heir apparent before working both up and down the enemy chain of command across multiple networks. Reece understood the methodology. Agnon was his version of crosscut targeting. Reece was not going to allow this network to evolve. He was going to destroy it. He was going to kill them all.

CHAPTER 43

Palm Springs, California

Saul Agnon wasn't the type to do much socializing. His work for Steve Horn and Capstone monopolized both his time and his energy. Though he didn't technically practice law, Agnon was proud of his attorney status, and maintaining his license required mandatory hours of continuing legal education. Each year he attended the Los Angeles Bar Association's Fall Retreat in Palm Springs, which not only satisfied his annual CLE requirement but was also a much-awaited chance to interact with other attorneys.

Agnon sat next to a redheaded litigator from a big L.A. firm at dinner but, despite his best efforts, couldn't convince her to join him for a night-cap in his casita. He hung around the late-night cocktail reception for a while but by 11:00 p.m. he was ready for bed. He had another long day of seminars to attend the next morning and, unlike most of the attendees, he actually enjoyed the material being presented. He wasn't much of a drinker and felt a bit tipsy from the three glasses of chardonnay that he'd consumed during dinner and the margarita that he'd enjoyed at the reception. He always got turned around at this resort, with its winding paths and dozens of identically designed guesthouses. It took him a full ten-minute walk in the clear desert night to reach his casita and another clumsy thirty seconds to fish his room key out of his blazer pocket and get it into the electronic lock the right way before he could open the door.

He closed the door behind him and was delighted to hear that the maid had turned on some classical music while performing the turndown service, though he did think it to be a bit loud. He removed his blue blazer and opened the armoire before reaching for a hanger, fumbling and dropping it on the stone floor. *Damn.* Bending over to retrieve it, he was suddenly pulled backward by strong arms that locked around his neck, legs scissoring around his torso while being pulled onto the floor. He was essentially lying on his back on the man's chest, being squeezed like he was in the clutches of an anaconda. He struggled to turn his head but when he did so, the assailant's arm moved tighter around his throat. He tried to scream but no sound escaped. With the blood supply cut off to his brain, he passed out in seconds.

Saul awoke after what must have been only a few moments: naked, bound, gagged, and blindfolded. The sound of Beethoven's Fifth blasted in his ears over the sound system in his room; even if he could scream, no one would hear him. His hands were restrained behind his back and his feet were somehow shackled. He tried to bring himself to his knees but was immediately shoved back down to the cold stone floor. Whoever had attacked him was still there and was watching his every move. His brain was foggy from the alcohol, but it took him only a few seconds to figure it out: James Reece had found him. The reality of what was happening hit Agnon in the form of complete, overwhelming terror. He felt the searing acid of vomit rise through his throat and retched as his dinner surged into his mouth. The cloth gag gave the sick liquid nowhere to go, backing it into his esophagus and filling his airway. Seconds after regaining consciousness from the rear naked choke, Agnon was drowning in his own vomit. The sense of panic was overwhelming. He gagged, snorted, and gagged again, all the while burning the precious oxygen for which his brain was beginning to starve.

Reece saw the man convulse and watched vomit shoot from his nostrils. He began flopping around like a fish on the deck of a boat, craving oxygen and choking on his own sickness. As much as he would have liked, Reece didn't come all this way to watch the man whom Holder's emails identified as a key contributor to the killing of Reece's family and SEAL troop drown in his own puke. He reached down to remove the cloth that he'd tied around Agnon's mouth, pulling it off over his head and removing the blindfold in the process. The man continued to writhe in agony as his head turned a deep purple color, the veins in his neck standing out like cables.

Reece wrenched the man's head back by his hair with one hand and stuck a gloved finger down his throat with the other to trigger the gag reflex. Vomit shot forward across the floor and Agnon's body convulsed as it cleared itself of the fluid. The rotten stench of stomach acid, food, and alcohol was overwhelming. Even with the surgical mask over his face, Reece had to turn away to keep from gagging. Puking on the floor was not a great way to keep one's DNA out of a murder scene.

An animal moan escaped from Agnon's throat, sounding like the death bellow of a large bovine. The good news was that he could breathe again. He didn't say a word as he lay naked on his side, panting for air with tears streaming down his face. What had been a normal human being ten minutes earlier was now a quivering mess, which was exactly what Reece wanted.

"Can you breathe now?" Reece asked in a voice devoid of sympathy. Saul nodded repeatedly without saying a word or even opening his eyes. Reece hoped that the guy's heart wouldn't fail.

When it looked like Agnon's respiration had returned to a normal range, Reece tied the vomit-soaked rag that had served as a gag around Saul's eyes and began dragging his limp body toward the bathroom of the resort cottage. He'd already prepared the area by folding two large bath towels over the side of the tub to prevent bruising the man's back.

Saul's compliance as Reece dragged him into position suggested that this process wouldn't take very long. Reece wrapped Saul's head with plastic wrap, covering his mouth but not his nose. He then pulled the attorney's body over the lip of the bathtub so that his head and shoulders were held below his waist and his feet stayed outside the tub, just off the tile floor. He straddled the smaller man and grabbed him by the throat with his left hand to get the angle correct while turning on the faucet with his right. The fixture had one of those handheld shower heads on a flexible hose, which Reece now held over Agnon's face. The stream from the massaging head flooded Saul's eyes and nostrils with water, which followed gravity downward and flowed into his sinuses, mouth, and throat. The angle of his head prevented the water from entering his lungs, thus he would not actually drown, though everything in the man's brain suggested otherwise.

Every fiber in Saul's body screamed for air, and it took all of Reece's strength to maintain his grip on the violently thrashing figure below him. Agnon coughed spastically to clear the water

313

from his throat but the plastic wrap acted as a one-way valve, letting the air from his lungs escape while keeping the water in his mouth. Though he didn't realize it, all his coughing accomplished was to speed up the process. The plastic wrap trick was something that Reece had learned from the CIA interrogators way back in the Wild West days just after 9/11, when Americans still had the will to win. Reece continued to spray water into Saul's nostrils as unimaginable sounds echoed in the confines of the bathroom. Good thing the casita was freestanding and the walls were thick.

After a count of twenty, Reece removed the stream of water from Agnon's face and pulled the man's body upright into a seated position on the urine-soaked bathroom floor. He pulled the plastic wrap down from Agnon's face so that it hung loosely around his neck.

"You know who I am, don't you, Saul?" Reece asked in an almost kind voice.

"I do, I do . . ." gasped Saul between hyper-ventilating breaths.

"Then you know why I'm here."

Saul shook his head violently. "I didn't . . . I didn't do anything . . . I just work for Horn. . . ."

"See? You're already bullshitting me. I can't have you doing that, Saul." Reece swiftly and violently wrenched Agnon back into the water-boarding position and resumed the spray of water. Without the plastic it was a bit messier,

314

but the net effect was the same. He was able to move the man from zero to ten on the punishment scale within a few seconds. Agnon's brain was quickly learning that doing anything other than complying meant instant and unimaginable torture. After Saul had spent another twenty seconds under the hose, Reece dragged him back out of the tub.

Reece had himself been waterboarded during SERE School after an escape attempt that the instructors deemed worthy of the treatment. He knew that as bad as the process of enduring the simulated drowning was, the threat of going through it again was the real motivator, or demotivator depending on your position.

"You ready to talk and tell me the truth?"

"Yes, yes . . . I am," Agnon gasped.

Reece stood and walked over to the bathroom counter, retrieving a small tape recorder and placing it on the closed lid of the toilet before pressing RECORD. He then let the man catch his breath for a few moments before he started asking questions. He began with an easy one.

"Who is Josh Holder?"

"He's a DOD agent. He's a D.C. guy, but he's out here for this project."

"Why him? Why is DOD involved?"

"He's the Hartleys' guy. He does work for them, double-dipping with DOD and J. D. Hartley's consulting firm. He was a liaison when Hartley was in Congress and has been a confidant of theirs ever since."

Reece took the conversation in a different direction. "Tell me about RD4895."

How does this guy know so much? Agnon thought.

"It's an experimental drug. A big company stumbled on it a few years back and saw its potential to prevent PTSD, some sort of neuron blocker. It seemed to work, but they couldn't get the safety profile worked out; the test animals kept getting tumors. They put it on the auction block, and Capstone bought it dirt cheap."

Reece looked at the nude, blindfolded form before him and knew that he'd broken him. The terror of the last few minutes combined with the looming threat of a repeat performance had taken away whatever spine Agnon had in the first place. Grabbing him by the arm, Reece hoisted Agnon to a standing position and led him back into the living area of the casita. The restraints around Agnon's ankles made the pace painfully slow. He unstrapped one side of the hospital restraints from Agnon's wrist and moved the man's arms to the front of his body. He then retied the restraints with Agnon's hands in the front and pushed him backward into a chair. Opening the door to the minibar, he removed two airplane-size bottles of Jim Beam and poured both into a glass that he then placed on the small end table next to Agnon.

He retrieved the tape recorder from the bath-room and put it on the table as well. Turning the classical music down, Reece removed the waterlogged and vomit-stained rag from Agnon's face and watched his eyes blink, slowly adjusting to the light. Wearing white Tyvek coveralls with a hood, a surgical mask, clear shooting glasses, and disposable paper booties over his shoes, Reece looked more like a lab technician than a commando. Agnon knew instantly that he wasn't going to survive this night and he resigned himself to his fate. Whatever will to fight he'd possessed had been broken down by those few oxygen-starved moments.

Reece motioned to the glass of bourbon on the table. Agnon suddenly realized how thirsty he was and reached hungrily with both manacled hands to pick up the glass. The brown liquid burned as it washed down his throat but it helped bring a calm over his body and broken spirit.

"So you were telling me about buying the drug. Why did Capstone buy it if the side effects were so bad? How did it have any value?"

"My boss is a risk taker. He doesn't go for the easy play, but he's also good at stacking the deck in his favor. He paid next to nothing for the compound. The United States is in a war with no end in sight, and if they could get the tumor stuff sorted out, the drug would be worth a fortune. In the meantime, the entire project was flooded with DOD funding, so the financial gamble was minimal."

"What do you mean, DOD funding?"

"We're playing with the house's money. This whole thing is being subsidized by the DOD. For the past two years, there's been one hundred million dollars in the Defense Appropriations Act for PTSD research, and all of that money goes to our fund, except for the ten percent we pay to Hartley."

"The SECDEF gets a ten-million-dollar kickback?" Reece said incredulously.

"Not directly. We pay her husband ten percent to be our consultant. Technically, contingency lobbying is illegal, but we pay him ten million for his services out of last year's appropriation to give everything the appearance of being aboveboard. It's obviously a sham, but nobody's looking too hard. People think that politicians are on the take and they're right, but it's not in the way that everyone thinks. Nobody takes bags of cash these days. If you did, you'd end up in federal prison. It's all done with undisclosed conflicts of interest. You show me a member of Congress who's part of the appropriations process and I'll show you a wife, child, or brother-in-law with a company that benefits from federal dollars. Everybody does it. The Hartleys are just playing on a different level."

Jesus.

"You guys don't have your own scientists, though."

"No, no. We contract with a lab in India. They pay pennies over there so you can hire PhDs for next to nothing. Boykin handled the science and the analytics. He's some sort of doctor turned accountant and financial analyst specializing in the health-care sector. He hatched the idea, and Mr. Horn gave the lab in India a timeline and a budget to rework the compound. They thought they had it worked out."

"How did it get tested on my guys?"

"With potential for this much money, you'd be surprised what people will do. I'm talking about tens of billions of dollars, which is a lot of money to spread around to make friends, not to mention the tens of millions that we're getting from Congress; that just gave everyone a taste. Mr. Horn put the offer out to a few of his close confidants, including Mike Tedesco. You get Tedesco and you get the Hartleys."

"You're telling me that the SECDEF arranged to test an experimental drug on a random SEAL troop? You bullshitting me again, Saul?"

"No, I wouldn't bullshit you, Mr. Reece. You know what a politician Admiral Pilsner is. He worked directly for Secretary Hartley at the Pentagon, and they became close. She has him on track to be the chief of naval operations and probably chairman of the Joint Chiefs. He's totally loyal to her. Of course, he was promised an enormous sum of money as well. She let him choose who to use, through Tedesco and Holder of course."

"You mean the admiral personally chose *my* troop to test out this drug?" Reece asked, his eyes narrowing.

"That's how it happened, Mr. Reece. I swear."

Interesting. Reece paused before continuing.

"How did you ever hope to get something like this approved? The FDA isn't going to accept results from some drug that you tested on people without their consent. I'm no expert, but I know there are all kinds of standards that have to be met. Phase One, Phase Two, all of that."

"That would be true normally, but when the president names the head of the FDA and they want a drug approved during wartime to help every man and woman in uniform, no one is going to ask a lot of tough questions."

"So now you're telling me that the president is involved? Is the freaking queen of England also part of this conspiracy?"

"No, not *this* president, the *next* president—Secretary Hartley."

No way! Reece thought. *How in the hell did I get mixed up in this shit show?*

"How did you get us to take it? I didn't take any pills or anything on this deployment."

"Remember the Tactical Performance Study that your team participated in?"

"Yeah, they took our VO_2 max and ran a bunch of cognitive tests on us."

"That was a cover for this. The vitamin B_{12} shots you were given in the second half of that study were actually RD4895. We did a baseline physical and psychological assessment. We assumed that everything was going well until the blood work came back from the last battery of tests before your troop deployed. White blood cell counts for a bunch of your men were off the charts and there were various other abnormalities that indicated that the compound hadn't been fixed."

"And that's when Boykin made the call to pull the plug and have us all killed?"

"I don't know. I really don't, Mr. Reece," Saul managed to get out through his tears. "How do you know so much about Marcus?"

"I found out about him a few days before I put a bullet through his brain in Wyoming."

Oh my God. This is real. He's really going to kill us all. Though Saul said nothing, his expression betrayed it all.

"How do you arrange a Taliban ambush half-way across the globe? You guys cut haji in on the billions?"

"We left it up to Pilsner on how to clean things up, all through Tedesco and Horn. They got to know each other through all those high-end fundraisers they throw for you guys, for the foundations and charities. That stuff is big business."

"So, Pilsner sets us up for an ambush and gets a bunch of Rangers and Army aircrew killed for good measure. How the hell did he manage that?"

"I don't know exactly, Mr. Reece. I just know that's how it went down." Saul took another long gulp of the bourbon.

"And Boozer and I survive."

"Yes, so Josh Holder makes your man's death look like a suicide, leaving only you remaining."

"What about Chinatown? How did you find me?"

"The SECDEF. She allocated a UAV to track you."

"*What?* She diverted a national drone asset to help kill me?"

"I swear it's true, Mr. Reece, I swear."

"Who is Humza Kamir?"

"Who?"

"Humza Kamir. The man you sent to kill me in Chinatown?"

"I didn't even know his name until you just mentioned it. That's the SECDEF's asset. I have no idea. Somebody they radicalize online in case they need some dirty work done that can be attributed to Islam."

Reece shook his head in disbelief. *Could that possibly be true?*

"Say that again? They do *what?*"

"They, they have this program where they radicalize at-risk individuals from target populations. They recruit them to what they think is a radical Islamic movement and then use them as expendable assets. I know it sounds crazy, but it's true. I swear."

Reece paused as the gravity of what Agnon had just told him sank in.

"Are you certain?" Reece asked, his voice icy and pointed.

"I couldn't believe it, either, when I first found out about it. In fact, I'm not even supposed to know about it. I wish I didn't. I think the Hartleys might have created it. I don't know. I just know it exists."

"Where do the Mexicans fit into all of this?"

"They were just contract labor. This isn't the movies, where you hire a hit man to kill someone. We pay some of the cops to make the arrangements with gang types to do it. Mr. Reece, I'm—"

Reece cut him off. "Don't fucking do it, don't even sit there and apologize for having my pregnant wife and baby girl shot down in our home by some fucking drug cartel. Trust me when I tell you that you don't want to do that."

Agnon sat silently, staring at the floor in front of Reece.

"If this doesn't work," Reece asked, resuming

his interrogation, "how are you planning to make money on it? You've got to be throwing some serious numbers at all these collaborators to get them to risk everything. How are they going to get paid if the drug is no good?"

"Well, now the drug works; there are no efficacy issues, at least not on the latest test rats in India. It's proving to be over twenty percent more effective than placebo. As for the adverse events, the tumors, we are confident that we have addressed that in the latest version of the product. The most recent test population has shown no such signs."

"You mean to tell me that you've tried this thing on another group of unwilling people? More SEALs?"

"Yes. Admiral Pilsner arranged for another group of candidates and they are doing just fine."

"You bastards!" Reece shot back, his voice laced with venom. It took all his strength not to snatch the life from Horn's underling then and there. Regaining his composure, he continued: "Okay, let's keep going. You haven't said much about your boss. Tell me more about Steve Horn."

Agnon took a deep breath. "Mr. Horn is a genius. He sees potential in things that others don't and he's relentless when he wants something. When he hears that I've been murdered, he's going to go into hiding and hire every security contractor on the planet to hunt you down. You'll never get to him."

"That's where you're wrong, Saul; I'm not going to murder you."

The look on Saul's face was a priceless mask of hope and shocked disbelief. Reece poured Saul another drink and grilled him for another hour about places, names, dates, everything he could think of that would be helpful in his quest. Saul's speech increasingly slurred, and his eyes narrowed to small slits. Eventually his head pitched forward as he passed out in the chair from the exhaustive waterboarding and the subsequent alcohol consumption. Satisfied that he had what he needed, Reece decided it was time for Saul Agnon to leave this world.

Reece opened his nylon pack and began laying out the instruments that would bring about the untimely death of Mr. Horn's compliant assistant. A lighter, a syringe, a metal spoon, a length of surgical tubing, and a small Ziploc bag containing powder. Reece wrapped the tubing around Agnon's left upper arm and tied it off tightly. He took the spoon to the bathroom, where he filled it partially with water from the sink before emptying the contents of the Baggie into it, forming a paste. Holding the spoon above the lighter, Reece watched the water boil the powder into a thin liquid. He then dipped in the tip of the syringe and pulled back the plunger, drawing the mixture into the plastic cylinder. Reece had done enough first aid training to be able to find a vein, and he quickly stuck the needle into the most prominent blood vessel protruding from the crook of Saul's arm. He pulled back on the plunger slightly and blood flowed into the syringe, spiraling through the liquid contents like the lava lamps Reece loved as a kid. He pushed down on the plunger, sending the liquid death into Agnon's bloodstream.

As the methadone, alprazolam, and carisoprodol flowed into Agnon's brain, they inhibited the respiratory response centers already hampered by his body's metabolization of alcohol. The mixture of chemicals had a cumulative effect on the brain's ability to measure carbon dioxide; Agnon's brain no longer sent the signal to his lungs that he needed to exchange carbon dioxide for oxygen and his body quite literally forgot to breathe.

His death came quickly. Reece placed the needle as well as the rest of the drug paraphernalia on the small table, alongside the empty liquor bottles and the half-full glass of bourbon. He pulled a trash bag from his pack, collecting the padded restraints from Agnon's hands and feet. In went the cloths that he'd used as a gag and blindfold and finally the length of plastic wrap that still hung around Agnon's neck. He carried the bag around the entire room, looking for anything that needed to be disposed of in order to sterilize the scene. He took the wet towels from the edge of the floor and threw them haphazardly onto the urine-soaked tile floor. He tied the trash bag off and dropped it into his pack, while the tape recorder went into a small compartment on the outside. Reece did one final sweep of the room before checking Agnon's nonexistent pulse and changing out of his lab clothes. Then, hanging the DO NOT DISTURB sign on the door, he exited into the early morning darkness.

Back at the condo, Reece sat at the kitchen table listening to the Saul Agnon interrogation tape. He made notes, stopping and rewinding the tape at more than one juncture to ensure that he had the details correct. If this was a lie, it was a well-crafted one. If it was the truth, it was mind-blowing. After reviewing his notes, Reece pulled a piece of paper from the bag in his pocket and removed the list. He unfolded it and looked at Lucy's drawing before turning it over and smoothing it flat on the table. With the pencil he'd been carrying in the bag, he drew a line through Agnon's name. He then added more names to the list based on his notes from his interrogation:

Josh Holder
~~Marcus Boykin~~

~~Saul Agnon~~
Steve Horn
CJNG, Mexico
Admiral Gerald Pilsner
Mike Tedesco
J. D. Hartley
Lorraine Hartley

It was time to take Marco del Toro up on his generous offer.

CHAPTER 44

Palm Springs, California

The housekeeper had respected the DO NOT DISTURB sign on the door of Casita 134 the previous day, but it was now well after the guest's appointed checkout time on Sunday and she had cleaned and restocked all the other rooms on her list. She tapped loudly on the door with her keycard.

"Housekeeping!"

But for the sound of classical music playing softly somewhere inside the room, silence.

"Housekeeping!"

Nothing.

"Housekeeping, I am coming inside!"

She inserted her master keycard into the slot and the lock clicked open. Reaching into the room and turning on the light as she swung the door open, her peripheral vision caught a human form slumped in a chair. She began to apologize for her intrusion until her eyes focused on the dead man, an odor the likes of which she had never experienced shocking her system.

"Dios Mio!"

She slammed the door shut and ran screaming for her supervisor.

• • •

When homicide detective Anthony Gutierrez arrived, the responding patrol officers had already cordoned off the scene. The officer outside the door nodded at the detective and motioned him inside the room where another officer was waiting. The smell of death hit Gutierrez's nostrils as soon as he crossed through the doorway. A quick glance at the body established that calling EMS had been a waste of time and resources.

The departed was naked and his entire body was devoid of color, except for his lower legs, which looked to be filled with dark red wine. Gravity had caused the man's blood, no longer under pressure from a beating heart, to pool in his legs. His eyes were closed and his mouth was open. But for the startling lack of color, the look on his face made him appear to be asleep.

The manner of his death was apparent from the array of drug paraphernalia on the table beside him: a syringe, a soot-colored metal spoon with the dried residue of what was likely either prescription drugs or heroin, a Bic lighter, a cocktail glass containing a small amount of brown liquid, and empty liquor bottles that appeared to be from the room's minibar. Surgical tubing was wrapped tightly around the body's left bicep and a puncture wound was evident on the forearm.

"Another overdose, Detective?" asked the patrol officer, almost rhetorically.

"Yeah, I'd say that's pretty obvious. Anything else in the room?"

"Nothing out of the ordinary. There's some puke on the floor over there, piss all over the bathroom. Looks like this guy was partying pretty hard."

"Who is he?"

The officer glanced down at a pocket-size notebook. "His ID and the name badge from his conference say he's Saul Agnon from L.A. The resort manager confirmed the room was booked in that name by a guy attending some lawyer conference."

"When's the last time anyone saw him alive?"

"All of the attendees have left the conference but, according to the maid, he had a do-not-disturb sign on his door all day yesterday. Maid came in at approximately two thirty-five this afternoon to clean the room and saw the body. She says she didn't touch anything. My guess is he's been dead since sometime Friday night."

"I'd agree based on the body. I'll call around to some of the folks at the conference and see if we can find out anything, but my guess is that this is a straight-up accidental overdose. Probably heroin or poly-substance. It's nothing like Northern California, but we still get at least one of these a month. Thirty-something white guys are dropping like flies."

"Can't imagine injecting yourself with that shit.

Makes my skin crawl." The officer winced at the mere thought.

"Addiction is a powerful force. This guy's a lawyer, probably makes more scratch than both of us put together, and he dies butt naked in a hotel room trying to get high." Detective Gutierrez shook his head. "I'll snap some pictures. Call the ME, and we'll get him bagged up and out of here."

CHAPTER 45

Point Loma, California

Reece slowed his Land Cruiser and eased into a parking space off the main drag in Point Loma, just across the bay from Naval Air Station North Island, the Navy's large real estate holding that occupied the majority of Coronado Island.

Reece had always liked Point Loma. There were some beautiful homes here, with great views of San Diego, its bay, Coronado, and the Pacific. He loved the smell of the ocean, and Point Loma was San Diego's maritime metropolis. He drove by the front gate to the Marine Corps Recruiting Depot, one of two boot camps where young recruits began their journey into the Corps. Crossing streets with names like Nimitz, Farragut, and Roosevelt, he passed yacht builders, boat repair shops, the exclusive San Diego Yacht Club, and a host of fishermen preparing for yet another day at sea.

Traffic had been light this early on a weekday, but Reece knew that a certain local coffee shop would be open and ready for business. The coffee shop looked like a small Victorian house, which it had been at some point years ago. With two stories and a charming front deck it could easily have been mistaken for an historic home, rather than the small-batch roaster it was. The inside was as appealing as the outside, with large overstuffed chairs and couches arranged among antique coffee tables of just the appropriate size. The walls were adorned with an assortment of old books, which always made Reece feel comfortable and at home.

As early as it was, Reece was not the first customer of the day. A girl in her early twenties sat pecking away at her laptop, probably a student from Point Loma Nazarene University, just up and over the hill, while across the room sat a grizzled old fisherman deep in thought.

Reece ordered a large black coffee. Ordinarily he would have added something sweet, but today he ordered it the same way his friend who usually accompanied him to this particular coffee shop would do it. Reece smiled, recalling how his larger companion would always make some comment about guys who spruce up their coffee, as he shook his head watching Reece add honey or sugar with a dash of cream, or worse yet, adding nothing because he ordered a latte.

Today, that Teammate wasn't there to give Reece a hard time about his coffee predilections. He was waiting for Reece farther up the road.

Reece fired up the Land Cruiser and headed up the hill, turning onto Cabrillo Memorial Drive. The higher Reece climbed, the more beautiful the view became, the homes and businesses retreating to give way to the natural beauty of the Pacific coastline.

Reece pulled into a small dirt lot facing east and took in the view. Naval Base Point Loma, home to San Diego's submarine fleet, was just coming to life below him, while across the bay he had a commanding view of North Island, Coronado, downtown San Diego, Imperial Beach, and on into Mexico.

His coffee sufficiently cooled, Reece rested his arm on the open window and took a sip of the strong black liquid that he was sure once flowed through the veins of the friend he had come to see, based on the copious amounts Reece had observed him consume on a daily basis over the years. Watching a *Ticonderoga*-class guided-missile cruiser pass through San Diego Bay into the open waters of the Pacific, Reece could not help but be impressed. That one ship contained more combat power than most small countries. Its imposing presence represented United States diplomacy abroad and traced its origins back to the Continental Navy during the Revolutionary War. To Reece, it looked like freedom.

Reece allowed another smile as he thought about how his friend would have been impressed that he knew the ship below was a *Ticonderoga*-class. Usually, when his friend would ask him to identify a certain ship in their wanderings, Reece would answer, "That's a big gray one." Reece's professional life had been spent studying the unconventional side of warfare: insurgencies, guerrilla tactics, and terrorism. On those subjects he was more than well versed.

Coffee in hand, Reece exited the cruiser and began the walk to meet his friend. It had been too long. The intermittent muffled sound from the sub base below would occasionally break over the hill to interrupt a distant lawn mower and the cadence of sprinklers on a section of grass across the street. The peaceful chirping of birds in a light morning breeze was the perfect complement to the serenity of Fort Rosecrans National Cemetery.

Reece ascended the steps into a small white nondescript building and entered his friend's name in the computer to locate his final resting place: section and gravesite number. He had made this trek with Senior Chief Martin Hackathorn on many an occasion, attending too many funerals together over the years. War does that. They always stopped at the small Victorian house coffee shop at the base of the hill before paying their respects to those taken too soon.

One becomes familiar with the layout of national cemeteries in times of war, and Reece was no different. He knew exactly where to go. It was a good spot.

Though he knew precisely where he was

going, Reece took his time getting there. He was dressed respectfully in slacks, his customary Salomon shoes, and a tucked-in button-up shirt. Black wraparound Gatorz sunglasses shielded his eyes from the early morning glare. A light jacket hid the Glock 19 concealed in his waistband, which he was sure was a violation of policy or law, probably both, and possibly even etiquette, but Martin would not want Reece to visit his gravesite unarmed, of that Reece was certain.

White headstones stood out in sharp contrast with the green grass of the rolling hills. One thing the country did well was keep up national cemeteries. Reece passed row after row in solemn respect; lives ending in dates 1914, 1877, 1966, 1944, 1917, 1898, 2006, 1900, and 2016 had found peace here. Those dates corresponded with events in a country that had seen little rest from war: the Indian War Campaign, the Mexican Campaign, World War I, Vietnam, World War II, the Haitian Campaign, Korea, the Spanish-American War, Iraq, and Afghanistan. Every generation seemed to be represented, and every generation had answered the call. This generation was the repository of that accumulated knowledge of war. Reece did not intend to let it go to waste.

Reece wondered where he would go when it was his time. With what he was about to do, he wasn't sure. He hoped they would honor the request in his will to be buried alongside Lauren and Lucy. He wanted to be next to them for eternity.

Reece didn't realize he had stopped walking, nor did he remember how long he had been standing there, coffee still cooling in his hand, eyes welling up, looking at the grave of his friend, the big man with the beard whose head Reece had last held when it wasn't even attached to his body.

Reece took a knee in front of the headstone, lowered his head, and didn't speak. His thoughts were focused beyond the grave. *Sorry, buddy,* Reece thought. *We never should have gone on that mission. I knew it and we went anyway. But, the truth of it is, we were set up before we even deployed. I'm the only one left. They took Lucy, Lauren, and our unborn son, and I don't have long. The bastards that killed you, killed us all back in this country during our work-up. Don't worry, though. I still have a bit more time. I know who they are now and I'm hunting them. They don't know it yet, but they will soon. I'm coming for them and I'm going to put them all in the ground.*

Standing, Reece took another look at the grave, emblazing the words etched there into his memory before turning to make his way back through the warriors of battles past.

Written on the headstone, under "Martin F.

Hackathorn, April 4th 1975–June 14th 2017, U.S. Navy, Afghanistan," was one simple word: PATRIOT.

Reece was coming.

Death was coming for them all.

PART THREE

THE
RECKONING

CHAPTER 46

Tijuana, Mexico

Marco had gotten Reece across the border without much trouble. The Range Rover that carried them south through Imperial Beach and Otay Mesa and into the San Ysidro border-crossing checkpoint was a version called the Sentinel. Built by Land Rover's Special Vehicle Operations unit in Great Britain, it could withstand armor-piercing incendiary bullets and shrapnel from hand grenades. With a 510-horsepower engine and a retooled suspension, it was a serious piece of machinery. Reece shuddered to think what it had cost. Up-armored Suburbans led and trailed the Range Rover, looking a bit like a presidential motorcade with a British twist. It seemed a bit high-profile to Reece, but this was Marco's department, and he seemed more than confident that he could get his friend back and forth across the border.

Reece couldn't help but tense up when they passed through the checkpoint into Mexico, but they drove through without so much as a pause. At midnight there was not the usual backup of cross-border daily labor, causing hours of delay at peak travel times that happened to coincide with San Diego's steadily growing number of commuters also going to and from work. Marco smiled watching Reece visibly relax as they sped south. Reece wondered how many Mexican and American laws he had just broken, knowing the contents of his load-out bag behind the seats.

Darkness enveloped the motorcade as it made its way into the heart of Tijuana. Things had gotten so bad there in recent years that the Navy had issued a directive forbidding sailors from partaking in liberty south of the border. The bars that used to bustle with U.S. military personnel from the second-largest naval port in the country were now just hosts to college students from San Diego and Los Angeles too young to get into the bars and nightclubs of Southern California.

Taking a sharp left down what appeared to be a dead-end alley, the vehicles abruptly turned into what looked to Reece like a garage chop shop. They pulled into spots obviously reserved for the boss as corrugated sliding doors came down behind them.

"We're here," Marco said, smiling.

"We're where?" Reece inquired, leaning forward to get a better look at his surroundings.

"My Tijuana offices."

Marco laughed as he saw a puzzled look cross Reece's face. "You expected better, *sí* ?"

"Well, it's a bit different from your usual digs."

"Ah, yes, it reminds me of my humble

beginnings. Plus, I can concentrate here without the unwelcome distractions brought on by success. Come," Marco continued, tilting his head in the direction of his door. "We have much to discuss."

Reece grabbed his load-out bag from the back of the Range Rover as Marco's security detail spread out into what looked to be their customary posts to keep an eye on surveillance camera footage of the surrounding area. A group of six nondescript cars were parked neatly in one corner of the garage. They looked like they would fit in nicely with Tijuana traffic and not arouse any suspicion if Marco needed to move around the city with anonymity. A small gym was set up in one corner of the garage along with an impressive array of wrestling mats.

"Is this how you've been beating me all these years? Sneaking into Mexico to train while I'm overseas?"

"Ha! One must do what one can. I know you read your Sun Tzu. Luckily tonight's foe has not," Marco called out as he bounded up a set of stairs to what Reece assumed would be his office overlooking the garage. Reece followed as hastily as he could, encumbered by the weight of his large bag.

Marco's office was neat and orderly, even minimalist. A row of security monitors lined one wall on the far side, allowing Marco to overlook the garage floor through large windows positioned to face the enormous doors.

"What business do you run from here?" Reece asked.

Marco looked his companion in the eye. "I have many businesses, my friend. I can run most of them from anywhere, but certain meetings and ventures require a place such as this." He paused. "Did you ever wonder how I got my American citizenship so quickly?"

"I assumed it was because your U.S. business interests would generate good tax dollars."

"Ah, yes, this is true. But I have other dealings that are of interest to certain agencies of your government."

"It's your government now, too," Reece reminded Marco with a nod.

"Very true, amigo, very true. I know it is hard to understand, but what we will do tonight will help both my business interests and our countries. I will explain more later. For now, you just have to trust me."

"I trust you, Marco. Otherwise I wouldn't be here."

"I know. Let's review those pictures again."

They had gone over the target package made up of the intelligence that Ben Edwards had delivered before crossing the border, but both men wanted to review it one last time. Reece knew Marco was the one person who could get him to his target. Marco had said yes without even knowing exactly what Reece had in mind. After hearing Reece out, Marco offered his security detail as an assault force but Reece decided against it; they could get him to and from his target and set up as a blocking element, but that was all. This was his war.

"Okay," Marco said when they had gone over it again. "When do we leave?"

"You said it was about twenty minutes to the target house," Reece said, looking at his watch. "Let's leave in thirty minutes, giving us a time on target of 0300."

"*Bien. Treinta minutos.* I will ready the men and cars. They will be, how do you say it? Our 'mobility package'?" Marco said, clearly pleased with his use of military lingo.

"Thanks, Marco. I won't forget this."

Marco nodded and left Reece alone to ready his gear.

The new Tijuana motorcade was a bit different than the one that had brought them into Mexico. Gone were the plush Range Rover and armored escort vehicles, replaced by unarmored, unre- markable everyday cars covered in dust and dents. Perfect for the night's mission. Reece just hoped they would start but was soon pleasantly surprised when he heard the engines crank up. It was apparent that the engines under the hoods were anything but ordinary. Marco smiled again, visibly enjoying surprising his friend.

"Sun Tzu," he said again, with a mischievous twinkle in his eye. "Deception."

Reece's current mobility package consisted of two cars that would be derelict vehicles almost anywhere in the United States but were an ideal fit for the streets of Tijuana. Marco and Reece were in the back of the lead vehicle. A driver and one of Marco's bodyguards sat in the front.

"*Diez minutos, Señor Toro*," said the big man in the front passenger seat.

Marco nodded. He started to say something when his phone chirped. "*Perdon*," he said, answering, "*Sí*," followed by a long pause. "*Sí. Gracias.*" Hanging up, Marco turned to Reece. "My source inside has left the building. Fourteen men. Six women. No children. The women are hookers from Mexicali. They have to import them for security reasons. They have one scout on the roof with an AK and one in the front room with a shotgun."

Reece nodded. His face was eerily calm. Marco had never seen his friend in work mode before, and even though he was not one to scare easily, inside he suddenly felt chilled. Reece was all business. Tonight that business was death.

"*Aquí*," said the man in the front passenger seat about ten minutes later, the car slowing to a crawl.

"Okay," Marco said. "This is it." He pointed to a dilapidated building at the end of the block.

"Reece, when you kill these men, will your journey be over?"

Reece paused. "I'm just getting started. Thanks, buddy. I'll be back in a few."

CHAPTER 47

Reece moved quickly and quietly from the sidewalk into the abandoned building Marco had identified on Google Earth across and adjacent from the target building. It was a construction project that looked like it had not been worked on in years. Reece felt good. He was dressed in his field cammies with full battle kit. It had taken more than fifteen years of warfare to dial his gear in to where it was today, and with tonight's op Reece would add yet another country to the list of places where he had applied his trade. The only difference between the gear from his last deployment to Afghanistan and tonight was that the helmet he wore was his nonballistic issued "bump" helmet, his Kevlar one having been lost to the ambush in the graveyard of empires. He was also not burdened with the two radios he usually carried; that gave him added mobility on this mission. His NODs gave him a distinct edge over his enemy, and tonight Reece planned on using them to his full advantage.

Though he was fairly certain the building was deserted, he cleared it methodically and smoothly. *Slow is smooth, smooth is fast.* As he moved to the roof he was transported back to another place and time, patrolling through the streets of Ramadi with his sniper team, setting up in the dark of night to await their unsuspecting prey from an advantageous position. Tonight was similar, except that he was alone, and these were the men who had killed his family.

Reece scanned the roof and moved to where he had a clear vantage point of the target house. It looked quiet. At first he thought Marco's informant had given them bad intel, since he didn't see the sentry on the roof. Another, more careful examination revealed the man sleeping in a chair, head back, an AK clearly visible propped against the railing next to him. Reece never would have used the roof during the day, but at night, with the technical advantage of his NODs, it offered a logical location from which to engage his first target.

Reece knelt down and rested his rifle on the railing. He settled the IR laser from the ATPIAL, invisible to anyone without a night-vision device, attached to the top rail of his M4 on the bridge of the sentry's nose. Pressing the trigger, Reece sent a 77-grain Black Hills 5.56 bullet directly into the man's face. Reece settled the laser onto the man's chest and put two more into his center mass just for good measure, his suppressor muffling the sound of the shots. Then he stood and made his way back to the street.

He passed Marco's vehicles as if in a blur, his movement smooth and steady, weapon up and trained at the front door of the target building. Locked. *Shit.* The informant was supposed to leave it open. If he had been with his assault team, Reece would have breached the door and begun clearing the house, as he had so many times throughout the war, but he was not with his assault team. Tonight he was the team.

Reece immediately switched to his secondary method of entry and moved to the side of the structure. *So similar to Ramadi.* Finding the outside pipe he had identified through Ben's imagery, he quickly slung his rifle and began to carefully work his way up the side of the building. *Not as easy as when I was an E4,* Reece thought.

Cresting the top of the building, Reece drew his pistol to cover the rooftop. Seeing only the dead sentry, he swung himself over the railing, holstering his pistol and bringing his M4 back around and into his shoulder in one fluid motion, before moving to the stairs leading down into the lion's den. Without knowing the exact layout of the interior, Reece was going to have to clear the entire building. Using angles much like a police officer with a flashlight and a handgun, Reece could instead use his NODs and M4 IR light/laser combo to clear each room. If he lost the element of surprise or the advantage afforded him by his night vision, things could go south in a hurry.

The building smelled of burnt cannabis, urine,

and sweat, a disgusting combination. Working his way into the first hallway of the third floor, Reece identified a partially open door to his left and closed doors to the other three rooms in the hallway. Pulling his M4 back at an angle into the crook of his elbow and body, Reece slowly pushed the door open. A lone figure could be seen lying facedown on the bed, wearing shorts and a tank top, sheets covering one leg. It looked like he was dead already. Continuing his scan of the room, Reece took everything in, his mind working to identify targets. *Clear, well, almost clear.* Reece leveled his laser at the back of the sleeping man's head and depressed the trigger, sending one round into his brain, which exploded onto the pillow and bed frame. *One down.* Reece held his breath. From the looks of it, these guys had been up partying most of the night, but it was never wise to underestimate your opponent.

Back into the hallway and on to the next room. Nothing to suggest Reece's suppressed shot had been heard. This door was unlocked and Reece opened it as quietly as possible. Two people were visible sleeping in bed. A grotesquely obese gang member lay naked, facing up, one leg draped over the side and resting on the floor. A petite young woman lay naked next to him on her back. Reece hoped that she partied hard enough to keep her from waking up. He didn't want to kill her, but if her waking up would compromise his mission he had no qualms about putting her down. Reece shifted his M4 to his left hand, gently releasing a small bungee cord that held a centuries-old tool that he and his men had learned still reigned supreme as one of the quietest ways to end a man's life. Reece raised the Winkler/Sayoc tomahawk, taking careful aim at the side of the sleeping man's head in the center of the temple, and drove it powerfully downward, through his brain, killing him instantly. Quickly Reece shifted to the woman and prepared to deliver her kill strike. She stretched and stirred, settling back into a comfortable sleeping position, unaware that the angel of death had passed her over this night.

Smoothly securing his 'hawk back into the sheath, he transitioned the M4 to his primary hand and moved back into the hallway. Two more doors on this floor. Eleven more men and five more females to contend with if the intel was correct. Next door. Locked. *Fuck*. Reece reached for his lockpicking set. No sense in kicking in a door and alerting a numerically superior force to his presence. Clicking on a small green LED light on the side of his helmet attached to a flexible neck allowed Reece to direct it appropriately. He slightly tilted his helmet up to allow him to see under his NODs to work the lock. As he inserted the first pick, the door began to move.

Reece's right hand moved back to his M4,

bringing it up while at the same time he identified his threat. Standing in front of him was a young woman wearing only panties, and behind her, sitting awake on the bed, was a fighting-age male clearly just getting out of bed and unsure of what was happening. Reece's left hand clamped around the throat of the girl in front of him as he made entry into the room. Sensing commotion at the door, her male companion stood up to make sense of what was happening, only to catch two rounds in the stomach from Reece's M4, fired from a position of retention. Reece drove the young woman into the floor, firing three more rounds into the target before him. Letting out a loud grunt, the barely awake man absorbed the next three rounds in the upper chest and neck, grabbing helplessly at his throat as blood sprayed from the deadly wound, sinking to the floor in a gurgle of death throes.

Reece quickly scanned the rest of the room to ensure it was clear and then yanked the young prostitute to her feet by the throat and onto the bed. "*Por favor, no*," she managed to cough out, "*por favor, no*," Reece had no reservations about sending her to the afterlife but wouldn't do so unless it were absolutely necessary. Pulling her up again by the throat, he moved her across the room back to the doorway, pinning her against the wall so he could look out into the hallway with his NODs. Still quiet. *Frogman luck,* Reece thought.

"*Por favor, no*," she whispered again, her eyes wide with fright.

"*Silencio*," Reece hissed, pushing her down to her knees and then forcing her to prone out on the floor. With an efficiency based on years of practice and execution, Reece pulled plastic zip ties from his plate carrier, quickly binding the young woman's hands and feet. Looking around the room, Reece settled on a sock near the dead man's shoes and stuffed it into her mouth, securing it with another zip tie. He then ushered her to her feet and back onto the bed, using a third tie to secure her to the metal bed frame.

"*Silencio*," he ordered again in a hushed tone. Her terrified eyes acknowledged understanding.

Reece moved back to the side of the door and ejected his partially used magazine, replacing it with a fresh one. Stowing the other away in case he needed it later, he examined the hallway yet again. Still quiet.

If he had had his troop with him, the building would have been secure by now. As this was a solo mission, Reece still had a ways to go.

Last door of the top floor. Unlocked. Reece pushed it open. His first thought was *how in the hell could these people not have heard the commotion next door.* His next was, *how in the hell could I not have heard them through the wall.* Two naked and heavily tattooed gang members were pounding away at one of the prostitutes.

She was on her hands and knees, taking one man from behind while taking the other in her mouth. Even with a small candle burning on the ground in the corner, none of them noticed the door inch open or the muzzle of Reece's rifle rise to chest height and fire two rounds into the upper back of the man working away at her from behind. If the other man noticed the reason for his friend's demise, he didn't show it. As the first dead man fell forward and collapsed onto the back of the woman in front of him, his partner in crime looked down in amazement to see his chest suddenly erupt into an unnatural violent mess of blood and tissue. His mind was just starting to realize what had happened when Reece's next round found its way through his left eye socket, tearing through the rational-thinking hemisphere of his brain and sending him down in the most unnatural of positions against the bloodstained headboard. Reece moved his IR laser back to the first man and put a security round in his head before swiftly committing to the room and kicking the first man off the female. She stayed facedown, not moving. For a second, Reece thought he had accidentally shot her, but then he realized the blood and tissue that covered her body were not her own; she was merely in shock from the two men she was just having sex with suddenly dying on top of her, showering her in a bloody mist.

Reece let her live, zip-tied her to the bed, performed another tactical reload, retaining the semi-used magazine, and moved back into the hallway. *Clear.*

Six down. Three prostitutes of the six total alive on the top floor. Eight more hostiles and three more noncombatants to contend with. *Move.*

Reece had become an instrument of death. Nothing felt more natural to him than moving through a target. He had done it at all tactical levels on the battlefield and now he was progressing through a new target, one that had no idea what was coming.

Down into the stairwell, scanning, clearing, processing every detail, weapon up and ready.

As Reece slowly pushed open the door to the second floor, he first sensed and then saw movement, meeting a juiced-up gangbanger in boxers running down the hallway with a stainless steel revolver in his hand. He must have heard or sensed something amiss upstairs. The sixth sense at work. He caught five 5.56 bullets in the chest as Reece shot him down. Killing men in close quarters was not as easy as the movies or local defensive weapons courses would have one believe; sometimes men die hard. There was no magic formula in the real world that would guarantee that someone would go down and stay down. The "two to the body, one to the head" popularized as the Mozambique technique was quickly dispelled in the realities of modern combat. Reece and his men shot their targets down; whether it took one shot or ten, you shot them into the ground.

A light switch was thrown at the end of the hall, and it erupted in a cheap flickering glow. Reece saw the man at the end of the hall, who had taken away the advantage of night vision, wearing jeans and a T-shirt, tattoos up the side of his neck and bald skull. Reece's shot down the hallway missed his mark as he pushed his helmet back on his head to see under the NODs in the new, lighted environment. The T-shirted man scrambled for his open door.

Wanting to get to him before he could get to a weapon, Reece charged down the hallway firing the M4 into the open door of the T-shirted man's room, clearing it by taking the angle and firing as he went. Not the usual protocol, but without a team of highly trained assaulters behind him, he needed to improvise.

As Reece attempted to get a better angle on the door, a heavily tattooed arm shot out of the room, grabbing his barrel and pinning him to the end of the hallway wall. *Jeez, this guy is strong.* With the M4 pushed against Reece's chest, it was combat ineffective. Reece grabbed the shaved tattooed head in front of him, smashing his helmet and NODs into the man's face twice before pushing both of them off the wall and back into the open door to the room. Reece registered a female voice screaming and saw a naked woman out of the corner of his eye, grasping desperately at sheets as she watched the death match taking place in front of her. Reece's kick off the wall propelled them both into the small bedside table, sending them crashing to the floor. His opponent was heavily muscled and outweighed Reece by a good twenty pounds. Landing on top of Reece, he wound up to deliver a crushing blow to the commando's face. Reece brought his head forward as the punch came down, connecting the man's fist to Reece's helmet.

It's strange the things one notices in combat. Through the screams of the naked prostitute, the flickering of the lights, and the crushing weight of the gangbanger on top of him, Reece saw the bandage. It was not professionally done but Reece knew instantly what it was: the bandage of a gunshot wound. This was the man Lauren had wounded protecting their daughter. A rage like he had never known boiled up inside him. Locking the bigger man's right arm to his body and trapping his right leg with Reece's left leg, Reece executed a jiujitsu move called the *uma-plata*, sending his enemy over and onto the ground. In one fluid movement practiced many times in training, Reece pulled a sharp dagger from its position on his plate carrier and sank it into the throat of his wife's killer. The eyes in his shaved head opened wide as he continued to struggle. Reece pushed down harder, withdrew the blade, and reinserted it with a sawing motion across his opponent's throat until his squirming stopped and he lay dead in a growing pool of blood.

Reece had no time for reflection. Bullets cascaded into the room from directly across the hall. AK fire. Reece knew the sound well. The rounds were being sprayed into the room without any real discipline, racking across the back wall and cutting across the upper body of the screaming prostitute, silencing her forever. Reece grabbed a frag grenade from a pouch on his belt, pulled the pin, and sent it careening into the adjacent room. Luckily, the construction was cinder block and could take a solid hit. When the grenade exploded, it sent debris flying into the hallway and into the room Reece now occupied. Taking advantage of the confusion from the blast, Reece flew across the hallway. There was no need for security rounds. One gangbanger and one woman lay dead, their bodies mangled from the violent blast, contorted into unearthly positions that signified death.

Nine targeted individuals down. Three females upstairs alive. Two females dead on second floor.

Now on the opposite side of the hallway from the stairwell, Reece reached out and killed the lights that still flickered after the grenade blast. Adjusting his NODs, he did another tactical reload and scanned the hallway from a position of cover inside the room that the grenade had rendered clear.

One door was still closed on this floor. Reece cleared the room that the man with the handgun appeared to have come from. A larger woman in a dirty shirt was crouched in the corner, knees tight to her chest. Her eyes were closed and she appeared to be praying. Reece let her be and moved to the closed door. Twisting the knob and throwing it open, he flattened himself against the hallway wall, half expecting a hail of bullets to burst through. Instead there was nothing. Reece slowly cleared around the door so he could see as much of the room as possible. Still nothing. He then made entry. Quickly sweeping the room and clearing all corners, he discovered it empty. *One floor to go.*

Reaching the stairwell door, Reece took a breath. *Time to finish the job.* Pushing the door open, Reece cleared both up and down the stairway. He began to work his way down when the first floor came alive with the sounds of war. Reece positioned himself so he had a clear view and line of fire to the first-floor stairwell door. He could clearly discern AK fire and what sounded like M4s and shotgun blasts. He heard yelling and commotion in Spanish getting closer to the downstairs door. More shouting and more gunfire. Suddenly the door Reece was covering flew open and in stumbled what were clearly two hostiles. They started to charge up the stairs when Reece cut them to shreds, the door slowly closing behind them. Reece refocused on the door, saw it begin to open, and began to apply pressure to his trigger.

"Reece! Reece! It's me," came Marco's voice up the stairs. Reece checked up as he saw his friend cautiously inch his face into view.

"Okay, I see you, buddy!" Reece called out. "You clear down there?"

"*Sí*, my friend!" came the reply.

"Coming down!" Reece shouted back.

Reece descended the stairs, weapon at the ready, all senses heightened and alert. He stepped over the two bodies at the bottom of the stairs as Marco opened the door for him. In the hallway were Marco and three of his security detail. Strewn on the floor were two more dead gangbangers and one dead woman. One of Marco's detail had another man on his knees, head against the wall.

Reece turned to Marco. "Well, that didn't work out as quietly as I thought. How long until the police get here?"

"*No policía esta noche, amigo.*" Marco sounded confident. "The night is ours. We saved this one for you," he said while motioning toward the man on his knees. "Do you want to ask him any questions?"

Reece looked at Marco and back to the prisoner, his eyes cold as ice.

"No," Reece said as he walked toward their detainee, lowered his M4, and executed him on his knees. "Let's go."

Marco looked at his security detail, shrugged, and headed for the door.

CHAPTER 48

Bird Rock, California

The sun was coming up over the San Diego skyline when Reece returned from his foray south of the border. He'd thanked Marco profusely for his generosity and loyalty and was told, "It was nothing, amigo." The events of the past weeks had caused Reece to sit back and take stock of his friendships. What he'd learned about loyalty was surprising. Some friends had leaned in hard to help in his time of need, while others had backed away. Some would have thought that his fellow SEALs would have rallied around him, but with the exception of Ben Edwards, that hadn't been the case. Most of his closest friends in the Teams had been killed in the ambush; others were probably too scared of retribution from Pilsner. It was a disappointment, but still, Reece couldn't blame them. Old friends like Marco and Liz, as well as new friends like Katie, had been there for him in ways that he'd never forget. The truth was that most SEALs he knew just needed to stay focused on preparing for war. That was their job, and any distraction from it only hindered mission success. That was how it had to be.

From the outside looking in, one would think

what Reece had done just a few hours earlier would cause thoughts of introspection, regret, and possibly even confusion. Movies and books often portrayed soldiers having a difficult time taking a life in combat and then struggling to deal with the psychological aftereffects of their actions.

To Reece killing was one of the most natural things one could do; it was hardwired into his DNA. If he were to think about it, Reece would conclude that the only reason he was alive today was that, throughout history, people in his lineage had been good at fighting to defend the tribe and at providing sustenance for their families. Killing was not so much about taking a life, it was about sustaining life: the lives of your countrymen, your unit, your family, yourself. That Reece did it exceptionally well did not bother him. Killing was what he did better than anything else.

He remembered being surprised by the feeling he experienced the first time he killed another man in combat. If one was to trust the experts, he should have felt instant remorse, regret, and confusion, even anger. It was as if society expected those who have taken lives in defense of their nation to immediately require counseling to assist them through their grief. Perhaps that convenient narrative allowed civilized society to better deal with their detachment from the realities of warfare, while sending young men to die in the mountains, jungles, deserts, and cities of foreign lands difficult to find on a map.

The truth was less complex. The truth was primal.

Reece felt no such remorse. The first time he killed and every time thereafter, he had felt a different emotion: *relief.* Relief might seem like an odd reaction, especially to the uninitiated. It was not relief in the sense that Reece discovered he *could* kill; he had never really worried about that. It was relief in the sense that his training, his skills, his instincts, his intellect, his dedication to understanding his enemy and the conflict in which they were engaged had not been found wanting. It was relief to be *alive.* Reece had a natural ability not just to fight but also to lead. Those two attributes had drawn his men to his side and built a trust not found elsewhere in polite society. It was what Reece was born to do.

He didn't do it because he liked it. He did it because it was required to ensure the survival of his men, his country, and his family. It wasn't that Reece felt no emotion from his years in combat; he was far from a sociopath. In combat units, sociopaths got good people killed and were weeded out as soon as possible.

When the topic came up in preparation for war, Reece would share with his men a story of the most important shot he had taken in combat. He framed it as the most important shot he didn't take. In an exceptionally brutal firefight in the streets of Fallujah, with bullets flying past and enemy mortars coming in, Reece cleared a dusty street corner and brought his rifle up, putting a man dressed in the black garb of the enemy into the crosshairs of his ACOG. At that point, anyone in the streets of Fallujah was considered a viable target by the commander's interpretation of the rules of engagement, but something about this didn't look quite right. The man was on a bicycle, riding slowly away from the fight. Could he be attempting to flank or attack elements in the rear? Possibly, though something about the man's body language and the way he rode the bike suggested otherwise. Reece couldn't quite figure out what it was, but his gut instinct and his morality caused him to remove his finger from the trigger and watch the man until he rode out of sight. Reece had reached down, switched frequencies on his MBITR, and transmitted a description of the man and his direction of travel to support elements in the rear. As he was about to sprint across the street to continue the push to retake the city, a mortar exploded on the opposite corner, forcing him back against the building and showering him with debris and dust. Had Reece not paused and watched the man in black ride away from the fight, or had Reece killed him and moved on, he would have been standing exactly where the mortar had landed. The man on the bicycle, moving away from the battle, had probably saved Reece's life.

Combat was also about discretion, and he never regretted not taking that shot. Sometimes the most important shots in battle are the ones not taken.

Reece understood that killing was necessary; it was his duty; it was his calling; and he wasn't about to stand back and let someone else go into the fray when his country was at war and he was of able mind and body. This is what Reece did. He would have liked nothing more than for future generations to never experience war. He also knew that if history was any indication, war was something to always prepare for.

Reece stripped off his blood- and sweat-soaked cammies, dropping them onto the floor of the condo's garage. He broke down his M4 for cleaning, the insides caked with carbon blowback from using the suppressor. As per his post-op ritual, he replaced the batteries in his NODs, ATPIAL laser, and flashlight. His helmet along with his rifle went to the bedroom with him. *Be prepared, Reece.* He leaned the carbine against the nightstand and picked up his phone for a Signal and SpiderOak check. With no activity on either account, he shut it down before showering off the blood, dirt, and grime of the past few hours, until finally pulling the sheets over his head to grab a few hours of much-needed rest.

BANG BANG BANG! Reece rolled out of bed and grabbed his M4, training the suppressed muzzle on the bedroom door. He heard a muffled voice that sounded like it was coming from the top of the steps outside. "It's me, bro! Let me in!" *BANG BANG BANG.* Reece lowered the muzzle and shook his head. *Fucking Ben.* Holding the M4 loosely at his side by the pistol grip, he walked out of the bedroom wearing a T-shirt and boxers to let his friend in through the front door.

"*Viva Mexico!* I brought you some tacos. Wasn't sure if you had time to stop and eat while you were down there." Ben was as chipper as ever. He looked Reece up and down and winced. "Do you just hang out all day in your drawers now, bro?"

"Just trying to get some sleep," Reece answered wearily.

"Still haven't shaved? You're not going hipster on me, are you? Though, it does nicely complement those undies. Do you think you're going back to Afghanistan or something?"

"Or something," Reece muttered, still waking up.

"Dude, you have the three-letter agencies going crazy," Ben continued, throwing a fat dip of Copenhagen into his mouth. "Your little excursion to Margaritaville has the DEA and my people all excited. They have no idea what the story is. The DEA thinks the Sinaloa Cartel is making a big move on New Generation, and the CIA is convinced that the Zetas made the hit and are trying to push their way into Baja. They definitely don't know it was some gringo from San Diego who hangs around in his underwear all day."

"It was good, Ben. I got the guys that . . . I got the men that killed Lauren and Lucy." Reece struggled. "And, I found out some other stuff that's gonna blow your mind." Reece took a bite of his taco and waited until he'd swallowed to finish his thought. "This whole thing was some kind of shady clinical trial. Capstone Capital is promising those involved billions and they've sold their souls for cash."

"Are you sure?" Ben asked.

"Absolutely. This shit goes really high up the food chain. Even Pilsner was involved. He's the one who put the drug into my troop and ultimately the one who sold us out overseas. They have new trials under way right now with a new group of SEALs. I just can't figure out the mechanics of how they got us ambushed in Afghanistan."

"I can," Ben replied with uncharacteristic seriousness. "We watch a lot of the big Islamic groups in the States for obvious reasons, big mosques, charity groups, that sort of thing. We're not supposed to work on U.S. soil, but we do it interagency style so it's all 'legal.' Of course, lots of innocent people come and go in those communities, but every once in a while there's something that doesn't fit. A few months ago, I saw some traffic on a Navy O-6 making regular

371

visits to an Islamic charity group in San Diego. It's one thing to have some enlisted guy decide he's going to follow Allah, but a high-level officer to start meeting with questionable Muslim groups is out of the ordinary. You want to know who the O-6 was?"

"You know I do."

"Captain Leonard Howard, the admiral's JAG."

"Fuck me."

"No, fuck him, bro. His visits with the imam stopped just before you guys got ambushed overseas. They haven't met together since."

Reece had another name to add to his list.

"This thing looks like a target package," Reece stated, taking the thick file from Ben and beginning to leaf through it.

"That's because it is, bro. Everything you need is in there. The imam that Howard met with is Hammadi Izmail Masood. He lives in the mosque. It is more of a mini-compound really, though surprisingly open. You would think they would be a bit more security conscious. They call it the Islamic Center for Peace and Prosperity of Southern California. The mosque should clear out Wednesday after Ishu. Do you know what that is?"

"Yeah, evening prayer. When does it go down this time of year?"

"Nine thirty. It will be fairly packed but will

empty out quickly. I've already set you up with an alias and a backstory. You even have an appointment with Masood after prayer, so you have two days to get ready."

Reece eyed Ben quizzically. "That's not really my style."

"Trust me. This will work. This is what I do now, remember?"

"What? Set up assassinations of Islamic clergy on U.S. soil?"

"Reece, we missed this one. We had this guy in our sights for over a year and we missed it. If we hadn't, maybe your troop would still be alive. Your government let you down. We knew this guy was as bad as they come. Outwardly he condemns terrorism and is the face of moderate Islam in Southern California, posting videos on YouTube disparaging Islamic extremists and calling for an end to violence. In reality, his group is a conduit for funneling money to ISIS. I'm talking millions of dollars. While he preaches peace, his money helps ISIS behead Americans on camera for the world to see."

"I thought ISIS was focused on Iraq, Syria, and the Levant? Why would Howard go through an ISIS guy to set up an attack in Afghanistan?"

"Don't be fooled, bro. Al-Qaeda and ISIS are not as far apart ideologically as it would seem. It's all about the caliphate, man. Twelfth-century shit. ISIS used to be AQ in Iraq, remember?"

"Oh, I remember," Reece said, thinking of the blood and energy he and his men had invested in hunting them down over the years, "but I thought they had a very public split not long ago."

"Well, they did. ISIS is the new kid on the block. Very popular, and far surpassing AQ in fundraising. That, along with their vicious attacks on Shia and even moderate Sunnis, have run counter to more recent AQ proclamations of Islamic unity. They appeal to the next generation of jihadi and are much more adept at recruiting, specifically using social media, than AQ ever was. AQ's message was to join up because Islamic lands are under attack by the West. ISIS flipped it around. Their messaging is all about being on the offensive. Very powerful stuff and something we haven't even begun to counter."

"That doesn't answer the question as to why Howard and Pilsner used them instead of AQ or Taliban."

"That question is exactly why they went the ISIS route: to throw people off the track. Logically it would make sense to use an AQ- or Taliban-affiliated network, but if you want to throw up a roadblock, use ISIS."

"Unbelievable," Reece said, shaking his head.

"Recently, ISIS and AQ leadership have recognized the power of collaboration. They can be a much more effective force if their energies are focused on destroying us instead of each other. Pilsner and Howard have access to the same intelligence channels that I do and they would have known the same thing. ISIS and AQ can channel resources and kill us today, then work out their differences tomorrow."

"So, the government wants Masood dead, and you figured I am a good guy to get it done?"

"Not exactly, brother, though he does need to die. This guy has funded more terrorism than the Blind Sheikh ever could have hoped to back in the day, yet he promotes himself as a moderate Muslim, denouncing all violence and terrorism. He was the connection to the Pakistani Taliban who planned and executed the ambush of your troop in Afghanistan. I know you are going to take him down. Least I can do is help. My superiors don't know anything about this. It's totally off the books."

"So how does the alias and backstory work?" Reece asked, back on task.

"You are a graduate student at USD in international business and have an elective world comparative religion class. You want to interview Masood for a paper you are writing on world religions and politics. Part of the mandate for their Islamic center is outreach, so this is not an odd request. They are very open and inviting. I have Masood's cell and center business phone numbers under surveillance. If he calls to check out your creds at USD, I divert the call and

confirm your enrollment in graduate school."
Ben smiled, obviously quite proud of himself.

"And, do me a favor," Ben continued, handing
Reece a small package, "leave this with the
fucker when you kill him. Wish I could go with
you on this one, buddy. Hypocrites drive me
crazy."

Reece had checked and double-checked his gear
for the next phase of his mission of vengeance.
All there was to do now was wait, but there was
somewhere that he needed to go first.

He steered his Cruiser through a quiet
neighborhood and parked at a small church,
continuing on foot. The streets were deserted
at this late hour; anyone attempting to follow
him in a vehicle would be easy to spot. Still, he
took an indirect route, winding his way through
a maze of residential streets, the silence broken
only by the occasional barking dog. His path
took him down an alley where he stopped and
pretended to tie his shoe. Satisfied that no one
was behind him, he cut between two homes and
paused at the base of a large eucalyptus tree.
Grabbing on to the lowest branch, he scrambled
up the trunk and straddled a massive fork. Taking
off his pack, Reece removed his bump helmet
with its attached NODs, securing them to his
head. The dark suburban scene was suddenly
bright green through his goggles, thanks to the

amplified illumination of the half-moon and stars. He scooted out on the branch until his feet dangled over a wooden privacy fence. Taking advantage of his night vision and his elevated perch, Reece carefully scanned the area for any sign of movement. Seeing nothing out of place, he swung his leg over the limb and dropped into the soft grass of his backyard. Drawing the Glock from his waistband, Reece moved to a knee and took in the scene silently for a full two minutes.

The house was dark and appeared from the outside to be undisturbed since he'd last left it. He walked across the yard and peered over the side gate toward the front of the house, where he saw Lauren's Cherokee in the driveway and the police tape still strung around the massive eucalyptus that had been the centerpiece of his lawn. The base of the tree had been converted into a makeshift shrine by the neighbors, with cards, handwritten notes, candles, and stuffed animals covering a significant portion of the front yard.

Reece holstered his Glock and activated the IR illumination on the side of his helmet before retrieving a Strider SMF folding knife from his pants pocket. Seeing no sign of a booby trap, Reece slipped the knife's blade between the upper and lower panes to the window of his small guest room, disengaging the lock. *Here goes nothing.* Reece slid the lower pane upward;

the window opened easily: nothing exploded. Reece exhaled in relief. He took off his pack and lowered it through the window. Twenty years of training and more than a decade of urban combat had taught Reece that there is no graceful way for a grown man to climb through a window. He boosted himself up and rolled forward through the opening. The Glock came out and Reece slowly and painstakingly cleared his home, room by room and closet by closet.

Moving into Lucy's room, Reece removed his helmet and sat on the tiny bed, surrounded by relics of her short time on earth. As his eyes adjusted to the darkness, he took in the sights and smells of his little girl's sanctuary. Her room was perfectly intact, as if some invisible force had protected it from the hundreds of indiscriminately fired rounds that shredded the rest of their home. As he sat there among his daughter's belongings, it was as if nothing bad had ever happened.

A tiny ceramic impression of her newborn footprint sat on a shelf next to a framed photograph of their young family taken at her christening. He stood smiling in his only suit, holding Lucy in her heirloom gown. A beaming Lauren stood by his side in a black dress that complemented her fit frame, her arm around Reece's back. *Damn, she looked beautiful.*

The photo brought him back to those two weeks of leave following a past deployment when he was able to spend nearly every day with the two loves of his life. Looking back on it now, it was the happiest time of his life. Reece knew that he would never feel such happiness, pride, or contentment again.

On Lucy's bed was a camouflage Team Seven blanket with her name, date of birth, and weight embroidered on it in pink—a gift from his troop. He ran his hand across the smooth fabric, feeling the threads where her name was written just like he was touching the blond curls on her head. He sat there for hours, taking in the sights and smells of his past in silent meditation. He didn't let outside thoughts invade his tranquility; this was time with his family.

Reece made a few stops at various stores in San Diego the next day: a tuxedo shop, two electronics stores, a fabric retailer, and a hardware store. He paid cash for everything, just to slow down any investigations that could be under way. He purchased a white tuxedo vest, a yard of white nylon fabric, heavyweight thread, a box of three-inch framing nails, insulated copper wire, a small wired lightbulb, a silicone-controlled rectifier, a safe arm switch, a nine-volt battery, and three prepaid cell phones.

Reece laid out the items from his shopping trip on the kitchen table of the safe house alongside Lauren's sewing machine, which he'd dug out of Lucy's closet after his vigil in her room. The Bernina machine had been a gift from his mother. Lauren, God love her, was not one for sewing and he was sure that she'd never so much as plugged it in. He laid the white tuxedo vest on the table facedown next to two M112 1.25 pound blocks of C-4 plastic explosive. Using a fixed blade, Reece cut the wrapping from the two explosive blocks to expose the claylike contents. The two blocks were combined into a single mass, which Reece rolled flat using a rolling pin. C-4 is an extremely stable explosive that would need a lot more than a rolling pin to set it off. Even so, modifying military explosives was technically a violation of more than a few regulations, and having seen the mangled bodies of insurgents whose homemade concoctions went off ahead of schedule, Reece took his time. Pushing those thoughts aside, he continued to shape the mass until he was satisfied with its size and thickness.

The nails came in strips of twenty-five, designed to feed into a carpenter's nail gun. Reece placed the nail strips on top of the explosive and pressed them into the surface until the entire face was covered with steel. He then moved the explosive sheet onto the vest and covered it with the white nylon fabric. Using scissors, he cut the material until it covered the deadly mix and pinned it in place. This was going to be the hard part; Reece hadn't used a sewing machine since ninth-grade home economics class and he wasn't exactly a master at it then.

Nearly every military unit had men who were gifted at sewing. Before the war created an entire industry of custom tactical nylon-focused gear companies, SEAL parachute riggers trained in sewing to repair parachutes would make side money customizing nylon gear for their teammates. Unfortunately, Reece had never spent much time in the riggers' loft learning that particular skill. The good news was that it didn't have to be pretty; it just had to hold everything together. After watching several YouTube videos on the basics of sewing, he fed the vest fabric into the machine.

Reece was confident that his future career would not be as a tailor but he got the job done. Leaving a small opening on the bottom right-hand corner of the nylon, he tied off the heavy thread to secure the stitches. He held the vest upright to test his work and, to his relief, everything stayed in place. Next Reece removed two of the three prepaid phones from their boxes and plugged both into their wall chargers. He used each phone to call the other to ensure that they functioned, that the numbers were correct, and that any cell phone carrier welcome texts or remote updates had all come through. He had seen even experienced terrorist bomb makers forget to do this and end up splattered across a wall when an unexpected text completed the circuit. Using a white paint marker, Reece drew a large X on one phone and wrote that phone's number on the back of the other. He also entered the phone number as a contact on the second prepaid model.

This is where things could get tricky. Reece wished he had an EOD tech to help him, but luckily, information that would have been tightly controlled when he first entered the Teams was now freely available to the world on the Internet. He pried the back from the phone marked with an X and poked around until he could determine which wire did what. He identified those leading to the vibration mechanism and clipped them free of their attachment, twisting the wires from the lightbulb onto the vibrator wires and dialing the number that he'd placed into the other phone's contact list. The phone on the table began to ring, illuminating the bulb. Satisfied that sufficient electrical current was flowing from the detached wires, Reece added the safe arm switch, which controlled the flow of electricity from the phone to the more deadly end of the device, and tested it in the on and off positions to ensure it would break the circuit to the cap. He then wired in the silicone-controlled rectifier designed to hold back the energy until hit with a trickle of electricity that would allow the full charge into the cap.

It was always hard for Reece to believe how these basic devices could cause such widespread terror and destruction, how a few hours of shopping could result in a mechanism for war. He disconnected the light and removed the battery from the phone, just to be safe. He then carefully removed a blasting cap from its plastic case and twisted its two wires onto those from the phone and nine-volt, wrapping the connected wires in electrical tape and slipping the device into the vest pocket. He pushed the blasting cap through the hole he'd left in the nylon fabric and buried it into the C-4 inside. He double-checked everything to ensure that he hadn't made any errors, then hid the vest under the bed in the second bedroom. He would use the phone plugged into the wall to charge both batteries and would place a battery into the vest phone just before it was ready for use. It would only get called once.

CHAPTER 49

San Diego, California

Wednesday came quickly, though Reece did have a chance to rest, regroup, and reflect on his personal jihad. He did not question the righteousness of his cause. His only prayer was that he get to the end of his list before the authorities or the tumor took his life. *Prioritize and execute.*

Reece hoped he looked the part. What did a master's business student taking an elective in comparative religion look like, anyway? Reece had spent a year at the Naval Postgraduate School studying defense analysis with an emphasis on combating terrorism and asymmetrical warfare. He remembered his professors wearing a lot of tweed coats, so he picked one up, along with some nonprescription horned-rimmed glasses. A leather cross-body satchel completed the look.

Reece tried to put on his least menacing expression before exiting his Land Cruiser and heading toward the mosque, passing an auto body shop and an abandoned warehouse as he walked. It wasn't the best part of town but it wasn't the worst, just a neglected neighborhood that you would move out of as soon as you had the chance. Reece felt naked leaving his pistol in the car but he didn't know if he would be frisked before meeting Masood or if he would have to walk through a metal detector. If it had been a legitimately sanctioned mission he would have forwarded those questions to his intelligence department in the form of an RFI, or request for information, but not having his accustomed support network, he was on his own to improvise.

The satchel held the instrument of Masood's impending death. Reece just hoped he could get in front of the imam alone. The target package had stressed that in order to maintain credibility and cover for action, the mosque was a legitimate force for good, performing religious services in accordance with moderate Islamic doctrine: officiating marriages, offering family counseling services, and helping San Diego's downtrodden. That their masjid's moderate outward stance was really a front for ISIS would have surprised more than a few of the faithful. Reece wondered what those Muslims who willingly gave money to Masood in accordance with the Third Pillar of Islam would do if they knew it was going to further the radical militant branch of their religion in the guise of charity.

Approaching the mosque along an avenue with more than a few burnt-out streetlights, Reece found himself walking down a different street in a different war: the streets of Baghdad's

Al-Jihad neighborhood, in the Al-Rashid District, 2006. After the Al-Askari Mosque bombing in February, the country had descended into anarchy. Sunni-on-Shia violence escalated to the point of civil war, with bodies stacking up in the streets by the thousands, making an already tumultuous situation even more chaotic.

Reece had been assigned to a CIA covert action program at the height of the insurgency: a small group of American advisors running a top tier Iraqi special operations force. Even though Iraq was technically a sovereign country and the unit was Iraqi, and totally off the books as far as the United States was officially concerned, they still had to get permission from both senior U.S. military leaders and CIA officials to enter mosques because of the political constraints of having U.S. personnel assigned in an "advisory" role.

In the midst of that carnage, Reece's team had tracked a high-value individual to a mosque in the early morning hours, and had him fixed with human assets on the ground and technical surveillance in the air. Mosques were routinely used by the enemy as places of sanctuary, where they could plan and hide with impunity. Even though the Law of Armed Conflict clearly stated that a religious site would lose its immunity if it were used for a military purpose, U.S. senior military and political leaders were so scared of the fallout from hitting a religious site that they in effect allowed the enemy to plan attacks against U.S. forces from them without fear of reprisal. The insurgents knew it and took full advantage.

Reece had used the gray area in which his unit operated to skirt that technicality and had thrown the enemy off base with a highly successful campaign focused on targeting the insurgents where they felt safe and secure. The CIA side of the house, along with their attorneys, were in full support, but when the senior Army general in Iraq found out about the program he had his chief of staff read Reece the riot act. He demanded Reece call him for approval if they needed to hit someone using a mosque as refuge, which is how Reece and his team ended up waiting for more than an hour as the general took his time deciding if he should grant permission for Reece's predominately Iraqi unit to enter the entirely Iraqi mosque. That delay provided enough time for enemy elements in the Al-Jihad neighborhood to surreptitiously surround Reece's small force.

Unfortunately for the enemy, Reece had quietly moved snipers into overwatch, had multiple aircraft circling and a QRF of Bradley Fighting Vehicles staged four blocks away. What could have been a surgical spec ops direct-action capture/kill mission turned into a forty-minute gun battle. Miraculously, Reece's force emerged relatively unscathed. Perhaps that is where Reece's distrust of senior officers began.

Tonight's crusade was personal and had nothing to do with sensitivity toward Islam or the Law of Armed Conflict. Tonight was different. Reece was under no constraints. He was unhindered by rules, regulations, laws, or societal norms. He was on the warpath, and his appetite for revenge was insatiable. Hammadi Izmail Masood had facilitated the worst loss of life in U.S. special operations history, and tonight he was going to pay.

CHAPTER 50

Reece passed a vacant lot filled with weeds and approached the small domed building from the sidewalk, joining two other worshippers headed inside for evening prayer. He attempted to slouch his shoulders a bit in an effort to look less threatening as he passed a wrought-iron gate and walked up the entrance steps.

A young Middle Eastern–looking man occupied an office just inside the building to the right with a sign in English reading: "Welcome. Front Office."

"Ah, excuse me?" Reece said.

"Yes," he responded cordially, rising from his desk and approaching Reece.

"*As-salāmu 'alaykum*," he said, using the traditional Arabic "peace be upon you" greeting, which Reece had heard many times the world over.

"*Wa 'alaykumu s-salām*," Reece responded, shaking hands and then touching his right hand to his heart. "I'm Draper Kauffman from USD. I have an appointment with Imam Masood after evening prayer. I was invited to observe tonight as well but don't know exactly what to do," he continued with a warm smile.

"Ah yes, you are the master's student from

USD. It is our pleasure to host you tonight. The prayer room for men is downstairs. We have another for women upstairs. Please remove your shoes. You may observe from the back of the room and then afterward Imam Masood will talk with you about the virtues of Islam and the noble work of the center as well as answer any other questions you may have."

"I hate to impose. Thank you so much for having me. This comparative religion class is part of my international business program, but I am really excited about it."

"We do this all the time, so it is no imposition. In fact, community outreach is one of the guiding principles of the center."

Reece descended the narrow staircase. Donations certainly had not been used to update the facility. Reece guessed that the humble surroundings were what drew many of the patrons to this particular Islamic center.

There were only about a dozen people preparing for evening prayer when Reece entered the room. They were performing the ritual ablution at a large round sink, washing in accordance with traditional Islamic practice. Reece skipped the washing and took his place in the observation area behind the congregates. All were men in conservative dress. A few more than half looked to be of Middle Eastern ancestry, with the remainder a mix of African Americans and Caucasians.

The room was exceptionally clean and sparse, which allowed those gathered to clear their minds and arrange their prayer mats facing East toward Mecca. Reece recognized Masood immediately from the target package photos and YouTube videos he had studied in preparation for this evening's mission. Masood took his place as imam at the front of the assembly and began the *salat* in Arabic. Reece's Arabic language skills were terrible, but he knew enough to recognize a few words and phrases. Masood began with "*allahu akbar*," reciting the traditional opening and then transitioning the service through the different phases of prayer: standing, bowing, prostrating, and sitting. Reece knew this ceremony was the formal way of subjecting oneself to, and remembering, Allah. There was a certain beauty to the service, a focus and devotion that Reece couldn't help but admire.

There was no doubt that there was a crisis in Islam, and it was playing out on the world stage in a spectacle of violence. Reece had experience with Muslims running the gamut from those who were Muslim in name only, to those who adhered to the pillars and tenets of Islam as best they could—similar to Christians who went to church on Christmas and Easter—right down the line to those Muslims who had been indoctrinated by an archaic ideology of hate that pursued a political agenda and would stop at nothing short of seeing all nonbelievers put to the sword. Those were the ones who could only be stopped with a bullet to the head, and at accomplishing that, Reece was exceptionally good.

Masood finished with the *taslim*, "*Assalamu alaikum wa rahmatullah*," before quietly making his way to the back to greet Reece.

"Mr. Kauffman," he said, in a heavily British-influenced Pakistani accent, "welcome to the center. Thank you for coming."

"Thank you for having me. The *salat* was beautiful. I have always respected the value and ritual of daily prayer. It would be a better world if more people took the time to give thanks and remembrance as you do."

"Thank you. That is why we are here. To give believers a safe place in which to practice the facets of Islam and raise awareness about the pillars of our faith. Please join me in my office, where we can have tea and continue our discussion."

Reece followed Masood back up the stairs and down a short hallway to his small office, stopping at the front of the mosque to say good night to the man who had greeted Reece upon his arrival and was just getting ready to depart. Masood moved with a fluid grace that belied his fifty-five years of age. His hair was black and cut short, which contrasted with the gray of his close-cropped beard. He wore earth-tone slacks and a long-sleeved button-up shirt without a collar instead of the more traditional *thawb*, probably in the spirit of Southern California inclusiveness.

"Please take a seat," Masood said, gesturing to one of two modest chairs in front of his desk as he set an old teapot on a single-burner electric hot plate on a small table positioned against the wall: an improvised tea-making station. Reece wondered how it hadn't burned the place to the ground yet. The room seemed to Reece what he presumed the office of a professor at an underfunded community college would look like. There were stacks of papers on the desk and a small bookshelf behind it, adorned with what appeared to be numerous religious texts. The walls were bare save for one framed work of Islamic calligraphy.

Masood noticed Reece looking at the painting.

"Beautiful, isn't it? It's a rendition of a Mir-Ali Heravi Tabrizi. Brilliant calligrapher from the fifteenth century. It is a reminder that the Islamic Golden Age was really not that long ago."

"I thought the Golden Age ended earlier than that," offered Reece.

"Some scholars would suggest that, but the evidence proves it lasted up through the sixteenth century. This is to remind me of how far we have fallen and how much work there is to be done. Call it . . . *inspiration*." He smiled. "The Holy Qu'ran states that 'God does not change the condition of a people until they change what is in their hearts.' My calling is to help change what is in their hearts. Now, how can I assist you this evening?"

"Well, first of all, thank you for taking the time. I'm in a fairly ambitious international business program at USD, and one of my electives is comparative religion. It's a team project and my part is to interview a well-respected Muslim leader about the current state of Islam in the world today."

"Well, that certainly is a topic I spend a lot of my time researching and speaking about at the center and as a guest speaker around the country. As you probably know, Islam is the second-largest religion in the world as well as the fastest growing."

"Why do you think that is?" Reece inquired.

"Islam is a way of life. It is about subjugating oneself to Allah and following the Pillars of Islam. It offers a code to live by that is appealing to a mounting number of adherents. It will be our Golden Age once again, but this time through inclusiveness."

"What do you say to those who point to the draconian measures some Islamic countries take to control their populations and force adherence to sharia law, like throwing homosexuals from buildings to their deaths, flogging young girls who want to go to school, and beheading nonbelievers?"

"The role of the center is not to compel non-believers to join Islam. The Prophet Muhammad, peace be upon him, says that 'there is no compulsion in religion' and we certainly do not believe in subordinating U.S. law to sharia law. Those who practice the abhorrent punishments you mention do nothing but hurt the cause and turn world sentiment against those of us who espouse the true tenets of Islam. We are a religion of peace that some have hijacked for their own self-serving, destructive means. In fact, I use Friday prayer to call for peace and unity. I have been condemned by some, but if we are going to live together in harmony we must learn to accept each other's differences. The United States is the perfect place to show the world how both Muslims and non-Muslims can work and live together in peace."

This guy was polished. He had the air and presence of an academic, with the charisma of an elder statesman.

"Why do you think the intolerant brand of Islam is currently flourishing in the Muslim world?" asked Reece, trying his best to sound like a grad student.

"It saddens me deeply to have to agree with you, Mr. Kauffman. Corrupt politics and sluggish economic conditions plague much of the Muslim world. Radical Islam does not represent the vast, vast majority of Muslims worldwide, and almost all of those killed in Islamic terrorist attacks are in fact Muslim," he said, shaking his head. "The answers, though, also lie within the religion. Islam was once a force for good throughout the world and can be again. Education is the key, Mr. Kauffman. Education is the key."

"Sir, do you mind if I use my computer to take notes?" asked Reece.

"Not at all. Be my guest."

"How are statements about peace, unity, and responsibility like those you just made interpreted in the Islamic community at large? Do you worry about your safety?" Reece continued as he reached into his satchel, removing an old laptop computer.

Instead of recycling old computers or selling them, Reece and Lauren had just stacked them in a closet in the name of data security. This particular one was state-of-the-art back in 1998. He had taken it from his home during the previous night's visit. It was quite a bit larger than today's ubiquitous MacBook Air, and with the keyboard, internal components, and touchpad removed it fit Reece's Winkler/Sayoc Tomahawk perfectly.

"Statements of inclusiveness and tolerance are not always received favorably by those with differing agendas, nor is criticism of Islam, as you are no doubt aware. It pains me to say that other imams have even issued fatwas against me, but those who have done so do not have the legal authority necessary for them to be legitimate, nor do they truly understand the history and intent of a true fatwa. So I feel as safe as one can in these times of trouble."

Reece studied the older man's face. Everything he was saying squared with Reece's studies and firsthand experience in the Muslim world. How could he talk with Reece with such authority and logic about the state of Islam and then facilitate the same terror he was condemning with such conviction? *How can this guy be such a good liar? He should run for political office.*

"Hammadi," Reece said, intentionally switching to the imam's first name and wrapping his hand around his tomahawk's maple-wood shaft, hidden by the open laptop screen, "do you know Captain Leonard Howard?"

Masood paused, successfully hiding his surprise. "No, that name is not familiar."

"Oh, you may have forgotten. He's the Navy attorney that contacted you to arrange the ambush of my SEAL troop in Afghanistan by your friends in the Pakistani Taliban. How much did it cost to have my men killed?"

This time Masood did not try to feign ignorance or redirect. Instead he paused and took a deep breath, his eyes narrowing.

"Ah, James Reece. I did not recognize you. You look different from your picture in the paper from your wife's and daughter's funeral. The beard suits you well, and the glasses are a nice touch. Too bad your family were *kafir* and are now in the fires of hell." He spat out *kafir* like it was the most vile word in existence.

Reece slowly closed the lid to the laptop and placed his 'hawk on top.

Masood's eyes looked questioningly, almost unbelievably, at the ancient weapon in Reece's hand and then back to meet Reece's icy stare.

"You should be happy, Masood. Dying like this makes you a *martyr*. Now, that may or may not be true, and it really doesn't matter to me in the least. What matters to me is that you die, just like the true believers you send out to sacrifice themselves for the cause. Tonight it's your turn."

As Reece stood to deliver his justice, Masood lunged for his desk drawer with surprising speed, bringing out a small CZ 75 Compact 9mm pistol. If he had kept it with a round in the chamber he might have had a chance, but the time it took to reach the slide and chamber a round was more than enough time for Reece's swing to connect with his quarry's hand in its attempt to bring the weapon to bear. With the heaviest part of the tomahawk resting in its head, it hit the inside of Masood's right wrist with its full force, destroying bones, muscles, and tendons, while severing arteries and veins and sending the CZ pistol clattering to the floor.

Masood screamed out in pain, grabbing at his right hand, which only remained attached by a thin shred of muscle and skin, smothered in the slippery ooze of its altered state.

Reece moved with the precision of a man who was no stranger to violence, unfazed by the coppery scent of fresh blood in the air or the primal screams of the man he had come to kill.

It was then that the headache dropped Reece to the ground.

The blinding pain was like a thousand shards of crushed glass grinding together inside his brain. This one lasted longer than his previous episodes but not long enough for Masood to reach his CZ.

It had taken the imam a few seconds to realize that this was his opportunity to escape or go for his pistol. He chose the latter and was two steps into his dash for the gun when Reece's tomahawk buried itself in the back of his upper thigh, sending him crashing to the floor.

Coming out of his incapacitation, Reece grabbed a handful of Masood's loose clothing to twist himself upward and swing the 'hawk down in a powerful arch, terminating in his prey's upper back, just shy of his spine. Using the embedded hawk as a fulcrum, Reece pulled himself into a kneeling position over the broken body beneath him.

Reece had to give his adversary credit. Even

with one severed hand, a thigh cut to the bone squirting blood profusely, and a tomahawk embedded in his back, he made one last effort to reach for his weapon with his good hand. Rotating the tomahawk to the side, Reece disengaged it from Masood's back and used it to keep him from his pistol by slamming it down like an angry hammer, cutting off four of Masood's five fingers, which stretched out to claw for the gun. Another bloodcurdling scream escaped Masood's lips and was cut short by one last swing of the 'hawk, the tip of its blade shaped into an evil spike by the master bladesmith who had crafted it for this exact purpose, carving its way through Masood's temple and into his brain, causing a massive intracerebral hemorrhage, and making him a martyr for the faith.

Reece extracted the tomahawk from Masood's crushed skull and looked to the door. No footsteps in the hall betrayed a visitor. No alarms. Nothing to signify anything amiss.

Still, Reece had to work fast.

Cutting off a head was more work than one would think, even with a razor-sharp tomahawk, and Reece had to press Masood's head into the floor with his left hand while chopping through the neck, gristle, and spine to finally free it from the body with his right. Reece did not relish decapitating a human body, nor did he hesitate or shy from the task. Sixty-eight U.S. servicemen were dead because of the conspiracy that this piece of meat helped facilitate. It was time to send a message to the others that he was coming for them, too.

Putting the decapitated head into his satchel, Reece moved down the dark hall toward the exit, tomahawk at his side but ready nonetheless. He paused at the front door, looking outside through the glass. Nothing moved. Just gloomy streets in a part of town no one cared much about. Turning off the exterior light, Reece descended the steps toward the sidewalk, pausing only momentarily at the wrought-iron gate to impale the head of Imam Hammadi Izmail Masood on a sharp vertical spire, tossing the black flag of ISIS that had been in the package Ben had given him at the safe house over it for good measure.

The night's work was just getting started.

CHAPTER 51

Reece needed to regroup. He was not yet done, and he had some preparations to make before launching his next mission.

These damn headaches might just get me killed before I can finish the list, Reece thought as he made his way back to the safe house to refit.

Reece took out his notes and the poster board floor plan of Holder's apartment and reviewed them thoroughly. A lot had transpired since his last visit, and he didn't want to rely on his memory. He studied the video he'd shot in the model apartment as well, to ensure he knew the layout back to front. He had continued to practice picking the lock identical to Holder's every chance he got and had become quite adept at working it not only quickly but also quietly. Stealth would be the key on this one. If he blew it, there would be no hiding what had transpired.

He went to his stack of gear in Ben's garage, retrieved his issued Heckler & Koch Mk 24 Mod 0 handgun, and threaded on the long black suppressor. This .45-caliber pistol was the smaller replacement for the old Mk23, a behemoth of a handgun that was a perfect example of bureaucratic blundering. To create something so heavy and cumbersome that when it came time to go to war it was left to gather dust in the armory was typical of the military's procurement and acquisition process. He then pulled a length of 550-cord from a kit bag and cut it with the folding knife clipped inside the pocket of his pants. He wet one end of the cord with his mouth and fished it through the lanyard loop molded into the handgun's grip. He ran the other end of the cord around the back of his neck until the suppressed handgun dangled at his belt line. Reece then tied the other end of the cord off and wrapped the large loop repeatedly around the grip before applying a small piece of rigger's tape to hold it in place. He arranged the remainder of the gear he would need and double-checked that everything was in order before loading up the Cruiser with what looked to be enough equipment to sustain him through a deployment. Putting on a pair of dark gray running pants, a black fleece pullover, and a pair of lightweight running shoes, he picked up his backpack and headed out the back door.

It was a weeknight and the traffic was almost nonexistent at this hour. He steered off I-5 and pulled into the parking lot of the medical office. He turned off the motor and headlights, sitting quietly in the vehicle with the windows down for nearly an hour, taking in the sights and sounds, or lack thereof. He pulled on a set of nitrile gloves and then reached into the pack on the passenger's seat and removed the handgun, unraveling the long loop of cord before slipping it over his head. He unzipped his fleece jacket and dropped the .45 down inside.

At 3:00 a.m., he climbed out of the vehicle, put on his unzipped pack, and pulled the waistband of his dark workout pants up and over the dangling handgun's suppressor. There's no great way to conceal a suppressed handgun, particularly when you're not wearing a belt. The 550-cord loop kept the gun inside his waistband, where it wouldn't flop around, but also allowed him enough slack to fire the gun at a close range target if the need arose. It wasn't ideal, but it would work.

He climbed cautiously over the short chain link fence, being careful not to let the handgun catch on anything. After crossing the well-lit parking lot, he stopped next to Holder's building and slipped the smaller PVS-18 night-vision mono scope attached to what operators referred to as a "skull-crusher" to his head. The skull-crusher was essentially a steel headband sturdy enough to carry the weight of night optics. It was lightweight and less bulky than a helmet, though its downside was how it got its nickname—it hurt your skull like hell. Carefully, he approached Holder's door and listened. *I hope this asshole isn't an insomniac.* He slipped his picks into the lock and slowly rotated his hands to unlock the door. Thanks to his lube job last time around, the door swung open without making a sound.

He stepped into the dark living room of the apartment and quietly shut the door behind him. The pitch-dark room became visible in various shades of green and black as he scanned with the small night scope. The ambient light in the apartment, from the digital clock on the microwave to the standby light on the television, glowed brightly. Reece drew the suppressed HK and held it at the position of retention against his chest. He stood perfectly still for what he thought was about a minute, listening for any sign that he'd awakened his target, thankfully hearing nothing but the hum of the appliances. He moved slowly down the hallway, conscious of every movement so as not to make a single unnecessary sound. He reached the door to Holder's bedroom and once again stopped and listened for any sign of movement. Satisfied, he reached out and touched the doorknob with his gloved hand. Turning the knob as slowly as his patience allowed, he cursed silently to himself as barely audible clicking sounds came from inside the doorknob assembly. He opened the door with his left hand while gripping his handgun with the right, his body bladed to the right to make it difficult for someone hiding behind the door to wrestle the gun from him.

Josh Holder was lying spread-eagle on his

back, wearing only a pair of dark briefs; the sheets were pushed down to the foot of the bed. *This guy must get night sweats.* Reece stepped into the room slowly and, on top of the dresser, found what he was looking for: Holder's DOD-issued SIG 9mm, tucked inside a Kydex belt holster. The handgun was a smaller version of the one Reece had used during his time with the Teams.

He had struggled with this part of the plan for days, debating whether to do what was smart or what was just. Shooting Holder with his own gun would look to the investigators like a probable suicide and would likely buy him a few more days of surprise before the net tightened. On the other hand, he couldn't think of anything more righteous than killing the man who had somehow gotten the drop on Boozer with his friend's beloved cartridge. The fact that the .45 ACP was suppressed was icing on the cake and decreased his chances of being seen or heard as he made his exit. He decided that he'd shoot Holder with the .45, pick up his empty brass, and then leave the man's 9mm lying cocked on his chest with a round missing from the magazine. It wouldn't fool the detectives very long, but then again, it wouldn't have to.

Reece was standing over Holder's supine form to determine the best angle for his shot, considering it was supposed to look like a suicide, when Holder emitted a surprising gasp and his torso catapulted upward to a sitting position, his eyes opened wide. The man's sudden movement startled Reece, who hesitated for a brief moment before shoving the HK's suppressor directly into Holder's open mouth—he could feel Holder's teeth shatter from the violent intrusion—and quickly squeezed the trigger.

The muffled sound was amplified by the acoustics of the small bedroom as Holder's brains splattered instantly against the white drywall, his body collapsing backward onto the bed. Reece didn't panic, but Holder's nightmare certainly startled him. *That's for you, Boozer.*

Reece grabbed Holder's SIG from the dresser, pulling it from its holster, ejecting and retaining a round, and leaving the hammer cocked to make it look as if it had been fired, then dropped it onto Holder's bare chest, picked up his .45 brass, and backed out of the room. He shut the bedroom door and flipped his NODs upward as he hurried toward the front door of the apartment. He wasn't sure if his .45-caliber round had penetrated the drywall and ended up in the neighbor's flat-screen or dishwasher or if it would have been intrusive enough to wake them up at this hour of the night. If it had, Reece figured he had about thirty seconds to spare until that neighbor called 911, came to investigate, or both.

He closed Holder's apartment door behind

him and pulled his lock picks out of his pocket, fumbling in his rush and dropping one of the picks to the ground. *Get your shit together, Reece. Relax, work the lock.* He took a deep breath, inserted the picks into the lock, and got the door secured once again. Then, taking off across the parking lot at a dead sprint, he leapt over the fence like an Olympic hurdler. Tossing his pack on the seat, he started the Cruiser and slowly drove away from the scene, waiting until he was around the backside of the medical office before he turned on his headlights and pointed his truck in the direction of Orange County.

CHAPTER 52

Capstone Capital Corporate Offices
Los Angeles, California

Steve Horn thrived on being in control, but under the current circumstances, he did not feel in control at all. He sat in his office, unable to summon anyone who could bring him all the answers. His right-hand man, the glue that kept this project together, had died of a drug overdose, of all things. The toxicology reports hadn't come back yet but the detectives were certain it was what was termed a reckless overdose, the same type they saw all too frequently. He checked with his own independent sources in law enforcement, who all confirmed that, yes, this thing walked and talked like a run-of-the-mill prescription drug death.

The circle of people "in the know" on this project was extremely small, as it had to be by necessity. First of all, there was only a finite amount of money to go around; you could only make so many nine-figure promises before running out of equity. Second, the sensitivity on this investment was off the charts. Fewer than a dozen people on the planet knew all of the pieces to this puzzle, and one of them was dead. Horn couldn't help from wondering whether one thing had anything to do with the other.

The office door opened suddenly and his assistant Kelsie burst through with a look of panic on her face. "Mr. Horn, I'm so sorry but that was Detective Weatherly on the phone. He said that Josh Holder was found dead in his apartment early this morning. They say he shot himself. He was always so sweet to me, Mr. Horn." She burst into tears and sank into one of the large leather chairs facing Horn's desk, her head in her hands.

That was no fucking suicide. Horn grabbed his iPhone and scrolled down to find Marcus Boykin's name. He touched the screen to dial his mobile number and heard it go straight to voice mail. On a hunch, he typed Boykin's name into the search bar on his desktop computer. The first link sent chills down his spine.

www.wyomingnews.com
STAR VALLEY MAN KILLED
IN HUNTING ACCIDENT
Marcus Boykin, 57, of Star Valley Ranch was found dead in his vehicle . . .

"Kelsie, get me Mike Tedesco on the phone! *NOW!*"

CHAPTER 53

Naval Special Warfare Command
Coronado, California

During the drive from his home, Tedesco had accepted his fate as atonement for his actions. His heart was filled with an immense sense of regret for getting himself mixed up in this project in the first place. *Goddamn Steve Horn.* At least his family wouldn't be harmed; in that he found some comfort. In his last act he had found his courage.

Mike Tedesco took a deep breath and opened the door of his Bentley coupe. Despite the lightweight blend of his bespoke Savile Row suit and open collar, he was sweating profusely. His knees were weak as he began the short walk to the building's entrance. The guard inside the door recognized him immediately and handed him a visitor's badge through the slot under the bulletproof glass. Tedesco walked the halls in a fog, unable to focus or wash the blank look of despair from his face. Those who recognized him regarded him with great curiosity. The man who usually walked these halls with an aristocratic air of confidence, great charm, and an impeccable appearance now looked like he was on his way to the gallows.

The admiral's aide rose from his desk as Tedesco walked past him to open the doors into Pilsner's office. "Mr. Tedesco, is the admiral expecting you?" he asked in vain as Tedesco opened the paneled door and walked inside.

Admiral Pilsner was sitting behind his desk in a starched khaki uniform, his nose still bandaged but the deep black eyes fading out to a grotesque purple and yellow. The look on his face indicated surprise. It wasn't like Mike to drop by without his assistant calling ahead first to arrange it. He was even more surprised at Tedesco's disheveled appearance. Tedesco stopped a few feet short of Pilsner's desk just as the admiral's aide stumbled through the door behind him.

"Sir, I'm sorry, I tried to intercept him—"

"It's okay, Mr. Tedesco is always welcome in my office, you know that. Have a seat, Mike. What's the problem? You look terrible."

Just then, a cell phone began to ring from inside Tedesco's coat. The ringer was set to sound like an old-fashioned dial telephone. *Riiinnng. . . . riiinnng. . . .*

"Mr. Tedesco, you can't have a cell phone in this building!" cried the aide, who strictly obeyed the security protocols of WARCOM.

Tedesco retrieved the phone, which appeared to be a cheap prepaid model, and held it across the table for Admiral Pilsner. "It's for you, Gerald," he said in a tone that haunted the room.

The admiral accepted it with disbelief and looked at the phone dumbfounded, as if he'd never seen one before. Slowly, he put it up to his ear. "Hello, who is this?"

Mike Tedesco closed his eyes. This was to be his penance.

"This is your executioner, you fucking disgrace. You wiped out my troop and my family, and you did it all for money and a promotion. I'll see you in hell, motherfucker."

James Reece hit SEND on a second cell phone, connecting a call to the one strapped to Mike Tedesco. The phone received the incoming call and sent a burst of electrons to a cluster of wires leading to a blasting cap loaded with PETN. The blasting cap detonated and forced a high-explosive response from the 2.5 pounds of C-4 sewn inside the suicide vest worn underneath Tedesco's dress shirt.

Tedesco's body tamped the force of the explosion, forcing all the energy forward toward Admiral Pilsner's desk. That energy turned the strips of framing nails embedded in the face of the C-4 into red hot shrapnel moving at well beyond the speed of sound, shredding Admiral Pilsner's face and upper torso like a dozen shotgun rounds. The blast sent chunks of his charred skull through the massive windows, which exploded instantly from the overpressure, propelling thousands of shards of glass onto the beautiful beach below. Tedesco's body was cut completely in half by the blast, and the parts of Admiral Pilsner that extended above his massive wooden desk simply ceased to exist.

Reece set down the cell phone on the late Mike Tedesco's dining room table and looked at Tedesco's widow, who sat just feet away, gently rocking their newborn infant. Janet Tedesco quickly went back to stroking her baby's head but she thought she detected a hint of sadness in the big man's eyes. When she looked back up, he was gone.

CHAPTER 54

San Diego, California

Leonard Howard had been somewhat of a failure in the civilian practice of law. He did well academically in law school but was unprepared for the chaotic workload of a civil litigator. He also found that, despite his dreams to the contrary, he was abysmal in the courtroom. Whenever the partners would send him in to cover a routine motion hearing, he would panic. His confidence would shatter, his mouth would go powder-dry, and his voice would crack.

He was quickly let go from the firm and found himself adrift. There was only one place where a lazy lawyer who was scared of the courtroom could thrive: government service. A law school friend told him about the Navy JAG program, and he was immediately sold. The uniform brought him instant pride and prestige, and the complicated bureaucracy of the military gave him an environment in which to excel. He particularly loved signing his emails "Judge," an unauthorized way to psychologically elevate himself through the electronic communications medium.

More than two decades into his uniformed service, Howard had risen to the rank of captain and was the judge advocate general of the Naval Special Warfare Command. When his friends and neighbors in the San Diego suburb of East Lake mistakenly referred to him as a SEAL because of his work on the staff of a SEAL flag officer, Howard never corrected them. Admiral Pilsner treated him like a trusted ally, and together they wielded the full power and influence of the U.S. Navy against anyone who stood in their way. It was very much "us" versus "them." Pilsner's political connections had made him a likely candidate to run the Pentagon, and Howard would rise alongside him as his most trusted confidant.

Captain Howard had an appointment that morning and would be arriving to work at WARCOM later than usual. Most men his age were long past the stage of needing braces on their teeth, but Howard's teeth had been in such horrible shape from a lifetime of neglect that his wife had finally convinced him to do something about it. She secretly hoped it would help his chronic halitosis as well as his appearance. The Navy denied his application to have braces put on, citing the purely cosmetic reason of his request. Unfortunately for him, the same bureaucracy in which he prospered could also be an insurmountable hurdle to climb. He shelled out the money to pay for the braces himself and had a regular visit with his civilian orthodontist out in the suburbs.

He turned off his cell phone during the office visit per the sign on the door, powering it back up as he walked outside to what they now called a sports activity vehicle.

His Navy-issued BlackBerry came alive with every conceivable alert when he turned it on and it reconnected to the network: voice mails, text messages, and emails had all come through while his device had been turned off. He scanned the emails first and stopped in his tracks as he opened the most recent message:

EXPLOSION AT WARCOM: 2 DEAD, EVACUATE IMMEDIATELY

He checked the voice mail from his deputy, a wave of nausea coming over him when he heard the news that Admiral Pilsner had been killed by an explosion in his office, likely a terrorist attack.

He immediately hit his local news app to see if there was more updated information available. Heart pounding, blinking to clear his vision, Howard tried to fight back what felt like an anxiety attack as he read the headline in shock.

LOCAL MODERATE ISLAMIC LEADER DECAPITATED IN BRUTAL HATE CRIME.

Instantly clicking on the link, he read:

San Diego Imam Hammadi Izmail Masood was murdered late last night in an apparent hate crime. His decapitated head was found this morning by neighbors, impaled on the spike of a wrought iron gate to the mosque where he lived and served as the director of Islamic Services for the Islamic Center for Peace and Prosperity of Southern California.

Without hesitation, he dialed his wife's mobile number. "Amy, listen to me, don't talk. Go get the kids out of school right now and take them to the airport. I'll meet you there. No, I don't have time to explain, and yes, it has to do with what you're seeing on the news. Gerald is dead. We have to go now. I'll meet you at the ticket counter. Throw some warm-weather clothes in a bag and go."

Leonard Howard climbed into his BMW X3 and sped out of the parking lot toward San Diego International Airport.

CHAPTER 55

Alpine, California

By the time the news of the explosion broke, Reece was on the road to the town of Alpine, in the mountains northeast of San Diego. Forty minutes later, he was winding his way up the dirt road toward the Canyon, a private thousand-yard rifle range owned by his friend Clint Harris. Harris had hoped to turn the site, built on an old runway high in the hills, into a full training complex for military and law enforcement use. Unfortunately he'd been sued by environmental groups and tied up in litigation ever since. He could still use the range for private guests; he just couldn't run it as a business until the lawsuits were settled.

Harris was a smart and successful businessman and was no joke with a rifle. He had spent time behind the scope in Southeast Asia, and even at sixty-eight years of age, he could still match and often surpass the skills of Reece's top snipers. He loved having Reece and his operators up to the range to train so he could test himself against the best. Harris was also an "off the grid" kind of guy and had no great love for the federal government. When Reece had approached him with this ask, he agreed without hesitation. Even though Harris didn't have a family, he risked imprisonment and financial ruin if he were ever discovered to have aided Reece's escape.

Reece knew the combinations to both gates en route to the compound and steered directly toward the open roll-up garage door where Harris stored and maintained the vehicles used on the training site. Harris backed a Polaris Ranger utility vehicle up to the tailgate of Reece's cruiser and was busy transferring gear, including a parting gift from Marco, from the cruiser to the Ranger before Reece could get the vehicle into park. Marco had his driver deliver a backpack filled with $100,000 in multiple denominations of U.S. currency soon after their Mexico excursion so that Reece would not be able to refuse it. Inside was a handwritten note reading, "Just in case you need traveling money, my friend. Keep the change.—Marco." Reece jumped out alongside Harris and helped him continue loading the heavy Pelican weapons cases and bags into the bed of the Ranger.

"Can't thank you enough for this, Clint. I mean it."

"You'd do it for me, Reece, that's all that matters. Now say goodbye to your girlfriend here; I promise it'll be a quick death."

Reece patted his beloved Land Cruiser to say goodbye after many years of faithful service. He knew that it would be gone by sunrise the next morning, probably at the bottom of the nearby Loveland Reservoir. Harris pulled the chains to lower the garage door and they both climbed into the Ranger. The noise of the Polaris's engine made it too loud to talk as they drove the short distance to the range. There wasn't much to say anyway. Harris stopped at the north corner of the long, flat range and pulled a Motorola radio from his belt.

"Tider, this is the Canyon, do you read me?"

"I've got you, Canyon, I'm five minutes out," replied a female voice with a southern accent that was discernible, even over the scratchy radio signal.

"Roger, we're ready for you here. You've got light winds from the west, less than three miles per hour. Range is clear."

"Roger, Canyon, see you in five."

"There she is." Harris pointed to a speck on the horizon directly to the north. As the speck grew closer, Reece could hear the humming sound of a turboprop. The aircraft flew directly over their position before making a sweeping turn that put it in line with the opposite end of the old thousand-yard runway. With the gears folded down and locked, and with the flaps at full extension, the pilot put the Pilatus PC-12 NG down just ahead of the impact berm, taking advantage of every foot of available runway.

The sleek single-engine aircraft was painted

silver and looked very much like a bird of prey. The plane's deceleration was rapid and, within seven hundred yards of the landing spot the plane was taxiing at normal speed. The pilot passed the men in the Polaris and turned the plane 180 degrees, pointing the nose back in the direction it had come from. The plane came to a stop and the engine's RPMs decreased audibly as it went into ground idle, the engine continuing to run with the props feathered so as not to create any thrust. A few seconds later, the engine shut off and the prop began to slow.

Almost immediately the cabin door on the left side of the aircraft folded downward and all five feet, five inches of Liz Riley stood in the cabin door. She was wearing aviator sunglasses and her hair was pulled back into a ponytail, covered by a crimson University of Alabama ball cap. She looked like she'd walked out of a CrossFit class instead of the cockpit of an aircraft, wearing a gray tank top and tight black nylon yoga pants. Her shoulders and arms were muscular without being masculine, courtesy of the gym addiction born during the rehab from her wartime injuries. Her right shoulder and part of her right arm were highlighted in a mural of intricate tattoos. She hopped swiftly down the steps of the Pilatus and embraced Reece in a bear hug.

"I'm so sorry about everything, Reece, I really am."

Reece returned the hug firmly, Liz being the closest thing to a sister he'd ever had. "Your turn to save my ass, Liz."

"Gladly! Let's get your gear loaded and get you out of here."

Liz grabbed one of the kit bags and ran up the steps into the aircraft's cabin. She set the bag down and stood in the door.

"Y'all hand that stuff up to me. I need to get the balance right."

The men began offloading the Ranger's utility bed onto the deck of the aircraft while Riley placed the various bags and cases in spots of her choosing. She wasn't the kind of girl whom you offered to help with the bags. She stood at the front of the cabin, pointing at the various items of kit as she made calculations in her head.

"Okay, boys, we're loaded. Get in, Reece."

Reece embraced Harris in a half handshake, half hug.

"See you when you get back," Harris said.

Reece nodded with a look that was unmistakable in its meaning. *I'm not coming back.* Then he climbed the steps into the cabin. Liz pointed at his seat in the cockpit and pulled the stairway door up, securing it. She climbed nimbly into the left seat, put on her headset, and talked herself through a rapid preflight checklist. Satisfied, she started the engine and ran the throttle up to full power, watching the tachometer rise. With the engine screaming, she released the wheel brakes and applied pitch to the spinning propeller blades. The aircraft surged forward, pushing Reece back into his seat as it accelerated down the dirt strip. Seven hundred yards from their starting point, Liz pulled back on the yoke and the nose pointed rapidly skyward. The Pilatus cleared the impact berm by a healthy margin and gained altitude as the landing gear retracted into the fuselage.

Liz turned the aircraft east and spoke for the first time since she'd assumed the controls. "So, where to, Reece?"

CHAPTER 56

Capstone Capital Corporate Offices
Los Angeles, California

Horn had his assistant arrange the video-conference in the same frosted glass room at Capstone where he'd hosted J. D. Hartley. This time it was Secretary Hartley calling, and it would take all of his negotiating skills to talk her down. He had to keep this deal on the rails or everything would be lost. The large LCD screen went from solid blue to an image of the secretary's conference room at the Pentagon. One of Hartley's aides confirmed that the video was live and then exited the camera's view, presumably to summon the secretary herself.

Lorraine Hartley without professional makeup and lighting was not a pretty sight and the video image did not help bolster her appearance. She looked exhausted and stressed; clearly she was not happy with the way things had spun out of control.

"Horn, I cannot believe that I let you and J.D. talk me into this thing. Pilsner is dead, Steve, blown out of his office window like confetti, and one of my best fundraisers is dead with him."

"Madame Secretary, I am deeply saddened by

the loss of the admiral and Mike. Both were great men."

"Oh, save me the condolence act, Horn. They were hardly great men. All I care about is this thing staying under the radar—and with the bodies piling up, that is *not* what is happening."

"Madame Secretary, I understand why you're upset; I really do. These are setbacks to be sure, but let's be honest, those men had served their purpose on this project. We now have less equity to share and, better yet, a platform to catapult you into the White House. This is your moment, Madame Secretary."

"What are you talking about? How is this mess going to do anything other than land me in prison?"

"No one is going to prison, Lorraine. This is exactly the kind of issue that you need to establish yourself as a strong leader. Don't let that lame-duck president be the face of this thing. Call a primetime press conference and tell the public about James Reece the terrorist. He'll have every hick-town cop in the country chasing him, and we know he won't let them take him alive. You'll look like you're already in the Oval Office and you can use it to pass that domestic surveillance bill that you've been trying so desperately to get through Congress. The public will be scared shitless, and you'll be their savior."

"You make a good point, Steve: we could really

capitalize on this. But how do we know Reece isn't coming after us?"

"I have an asset that I've been holding in reserve, Lorraine, who can lead him right to his own demise. Get your best military or law enforcement units to hunt him down and tighten the noose, and my guys can finish the job. We give credit to whoever you want to owe you one and we move forward with the next round of trials. This thing is going to work, Lorraine. You're going to be president, and we're going to make billions with a *b*."

"I'm giving you one last shot on this, Horn. This had better work or I'll make sure you never see another dollar out of this agency's budget."

"It will work, Lorraine, trust me."

CHAPTER 57

Riley had flown VFR out of North Las Vegas Airport, where she had returned in order to file a flight plan back to her home field in Texas. So long as she obeyed the visual flight rules no one would question where she flew or, more important, where she'd landed. Once they were back on the ground in Nevada, Reece stayed in the cockpit, wearing a hat and sunglasses, while Riley filed her flight plan and supervised the refueling of the aircraft.

Liz got permission from the North Vegas tower to take off and they began the long trek to East Texas. Reece trusted Liz Riley in a way he trusted few, if any, other people in his life. He hadn't told the whole story from start to finish to anyone and doing so took up most of the nearly four-hour flight.

He started at the beginning, during the peculiar pre-mission planning before the ambush, all the way through the tragic events that followed. He told her about the tumors, the unauthorized clinical trial, and the involvement of the Hartleys. He told her how he'd created the list and had been working his way down it as efficiently as possible. The truth was, Reece wasn't a cold-blooded killer, and he needed Riley's moral compass to lean on. He wanted to ensure that he was doing the right thing, the thing that would make his men and his family proud. Liz was a good listener, never interrupting, letting Reece's discourse serve as his confessional.

It was not lost on Reece, or on Liz, that he was transforming into an insurgent. His methods of killing blending his skills as an operator with the lessons he had learned over his years in special operations studying terrorists, guerrillas, subversives, and assassins. If he had spent time thinking about it, he would have realized that his physical transformation matched the psychological one taking place within. He had raided the armory of his enemy and adopted clothes to blend into the populace, his long hair and beard making him look more like a logger from Oregon than a military man.

Reece had always taken a hard line against prisoner abuse, regardless of what atrocity that prisoner had just committed. Even in the hard-core world of the SEAL Teams they were called anything but prisoners, *detainees* being the more polite term, though Reece always thought that sounded more like what cops did at traffic stops than what happened in war. As soon as they were flex-tied, their safety became the responsibility of the troop. Reece had no tolerance for any violence against the enemy once they were cuffed and under his control. It was one of the things that differentiated the United States from the enemy. Now Reece had violated that most basic tenet of warfare, executing a man on his knees in Mexico. He had desecrated the body of the dead imam and left his head impaled on a spike in front of the mosque, forced another conspirator to wear a suicide vest onto a military installation to assassinate a high-ranking officer, murdered a federal agent while he slept, put a long-range projectile through the brain of an accountant, and tortured an attorney before intentionally overdosing him on narcotics. All that was prologue; he was not yet finished merging his highly honed abilities as a warfighter with the guerrilla tactics used against larger, more conventional militaries by terrorists the world over. His skills were the perfect fusion of elite special operator and cunning insurgent.

"Reece, you are the strongest man that I've ever met, and I grew up around enough real men to know the difference. You've done it right your entire career, your entire life, and you don't deserve any of this. Lord knows that Lauren and sweet Lucy didn't deserve it. Most would have cracked under that pressure and crawled into a hole. I hope you don't regret anything that you've done to avenge your family and your men because, as far as I'm concerned, there's nothing that you could do to these monsters that would be over-the-top. There isn't a day that goes by that

I don't think about your risking your life to save my butt in Iraq. I will land this damn plane in Lorraine Hartley's front yard if that's what I need to do to help you."

"I hope you don't think less of me, but I can't let these people get away with this," he said with intensity.

"Reece, have I ever told you about my grand-father?"

"No, I don't think so. Your dad's dad?"

"No, my mother's daddy. He was the county sheriff back home. He was murdered in cold blood by some shitbag who'd just gotten out of jail. This was back in 1977, before I was even born. The guy that killed him sat on death row getting three squares a day for thirty years. Then some appellate court decides that he's ineligible for the death penalty. These big-city Harvard lawyers line up to defend murderers like him. Who's sticking up for us? I never got to meet my grandfather, and our family will never get justice. Your Teammates, those Rangers, the pilots and aircrew: none of those guys will get to hug their wives, coach their son's Little League games, or walk their daughters down the aisle. One of those 160th pilots, Chief Hansen, went to flight school with me. We all called him Swede because he looked like a huge Viking. He wanted to be an attack pilot, but he couldn't fit in anything other than a Chinook. He had a wife and three boys at home. He'd never even met his youngest, born just before he was killed on deployment. He was too mission critical to get emergency leave. My heart breaks for his wife and those boys. You'll never get to see Lauren or Lucy again or even meet your son. The system will protect the Hartleys, and they'll keep getting richer and more powerful. She'll be in the White House, and you'll still be trying to get people to believe your crazy conspiracy theory. No, Reece, if you're looking for someone to tell you you're doing something sinful, you've come to the wrong place. You hunt down every one of these fuckers and do justice for your family and all of those warriors' families." She paused. "Kill them, Reece. Kill them all."

Unsure how to respond, Reece remained silent as Liz collected her thoughts.

"I'll do anything that I can to help," she said softly.

"Thanks, Liz, you're doing enough already. I hate it that you're sticking your neck out this far for me. Sooner or later they're gonna figure out that you were involved."

"Maybe they will, maybe they won't. Whatever happens, it'll be better than getting tortured and gang-raped by a bunch of jihadis in Iraq. Pretty sure the FBI can't cut my head off. I owe you my life, Reece, and besides, y'all are like family. They murdered the closest things to a sister and a niece I've ever had."

CHAPTER 58

Ghost Rose Ranch, Texas

Liz Riley's employer kept both of his planes in a hangar on his ranch between Houston and College Station. Liz lived on the property in a small but well-appointed and clean cabin, which would be Reece's home until he could figure out his next move. Only a skeleton crew of staff were on the ranch, with the boss out of town, and none of them would bother Miss Riley's guest. She landed the Pilatus on the paved private airstrip and taxied toward a hangar that looked as clean as an operating room.

"Welcome to Ghost Rose Ranch," she said, shutting down the engine and beginning her postflight checklist while Reece climbed back into the passenger cabin.

"Just leave your gear in the plane if you want to, no one will bother it," Liz called from the cockpit. Reece nodded and found a small overnight bag that contained some clothes and toiletries, then opened the hatch and let down the stairs. He was desperate to stand on solid ground and stretch his legs after spending half the day in the small airplane. He paced around the hangar as Liz attended to the plane. Eventually she too climbed down the stairs and went through a series of stretches to loosen up her stiff body.

"How's your back?" Reece asked, referring to the injury that had ended her career as an Army aviator.

"It's okay. It gets stiff when I spend all day in the plane, though. Nothing that a glass of Pinot Grigio won't fix."

She flew like a man but drank like a girl. Reece always thought her to be an odd paradox of tomboy and girly-girl and he was constantly surprised by things that she said or did that made her seem too much of either one or the other.

A Ford F-350 King Ranch truck pulled up in front of the hangar and a small man in a western shirt, jeans, and boots tipped his Stetson to Liz and nodded his head at Reece.

"Señora Riley."

"That's Ernesto," said Liz. "He'll drive us to my place. Don't worry, he knows how to keep his mouth shut."

They climbed into the pickup and Reece took in the sights of the sprawling ranch as they made the ten-minute drive to Riley's cabin.

Islamorada, Florida

It had cost Leonard Howard a fortune, but he had been able to get himself and his family on a red-eye flight from San Diego to Atlanta and then down to Fort Lauderdale, where they rented a car for the drive to Islamorada in the Florida Keys. They arrived at the rental house exhausted, but happy to be safe, and as far away from San Diego as the U.S. borders allowed. That nut job Reece had to be operating without any kind of support, and there was no way he'd be able to make his way across the country without being captured. Besides, how would he ever find them here with no intel assets?

Howard and his family had lain low the first day and caught up on sleep but now they were growing more comfortable with their tropical surroundings and were beginning to explore a bit. His teenage son and daughter complained at first about the lack of a beach near the house but quickly realized that a world of aquatic wonders lay just below the water's surface, among the flats and reefs that made the Keys a snorkeling and diving destination. Howard bought them snorkeling gear at a local dive shop and they spent most of the day exploring their new world. Leonard and his wife were satisfied sitting on the porch and reading. She read architectural and interior design magazines while he read a new Brad Thor novel he'd picked up in the Atlanta airport. This is the way they'd live the rest of their lives once he cashed in on what he and the late Admiral Pilsner simply called "the Project."

Reece followed Liz up the steps of her cabin and into the small living room. "Can I get you anything?" she asked as she headed for the kitchen. "I've got beer, wine, water, not much else. . . ."

"I'll take a beer, I guess, and maybe some lights. This place is like a cave," Reece said, squinting at the photos on the mantel. There were pictures of Liz in her flight suit in front of her Kiowa in what was obviously Iraq, one of her father pinning on her wings at flight school graduation, and another that stopped him short: Liz, along with Reece, Lauren, and Lucy, all smiles at Christmas, happiness frozen in time.

Liz walked back into the living room carrying a bottle of Coors Light for Reece and a glass of white wine for herself. "I finally get a man back to my place and he's the one non–family member I can't have fun with."

Reece quickly recovered and pulled himself away from the photo.

"Are family members off-limits where you come from? I didn't realize that," he joked.

"I'm from Alabama, asshole, not Tennessee." Riley punched Reece on the upper arm as she sat down on the couch next to him. "You can use my Wi-Fi if you need it. We can't get a landline out here so it's all via satellite. I think it's secure but

I can't promise anything. You know how risky that stuff is these days. I got three prepaid phones for you as well. I wouldn't use any of them more than once, if I were you."

"Okay, thanks."

It was risky but necessary. Reece connected to the Wi-Fi signal and checked his SpiderOak folder for a message from Ben Edwards. He found one that was nothing more than a series of numbers and letters followed by "JAG." It took Reece a moment to realize that the characters were grid coordinates and that Ben was leading him to a loose end, one of the few remaining names on his list.

"What do you have there?" Liz asked.

"A message from Ben," Reece responded. "Looks like it's the location of my next target."

"Good ol' Ben," Liz said, reminiscing. "I remember him hitting on me constantly when I visited you and Lauren out in Coronado. I think he had just been picked up by the Agency. He always gave me the creeps. I think he was married at the time and his wife was right there!"

"Sounds like Ben. He always had a bit of trouble with those wedding vows."

"Where's the target?" Liz asked.

"Florida. The Keys."

The problem was getting there. It was the most bottlenecked spot in the United States, with one road in and out and surrounded by water on all sides. If this were a SEAL mission, the water would be the easy way in. They could use aircraft, a larger vessel, or even a submarine to drop him and his men in CRRC Zodiac boats offshore, where they'd ride as far as they could before swimming in silently below the surface using closed-circuit breathing apparatus gear that left no telltale bubbles to give away their positions. The irony was that, despite being a highly trained maritime commando, Reece didn't have access to so much as a canoe.

Reece had spent some time in South Florida as a kid but that was decades ago and that part of the country had changed dramatically since then. Before the war he and his Teammates had conducted demonstrations for the crowds at the UDT/SEAL Museum in Fort Pierce, so he did have some semi-local contacts. He'd hit it off while he was down there with some really good local guys who liked to spearfish and had kept in touch with a few via email. Still, he didn't know them well enough to reach out for help as the most wanted man in America, which he suspected he was well on his way to becoming as law enforcement began putting the puzzle together.

He also knew that there were some small private airstrips in South Florida where the more entrepreneurial and sophisticated black market businessmen had brought in bales of contraband marijuana known as "square grouper" during the

1970s and '80s, but the feds still watched them closely as part of their counterdrug efforts. He couldn't think of another way in that gave him a reasonable chance of getting out and decided he'd have to rely once again on the generosity of his friend Marco. Reece excused himself and walked out onto the cabin's front porch. He used one of the throwaway phones to reach out to his Mexican benefactor and, sure enough, Marco had contacts in Miami who would arrange for no-questions-asked transportation. There would be a car waiting for him at the FBO at the Opa-Locka airport, northwest of Miami.

"So, it looks like you won't get to have a man stay overnight after all," he told Liz as he walked back inside.

"Where to then, my fugitive friend?"

"Miami, then I'll drive down to the Keys. How long would it take us to fly there?"

Liz looked toward the ceiling and did some quick math in her head. "Probably three and a half hours, depending on the winds."

Reece looked at his watch. "Maybe we will have a sleepover; too late to pull this off tonight. I need to look at the imagery and do some planning anyway. Does this cavern have a guestroom?"

Early the next morning Liz filed a flight plan and they headed for the Sunshine State. Their flight path straddled the white sands of the Gulf coast and the forgotten shorelines of the Big Bend as the Florida peninsula arched southward toward the Caribbean. After passing over Sarasota, Riley turned due east, crossing the seemingly endless expanse of islands and Everglades.

What looked like a solid wall of saw grass from ground level appeared more like hundreds of intertwined snakes from above. Small rivers, creeks, and streams ran among clumps of dry or semidry land where vegetation grew. Navigating it by water would be nearly impossible.

The desolate habitat, far more varied than most believed, was a stark contrast to the highly populated coastlines of Florida that attracted tourists the world over. This must have been what all of South Florida looked like before men came with dredges to turn a sea of grass into a concrete jungle. When hurricanes came to reclaim the ancient swampscape, they built taller levees and deeper canals to hold back the tide of nature. The westernmost barriers of the levee system drew across the state like a line in the sand between raw beauty and manufactured civilization. Cookie-cutter neighborhoods stretched eastward toward the Atlantic, and a gridlike maze of asphalt snaked with traffic.

Reece stayed in the plane while Liz checked in with the FBO and located his ride, a 2004 Dodge Ram truck with keys under the mat. She returned to the plane and gave Reece a thumbs-up.

"Your ride is there, just like your friend said it would be. You sure you don't want me to come along and help out?"

"No, Liz, this is my show. You're sticking your neck out further than I want you to as it is."

"Did you see me getting my head cut off by some hooded asshole on YouTube? No? Oh yeah, that's because some SEAL I'd never met before stuck his neck out for me."

"Well, I'm glad I saved your ass back then 'cause I sure needed you this week."

"Go do what you gotta do and call me if you need a hot extract. There are airfields all over down here: Marathon, Key Largo, Tavernier; there's even a private strip down on Summerland Key that I could probably talk my way into. You call and I'll be there."

"Liz, I seriously can't thank you enough. I'll see you in a few hours."

"Be safe, Reece, be safe."

Reece started the truck, cranked the air-conditioning, and headed out into the southbound surface streets of Miami. There is the Miami that tourists see, with brilliantly lit skylines, art deco architecture, and white sandy beaches, and then there was this one. Much of Miami's population is made up of first- or second-generation Americans, immigrants from third-world, Latin American, and Caribbean nations who found refuge in the opportunities offered by Florida's growing economy. The predictable results of that mass transplant are entire neighborhoods that appear to have been plucked from Havana, Bogota, or Port-au-Prince: places where iron bars cover every window and doorway, English is rarely spoken or read, and the occasional chicken, pig, or even cow can be found in an urban backyard. Reece had done some drug interdiction operations as an enlisted SEAL down in South America during the pre-9/11 days, and the sights and sounds of these neighborhoods brought him back to those more innocent times. He made his way south and west onto the Palmetto Expressway, pulling into an aggressive flow of traffic that would give L.A. a run for its money.

Reece chuckled as he thought of a trip to Miami a few years earlier, when he and some Army special operators staged a mock attack on a prison facility that was set to be demolished. The troops snuck ashore and planted breaching charges to blast their way through the thick concrete walls of the erstwhile correctional facility. When the charges detonated, residents of a nearby housing project thought that they were being raided by SWAT teams and rushed to flush narcotics down the toilets. The effect of hundreds of toilets being flushed nearly simultaneously overwhelmed the utility infrastructure, and it took hours for the area to regain normal water pressure. They probably took more drugs off the street inadvertently that night than the local police would have seized in a month.

Reece finally made his way to Florida City and down into the string of islands known as "the Keys." The roughly one-hundred-mile chain stretched along the roads and bridges of a single highway, with each mile designated by a numerical marker that counted down to zero as you headed toward Key West. Just about every location in the Keys was referenced by its corresponding mile marker. As you counted down the mile markers and migrated farther south on U.S. 1, you saw fewer signs of Miami's influence and more artifacts of Old Florida. The long-standing roadside motels and dive restaurants, relics from the 1950s and '60s, reminded Reece of road trips with his parents and grandparents as a kid. If only his children could have lived to know such carefree days.

CHAPTER 59

Islamorada, Florida

Amy Howard was taking an afternoon nap while the kids watched a movie on the large flat-screen television in the living room. Leonard asked the children if they'd like to join him for a walk, but they declined. They were both at the age where they preferred to spend as little time with mom and dad as possible and they were worn out from snorkeling all morning under the Florida sun.

Howard wore a wide-brimmed sun hat, light-weight nylon Columbia fishing clothing, and Teva rafting sandals as he walked down the coquina driveway toward the access road to U.S. 1. A sidewalk paralleled the highway before connecting to a nature trail that offered a dry look at some of the miles of mangrove swamps that formed the core of the local ecosystem. At one point, the trail entered a cathedral of overhanging trees, which provided some welcome shade from the blazing sun. Despite the slow pace and the short distance he'd covered, Howard was already sweating in the oppressive humidity. He couldn't imagine this place in August. As pretty as it was here, he'd take California any day.

He heard what sounded like footsteps behind

him and turned to see the source of the sound. When he did, he was hit in the jaw by a blow that sent the world to black and him toppling down onto the concrete sidewalk. He awoke with a man astride him, raining blows down on his face. He tried to bring his hands up to block the punches, but his arms were pinned down by a death grip from the man's thighs. Reece had pummeled Howard's face to a bloody pulp, but stopped himself before beating the weaker man to death. That would have been too painless an end for the man who sold Reece's troop out to the Taliban out of pure greed. He took off his leather belt and looped it around Howard's neck like a leash, dragging him off the sidewalk and into the mangrove swamp, the JAG crawling behind him as best he could. When they were fifty yards from the trail, Howard's arms gave out and he became dead weight. Reece dropped the belt, letting the man's head fall to the soft ground before picking the lawyer up in a fireman's carry and wading into the water. The mangroves were like a maze and Reece had to pay attention to find his way back the way he'd come. He was more than a little relieved when he rounded a corner and saw the bow of the "borrowed" Hewes flats boat riding low against the water. He tossed the semiconscious Howard over the gunwale and bound his hands and feet with flex-cuffs for the ride.

Off the main chain of islands that were bisected by the highway and railroad were numerous islands of varying sizes and shapes that were accessible only by boat. Reece steered the Hewes northward across the clean waters of Florida Bay in search of a suitable spot away from the prying eyes and ears of civilization. He didn't have to go far. The shallow draft of the flats boat allowed him to cross over countless underwater obstacles by simply raising the outboard motor. Standing on the poling platform in shorts and a T-shirt and moving the boat with a long fiberglass pole, he looked to any observer like just another angler looking for bonefish in this world-class fishing destination. Reece found a protected cove where he could pull the boat in close to the shore and dropped anchor.

The admiral's JAG had regained consciousness and was jabbering on endlessly, taking no responsibility for his part in the plot to kill Reece's troop and family, begging for his life, and blaming everyone he could think of for the current predicament. Reece cut the plastic ties binding Howard's feet and tossed the senior officer over the side, watching him flail wildly until he discovered the water was only chest deep.

Reece slid over the gunwale and shoved the naval judge advocate toward the mangrove-tangled shoreline. Howard tripped constantly on the exposed roots of the native trees and it took them what seemed like an eternity to reach the dry sandy ground of the island. The JAG fell to his knees in front of a sabal palm tree and began to pray loudly. Reece looked down in disgust at a man who would seek the help of God after sending so many good men to early deaths without remorse. Howard's hat had fallen off somewhere, and Reece attempted to grasp a handful of the man's balding hair, but what was left after the military-regulation haircut slipped through his fingers. On his second attempt, Reece grabbed the petrified attorney by the throat and hoisted him skyward, holding an evil-looking blade in the other hand.

"Stand the fuck up!" he growled as he yanked the captain to his feet and shoved him back against the tree. "I want you to know what's happening to you. You are a traitor, a coward, and a disgrace to the uniform you wore. You served sixty-eight good men up to the enemy on a silver *fucking* platter so that you could rise alongside that shitty excuse for an admiral. You are the lowest piece of human shit alive. Look at me! Look at me when I talk to you, motherfucker!" Just as his enemy had lost control in their quest for power, Reece lost control and succumbed to the primal need for vengeance, all the emotions of the past several weeks boiling to the surface as he stood in front of the Navy attorney who had facilitated the deaths of his men half a world away.

"I don't know what you're talking about, Reece. I'm just a JAG. I don't know what you're saying," Howard pled with his eyes closed, blood still streaming down his battered face.

His denial sent Reece over the edge with rage. It was time for Howard to die. Reece slashed him across the lower abdomen with the curved blade of his razor-sharp Half-Face karambit knife, splitting the lawyer's abdominal wall and sending his intestines spilling out onto the marshy ground.

Howard released an animalistic screech and grasped for his bowels, desperately trying to shove them back inside the gaping opening. The wound bled surprisingly little.

"My God, my God . . ." were the only words he could muster, repeating them over and over in agony, his pleas for divine intervention going unanswered.

Reece showed no mercy, dropping the karambit to the ground and pulling his Dynamis Razorback belt knife from his waistband. He wielded the knife with violent grace, deftly skewering Howard's intestines with the tip of the blade, but carefully not severing them, then jammed the tip of the knife into the soft, pulpy trunk of the tree, tethering the JAG to it with his own entrails.

"Walk," Reece said in a calm voice that

contrasted sharply from the screams of rage he'd used just seconds earlier. "Walk around this tree or I'll gut your kids while you watch."

Leonard Howard stumbled forward in shocked silence, making his way slowly around the tree's circumference, all the while wrapping himself tighter and tighter to the trunk with his own intestines, finally collapsing to the ground, convulsing in tears with his back against the trunk.

"Please, please, don't leave me here. Please," he breathed. "I'll tell you anything you need to know."

"That's just it, Howard," Reece said, leaning in close. "I've already got what I need. Now I'm just going to watch you die."

"I . . . didn't . . . want . . . to . . ."

"You didn't want to what? You didn't want to kill my troop? You didn't want to kill my wife, my daughter . . . my son? Not good enough, Howard. Not even close. Don't worry, you won't die in vain. Your death serves a purpose. You get to send a message to what's left of your band of conspirators. If you're lucky, you'll go into shock before the rats start eating you alive."

Gazing up at his killer, Howard remembered the look Reece had given him back in the admiral's office in what seemed so long ago. *Death.* Reece stared into the hollow eyes of the dead man at his feet, his stomach a gaping hole that would provide ample sustenance for the creatures of the swamp. The bowel smell overwhelmed Reece's nostrils. Howard was already attracting flies and mosquitos. The crows and rats would come next, followed by the crabs. An American crocodile was not out of the question in these parts. He would probably live for several hours as he was slowly eaten alive by the jungle, so long as his heart held out. It would be a couple of days before anyone would find what was left of his body and that would be just enough time for Reece to prepare the final stages of his plan.

Reece wiped his karambit clean on Howard's soaked pant leg and walked swiftly back toward the boat, the SEAL-designed Razorback blade securing Howard to the tree leaving no question as to the identity of the JAG's executioner.

Reece didn't reflect upon what had possessed him to inflict such a ruthless act, but he was a student of warfare; it had come from the deep recesses of his subconscious memory. The Incas had devised this gruesome method of execution centuries ago in order to send a message. North American tribes, including the Shawnee, had used it as well. Sendero Luminoso in Peru adopted it in the 1980s as a brutally effective method to win the minds of locals and dissuade the government from being overly effective in their efforts to eradicate them. While the indigenous tribes and the modern terrorist group did it to strike fear into the souls of those that opposed them, Reece did it as the visceral act of a man overcome by rage.

Let those whom he hunted lose sleep wondering if they were to meet with a similar fate.

CHAPTER 60

The drive north was frustrating. The lone artery that runs the length of the Keys was choked with tourists, residents, and fishermen towing boats to various points north. To a man who had just blown up an admiral in his office, shot a federal agent in his bed, decapitated a terrorist, and left a man disemboweled and dying in a mangrove swamp, the stop-and-go traffic was maddening.

Reece would be hard to recognize with his hat, sunglasses, and beard but a driver's license check would bring the full weight of U.S. law enforcement scrambling in his direction. A simple traffic stop would likely result in the end of Reece's mission. He was careful not to speed when the traffic let up enough for that to be a possibility and he used his turn signals like a teenager trying to pass driver's ed. North of Key Largo, traffic relented a bit, and the flow northward toward Miami put him slightly more at ease.

Reece tensed as the truck reached the southern end of Miami's suburban sprawl. Aggressive drivers cut in and out of lanes and, at three miles per hour over the posted speed limit, Reece felt like he was driving a farm tractor. He sped up a bit to stay in the flow of traffic but maintained his position in the right lane. He glanced down at the folded-up map on his lap and prepared to merge onto the Palmetto Expressway for his return to the airfield. As he eased the pickup onto the access road for 826, he was suddenly cut off by a tricked-out orange Honda Civic that looked like a prop car from one of the Fast and Furious movies. He hit the brakes to avoid colliding with the tiny coupe and heard a screech of tires followed by the crunch of metal and plastic. Reece's head slammed backward in the headrest as the inertia of the rear-end collision pushed his borrowed truck forward and then to a stop.

Fuck. It was a hard hit but Reece was none the worse for wear. *I can't believe this whole thing could go south over a fender bender. Think, Reece. You'd better talk your way out of this one.*

Reece looked in the side mirror to see a morbidly overweight man, roughly his own age, climb down from his lifted Ford Excursion. The driver was walking directly toward Reece's driver's-side door, as swiftly as his considerable bulk allowed. Reece took a deep breath and forced a smile as he opened the truck door and stepped out to meet the fast-approaching driver.

The other man was within arm's reach by the time Reece had his feet on the ground. Dressed in orange and green Miami Hurricanes athletic shorts and a white tank top that showed off his heavy investment in tattoos, the large man carried himself with the air of a bully, one of those guys who act as if their size comes from muscle rather than fat. He pointed his finger toward Reece's face and tilted his head forward to look over his mirrored sunglasses. The man's face was red with anger and spittle flew from his lips as he shouted.

"*Oye!* You wrecked my truck, you *gringo maricón!*"

Reece raised his hands in mock surrender.

"Sorry, man. That guy cut me off, and I had to slam on the brakes to keep from crashing into him. I'm sure we can work this out, I've got good insurance." *I have no idea who this truck is registered to or whether it even has insurance. I wonder whether USAA will drop me for being a domestic terrorist?*

Their accident was backing up traffic. Horns were blowing and impatient drivers began crossing the diagonally striped merge lines to drive around them and access the Palmetto. The man stepped even closer to Reece, well inside his reach.

"Fuck your insurance, *punta*, you're gonna pay me for this shit right now or I'm gonna shoot your fucking ass." It was doubtful that this guy had a gun in his elastic waistband but he probably had one in the car.

"Easy, friend, easy. Let's just exchange information and get on our way. We don't need to wait around for the cops to come."

A woman, who Reece assumed to be the man's wife or girlfriend, stepped out of the passenger side of the truck screaming in Spanish and waving her arms. As Reece tried to calm the man down, whatever she was saying appeared to make him even more agitated. She kept pointing at the damage and screaming while Reece pled with the man to relax.

"My wife is calling the cops right now, this shit is all your fault."

"We don't need to do that, man, I can pay you cash. Just follow me to an ATM."

The driver turned his head to look back at his wife.

"Too late," was all he said before Reece's left arm encircled his antagonist's right arm, tying it up and rendering it useless while at the same time driving his right hand straight up, palm open, into the underside of the man's chin. The force of Reece's blow broke the jaw and destroyed what was probably a bad set of teeth anyway, but more important, it caused the man's brain to hit the back of his skull and bounce back inside his head, sending a shockwave through his nervous system and knocking him immediately unconscious. The man's knees buckled, and gravity sent all 380 pounds directly downward. His head smashed on the asphalt street with a sickening *thunk*. His female companion jumped from the car screaming, a phone pressed to her ear.

Reece leapt into the driver's seat of his truck and pulled the shift lever down into drive. He slammed on the accelerator and felt the truck strain as the tires spun, barely moving forward. The accident had entangled the two heavy vehicles into one gigantic train of steel. Reece put the Dodge in neutral, pressed a button on the left side of the dash to engage the four-wheel drive, and put the truck into its lowest gear. He accelerated forward, dragging the heavier Ford SUV behind him as the engine raced to produce enough torque. He knew he couldn't travel far this way, but for now, it was all he had.

I've gotta get out of this truck. He drove up the sweeping overpass toward the expressway, leaving the fat man's hysterical wife behind, and glanced down at the map to determine his next move. The map gave him an idea. As he reached the middle of a long turn, he swerved right and then left as he slammed on the brakes. The two trucks slid into position, blocking both lanes of the highway overpass from one concrete guardrail to the other. He engaged the parking brake on the Dodge and put the keys and map into his pocket. He slid over the bench seat to the passenger side and grabbed his backpack from the floorboard as he opened the passenger door. Horns were already blowing as he climbed over the guardrail and dangled from the edge. *Fuck me.* Reece released his grip, dropped his chin to his chest, and placed his feet and bent knees together to prepare for what was surely to be a painful impact.

It had been almost twenty years since the Army black-hat instructors at Fort Benning had taught Reece the parachute landing fall, or PLF for short, but there are some things that you never forget. The balls of his feet hit the gravel and he rolled to his side, distributing the impact of the fall from his feet, onto his calves, thighs, hips, and back. The technique, developed to allow rapidly descending parachutists to avoid injury, also worked well for a man on the run to drop from a highway overpass onto the railbed below. Reece's body had endured lots of wear and tear since his jump school days as a young SEAL, and he lay still for a moment to assess his body's condition. He felt hurt, not injured, so he rolled into the prone position and up into a kneel. His right knee buckled slightly as he put his weight on it but he was able to hobble forward with minimal pain.

None of the commuters seemed to notice or care that a man had climbed onto the Metrorail platform from the rails below. They were all too engrossed in their smartphones. A young boy did notice, but when he tried to tell his mother that a man had fallen from the sky and landed on the tracks, she nodded at him while continuing her online shopping spree. Dadeland was the commuter rail system's terminus, and a train arrived after less than a minute of waiting.

If anyone outside Miami had ever heard of Dadeland, it was probably because of the 1979 "Dadeland Massacre," a bloody shoot-out in a parking lot that came to symbolize Miami's epidemic of drug violence. Reece hoped there wasn't going to be a second bloody shoot-out in Dadeland but he was ready, just in case. He unzipped the backpack to allow him access to his handgun and held the bag down at his left side as he stepped onto the train. The entire side of the Metrorail car was painted with a Wi-Fi advertisement, which prompted Reece to retrieve his iPhone from the back pocket of his pack. He prayed they hadn't found a way to track it but he had no choice other than the "burner" phone he was saving for a last resort. He powered up the device, connected to the Wi-Fi signal, and opened the Signal app.

had to ditch the truck. on the metro heading north from the Dadeland station green line. need to plan an extract soon, cops probably looking for me.

Liz Riley must have been looking at her phone since her response came back almost immediately.

I'll make a plan, wait one.

458

Reece pulled the map out of his pocket and began looking at options. The SEAL in him told him to go to the water but there didn't appear to be a maritime route to an airfield unless he could get ahold of a boat. He looked up, hearing sirens, but they were headed away from him, toward the crash scene. His phone vibrated.

> *Unless you have to bail, stay on the green line until the Okeechobee station——looks like 20 stops. I'll get a ride and pick you up there.*

Reece consulted the station map on the wall of the metro car and looked down at the map. *Shit. I'm gonna be stuck on this damn train forever.*

> *Ok. I'll let you know if I have to divert. What are you driving? If it gets hot, leave me and I'll make my own way.*

Reece moved to the front of the car and leaned against the corner so that he could see the entire space. Everyone appeared to be engrossed in their phones, and no one paid him any attention. Apparently between the beard, the ball cap, and the sunglasses, he wasn't recognizable from the media reports he assumed must be out by now, though he had yet to see any.

As the train worked its way north, Reece

examined the South Miami landscape, keeping a sharp eye out for any sign of law enforcement activity. Then it was through the University of Miami campus, passing next to the baseball field. He breathed a sigh of relief every time the doors shut and the train continued northward.

The tracks paralleled U.S. 1 and took Reece north through downtown Miami and its towering skyscrapers. Reece couldn't believe how the city's skyline had changed since his last visit here. The ride continued through some slum areas north of downtown before turning westward into mainly residential areas. From the train Reece could view the roofs of tract homes arranged in perfect grids as far as the eye could see. The scene reminded him a bit of some of the crowded cityscapes that he'd seen in places like Baghdad and Manila. After a painfully long train ride, the station diagram indicated that Reece was one stop away from Okeechobee. He pulled the iPhone out and saw that he had a message alert. He logged back into Signal and saw a new message from Liz.

Out front. Black Honda minivan. All clear.

Reece scanned the area around the approaching station as much as possible through the train's windows. The car came to a stop and the doors jolted open. A few passengers disembarked quickly and fewer still brushed past them to board the train without a sliver of courtesy or patience. Reece had figured out the timing of the stops after enduring station after station, staring intently at the screen of his phone as the passengers came and went. When he knew he had a second or two before the doors began to close, he feigned surprise and sprinted off the car. Anyone who had been shadowing him from inside the train would be heading off to the next station without him. A quick glance back at the platform confirmed that no one had exited behind him.

Reece pulled his hat down tight to remain as protected as possible from any facial recognition cameras that might be at the station. Grant money from Homeland Security had helped create a surveillance state in population centers across the nation, and mass transit systems were some of the most popular sites.

The rail platform was elevated above ground level, which allowed Reece a good vantage point from which to observe the area. Looking over the rail, he spotted Liz's borrowed minivan idling next to the curb below. Nothing appeared out of the ordinary, but this was exactly the kind of choke point where ambushes took place. Reece made up his mind that, if things went bad, he would not involve Liz any further. She'd done more than enough by now and had long since repaid her debt. He had a hunch that, at this point in the game, she was helping out of her own anger over the murder of her friend Lauren and her adopted niece, Lucy. Getting one of the few true friends he had left in the world arrested or killed wasn't part of Reece's plan.

It's now or never. Reece took a deep breath and tightened his grip on the handgun inside his backpack. As he made his way quickly down the stairs, he heard the sliding doors open on the van. Liz obviously had eyes on the steps in her rearview mirror and had pressed the button to open the automatic doors. He saw the van's brake lights come on, indicating that Liz had put the vehicle into gear and was ready to go. He scanned the parking lot as inconspicuously as possible as he walked down the sidewalk that ran parallel to the van. His knee still throbbed a bit from his PLF onto the platform but he was confident that the injury was relatively minor and he could run if he had to. As his forward progress brought him alongside the van, he reached in and grabbed the inside handle, slinging himself into the backseat. The van lurched forward as soon as his feet left the sidewalk, and Liz sped toward the station exit.

Reece drew the Glock from inside the pack as the sliding doors began to close, alert for anything out of the ordinary. Liz turned underneath the rail line and onto West Twentieth Street, making a quick turn left and then gunning the engine to merge onto the Hialeah Expressway. If the feds were going to make a traffic stop, they would have done it before now. She glanced up into the rearview mirror through her aviation glasses.

"You okay, bubba?"

Reece breathed a sigh of relief.

"Better now. Thanks for the pickup. How'd you get wheels?"

"FBOs almost always have cars or vans that you can borrow. They make so much money selling you fuel that they'll do anything to make you happy. Did you wreck your friend's truck already?"

"I did. I'll tell you about it in the air. People here drive like shit."

"You've destroyed two perfectly good vehicles in like twenty-four hours. People are gonna stop lending you stuff."

As they drove eastward, paralleling the Metrorail tracks, it became obvious that they were retracing Reece's path from just minutes earlier.

"Don't say a word, Reece, I've never been to this city in my life."

"I didn't say a thing, Liz. Just do your thing."

They turned left at East Eighth Avenue and the neighborhood became even more residential. It occurred to Reece that if he had to bail out of the vehicle, this maze of houses, fences, and small backyards would make pursuit difficult unless the cops brought in a helo. He took note when they crossed a small canal, undoubtedly made when the land was drained to make it a hospitable suburbia. As they neared the airport, the scene became increasingly industrial. Their path took them through warehouses with loading docks, building supply companies, and auto repair shops. Reece was pretty sure he'd seen a gunfight scene in an old episode of *Miami Vice* that was filmed in this area.

"Anything hit the news about me yet?" Reece asked.

"Not yet. I figured it would have by now. They are still saying the attack on the admiral was either terrorism or workplace violence, depending on which news channel you watch."

"They know. All they need to do is talk to Tedesco's wife, and the pieces will fall into place. They're probably figuring out their plan before hitting the news outlets."

Reece could hear a private jet on final approach above them as Liz drove north through an intersection. The light turned yellow as she crossed the parallel street, and she hit the accelerator so as not to run a red light. As if in slow motion, the light turned red above them as a green and white Miami-Dade Police Dodge Charger sat at the traffic light to their right. The police car turned right and sped up behind them.

CHAPTER 61

"Oh shit, Reece. So sorry."

The Charger maintained its pace just a few feet behind the minivan for an agonizing ten seconds.

"Maybe he won't pull us over?" she said hopefully.

Just then the red and blue light bar illuminated and the siren let loose a short blast that made Liz jump in her seat. She checked her mirror as she engaged her turn signal and pulled over to the curb.

"Don't say a word, Reece, and please don't shoot him," Liz said, remembering her grandfather.

"Check."

Reece faced forward and slipped the Glock under his right thigh, putting both hands on his knees, where they would be easily seen. Liz put the vehicle in park and removed the University of Alabama ball cap from her head. She quickly pulled the elastic band from her ponytail and flipped her head side to side to let her hair down. With her right hand she tugged at her tank top to expose as much cleavage as she could and put on her most seductive smile.

The officer who appeared at the window was young, fit, and Latin, with a uniform that was meticulously pressed. Liz thought he looked like a guy you'd see in a Spanish-language soap opera, which made her own acting performance that much easier. She pulled off her Ray-Bans to give him a look into her blue eyes. Her ample southern accent became even more pronounced as she addressed the officer while sounding like a character from *Gone with the Wind*.

"I am so sorry, Officer. That light changed, and I didn't know what to do."

Despite the gravity of the situation, Reece nearly burst out laughing.

"Can I see your license, registration, and proof of insurance please, ma'am."

"Yes, sir, of course."

She retrieved her license from a small zippered bag on the passenger seat and opened the glove box to look for the rest of the documents. When Reece noticed the officer's eyes shift to check out Liz's fit body instead of watching her hands for a weapon, he was pretty sure that her acting job was paying off.

"This is a loaner van from the airport's FBO, so I hope it has everything in here."

She was relieved to see a short stack of paperwork when she opened the compartment, and grabbed the entire pile. She thumbed through the documents on her lap and quickly found a Florida vehicle registration sheet and a small insurance card. She placed her license on top and handed the stack to the stone-faced officer.

"I'm so sorry, I'm a pilot and had to pick up my client in Miami Lakes. I don't know this area and was trying to do too many things at once."

The officer glanced at Reece in the backseat and held his stare for several seconds, clearly sizing him up. Despite his disheveled appearance, Reece put on the most pleasant face possible. "I'll be right back, ma'am."

The officer retreated to his patrol car, where, Reece assumed, he was running both Liz and the van in his computer database. They were about to find out very quickly whether he was the subject of a nationwide manhunt and if anyone in the law enforcement community had tied him to Liz Riley.

I don't want to shoot this poor bastard but hope is never a good plan. If there is even a hint he is onto us, I need to disable him, his vehicle, and his radio and drive east to find a marina. Steal a boat and head offshore. Think with your dick, Officer.

Reece shifted his eyes between the watch on his wrist and the rearview mirror, counting the minutes and looking for any sign that the officer was making a radio call. Four minutes passed before the door opened on the police car. Reece studied the officer's body language as he approached. His right hand held a metal ticket book, not his sidearm, and his left hand hung calmly at his side. His stride showed swagger rather than fear. Any sane human approaching someone who they thought was an armed and dangerous domestic terrorist suspect would approach with more caution or stay in their car and call in SWAT.

The officer rested the metal ticket book on the van's windowsill where Liz could read it.

"Ma'am, I've written you a warning for failure to obey a traffic control device, which would have cost you two hundred and four dollars, and three points on your license. If you're a pilot, you should be more careful than that. Please sign the warning on the bottom line."

Liz leaned forward to sign the warning and made sure to allow the officer as much of a view down her tank top as possible. It worked, as he paid no attention to Reece whatsoever.

"That is very understanding of you, Officer. Thank you so much for not giving me a ticket."

"Yes, ma'am, please have a good day and try to be more careful. This copy is yours. If I pull you over again, I'm going to have to write you a ticket."

"Yes, sir, I promise that won't happen."

The officer finally broke into a smile and nodded to Liz.

"Please have a safe flight, Miss Riley."

"Oh, I will, thank you so much, sir."

The officer was nearly blushing as he turned

to walk back to his car. When he got to the rear of the minivan he came to a dead stop, paused, and turned back toward the window. Reece subconsciously flexed his right hand and took a deep breath to fight his racing heart rate. The officer stooped downward so that he had a direct view at Reece.

"Sir, why don't you have any luggage?"

Reece did his best to force a smile. "I just flew down here to look at some real estate. I didn't stay overnight so what little I brought is in the plane."

The officer stared at Reece for a moment, looked back at Liz, and nodded his head.

"Safe travels."

Holy fuck, that was close.

Liz started the van and put it into gear, pulling onto the road before the officer had even returned to his Charger. Reece felt the surge of euphoria that always followed a life-or-death encounter. His head began to swim with endorphins the way it usually did after a successful mission or firefight overseas.

"Reece, do you mind if your pilot for this evening is intoxicated?"

Reece exhaled a giant lung full of air. "I'll tell you what, I have never been so glad to have a hot female gym rat for a pilot."

Liz looked back at Reece in the mirror and flashed an embarrassed grin. She immediately pulled her top up and reached over to put her hat on.

Ten minutes later, she was all business as she meticulously went through the preflight checklist. Neither Reece's nor Liz's blood pressures began to return to normal until they were wheels-up over northern Dade County.

CHAPTER 62

The Pentagon
Arlington Country, Virginia

Generals Lewandowsky and Stuart waited in the secure conference room. They were given specific instructions not to include any deputies or aides in the meeting, which was highly unusual, if not unprecedented. Lewandowsky was nearing the end of his tenure as the chairman of the Joint Chiefs of Staff. He had been a stud fighter pilot, one of the few fortunate enough to see air-to-air combat during Operation Desert Storm. He also played the political game well enough to have risen to the pinnacle of the military food chain. Mentally, he already had one foot out the door as he looked forward to sitting on a few corporate boards in retirement. He had a laid-back demeanor that made him well liked among both his fellow generals and the men serving below him.

Ewell Stuart was very much the opposite: intense, opinionated, and decisive. A native of rural Virginia and direct descendant of Civil War general J. E. B. Stuart, General Stuart was probably liked by no one, but respected by all. He'd spent his early career as an infantry officer

in the Ranger Battalions before being selected for the Army's Special ████████████ at Fort Bragg. He was currently in charge of the Joint Special Operations Command, ████████████████████
████████████████████████████████
████████████████████████████████
████████████████████.

Neither man liked or respected Secretary Hartley, though both understood and valued the U.S. tradition of civilian control of the military. Hartley was a pure politician, checking the SECDEF box to build her credentials for a White House run. It wasn't just that she was a phony who didn't take the job seriously, it was her blatant practice of funneling every dollar she could muster through her husband's consulting firm that they found so offensive. If you wanted to sell a fighter jet, aircraft carrier, or armored vehicle to the military, you'd better hire J. D. Hartley. Want the contract to run the mess hall at Bagram? Retain J. D. Hartley. The Hartleys treated the Pentagon like the world's largest ATM machine.

Like many politicians, Lorraine Hartley had started out with good intentions. As a college student, with the help of a few of the more radical faculty members, she became outraged at what she came to see as injustices imposed by the U.S. government on countries around the globe. When she met J.D., she found a partner who would help her change the world. After J.D.'s election to Congress, their lives transformed dramatically. Everywhere she went, she was told how great she was, how smart she was, how talented she was. Before long, she was believing every word of it. The entitled behavior of both Congressman and Mrs. Hartley became increasingly outrageous, but in D.C. there were always suit-clad enablers willing to keep things quiet. By the time she was appointed secretary of defense, Madame Hartley had become the epitome of what her twenty-year-old self had sought to stand up against.

Both men had busy calendars, and it was fifteen minutes after the scheduled meeting time when the SECDEF finally arrived with her deputy secretary and young female aide carrying an iPad. The message was clear: you can't bring your staff, but I can bring mine. You weren't supposed to bring electronic devices into a secure room such as this, but neither man was willing to fall on a sword over that point. She greeted both men with a plastic smile before taking her seat at the head of the conference table. She was wearing a classic black suit made by St. John Knits, her usual attire. Her propensity for wearing all black, concocted after a focus group determined she was "most trusted" in that color, combined with her sour demeanor, was the reason for her nickname among the military officers who worked around her: "the Undertaker." Though no one ever dared use the moniker in front of her, her network of civilian rats let her know that she was so named. The fact that she was viewed as intimidating and insensitive pleased her.

The Joint Chiefs don't have direct command authority over military units; that structure flows directly from the SECDEF to the combatant commands. Though previous SECDEFs relied upon the Joint Chiefs for their advice and expertise, Hartley rarely did. Secretary Hartley acted as if Lewandowsky weren't even in the room as she directed her comments only to General Stuart.

"I've just come from a meeting with the secretary of homeland security. The blast that killed Admiral Pilsner came from a suicide vest. The man wearing the vest was a financier with no terror connections, and he did so because his family was being held hostage." She left out the fact that she'd known Mike Tedesco for well over ten years. "The man who strapped the vest on him was a SEAL officer, the one who led that shit show in Afghanistan that got everyone killed. We have reliable information that he's hiding out in some shack in New Hampshire; my people can provide you with the details. General Stuart, I want your SEALs up there as soon as humanly possible. One of our contract security firms will send a team to accompany them."

"I'm sorry, ma'am, but, as I'm sure you're

aware, the Posse Comitatus Act prevents us from using military forces in such a role on U.S. soil. This is an FBI mission," Stuart responded.

"I didn't ask you for a legal opinion, General. I went to Harvard Law School and don't want or need you to tell me what I can and can't do. I'm telling you to get your SEALs on a plane and get their asses to New Hampshire."

"I cannot give that order, ma'am. It violates the Constitution."

"Fuck the Constitution!"

The SECDEF's aide, who hadn't said a word thus far, glanced up from her iPad and interrupted. "Actually, Madame Secretary, it's not in the Constitution. Posse Comitatus is part of the U.S. Code, it's federal law. It didn't even apply to the Navy until 1992."

The SECDEF looked annoyed at her aide for the correction, but directed her anger back at General Stuart. "What are you, a fucking Eagle Scout? You give that order or not only will I demand your resignation and get it, but I will make sure that your beloved command is defunded into obscurity and that your men are reassigned to conventional units. You will be responsible for the death of special operations."

Stuart sat back, stunned.

"What's it gonna be, Stuart, are you gonna give the order or do I have to keep firing generals until I find one that will do his job?"

CHAPTER 63

████████████████████████████████

████████████████████████

Senior Chief Fred Strain had sent the recall text out to the Iridium satellite pagers of the operators in his assault team less than an hour ago. There was no excuse for missing that recall and now each member of his eight-man team was assembled in the conference space attached to their squadron room.

"All right, guys, this is a frigging crazy one." Fred was trying to stop swearing so much. He gave it up along with drinking after his wife gave him an ultimatum: stop drinking or leave the Teams. Fred had stopped drinking.

He almost shook his head as he chose his next words carefully.

"We are going after one of our own. Are you all aware of what happened at WARCOM?" Heads nodded up and down. It had been hard to miss. The media loved the SEALs these days. Even before the bin Laden mission catapulted them to cult hero status, there had been movies, books, video games, and other high-profile missions that had brought them into the spotlight. "You are not going to believe this, but the evidence is pointing to a SEAL as the perpetrator."

Looks of disbelief were shared among the group. Nobody liked WARCOM, and everyone had an intense dislike for the current admiral, but to blow him up? That seemed a bit out there. The current working theory in the media was that it was an Islamic terrorist group seeking retribution.

"Who's the guy, Senior?" one of the younger SEALs asked.

Fred paused; he almost couldn't bring himself to say it. "Lieutenant Commander James Reece."

"No fucking way!" the younger SEAL shouted, shaking his head. "No fucking way! He was my platoon commander before I came here. Total stud! Prior enlisted. He gets it. No way that guy did this."

Enlisted SEALs' contempt for officers was well documented. Every now and again there would be one who broke the mold, who was admired for his leadership, battlefield prowess, aggressiveness, and character. James Reece was one such man.

"Sorry, Smitty. It looks like it's true."

"Well, if he did this, he had one damn good reason."

"Doesn't matter the reason, Smitty. He did it. Plain and simple. I knew him as well. We were paired up in sniper school and operated together back in the early days. As solid as they come. His family has a long history in the Teams."

"Did he skip the country, Fred? Is that why they called us in?" another SEAL asked.

"Well, now here is where it gets a bit convoluted. You are all going to be asked to sign additional nondisclosures for what is about to happen."

"Really?" Smitty piped in. "More nondisclosures? You mean the hundred other ones we signed don't cover this? What the fuck, Senior?"

"Just listen up, Smitty, and let me get through this."

"Sorry, Senior."

"Okay, this is an unprecedented situation. This SEAL, who as we can see from what he did at WARCOM, is not your typical officer who just does his two platoons and then goes to a staff job for the next fifteen to twenty-five years—this guy knows what he's doing. A SEAL domestic terrorist. It's bound to hit the news soon. They are still calling it an act of terrorism, but that's going to change in short order, and we want to be up and out of here before it does so it doesn't put him more on edge than he already is. He is still in the country and the SECDEF wants him apprehended as soon as possible."

"Fred, I haven't been paying much attention to the west coast stuff in the news. How many people did he kill at WARCOM with that blast?" asked one of the Team's more laid-back guys, who looked like he was in a perpetual state of drunkenness.

"That's just the thing, only two: the admiral and some L.A. finance guy. The admiral's aide had his eardrums blown out but other than that, no one else was injured. Apparently he wrapped this L.A. guy in an S-vest, took his family hostage, and made him detonate himself in the admiral's office."

"No way!" said the laid-back operator, finally showing signs of waking up. "That's hard-core shit. I'm starting to like this guy."

"Cut it out, Paul," Fred said curtly. "This is serious business. We cannot underestimate him. This is a mission just like any other. Put the fact that he is a SEAL out of your minds except in the context that we are going up against a formidable adversary. He's had a lot of the same training that we have and has seen his share of combat. Whatever his beef was with the admiral and this finance guy is none of our concern. What is our concern is planning a mission to kill or capture this HVI," he said, intentionally verbalizing the high-value individual terminology used overseas.

"Hey, Fred, you said he was still in the U.S.," commented one of the more thoughtful SEALs in the group. "How can we go after him here? Doesn't Posse Comitatus still apply?"

"That's where the nondisclosures come in, gentlemen. SECDEF has suspended Posse Comitatus through an executive order signed by the president. We will be operating on U.S. soil, using all assets at our disposal to kill or capture our target."

"What? Can she even do that? Why us? Why not just use HRT?" the SEAL asked, using the acronym for the FBI's elite Hostage Rescue Team.

"SECDEF wants us . . ." Strain hesitated. "She wants us because, according to her intelligence sources, Reece's next target is the president."

Eyebrows went up around the table as the gravity and complexity of the situation unfolded before them.

Fred paused, scanning the room. "If anyone has a problem with going after this target or operating on U.S. soil, let me know now."

Nobody moved.

"Okay then. He's in a cabin in the mountains of New Hampshire. I don't know how they know this. The target package is slim. It says single-source HUMINT with no technical corroboration. Like I said, this is a weird one. There is a bird waiting on us at NAS Oceania," Fred continued, referencing the naval air station down the road from base. "We need to be airborne in an hour. We will cover specifics when we land in Vermont. From there we will make our way into New Hampshire. There is no time to more fully vet this or let it develop. SECDEF wants this done yesterday, and we are the force of choice. Any questions?" Fred looked from one operator to the next.

Fred regretted the next words that came out of his mouth as soon as he said them. "You don't have to like it. You just have to do it." *What a dumbass thing to say*, he thought.

"Smitty, a word please," Fred said as the crew got up to grab their gear and head to the airfield.

"Yeah, Senior?" Smitty asked as soon as the door was closed.

"Smitty, you are one hell of an operator, and I'd want you by my side going through a door anytime."

"But . . . ?"

"But, you won't be coming with us on this. And," the Team chief quickly added, "before you protest or say anything else, this is not your decision. I am ordering you off the mission. I can't have guys that know and respect Reece on this op. I know you understand."

Smitty tried to hide the relief on his face. He was conflicted like never before. He couldn't let his Team down, nor could he go after the man he looked up to as the best combat leader he had ever worked with, someone he would follow into the fires of hell. Taking the decision out of his hands was the sign of a good leader.

Smitty simply nodded, bowed his head, and walked from the room without his usual energy.

Fred took a breath. "Son of a bitch," he whispered to no one but himself. Taking another deep breath, he strode from the room to ready his gear.

CHAPTER 64

The Pentagon
Arlington County, Virginia

The story preempted every network broadcast and monopolized the cable news channels. Off-the-record quotes from "senior officials" at the Department of Defense were used to tease the story, ensuring massive coverage. Anchors gave viewers a countdown to the prime-time press conference that would be given by Secretary of Defense Lorraine Hartley, while reporters broadcasting from the dozens of satellite trucks crowded in front of the gates of the Naval Amphibious Base Coronado referenced reports of a "domestic terrorist" being responsible for the blast that killed decorated SEAL Admiral Gerald Pilsner.

At 8:00 p.m. Eastern Time, Secretary Hartley strode confidently toward the blue lectern at the Pentagon in a somber black suit. Her face exuded competence and control, a steady hand during these tragic times. *Never let a tragedy go to waste.* All that was missing from the scene, she thought, was the Presidential Seal on the podium.

"My fellow Americans," she began in a voice devoid of her usual New England accent. "It is with great sadness that I address you today to report yet another case of violent extremism in this great nation. This week a respected California businessman's family was held hostage by a domestic terrorist who forced the man to wear a suicide vest onto a military installation. This act of terrorism took the life of a great American hero and the commander of all U.S. Navy SEALs, Admiral Gerald Pilsner. Tragically, the admiral's killer was one of his own SEAL officers, a disgraced extremist veteran who faces criminal charges for his negligence as a commander in combat, negligence and incompetence that lead to the deaths of over sixty SEALs, Army Rangers, and Army pilots and air crewmen. It was, and is, the worst special operations disaster in American history. The man responsible for this unprecedented disaster is Lieutenant Commander James Reece. It is thought that his guilt over the ambush in Afghanistan drove him to target Admiral Pilsner and it is suspected that he is also responsible for several other murders over the past weeks in Southern California, including the atrocious slaying of a peaceful Muslim cleric and another vicious killing just this week in the Florida Keys where he took the life of another American hero, U.S. Navy Captain Leonard Howard."

Secretary Hartley paused for dramatic effect, the silence broken only by the shutter clicks of the print photographers' cameras.

"Lieutenant Commander James Reece is at

large and should be considered well armed and extremely dangerous. A nationwide law enforcement effort to locate and arrest him is already in progress but, unfortunately, the labors of our brave men and women in law enforcement are being hampered by extremists on the right who have put so-called privacy concerns over the safety of Americans from the scourge of terror. I have asked the president to sign an executive order enacting various emergency measures necessary to catch Mr. Reece and prevent others like him from murdering their fellow citizens. I also call on Congress to act swiftly to pass the bipartisan Domestic Security Act so that we can all live safely and without fear. Since 9/11 we have looked outward for the threats of terror. This xenophobic focus on so-called foreign terrorists has caused us to overlook the true threats to liberty brewing here at home. Extremists such as Timothy McVeigh, Randy Weaver, Eric Rudolph, and James Reece should be the real targets in our fight against terror. I stand ready to defend this nation from *all* enemies, foreign and domestic, and with your help, we will bring James Reece to justice, or we will bring justice swiftly down upon him. I'll take your questions."

An attractive female reporter from one of the networks stood and was recognized for a question spoon-fed to her earlier by Hartley's Press Secretary.

"Secretary Hartley, is it true that Commander Reece's pregnant wife and daughter were murdered in their home several weeks ago and that James Reece is suspected of committing those murders?"

"That's right, Meredith, and, yes, we do suspect that he was involved. This also brings up another point about the mental health of our men and women in uniform. Mental health and PTSD are serious issues that we as a nation must address. I call on our scientific community to dedicate their resources to addressing these problems. We need to declare war, not on members of our community who are of a certain religion, but on post-traumatic stress disorder. Next question, yes, Andrew?"

Andrew Harrison was a reporter and legal expert for one of the cable news networks.

"Secretary Hartley, can you confirm that James Reece used 'assault weapons' with high-capacity clips for some of the murders in California?"

"Yes, Andrew, we know that he used a military-style AK-47 machine gun with an illegal clip to kill a Muslim American cabdriver in Los Angeles. That man's only offenses were having dark skin and worshipping a different God. Now his wife is without a husband and his children are without a father. One more question."

William Brantley was the elder statesman of American broadcasters, with a career that spanned back to his time as a young war correspondent in the closing days of the Vietnam War.

"Madame Secretary, perhaps this isn't the time for such a question, but you've led this nation steadfastly through *so many* tragedies. Will you announce for us your intention to run for president of the United States?"

Don't lay it on so thick, William. "Thanks, William, but this isn't about me. This is about the American heroes who have paid the ultimate price to defend our nation. This is about bringing a terrorist to justice. Thank you all, God bless the victims of these tragedies, and God bless the United States of America."

The secretary stood for a full five seconds and stared into the television cameras before turning to exit stage right.

I nailed it.

Angels Camp, California

Katie Buranek watched the secretary's speech, aghast. She was a bit shocked that Reece had apparently turned Mike Tedesco into a human claymore mine in Pilsner's office, but even more, she was disgusted by the outlandish allegations made against him. She could buy that he'd killed Pilsner and Tedesco, God knew they had it coming, but there was no way that he had anything to do with the death of his wife and child. She knew firsthand that the story about Reece "murdering" the cabdriver was a lie, even down to what type of weapon he'd used. She was also confident that Reece was no extremist. He never once mentioned politics in any of their conversations. To paint a hero like James Reece as a xenophobic fascist was an affront to everything she knew about the man and his family, whom she so admired. It was time for her to get in the fight, this time wearing her journalist hat, working an editorial that would likely be the sole voice against the Hartleys' massive public relations machine.

CHAPTER 65

Coös County, New Hampshire

Fred still believed in the Constitution. He had dedicated his life to supporting and defending it. Like many senior enlisted SEALs, Fred had his college degree. Unlike most SEALs, he was also working on a master's degree in philosophy, of all things. He loved history, specifically the history of warfare, but he tempered that with the peace that studying philosophy brought him. His guys sometimes called him the warrior-poet, a title he wore with honor. That the president and SECDEF had suspended Posse Comitatus bothered him. He was old enough to remember the fiascos that were Waco and Ruby Ridge in the early 1990s. He was just a kid at the time but remembered the political firestorm that ensued when it was discovered that ██████████ advisors had been on the ground assisting the ATF at Waco. Federal government overreach was still something about which most Americans were extremely apprehensive.

What had caused Fred even more concern was the group of men who met him and his team at Mount Washington Regional Airport in New Hampshire. Twenty private security contractors from a firm called Capstone Security were awaiting him. A call back to his command confirmed that the SECDEF had already personally called to ensure the SEALs would support the contractors. The reason for the support role, he was assured, was some legal necessity related to Posse Comitatus. Fred was enraged. This was complete bullshit. These security contractors were not here to apprehend Reece, they were here to assassinate him. Fred knew the law and understood the Constitution. He also knew he had pledged an oath to obey the orders of those appointed over him. It was these two conflicting allegiances that gnawed at his soul.

Speeding over mountain roads brought him back to the moment.

"Slow down, Clarke," he ordered gruffly. "We need to get to the target in one piece."

The UAV on loan from Department of Homeland Security showed no signs of life at the mountain cabin. Far removed from the paved roads of the New Hampshire countryside, it looked like an idyllic retreat, at least from the feed Fred was watching on the iPad mini in his lap.

Fred moved his HK 416 rifle to the side and tapped the transmit button on the MBITR radio secured in the gear on his plate carrier. "Lead, slow it down," he cautioned to the first vehicle in the convoy.

They all wore their gray shipboarding kit, minus any flotation, so as not to look overtly military. The gray, nondescript uniforms made them appear more like a big-city SWAT team than a group of battle-hardened SEALs. The only giveaway was that each operator's helmet did not match the unexceptional gray of their uniforms and body armor. Operators could become attached to their helmets. Helmets of multicam or AOR1 desert digital camo sat in their laps so as not to alert local citizens that war had come to town.

"What? You getting too old for this, Senior?" quipped one of the newer members of the team from the backseat of the rented Suburban.

"No. I just want us all to arrive at the drop-off point alive."

"Good copy, Senior," responded the younger man.

"Hey, Senior, why didn't they just use local cops to get this guy. I heard what Smitty said about him being a good operator and all, but he's only one guy and he's just a vanilla SEAL," Clarke said, using the unofficial, semiderogatory term ████████████████ ████████████████████████████████ used to describe those SEALs and Army SOF operators not in their particular units.

"Hey!" Fred responded with more emotion in his voice than he intended. "This guy is *not* just a vanilla SEAL, and you know I hate that term. He is an HVI. A domestic terrorist. He is our targeted individual. Do not underestimate him, do you understand?"

"Understood, Senior."

"That goes for everyone," Fred said, clicking his radio once more. "Listen up, gentlemen. We are one hour out. Do not, I say again, *do not* underestimate this guy."

"Good copy," came the trail vehicle's reply.

Fred settled back into his seat. The rental Suburban and Tahoe would get them as far as a drop-off point on the opposite side of a steep mountain behind the cabin. From there they would patrol in to observe from high ground. Then they would make entry under the cover of darkness and apprehend America's most famous domestic terrorist.

Reece knew they would come. He didn't know how many or exactly when, but he knew they would come. He spent little time pondering whom they would send. Would it be private contractors? A possibility, considering the resources of the conspiracy in which he found himself an unwitting pawn. Local sheriff? Reece hoped not. FBI Hostage Rescue Team? A probability, considering they had the authority to operate on U.S. soil. ████████████████████████ Maybe, depending on how desperate the SECDEF had become.

Whoever came for him was a part of that conspiracy. They were coming to prevent him from completing his mission and that was something Reece could not allow.

Reece felt no allegiance to anything or anyone. His sole purpose was to make those who killed his family account for what they had done. They had taken everything from him. Now it was his turn.

When they came for him, the last piece of the puzzle would fall into place. Reece prayed he was wrong, but even before he heard the helicopter he knew he was not.

His pursuers were instruments of a group of conspirators who had subverted the system for their own benefit. Power and money were formidable motivators to those in life with no purpose other than their own self-aggrandizement. Had Reece died in Afghanistan as they had planned, his family would still be alive, Horn and his cronies would be more wealthy than most ever dreamed possible, Admiral Pilsner would be on his way to a seat on the Joint Chiefs of Staff, and Lorraine Hartley would be on her way to the presidency. Unfortunately for all of them, Reece *was* still alive. He was alive and set on a reckoning, one that would see them all to early graves.

He was nearing the end of his journey and would soon join his wife and daughter. Just a few more people to kill, and, if he was right about an approaching assault force, there would be one more name to add to the list.

From his elevated position Reece had a clear view of the road leading to the remote dirt turnaround area where it appeared that hikers sometimes parked their cars. This time of year it was empty.

Reece heard the rotors of the chopper well before he saw it. Even at this distance Reece knew what it was. The helicopter didn't surprise him, though they should have kept it farther back until the assault had commenced. What surprised him was the number of people they sent. The lead black Suburban was followed by a Chevy Tahoe and two ten-pac passenger vans. Reece watched them exit their vehicles and gather into a loose formation. These were no hikers or Boy Scouts on a field trip. These were the men sent to kill him. It was an odd conglomeration of what looked to be military or paramilitary forces and private contractors. A few stood out as professional soldiers, while others appeared to give off an air of invincibility and arrogance. Two even lit up cigarettes. He counted close to thirty attackers.

It was time. The enemy had massed, was unaware, and was in the kill zone. Reece picked up the MK 186 wireless firing device that he had linked with a string of six claymore mines yesterday morning. The MK 186 was bulky and old but it worked. He had set them up in a classic L-shaped ambush, adhering to the old military adage *Keep it simple*. The Mk 48 7.62 machine gun lay next to him along with his M4 with M203 grenade launcher and two LAW rockets.

He looked back at the force readying to kill him and armed the MK 186 with the push of a button. In this game, you lived by the sword and died by the sword. The men 150 yards away and below him knew that well. It was their turn to die by the sword.

Something stopped Reece cold. He pushed disarm on the MK 186 and picked up his binos. Something about the way one of the men below moved gave him pause. It looked to be the leader wearing gray op cammies and gear. A bit of a beard and longer sandy hair gave him the appearance of a contractor, but his demeanor suggested something else. Reece focused the binos in on the man who was seconds away from being eviscerated into eternity.

Damn it, Fred, what are you doing down there? Reece thought, looking down at his old sniper school partner. *Some of them are your brothers, Reece. They're hunting you, but they don't deserve to die today. They have no idea the part they are playing in this game.*

Without another thought, Reece dropped the binos, grabbed his M4, and disappeared into the bush, leaving an empty target for Freddy Strain to ponder.

Only one person on earth knew he was going to the cabin.

Reece now knew the final name to add to his list.

CHAPTER 66

Katie Buranek's story went live on a lesser-known, though legitimate, news site at 5:00 a.m. Eastern Time. Her more mainstream outlets wouldn't touch it, fearing backlash from the administration in the name of limited access and IRS audits. Drudge picked it up by 6:00 a.m. and it was on all of the morning political talk shows an hour later. The conspiracy theorists bought into the story hook, line, and sinker. Talk radio hosts were jumping up and down over it by noon. Stories like this popped up all the time, but Katie's credibility as one of a few true investigative reporters left in the business gave this one legs.

She didn't make accusations, despite having the evidence to do so, but instead asked the readers to think for themselves. What was a Bentley-driving political bundler with close ties to the Hartleys doing in the WARCOM admiral's office in the first place? Why didn't the secretary of defense acknowledge her close relationship with Tedesco during her remarks? Why would a highly decorated SEAL with a half-dozen combat deployments suddenly go rogue and start taking out members of his chain of command? She had on-the-record quotes from former commanders, peers, and subordinates of Reece who all agreed that he would never do such a thing, a few throwing in the caveat "without a really good reason." They also agreed, to a man, that he would have never hurt his wife and daughter. And why would the SECDEF not accept the alibi that he was at Balboa Naval Medical Center when his family was killed, as the police investigators did? Why deal in facts when you can simply issue statements that the media will parrot?

Katie posed questions about Capstone Capital and its status as one of J.D. Hartley's clients. Why was a California-based private equity firm getting an annual $100 million appropriation out of his wife's budget? Wasn't the idea of having the spouse of a cabinet secretary lobbying her agency fundamentally corrupt? These questions, which the Hartleys had successfully avoided in the past, were now too juicy for the mainstream press to ignore and could seriously damage her chances of becoming the next president.

Hartley's communications staff was in full crisis mode, putting far more time and effort into this story than they ever did to any Pentagon issue. Though Hartley's close advisors were all technically DOD employees, they were political professionals who had followed her into the job and would follow her out. They decided that the best course of action was to stonewall and retaliate. They refused to acknowledge that the article, which they dismissed as "fake news," raised any real issues of substance and they attacked Buranek as a "conservative bomb-thrower," despite her history of equal criticism of both political parties. The secretary herself made no official statement in response to the article, instead coordinating a contrived scene with a friendly reporter as she and her staff walked into the White House for a briefing.

"These people have been attacking J.D. and me for years and they've always lied. Conservatives can't swallow that the real threats to America are among their own ranks. They're focused on foreign 'threats' when we are radicalizing our own citizens into extremism through talk radio and the Internet. This blogger is part of the problem, not part of the solution. We can be free from this fear with the passage of the Domestic Security Act."

Chew on that, Katie whatever your name was.

CHAPTER 67

Bennington County, Vermont

"What kind of a shopping list is this, Reece?" asked a skeptical Liz Riley.

Reece smiled. "It's one for the ages, Liz. Any questions about it?"

Liz and Reece had flown from Florida to a small private airport in Vermont used mostly by retired locals with a passion for flying and a few wealthy families from New York and Connecticut who liked to escape to the woods on the weekends. They were able to rent a small private hangar to use as a home base while preparing the final phase of their mission. Liz arranged it en route and explained to the manager that they were doing a site survey for her boss for an upcoming retreat. After Reece aborted the ambush of the assault force sent to take him out at Ben's cabin, he made his way back to Liz at the airfield to begin final preparations for the remainder of the list.

"A glassware chemistry set? Round-bottom flask? Catch flask? Clamps?"

"It's for distillation," explained Reece.

Liz raised an eyebrow and continued, "plastic five-gallon bucket, a wooden broom, fertilizer, high-yield stump remover, Liquid Fire drain cleaner, a bedsheet set, a string of Christmas tree lights, a hot glove, fifteen-inch-long, six-inch-diameter plastic PVC pipe with collar; copper bowls, coffee filters, candles, cold packs? You sure you need all this?"

Reece just nodded. "Any questions?"

"Let me see: um, concrete cleaner, pool cleaner, hydrogen peroxide, a set of shot glasses, a heat lamp, a wireless doorbell? Are you doing what I think you are doing, Reece?"

"Probably. Don't worry, Liz. This is for one person in particular. It will be precise and is meant to send a message."

"You certainly know how to send a message, my friend. Okay, I'm on it. Guessing you want me to spread this around and not pick it all up at Terrorism 'R' Us?"

He ignored her attempt at humor. "I've already identified the chemistry equipment on Craigslist. Just explain that your high school kid loves science and asked for a set for his birthday. Pretend like you have no idea what it's for. Everything else, spread out and pay cash. We still have plenty from the stash that Marco gave us. I have a list of stores here that should carry what we need," Reece said, handing Liz the list, which included addresses. "It's going to be a long day, Liz. Even though you could get all this stuff between a couple of hardware stores, a nursery, and a Radio Shack, visit multiple stores in multiple towns so it doesn't look like you are doing what you are *actually* doing."

"Is making this thing dangerous? I don't want you to blow yourself up. Or me, for that matter."

"It's not without danger, I'll tell you that. Remember the EFPs in Iraq?"

"Of course. Those fucking things," Liz said with disgust, shaking her head.

They both knew people killed and others maimed for life from the plague of explosively formed penetrators. A basic and effective weapon, EFPs consist of pipes, explosive chains, and metal plates that, when detonated, turn into molten slugs or "penetrators," focused from the high-velocity force of the charge and allowing them to slice through armored vehicles with ease. Although developed in World War II and later tested extensively by Hezbollah in Lebanon, they really came into their own and into the public consciousness following the invasion of Iraq. With significant assistance from Iran, they were smuggled into Iraq across centuries-old ratlines, predominately to Shiite militias and Badr Brigade splinter groups. Introduced to that theater in force in 2005, they would defeat the world's most technologically superior armor, causing death, destruction, and psychological terror. One of the deadliest asymmetrical weapons used against Allied forces in modern times, EFPs and other

Improvised Explosive Devices accounted for more than 50 percent of all U.S. causalities in Iraq and Afghanistan and untold suffering from the 33,000 physically wounded. The corresponding psychological toll was incalculable, but extended well into the hundreds of thousands.

For a minor investment in personnel and material, the enemy was able to bring a superpower to its knees. This rudimentary, cheap, and relatively small tactical weapon caused damage far in excess of its size and became a weapon of strategic importance. Reece had spent years of his life pressuring the enemy threat network in Iraq, mapping out, dismantling, and destroying IED cells throughout the country. Now, on home soil, he planned to turn this weapon against one of the men who stood to profit from the deaths of his troop and his family.

"And I need you to do me a big favor, Liz. I need you to get in touch with Raife."

Liz paused. Raife had been like a brother to Reece in the Teams. They had met in college and entered the Navy together, one as an officer and one enlisted. An event in Iraq years earlier had caused Raife to leave the SEAL teams under circumstances no one but Reece fully understood.

"Are you sure that's a good idea? Do you think he will help?"

"I know he will. It will just be better coming from you. You might have to do a little sleuthing to track him down. You can get to him through his family offices if you get creative. I hate to add this to everything else I need you to do today, but it's the only way."

"I got it, Reece. I still have his sister's contact information, so I'll get through to him somehow."

"Great. When you do, read him this," Reece said, handing Liz a folded-up note. "It's detailed instructions and a big ask, but I know he'll do it."

"I sure hope so," Liz said, reading through the note with a hint of skepticism in her eyes.

"Oh, and we need a Sprinter van."

"Oh, just a Sprinter van?" Liz quipped.

"I located a used one online not far away. It doesn't have the New York plates that I'm looking for but we can steal some along the way."

"Won't buying it in cash seem suspicious?"

"Possibly. It's a year old and it looks like the guy just needs money. If it does arouse suspicion, by the time it's followed up on it will be too late. I just need something that can blend into the New York delivery vehicle scene, and this should be perfect."

Liz looked at the floor, opened her mouth to say something, and then stopped.

"Liz?" inquired Reece.

"James, what happens when this is over?"

"Focus on the mission, Liz."

"I knew you would say that," she said with a hint of disappointment in her voice.

"I'm sorry you are so deep into this, Liz. That was never my intention and it's my one regret about this whole thing."

"Fuck you, James. I am in this because I choose to be. I want to be here and I want to take these guys down. They have it coming."

Reece nodded. "First thing we need to do is get you a wig or something for your shopping spree today. They will eventually piece this together, Liz. Have no misconception about that. A disguise might just slow them down a bit. I've talked with Marco. When this thing goes south—and Liz, it *will* go south—he's got a place for you in Mexico. I've been there. It's not the States, but you will run his Mexico flight operations and live on his estate south of Puerto Vallarta. He has lawyers who can help work on a deal to get you back to the U.S. and keep you out of prison. Whatever they tell you to tell investigators about me, do it. Unfortunately, that's the best I can do for you."

Liz bowed her head again. It was a lot to take in.

"Focus on the mission, Reece," she said, turning to go borrow the airfield's loaner car.

It took Liz a full day and into the evening to track down everything on Reece's grocery list. They had driven together to the home of the man selling the Sprinter van. Apparently his wife was not as excited about converting it into a small camper van as he was, so he was selling it to get them something she would enjoy as well. He had purchased it as a cargo van so he could outfit it himself, which made it ideal for the job Reece had in mind. If he thought it was odd that Reece stayed in the airport's vehicle, he didn't let on. He was just happy someone was willing to pay cash for his impulse buy. After Liz acquired the Sprinter she switched vehicles with Reece and began her quest for the items on her shopping list.

When Liz returned to the hangar later that evening she found Reece securing something to the inside of the Sprinter van. It was a desk he had liberated from a small office attached to the hangar. On the wall of the hangar was the outline of what appeared to be a large SUV.

"What's up, Reece?"

"Just getting prepped. How'd it go? Any problems?" Reece asked.

"Surprisingly few. I did some quick research on the more obscure items and came up with a backstory in case anyone started asking questions. Most of the guys were extremely helpful."

"I'll bet," Reece said with a knowing gleam in his eye.

"They all just seemed happy someone was buying their stuff," Liz said with a grin.

"Great. And how'd it go with Raife?"

"I got through to his sister, Victoria. She gave me his current contact numbers and said she would pass on the information. We also coordinated a place for me to drop off your gear for Raife after we part ways here. That was the best I could do."

"He'll take care of it."

"I sure hope so. How's your science experiment preparation going?"

"I'll be able to build the device with the materials you picked up today. Remember the July seventh bombings in London a few years back? Similar stuff. Though this one will be targeted and more precise. I am in no way an explosives expert, so I want you to stay clear as I do this. I could very well blow myself sky-high."

"You're a Navy SEAL, for Christ's sake. Can't you build a bomb that won't blow us up?"

"We have EOD guys that are the real experts in this sort of thing. I learned all this from studying the enemy overseas, taking down their bomb factories. They don't quite take the precautions we would here in our explosives courses in the States. Every now and then the enemy would do our job for us and blow themselves up by being careless. I wish I had a few more blocks of C-4, but I used what I had on the admiral, and my claymores are back in the New Hampshire woods, so I'll have to do this the insurgent way."

"What's this?" Liz asked, pointing to the vehicle outline on the wall.

"J. D. Hartley moves around New York in an up-armored Suburban. It's a serious setup. Withstands up to 7.62 ammunition and even smaller IEDs. We used the same ones protecting the interim Iraqi government officials back in Iraq. It seemed like everyone wanted to kill those guys. Anyway, that is a measured outline of a Suburban. I want to know exactly where I have to stop the van to line up the EFP I'll have secured on the desk in the back. The explosive will turn the copper bowl you purchased into a molten slug, which will cut right through the armor— and right through J. D. Hartley."

"What if he has someone with him?"

"Then it just wasn't their day." He paused, "Liz, I'll do everything I can to make sure it's just Hartley."

"When is this going down, Reece?"

"A reporter friend of mine contacted a paparazzi photographer she knows in New York City to ask about Hartley. She said she was doing a piece on him and wanted some up-to-date on-the-ground information. Apparently he is spending his nights with a blonde real estate agent in SoHo. I even have the address."

Liz watched Reece from across the hangar. If he blew himself up, he did not want her to die as well.

507

She watched as he cautiously emptied fertilizer into a bucket of water, stirring it with the broom handle before adding a golden-red fluid from the chemistry set catch flask. He then slowly poured what had then transformed into a milky white froth onto one of the bedsheets he had strung between a set of chairs. To Liz it reminded her of the jellies she would make with her grandmother as a child, watching the liquid slowly drip through cheesecloth over the kitchen table. Reece focused the heat lamp on the bedsheet and then moved to a table farther away from the concoction he had just created, presumably to limit the damage in case the next batch did not go as planned. From her vantage point, it was difficult for Liz to tell what he was doing. She could see him mixing shots of what appeared to be the pool and concrete cleaners with nail polish remover into the chemistry glassware, swirling it around and then pouring it into a coffee filter he had secured over a round-bottom flask. She could tell he was being as meticulous as possible during this portion of the process and she wondered whether this was the part where terrorists sometimes unintentionally exploded.

With pliers he pulled the bullet out of a 5.56mm cartridge case and poured the powder on the table. Liz was transfixed, thinking that at any moment she might watch as the man she was closest to in this world entered the next. From a string of red, green, yellow, and blue Christmas tree lights, Reece cut a single bulb, heating up the end with a candle, before dipping it into water to break off the tip. She knew this was a delicate part of the procedure as she watched Reece pack the cartridge case with his newly created mixture and place the broken light inside, securing it with hot glue. It dawned on her that from elements that usually brought happiness and joy, Christmas and swimming pools, Reece was brewing up a mixture of death.

When he was done, Reece stood and slowly moved away from the table. He looked tired and relieved.

"That went well," he said. "The good old 'mujahideen slam.' And, we're even still alive."

"Will wonders never cease," Liz replied, obviously as relieved as he was.

"It will take at least overnight to dry the urea nitrate on the bedsheets. That's the equivalent of TNT and will be the primary explosive. The heat lamps should help speed up the process. The dangerous part is done. Tomorrow I'll pack the PVC pipe with the explosive and place the copper bowl under the collar, set the firing cap I just made into the back, and attach the lightbulb to the wireless doorbell. Not bad for an amateur."

"I'm just glad we are all still in one piece," Liz stated.

"Me too. Let's get some rest. Over the next few days we're going to need it."

CHAPTER 68

New York, New York

Anthony Craig did not like his job. Well, it wasn't his job per se; it was the person his job required him to drive around New York that he disliked. As a young black kid growing up in Brooklyn in the 1960s and '70s, he had been headed down a dark path. That was until his father took a day off from his janitorial duties at an investment bank on Wall Street, something Anthony could only remember him doing that one time, in order to take him to lunch. Instead of getting a bite to eat, they had walked to the Marine Corps recruiting office on Chambers Street. The Marines had knocked the chip off his shoulder and turned his life around. After his father's early death from a heart attack, Anthony left the Corps and returned home to New York City. He married a woman whom he'd met at church and they raised two children, who were both now in college on academic scholarships. Now in his mid-fifties, he was proud of the life he had created. He was not proud of the man he was driving around.

It wasn't that J. D. Hartley treated him poorly; in fact, it was just the opposite. Despite Hartley's philandering, he was generally well-liked by everyone. Hartley was at a point in his life where his adultery was a part of his persona and even an element of his national identity. He had been elected to Congress from the great state of California despite being caught red-handed on multiple occasions in compromising situations, both financial and extramarital, but what was acceptable in California was not palatable to a national electorate. After a failed presidential election bid, he had let his wife take the spotlight as she worked her way through positions of power all the way up to secretary of defense. J.D. had occupied himself running his consulting company, lobbying and building his foundation with the mission of bringing computers and education to the third world. This allowed him to attend fundraisers where he was the toast of the evening, surrounded by adoring women who found his mischievous ways intensely alluring.

What offended Anthony wasn't the lifestyle or elitism of his current employer. It was the fact that J. D. Hartley had assumed from day one that, because Anthony was black, he was by default a liberal Democrat and supportive of the Hartley's political leanings. Anthony had seen liberal policies fail his community time and time again, promoting an entitlement culture that he believed was the cause of the problems, rather than the solution to them. In any event, Anthony was a man of God and a professional. He smiled and made small talk when necessary, always on time and always gassed up and ready to go.

Today his boss had made him wait longer than usual. Anthony had parked the Suburban right in front of the SoHo apartment where Hartley had spent the night with his latest mistress, a well-endowed real estate agent in her early thirties. He must have really been on a roll, as he'd spent the entire day with her in the apartment building, finally calling for Anthony in the late afternoon. The doorman allowed Anthony to park in the loading zone while he waited for the former congressman.

Anthony had the satellite radio set to a classical music station as he surveyed the Manhattan evening. He loved the hustle of New York and would never think of working elsewhere. The vitality of the people moving along the sidewalks, the constant stream of traffic, and the majesty of the buildings never got old for him. It was his city.

The melancholy of Richard Strauss's "Im Abendrot" filled the Suburban. Anthony loved classical music almost as much as he loved New York. Pairing the two was majestic. Knowing that the piece was written with the calm acceptance of death as its inspiration seemed in sharp contrast with the life surrounding Anthony's current piece of early evening New York energy.

A wave from the doorman signified that Congressman Hartley was headed down. Anthony exited his vehicle, pushing the heavy armored door open, and moved to the right rear passenger side to open the door as Hartley exited the building with a spring in his step.

"Good evening, Anthony," Hartley said with a confident smile full of magnificent white teeth as he approached the car in an immaculate navy blue suit and bright yellow tie. "Sorry to keep you waiting, but duty called."

"Good evening, Congressman," Anthony replied as he opened the door for his employer, shutting it behind him and making his way around the front.

The black Sprinter van almost knocked him off his feet.

"Whoa!" Anthony stammered as he regained his balance. "Hey!" He yelled at the Sprinter driver.

The van had pulled in right next to the congressman's Suburban, so close that it had knocked the left side-view mirror off the vehicle.

These young delivery guys are crazy, thought Anthony, bringing his arms up in an incredulous shrug as if to say, *Well, now what?*

As he moved back to the front of the Suburban, he got a good look at the driver of the van. With a full beard and unkempt hair, he looked more like a mountain man than a delivery driver. It was when he slid from the front seat and moved parallel and forward of the pinned vehicle that Anthony realized this was no delivery driver.

Time seemed to slow for Anthony as he looked through the front window to see Hartley in the backseat reading his paper, unmoved by the commotion caused by the Sprinter. Switching his attention back toward the van driver, he noticed something small and white in his left hand. He appeared to be looking not at Hartley and not at the Suburban but at the people on the sidewalk. It was only then that Anthony realized what was happening. He had to get Hartley out of the car. That was his last thought before a sound he had not heard since his basic demolition training in the Marine Corps thirty-five years earlier erupted from the Sprinter. Fire, deafening noise, and a shockwave unlike anything he had ever experienced reverberated through his body and sucked the air from his lungs. The congressman's Suburban rocked onto its side against the curb while the front of the apartment building absorbed an impact that Anthony thought might take down the building. Wide-eyed, he stared at the formerly peaceful streets that had just been transformed into a war zone. When he turned back toward the bearded man, all he saw was traffic and chaos.

CHAPTER 69

Reece turned the corner and ran east, blending in among the masses of humanity desperate to flee the site of the explosion. He couldn't help but think of similar images from television sixteen years earlier, images that sent Reece and his brothers to far corners of the globe in search of those responsible. *Improvise, Reece.* He saw an opportunity and reacted instantly, grabbing a wide-brimmed black hat from the head of a Hassidic Jew jogging in front of him. The man turned instantly to his left to recover his sacred hat, but Reece brushed past the man on his right side and continued forward. The sheeplike crowd sensed the lack of danger and began to slow as human curiosity started to set in. Much to Reece's shock, people began pulling out their phones to check news sites, take video, and even to post to social media accounts, lest anyone miss a single moment of their shared life experience.

Getting caught carrying a gun in New York City was an absolute no-go. As much as Reece loved his Glock 19 for its reliability and durability, it was a little big to conceal from a trained eye. Getting spotted by a sharp-eyed NYPD officer for carrying a concealed handgun would bring his mission to a screeching halt. He'd have a tough time talking his way out of the encounter, and shooting it out with the cops here was a really bad plan. He wasn't about to go unarmed at this point, though, so he had compromised firepower for concealment. The Glock 43 was a compact, single-stack magazine version of the larger Austrian pistol that shared its 9mm chambering. Reece's pistol had been extensively customized by Zev Technologies in Oxnard, California, and Reece could shoot it almost as well as he could its larger relative. With the slim but powerful handgun in an appendix holster, Reece could defend himself and potentially break contact if it were absolutely necessary. He desperately hoped that wouldn't be the case.

Reece slowed his pace to a jog and eased to the edge of the crowd. Switching to a brisk walk, he turned north down an alley, placing the hat atop his head. Removing his backpack as he walked, he took out a black Arc'teryx fleece and pulled it on. The disguise wouldn't bear close scrutiny but, along with his full beard, it would work at first glance.

The alley took Reece to another eastbound street, where he turned right and began looking for a cab. It had been years since he'd visited New York, and it took him a few tries before he decoded the meaning of the light bars on the taxi's roofs. Finally spotting an empty car, Reece walked out in front of it to block its path.

The driver stopped and he quickly climbed inside. "Brooklyn, Best Buy on Belt Parkway," Reece said, in his best Eastern European accent, uncertain whether his mimicry even matched his preposterous disguise.

The ordinarily bad Manhattan traffic turned to near-instant gridlock as news of the explosion spread across the borough. The rumor mill came alive with speculation, half-truths, and blatant lies, panic spreading like a wildfire in a gale. What should have been a short drive turned into a painful crawl. The driver, who appeared to be from somewhere in central Africa, turned up the local news station to listen to the breaking story. Reece braced for a description of the bomber and lowered his head as if in prayer. It struck him that now wouldn't be a terrible time to ask the man upstairs for help. *Please, God, all I've ever asked of you was to watch over my family. Let me avenge their deaths.*

Initial eyewitness accounts indicated the perpetrator was a male of Middle Eastern descent. The tall American of Scandinavian ancestry, dressed as a Jew from Eastern Europe, had to chuckle at the description. *Maybe Hartley has a point about our xenophobia after all.*

As they crossed into Brooklyn, Reece reached into the pocket of his jeans for the last of his throwaway cell phones. It was a flip phone, without the benefit of a full keyboard, so it took him longer than normal to type out the text message:

pick me up at mom's in 30

Darkness came early this time of year and so by the time the taxi made its way into the shopping area near Coney Island, night had fallen. Reece paid the hefty cab fare in cash, leaving a 20 percent tip, enough not to be remembered as a guy who stiffed the driver, but not generous enough to stand out. It would probably be too late by the time anyone tracked down the driver, but there was no use taking unnecessary chances. The other side could always get lucky. He climbed out of the cab into the chilly night air; the temperature had dropped into the high forties and it was starting to rain. *Perfect.* Reece stood for a moment and pretended to use his cell phone as the cab sped away in search of his next fare.

Reece walked south, past a hotel, a wholesale club, and a Mercedes dealership. As he passed through a relatively dark area between the lights of two businesses, he took the ill-fitting hat from his head and flung it like a Frisbee off into the weeds. He retrieved a battered ball cap from one of his old platoons out of his pack and pulled it on low and tight. The insignia would be meaningless to all but a few people, most of whom were dead. *See you soon, boys.*

Reece turned right on Bay Forty-First Street and headed toward the water. Airports and train stations were full of cops, surveillance cameras, and sophisticated software to track the comings and goings of passengers. Marinas, however, were what Churchill would have called the "soft underbelly" of transit, with minimal if any security or surveillance. The Marine Basin Marina was scheduled to close at 5:00 p.m. and the employees were too engrossed in their closing rituals to notice a solitary figure walk through the gate in the rainy darkness. Reece could see the running lights of his exfil ride floating just off the end of the marina's long pier. The boat, expertly driven, pulled close as he approached, the driver controlling the throttles to keep the vessel from smashing into the concrete pilings in the choppy waters. Reece walked off the end of the pier and landed on the deck with well-practiced grace. The driver seemed to take no notice as he accelerated the boat away from the shoreline.

"Thanks for the ride, Raife," Reece said as he approached the driver at the helm.

"Don't mention it, eh?" Raife Hastings replied without taking his eyes off the water. He spoke with a slight accent that most would assume to be South African. Reece knew better.

CHAPTER 70

Fishers Island, New York

The 38-foot Protector Tauranga bobbed in the dark waters of Fishers Island Sound, between Fishers Island, New York, and Ram Island, Connecticut. Located at the eastern tip of Long Island Sound, Fishers Island had long been associated with the military as a base for naval forces up to and through World War II. These days it was the lesser-known cousin to the Hamptons, though at only nine miles long and one mile wide, it was arguably more exclusive. Once a guardian to the waters of the northeastern United States, it was now an escape for the ultrarich, with two private clubs and one of the most sought after rounds of golf on earth. With less than 250 year-round residents, it was the perfect escape for the country's most discerning families. In late October few lights burned in the homes spaced generously along the shoreline. Reece had his thermal imager focused on one in particular.

They had timed it for a slack tide, as currents were exceptionally strong here. There was very little maritime traffic tonight due to the wind and weather, which both continued to build, but the triple 350-horsepower outboard motors of the Protector had no trouble holding station in the rough seas. Originally built for the New Zealand Coast Guard, its ridged fiberglass hull and surrounding inflatable chambered Hypalon tubes made it strikingly similar to the RIBs that SEALs had used in maritime operations for most of Reece's time in the Navy, though this one was built with luxury, not effectiveness in war, as its guiding design principle. Rain pelted down around them, but neither man seemed to care. *Good operating weather.*

Raife manned the helm. He had been quiet most of the trip. At two inches taller than Reece's six feet but with shoulders to match, he looked like an MMA fighter trapped in a cowboy's body who somehow found himself captaining a ship at sea. Wisps of dirty-blond hair snuck from beneath a black watch-cap-style beanie and betrayed the fact that this guy did not spend much time in a boardroom. The scar that ran from the corner of his left eye and ended just shy of his upper lip gave his rugged features a menacing look. Even though it was dark, his green eyes pierced the night like a nocturnal predator.

"Okay. I've seen what I needed to," said Reece, lowering his thermal. "Take me around to windward. I don't want to come right in on them. They probably expect that coming from a Frogman."

Raife nodded but didn't say a word. He pushed the throttle forward and the agile boat sprang to life, easily handling the choppy waves and turbulent weather for which it was engineered. Deftly piloting around the eastern tip of the island, he slowed his advance and maneuvered the Protector west. Anyone looking from shore would think he was just one more rich yachtsman who didn't check the weather and had bitten off more than he could chew, now making his way back home to Long Island in his expensive toy, choosing to avoid the notoriously hard-to-navigate shallow rocks of the Sound, termed "the Clumps."

"This is good," Reece told his larger companion. "Just over a mile offshore."

Katie had accessed her work database and spent hours sifting through public and private records of the Hartleys, attempting to piece together the SECDEF's most probable location. There had to be a place off the books where she would hole up. Then Katie found it. Hidden deep within the convoluted financials of the Hartley Family Foundation was a write-off for a Foundation Planning Office. The address was a post office box in New York but a phone number listed on one of the mandatory 501(c)(3) forms had a Connecticut prefix. Katie narrowed her search to counties bordering Connecticut and cross-referenced those with geo-data location information embedded in the newer digital photos taken of the couple over the last three years. Matching that data, Katie found what she was looking for. She passed the information to Reece via Signal and wished him luck.

Tracking down Steve Horn had not proven to be the most difficult of tasks. What tipped the scales toward the nautical utopia of northern New York came from Liz, who had activated her contacts in the aviation community. A day after the mission to kill Reece in New Hampshire had ended in a dry hole, a Gulfstream IV owned by Capstone Capital landed at Francis S. Gabreski Airport in Westhampton Beach, New York, where it remained with its pilots on standby. Utilizing her knowledge and associates in the industry, Liz had discovered that Horn had chartered a Eurocopter AS350 helicopter to make the thirty-seven-nautical-mile flight from Westhampton to Fishers that same day, as the airfield on the island was not nearly long enough to accommodate something the size of a Gulfstream. All signs pointed to Fishers.

Raife watched his former Teammate adjust the last of his gear he had liberated from his cage back in Coronado. Reece was dressed in a black wetsuit. The areas of his face and neck not covered by his beard were painted a pattern of black and dark green, and a Draeger LAR V rebreather was strapped to the front of his chest.

His M4 was secured inside a shoot-through waterproof bag to ensure that it would work when he got to shore. A waterproof backpack with a valve for ballast held his web gear and other over-the-beach mission essentials. Attached to his weight belt was an "attack board." This neutrally buoyant plastic rectangle about the size of a small laptop was built around the bubble of an exceptionally tough compass. It also held a G-Shock watch set to the stopwatch feature, along with a depth gauge, all illuminated by a tiny chemlite wrapped in black rigger's tape so that only a sliver of light escaped. These tools would allow him to navigate to his target undetected.

His gear ready, Reece stood, faced his friend, and extended his hand. Raife paused but clasped it in a firm grip. "Thank you," Reece said over the roar of the downpour, more sincerely than he'd ever said anything in his life.

"What you need has been put in place. It's confirmed."

"Thank you," Reece said yet again.

"I *owed* you," Raife said, clearly stressing the past tense of the word.

Reece managed a slight smile, then moved to the leeward edge of the Protector's inflatable sponson, pulled his mask over his darkened face, inserted his mouthpiece, and initiated the prebreathing sequence to purge his body of carbon dioxide before beginning his insertion on the pure oxygen rebreathing system. After a few minutes of breathing through the system on the surface he was ready to go.

"Hey, Reece? This evens us up," Raife said firmly.

Reece nodded and slipped into the dark waters of the Atlantic.

CHAPTER 71

J. D. and Lorraine Hartley had rented the Fishers Island home for the past fifteen years through a shell corporation attached to their family foundation. It afforded them both the anonymity they sometimes required as well as a healthy write-off for tax purposes. It sat just off a beautiful beach facing New London, Connecticut. Nothing like living the good life to help the world's downtrodden. Though not nearly as opulent as homes belonging to families with names like Rockefeller and Du Pont, it was not quite a shack, either. Despite their picturesque location, the Hartleys had been eyeing an estate on the east end of the island, closer to the golf course.

A rock stairway built into the cliff led to a perfectly manicured lawn above which a New England–style home straight out of a Currier & Ives print sat surveying its domain. J.D. had spent considerably more time there over the years since his untimely departure from politics. He found it was the perfect place to conceal his philandering ways from the watchful eyes of the paparazzi, not to mention his wife, who had proven much more adept at the political game than her ne'er-do-well husband.

Tonight that ne'er-do-well husband was missing

from the picture of classic east coast perfection. His body was confirmed to have been the one inside an armored Chevrolet Suburban outside the SoHo apartment of a blonde less than half his age. It took a few hours to confirm the identity of the congressman, due to the fact that there was not much left of him after he was eviscerated by a slug of molten copper that turned his armored car and his body into an inferno of melted steel, glass, flesh, and bone.

"How the fuck did that bastard find him?" Lorraine Hartley asked as much to herself as to the well-dressed Steve Horn next to her. She had enough trouble tracking down her husband. That Reece was able to do it with apparent ease made her even angrier. She noted the calm, composed demeanor of the man next to her. He was beginning to annoy her with how, even in their current predicament, he still maintained an element of style and poise.

Steve Horn swirled the Rémy Martin Louis XIII cognac in his crystal snifter, leaned back in the massive leather chair, and looked into the smoldering embers of the fire in the great stone fireplace before him, noticing that the secretary of defense seemed much more concerned with how Reece found her husband than she was with the fact that he was now dead. He chose his words carefully before responding.

"Listen to me, Lorraine," he began, sounding

almost condescending. "This entire venture has no doubt taken a turn for the worse. I made my money being strong when others were weak, looking for opportunity in the chaos. In this case, Madame Secretary, we have an opportunity, an opportunity to make even more money than before."

Lorraine Hartley couldn't believe what he was saying. Even at a time like this, he still thought about how to maximize profits.

"While Commander Reece has been running around killing everyone like a madman, he has also been stacking the deck in our favor and playing right into our hands. With Boykin, Holder, Saul, Howard, Pilsner, and now your husband, God rest his soul, out of the way, we stand to make a significantly greater sum of money, not to mention there are far fewer loose lips. With your capital still intact and with you the seemingly obvious choice to win your party's nomination for the presidency, you will be able to push FDA approvals for the vital drugs needed to inoculate our servicemen from the ravages of PTSD before they go into combat. Think, Lorraine, who better to push for this initiative than a female president whose very husband was murdered by a veteran suffering the effects of PTSD? Also, thanks to Commander Reece, you will be able to greatly expand the powers of the executive branch and pass the Domestic Security Act. We get richer and more powerful, and the country gets safer. *And we can all live without fear,*" he added for effect.

"Steve, you don't get it, do you? He is going to kill us all."

"Nonsense." He could see she was coming unglued. He could not have that in a commander in chief he planned to control. It was unbecoming.

"Do I need to remind you what he's done so far, Steve?" she said, almost on the verge of hysteria. "He cut off that Muslim cleric's head. He left it on a spike outside the mosque! He gutted poor Howard! My people tell me he was eaten alive!"

"Madam Secretary, I want you to listen very carefully to what I am about to tell you. What happens here tonight, perhaps tomorrow, perhaps the next, will catapult you into the White House."

Hartley looked at him incredulously. *Has he lost his mind?*

"We are not safe here, Madame Secretary. At some point very soon, that maniac Reece will make an attempt to kill us, which is exactly what we want. Our trap is set. It is time we finished this."

"You said my house here *would* be safe," she stated meekly.

"I had to get you here, Lorraine. It is nearly impossible to hide everything in today's age of information. Someone who knows how to dig will find it, and in this case," he said, pausing, "someone did."

CHAPTER 72

Reece's scan via both thermal and night vision from the Protector had yielded nothing out of the ordinary. Maybe they weren't there? Maybe he had missed his shot. Another headache had hit him on the way in, though this one was not nearly as severe as the one that almost crippled him in the mosque. He never knew which headache might be his last. Not knowing the speed with which his tumor was growing made it even more imperative that he finish the names on his list before joining his wife and daughter. The insertion via LAR V, a classic Frogman combat swimmer operation, allowed him to avoid the thermals and night vision of any security detail.

Ending up under the long-abandoned dock attached to a part of Fishers Island still owned by the Navy and occasionally used to monitor submarine activity off the coast, Reece used a pylon to conceal his combat peek, slowly scanning the beach, cliffs, stairs, and high ground of the long-defunct outpost. Conspiracy theories had swirled around the island for years that the prohibited area was operating some sort of biological weapons development lab, akin to the rumors surrounding Plum Island, to the south. Reece hoped tonight that the speculations were just that, rumors.

Reece unhooked his Draeger, flooded it, and let it sink away. Then he attached his fins to his weight belt and dropped them to the ocean floor before working his way under the dock to the rocky shore. He was committed. The rain and wind masked any noise he made removing his M4 from its waterproof bag and quickly transitioned out of his wetsuit and into his AOR2 woodland-patterned camouflage combat pants and shirt. He slipped his magazine carrier over his head and attached his pistol belt to his waist. Then, donning his bump helmet with NODs, he scanned ahead and moved toward the stairs.

At the top of the steps, Reece turned and headed northeast, coming to a kneel in a small clearing to listen and observe. The weather played to his advantage tonight, masking his movement and keeping civilized people indoors, where it was dry and warm. Reece studied the GPS he always kept on the stock of his M4, bringing back memories of the last time he had checked it, just prior to the ambush in Afghanistan. It would all be over soon.

Moving as if guided by the souls of those warriors who could not exact vengeance themselves, Reece pushed through the thick woods of the island paradise, past red oaks, American beech, and red maples, aided by the howling wind and pelting rain. It was a good night for a reckoning.

Sticking to the wood line, Reece skirted the meadows and ponds, giving the large homes he encountered a wide berth even though they were essentially abandoned at this time of year. Unencumbered by the usual weight of his body armor, he worked his way swiftly and silently toward his target. The thick shrubs and grasses, soft earth, and decaying logs through which he now moved reminded him more of Central America than what he had assumed he would find off the coast of New York. He would have loved to explore wilderness like this with his children, had they not been murdered by those he now hunted.

Arriving at what overseas he would have termed his "set point," Reece stopped again just back from the tree line, looking out at his target building. The rain combined with the humidity created by his body during his patrol from the Atlantic side of the island caused his NODs to fog up with irritating regularity, though it certainly was better than not having them at all. Reece settled into a comfortable position and observed his objective.

Finally he saw them, sitting out of the rain in the dry warmth of the idling SUV, with a commanding view of the water just to the side of the opulent home's driveway. The four men, who were undoubtedly supposed to be out in the elements patrolling the perimeter, were sitting in the Chevy Tahoe texting away to fight the boredom. Apparently they didn't think it was possible for him to get there this quickly, which explained the absence of a rear security element. Through his NODs he could see their faces illuminated by the light of their smartphones; all of them not only distracted from their jobs by the lure of the digital world, but their night vision ruined by the LCD screens. They undoubtedly had access to NODs, but none appeared to be wearing them.

Odd. The same senses that had kept him and his men alive on the front lines of the war on terror until that last deployment were now telling him something was wrong. *Last time you didn't listen to that voice you got your entire element killed, Reece. Last time I cared about keeping my men alive. Now it is just me, and I am already dead.*

Patience, Reece. No need to rush to your death. Make it count and finish the job. Keep scanning.

That's when he spotted the sniper.

CHAPTER 73

To the south, fifty yards off the main home, sat a quintessential guest cottage built in the same style as its larger companion. A flicker of light, perhaps from a headlamp or cigarette lighter, illuminated a window and then went out. Sometimes that's all it takes in this game.

It was a good position, an urban hide site, out of the elements, in control of the high ground with a commanding view of the water, dock, and beach below. The goons in the Tahoe were bait. The sniper was there to finish him. Their mistake had been assuming Reece would come directly from the sea; that, and not posting rear security.

Reece crept farther back into the wood line and worked his way into the dead space behind the cottage, stopping once again to look and listen for anything out of the ordinary. Satisfied that he had the critical element of surprise in his favor, he moved smoothly from tree to tree until he was standing at the entrance to the cottage, M4 at the ready. The door was unlocked and Reece slowly pushed it to the side.

"Hey, Tim, you're suppose to radio in before coming over!" the sniper said angrily, turning from his seated position at a table, set up the same way a bench-rest shooter would in competition. He was situated in the back of the small living area, furniture pushed to the side to give the gunman an unobscured view and clear bullet path down to the low ground. Reece's M4 spat once, the suppressor muffling the sound to an almost inaudible level, with the howling wind as a backdrop. The bullet impacted his would-be killer's head with a wet thwack, throwing brains and tissue over what Reece recognized as an Accuracy International .338 Lapua topped with a Schmidt & Bender scope. *Nice rifle.*

Reece approached the contorted body and, slinging his carbine, found the man's radio and headset, listened for a moment for any incoming radio traffic, and then attached it to his web gear before moving back into the storm.

One more group of contractors to deal with. To Reece it mattered little that they undoubtedly had wives, children, girlfriends, or parents waiting for them at home. To him they were mere targets, obstacles blocking him from his ultimate objective. To that end they were going down. When you lived this life, that was part of the contract. Don't let it be a surprise when the reaper comes to call.

Reaching into his pack, Reece readied the demolition charge, the last of his armory acquisitions from back in Coronado. It seemed like years ago that he had started preparing for this evening's mission, though in a way he had been preparing for it his entire life. Starting the timer on the MK147 time-delay firing device, Reece set it for a ten-minute countdown. He crawled on his hands and knees to the rear of the SUV and slid the demo as far forward as he could reach. Then, retreating from the vehicle, he set his sights on the mansion.

CHAPTER 74

Steve Horn was on his third brandy when he felt, rather than saw, the figure emerge from the shadows. Though he knew it was a possibility, he couldn't quite fathom how Reece had made it past the contractors; they were supposed to be the toughest mercenaries available. Even with one last fail-safe contingency plan still in place to kill the Navy commando, Horn was surprised by the fear the dark man in NODs appearing from nowhere instilled in him.

"Commander Reece!" Horn said in a louder voice than necessary, in an attempt to bolster his confidence and composure.

Lorraine Hartley jumped in her seat at Horn's abrupt shout.

Reece moved slowly into the room, lifting his NODs back on his helmet. His dark beard, face paint, and gear dripping rainwater only added to his intimidating appearance.

In front of the fire, sitting with Lorraine Hartley and Steve Horn, a brandy in one hand and what appeared to be a small box in the other, was Ben Edwards. Reece had expected all three. What he didn't expect was the fourth person; kneeling on the rug next to Ben, hands bound behind her back, a bandana running between her teeth and tied around her head, face battered and hair a mess, was Katie Buranek.

"You son of a bitch!" Reece hissed, raising the M4.

"Ah . . ." Ben said, holding up and shaking the box in his hand.

In response to Reece's questioning look, Ben brushed Katie's hair back with the hand holding his snifter, revealing multiple strands of what looked to be thin yellow rope wrapped around her neck.

"Yeah, that's det cord, buddy, and yes, this is a detonator," he said, shaking the box once more. "You don't have these little toys in the Teams yet, bro. In case you were wondering, my thumb has depressed the button here. As soon as it comes off, pop! Off comes Katie's head."

Reece kept his weapon trained on Ben but had a healthy eye on the SECDEF and Horn.

"You don't look surprised to see me, bro."

"I couldn't believe it when I finally put it together, Ben. I had my suspicions but the assault force at your cabin confirmed it. You were the only one who knew I was going there."

"Yeah, I figured that would cue you in. Mistake on my part. It did allow you to almost finish your list, though, which helped us out immensely, by the way. I still can't believe you had those guys in a textbook ambush and let them live. Getting soft, buddy."

"How could you be involved in this, Ben? How could you be a part of killing Lauren and Lucy?"

"Shit, bro, I didn't do that. By the time I was brought in, those decisions were made. The SECDEF here just wanted me to see what you knew about the tumors. I had no idea they were going to kill your family. Once they did, there was no turning back the clock. I'm sorry how it went down, bro, but this is bigger than you or me."

"So you kept it from me and then used me to kill off everyone who knew about the experiments. SECDEF gets elected, the Domestic Safety Act gets passed, and you all make your fortunes from RD4895."

"Everybody has a price, bro. Apparently mine has ten figures."

Reece stared at his best friend in a disgusted rage.

"That's why you never gave me any location information on this guy?" Reece asked gesturing toward Horn. "You needed him to keep this plan moving forward. You needed him in place for your payday?"

"You were always the smart one, Reece. And yeah, that was why you weren't killed at the condo. You were being so efficient tying up our loose ends while at the same time increasing our share of the profits that the logical business decision was to allow you to keep at it, up until now that is. I was actually nervous you would put it together quicker than you did. Those emotions got you, bro. Kept you from seeing the whole picture."

"And J. D. Hartley?" Reece asked, looking at the SECDEF.

Not able to even form a sentence, Lorraine Hartley looked in loathing at Steve Horn.

"Don't act surprised, Lorraine," Horn said in partial dismissal. "His death helps propel you into the White House with the sympathy vote. You haven't spent the night in the same house in years. He was a liability to your campaign as it was. Don't pretend like you are going to miss him."

"You concocted a plan to let Reece keep killing our business partners and didn't inform me?" the SECDEF asked Horn in shock.

"As much as I'd like to take credit for that part of the plan, I can't. It was all Ben's idea. Following your jihadi's failure to take him out on the streets of L.A., Ben went a bit further off the reservation and devised a plan that allowed Reece to continue his crusade, making us all richer in the process. When he finally read me in after Reece killed Holder, Tedesco, and Pilsner, I thought it was genius. Can't believe I didn't think of it myself."

Secretary Hartley shook her head in disbelief as Horn continued: "Ben's actually a lot smarter than he looks. Don't be fooled by the tattoos. He's been right about a lot of things, including the fact that Reece would make it past my contractors and into this very room; hence our insurance policy tied up on the floor there," he said, pointing at Katie. "Your friend had more faith in your skills than I did, Mr. Reece; well founded, it now seems."

"Here's what's going to happen, bro," Ben said. "Horn is going to make us all very rich. Almost everyone else who stood to profit from this is dead, thanks to you. Yeah, you will have to do a little time, but the SECDEF will pardon you with her newfound presidential powers, blaming your actions on the ravages of PTSD. I am going to disappear, never to be heard from again, and you and Katie can live happily ever after. Maybe they can even operate on that tumor of yours and save your life?"

Ben looked at Katie, her eyes wide with a mixture of revulsion and horror. "Oh, and Katie is just here to ensure you make the right decision. I'm sorry about your family, Reece, I really am. Nothing can bring them back now. Let's all do the smart thing. The pardon is a gift. Katie's life is a gift. *Don't* fuck this up, bro."

Reece looked at Katie, then back to Ben, his eyes the picture of resolve.

Horn broke the silence with a loud, slow clap, pulling himself out of his chair to take a more domineering position above the other conspirators.

"Ben, that was a lovely breakdown of the plan. Thank you, but I've had a change of heart. I am modifying the terms of the deal. Our negotiating power has shifted. Let's clean this mess up right now, shall we?"

"What do you mean, Horn?" asked Ben skeptically.

"Tonight, Commander," Horn said, turning his attention to Reece as if presenting an investment opportunity to a client, "you get to actually save a life instead of taking one. You get to save Katie. You get to save her by dying."

Reece hadn't dropped the M4, but he did shift it toward Horn, the SECDEF tensing up as the barrel passed across her face.

"Come on, Reece," Horn said in an almost bored, exasperated tone. "You are not leaving here alive. You are half-dead now from that tumor, if I understand correctly. If you kill any of us, Ben lets go of that button, and you kill the one friend you have left, who seems to be quite fond of you, by the way. Shoot yourself or let us shoot you, it matters not either way. Point being, you keep Katie alive, and we all move on with our liv—"

Horn never finished his sentence. The explosion from the charge in the driveway split the SUV in half, turning the Capstone Security men into human mulch. The blast shattered the multitude of windows on the mansion's front and sent a shockwave through every room.

Reece's first bullet caught Horn between his nose and mouth, forever leaving him with a look of surprise on what was left of his face. He was dead before he hit the ground.

"Nooo!" screamed the SECDEF, crawling up onto her chair, covering her ears with her hands. Reece's next two rounds found their way into her upper chest. A third to her head completed the job.

Reece settled back on Ben.

"What the *fuck,* Reece?" exclaimed Ben in amazement, holding up the detonator. "What the . . . ?"

Reece's M4 finished the night's deadly business, firing two 77-grain Black Hills 5.56 rounds at 2,340 feet per second directly into Ben Edwards's face at ten feet. His head snapped back, empting its contents onto the chair behind him, and his hand came off the button.

Katie screamed through the bandana that stifled her cries, but surprisingly her head stayed intact. Reece stepped forward and fired two more rounds into Ben's face, then slung his weapon and knelt down to help Katie.

He cut the bandana off her head before slicing the zip tie that held her hands behind her back. Falling forward into him, Katie sobbed uncontrollably.

"It's all right, Katie, it's all right," Reece repeated, stroking her hair and holding her tight to him.

"We have to go, Katie. We don't have much time, we have to go. Can you walk?" he asked, helping her to her feet and replacing his magazine with a fresh one from his chest rig.

"Yes, I can walk."

"Okay, follow me."

Reece led Katie outside, finding the shed he had identified on satellite imagery. Next to the shed was an old seventeen-foot Boston Whaler Montauk on a trailer. Gas cans were set between the boat and the shed. Reece picked up the first one. Empty. Then he picked up the second one and shook it. Plenty of gas. He handed it to Katie and picked up another. Full.

"Follow me," Reece ordered again, already moving back to the house.

"Pour that gas around the room, furniture, drapes, anything that will burn." Katie did as requested. It felt good to take action against these monsters who had grabbed her in the dead of night from her brother's home.

Reece doused the bodies with gas and then told Katie to run to the door. Looking down at the symbol on his father's old Zippo, Reece slid his thumb over the striker, grinding sparks off the flint and igniting the fuel to produce a flame. Tossing it onto Ben Edwards's body, Reece followed close behind.

It was still raining when they hit the street, the summer home beginning to flame up behind them and the SUV smoldering in the driveway.

"Airfield is four miles west. Can you run that far?"

"Yes, but why don't we take this?" Katie asked, pointing to an exquisitely restored 1973 two-tone forest green and alpine white Toyota FJ55 Land Cruiser parked next to the shed. Residents of Fishers Island loved their classic cars.

Reece couldn't suppress his grin, then looked back at the flaming house.

"I think I just melted the keys."

Katie smiled, opened the driver's-side door, and pulled a set from the ignition.

"It's a Fishers Island thing," she said.

"Well, that's working smarter. Let's go."

Reece took the wheel, and Katie squeezed in beside him. They were on the road before the volunteer fire department had their boots on.

CHAPTER 75

Reece looked at the luminous dials on his watch. Liz would be landing in six minutes. This was cutting it close. Her instructions were to wait for thirty minutes and then take off. If he didn't show up, she was to assume he was dead.

By the time they made the four-mile drive, Liz had already taxied to the north end of the runway, spun the plane around, and began readying for take off. Reece ditched the truck and moved Katie to the waiting aircraft. The door folded downward.

"Who is this?" Liz shouted from the cabin door, past the hot exhaust of the outtake.

"Liz, this is Katie. Katie, Liz."

"Well, get in and let's get out of here," Liz shot back.

"I'm not coming, Liz. I'm taking the secondary extraction. This is going to be a mess. I am not bringing you two down with me."

"Get in the fucking plane, James," Liz ordered impatiently.

Reece ignored her and turned to Katie.

"Take this," he said, pressing a minicassette recorder and thumb drive into her hand. "These are the only copies. Everything those bastards said in there is on the cassette, along with some other admissions from Saul Agnon. The thumb drive has all the emails and intel that Ben gave me to help back things up. That should keep you busy for a while. Somebody has to set the record straight for my men and my family. You might even get another journalism award out of it." He smiled.

"Where are you going, James?" Katie asked with tears beginning to stream from her eyes.

"I'm going to die, Katie. They killed me before I even left on that last deployment to Afghanistan. They killed all my guys before we even left. It's my turn now."

He ushered her up the steps. She was too shocked to say anything. Liz just glared at him with eyes that shot fire.

"Get in the plane, James?" she tried again.

"I love you, Liz, now get out of here."

As Reece stepped back to close the door, Katie turned sharply in her seat, snapping out of her trance.

"Reece, how did you know Ben didn't have that detonator connected? How did you know he wouldn't blow my head off?"

Reece paused, looked Katie in the eye, and over the sound of the wind, the propeller, and the rain, replied, "I didn't," before shutting the door and moving off at a run toward the marina.

EPILOGUE

Atlantic Ocean
Present Day

Reece awoke below deck, the sound of the Beneteau Oceanis 48 cutting through the water and the flapping of the sails waking him from his thirty-minute catnap. After throwing his feet out of his bunk he made his way topside and into the light. The storm that had kept him busy for the first three days after departing Fishers Island had subsided, leaving beautiful rolling seas and steady winds.

Raife's sister Victoria had sailed the Beneteau from their Martha's Vineyard home down to Fishers Island the day before Reece's assault, removing all the electronics per Reece's request. He had also instructed Raife to report it stolen, but somehow doubted he would. That Victoria could handle the massive forty-eight-foot sailboat on her own spoke volumes about her competence and seamanship; Reece was struggling to just keep the boat headed in the right direction. He had sailed as a kid, though nothing this large and complex. Luckily, the Navy had seen fit to send him to a civilian sailing school years ago. The idea was that he would have the ability to rent sailboats around the world and use them to conduct surveillance or to blend in with local maritime traffic and insert SEALs into denied areas. He didn't know how much longer he had to live. He doubted if he would make it to Europe or Africa before the tumor killed him. He was at peace and he was ready to leave the world behind. He thought about Lucy and cried for her, for the life she would never have, and he thought about Lauren and the second child they would never bring into the world. He was ready to join them.

One beautiful sunset turned into another stunning sunrise, and Reece continued to sail. Victoria had seen to it that the boat was filled with provisions for a long voyage: water, food, and medical supplies. What would he do if he were still alive when he reached the Old World or the Dark Continent? Turn south and continue sailing until the tumor took him? Maybe he would go for a swim and never surface? Maybe that would deliver him to Lauren and Lucy? He knew he wasn't long for this world, so he might as well continue sailing until the sea or the tumor decided it was his time. Either way, his work on earth was done.

Sitting on deck at the starboard helm steering station, the storm a distant memory, and with the blaze orange sun setting behind him to the west, Reece reached into his pocket and removed a Ziploc bag. Pausing, he slowly opened it and unfolded the paper within, drawing lines through the last of the names on his list.

~~Josh Holder~~
~~Marcus Boykin~~
~~Saul Agnon~~
~~Steve Horn~~
~~CJNG, Mexico~~
~~Admiral Gerald Pilsner~~
~~Mike Tedesco~~
~~J. D. Hartley~~
~~Lorraine Hartley~~
~~Leonard Howard~~
~~Hammadi Izmail Masood~~
~~Ben Edwards~~

He looked at the list without a hint of remorse. It was done.

Then, hesitating briefly, he turned it over and smiled, running his fingers over the crayon drawings of his beautiful wife and daughter under an arching rainbow, the perfect splendor of which only the young and innocent can capture. His eyes glistened over, and a tear fell onto his most treasured possession.

"I'm coming, baby girl," Reece whispered, rubbing his eyes. "I'll be with you soon. I love you."

With that, he moved to the stern and, watching

the sun drop below the horizon, he touched the paper to his heart and let it fall from his grasp, committing it forever to the peace and tranquility of the sea.

FBI Headquarters
Washington, D.C.

In the days following the revelation that Secretary of Defense Hartley and financier Steve Horn had been found shot to death and incinerated along with an unidentified body in a Fishers Island mansion, on the heels of Congressman J. D. Hartley's targeted assassination in SoHo, the conspiracy theorists went into overdrive, cluttering the Internet and airways with one explanation after another.

Congress appointed a special prosecutor to investigate and make sense of the mess because so many government officials were involved, all of them dead thanks to one Lieutenant Commander James Reece, current whereabouts unknown.

Things really got interesting when investigative journalist Katie Buranek published the first in a series of scathing stories exposing a conspiracy involving illegal testing of drugs on the nation's most elite special operators, the sharing of top-secret NSA-gathered intelligence information with certain individuals in the financial industry to assist in the assassination of innocent civilians, and a program of intentional radicalization of jihadi assets by elements of the U.S. government for domestic terrorist operations, leading all the way to the SECDEF herself. Ms. Buranek was uncooperative in assisting investigators to unravel the story, instead telling them to wait for her next exposé.

Among the piles of evidence collected by the special prosecutor was a cell phone belonging to James Reece of Coronado, California. Having not been used in the preceding weeks that Reece was on the move, it sat untouched on the dresser of his California home until it was subsequently collected by investigators.

Later, after it had been tagged, exploited, and stored into evidence, a call had come in and gone to voice mail.

Head and Spine Associates
La Jolla, California

"Um, hello, Mr. Reece, this is Dr. German. We've been trying to get in touch with you. We usually don't leave messages like this, but I wanted you to hear this as soon as possible. Your biopsy came back and, under the circumstances, it is the best news that we could expect. Your tumor is what's called a cerebral convexity meningioma, which is a very common and slow-growing lesion. Based on the type and location of the mass, I am very confident that I can remove it surgically. We are talking a seventy-five percent or better survival rate. It could be causing you headaches, which is nothing to be alarmed about. Please call us back and my assistant will schedule you an appointment for a follow-up. We can speak in more detail at my office. Again, sorry to have to leave this on your voice mail, but I didn't want you to worry needlessly. Have a great day, and enjoy your new lease on life, Commander."

GLOSSARY OF TERMS

AC-130 SPECTRE: A ground support aircraft used by the U.S. military, based on the C-130 cargo plane. AC-130s are armed with a 105mm howitzer, 40mm cannons, and 7.62mm miniguns, and are considered the premier close air support weapon of the U.S. arsenal.

Accuracy International: A British company producing high-quality precision rifles, often used for military sniper applications.

ACOG: Advanced Combat Optical Gunsight. A magnified optical sight designed for use on rifles and carbines made by Trijicon. The ACOG is popular among U.S. forces as it provides both magnification and an illuminated reticle that provides aiming points for various target ranges.

AQ: Al-Qaeda. Meaning "the Base" in Arabic. A radical Islamic terrorist organization once led by Osama bin Laden.

AQI: Al-Qaeda in Iraq. An Al-Qaeda-affiliated Sunni insurgent group that was active against U.S. forces. Elements of AQI eventually evolved into ISIS.

AT-4: Tube-launched 84mm anti-armor rocket produced in Sweden and used by U.S. forces since the 1980s. The AT-4 is a throwaway weapon: after it is fired, the tube is discarded.

ATF/BATFE: Bureau of Alcohol, Tobacco, Firearms and Explosives. A federal law enforcement agency, formally part of the Department of the Treasury, which doesn't seem overly concerned with alcohol or tobacco.

ATPIAL: Advanced Target Pointer/Illuminator Aiming Laser. A weapon-mounted device that emits both visible and infrared target designators for use with or without night observation devices. Essentially, an advanced military-grade version of the "laser sights" seen in popular culture.

BDA: Bomb/Battle damage assessment. The practice of assessing damage inflicted on a target from a stand-off weapon, most typically a bomb or air-launched missile.

Benghazi: A city in the North African nation of Libya and the site of the 2012 attack on the U.S. consulate. The U.S. ambassador to Libya, a Foreign Service Information Management Officer, and two CIA Global Response Staff members (both former SEALs) were killed in the attack.

Beretta 92D: A double-action-only 9mm handgun that is a variant of the 92F used by much of the U.S. military. The 92D does not use a manual safety and its bobbed hammer cannot be manually cocked.

Beretta 92F: Double-action 9mm handgun that has been the standard-issue sidearm for the bulk of the U.S. military since 1985, as well as a favorite of action movie propmasters. In 2017, the U.S. Army selected the M17, manufactured by SIG Sauer, to replace the Beretta.

Blind Sheikh: Nickname for Omar Abdel-Rahman, who is currently serving a life prison sentence for his role in the 1993 World Trade Center bombing.

BUD/S: Basic Underwater Demolition/SEAL training. The six-month selection and training course required for entry into the SEAL teams, held in Coronado, California. Widely accepted as among the most brutal military selection courses in the world, with an average 80 percent attrition rate.

C-4: Composition 4. A plastic explosive compound known for its stability and malleability.

C-5: Lockheed Martin "Galaxy" aircraft used as a military transport. The C-5 is one of the largest functional aircraft ever produced.

CH-47: Boeing "Chinook" twin-engine heavy-lift helicopter used by the U.S. Army. Often used in Afghanistan's mountains due to its high service ceiling, the Chinook is a large aircraft that resembles a flying school bus.

CIA: Central Intelligence Agency.

CJSOTF: Combined Joint Special Operations Task Force. A regional command that controls special operations forces from various services and friendly nations.

CRRC: Combat Rubber Raiding Craft. Inflatable

"Zodiac-style" boats used by SEALs and other maritime troops.

CZ-75: 9mm handgun designed in 1975 and produced in the Czech Republic.

Dam Neck: An annex to NAS Oceana near Virginia Beach, Virginia, where nothing interesting, whatsoever, happens.

DCIS: Defense Criminal Investigation Service.

DEA: Drug Enforcement Administration.

Delta Force: A classic 1986 film starring Chuck Norris, title of the 1983 autobiography by the unit's first commanding officer and popular name for the Army's Special █████████████ ████████████████████████████████████ █████████████████

DOD: Department of Defense.

DOJ: Department of Justice.

Echols Legend: A best-quality hunting rifle designed and hand built by gunmaker D'Arcy Echols of Millville, Utah. Considered by many to be the highest-quality sporting rifle ever made.

EFP: Explosively Formed Penetrator/Projectile. A shaped explosive charge that forms a molten projectile used to penetrate armor. Such munitions were widely used by insurgents against coalition forces in Iraq.

EMS: Emergency Medical Services. Fire, paramedic, and other emergency personnel.

EOD: Explosive Ordnance Disposal. The military's explosives experts, who are trained to, among other things, disarm or destroy improvised explosive devices or other munitions.

Eotech: An unmagnified holographic gunsight for use on rifles and carbines, including the M4. The sight is designed for rapid target acquisition, which makes it an excellent choice for close-quarters battle. Can be fitted with a detachable 3x magnifier for use at extended ranges.

FBI: Federal Bureau of Investigation.

FDA: Food and Drug Administration.

FOB: Forward Operating Base. A secured forward military position used to support tactical operations. Can vary from small and remote outposts to sprawling complexes.

Fobbit: A service member serving in a noncombat role who rarely, if ever, leaves the safety of the Forward Operating Base.

Frog Hog: SEAL groupie. Frequently sighted in and around Coronado and Virginia Beach watering holes.

Glock: An Austrian-designed, polymer-framed handgun popular with police forces, militaries, and civilians throughout the world. Glocks are made in various sizes and chambered in several different cartridges.

GPS: Global Positioning System. Satellite-based navigation system that provides a precise location anywhere on earth.

GRG: Gridded Reference Graphic. An annotated

aerial map or photograph with various sectors of areas of interest separated and identified by gridlines.

Hell Week: The crucible of BUD/S training. Five days of constant physical and mental stress with little sleep.

HK416: M4 clone engineered by the German firm of Heckler & Koch to operate using a short-stroke gas pistol system instead of the M4's direct-impingement gas system. Used by select special operations units in the U.S. and abroad. May or may not have been the weapon used to kill ███████████████.

HRT: Hostage Rescue Team. The FBI's elite counterterrorism and hostage rescue force, based out of Quantico, VA.

HUMINT: Human intelligence. Information gleaned through traditional human-to-human methods.

HVI/HVT: High-value individual/High-value target. An individual who is important to the enemy's capabilities and is therefore specifically sought out by a military force.

IED: Improvised explosive device. A homemade bomb, whether crude or complex, often used by insurgent forces overseas.

IR: Infrared. The part of the electromagnetic spectrum with a longer wavelength than light but a shorter wavelength than radio waves. Invisible to the naked eye but visible with night observation devices. Example: an IR laser aiming device.

ISIS: Islamic State of Iraq and the Levant, or Islamic State of Iraq and Syria. Radical Sunni terrorist group. Also referred to as ISIL. The bad guys.

ISR: Intelligence, surveillance, and reconnaissance.

JAG: Judge advocate general. Decent television series and the military's legal department.

JSOC: Joint Special Operations Command. A component command of SOCOM, ██████████ ████████████████████████████████████ ████████████████████████.

Kaffir: An Arabic term used by Muslims to describe a subset of society who have read and rejected the message of the Qur'an; or, a derogatory term for a nonbeliever of Islam.

Langley: The Northern Virginia location where the Central Intelligence Agency is headquartered. Often used as shorthand for CIA.

Law of armed conflict: A segment of public international law that regulates the conduct of armed hostilities.

LAW rocket: M-72 Light Anti-armor Weapon. A disposable, tube-launched 66mm unguided rocket in use with U.S. forces since before the Vietnam War.

M-1911/1911A1: .45-caliber pistol used by U.S. forces since before World War I.

M-203: A 40mm single-shot grenade launcher that can be fit to the underside of the M4 carbine to provide an indirect fire capability.

M4: The standard assault rifle of the majority of U.S. military forces, including the U.S. Navy SEALs. The M4 is a shortened carbine variant of the M16 rifle that fires a 5.56x45mm cartridge. The M4 is a modular design that can be adapted to numerous configurations, including different barrel lengths.

MACV-SOG: Military Assistance Command, Vietnam–Special Operations Group. A joint special operations unit consisting primarily of Army special forces, Navy SEALs, and CIA personnel during the Vietnam War. Many of their missions remain highly classified to this day.

Mahdi Militia: An insurgent Shia militia, loyal to cleric Muqtada al-Sadr, that opposed U.S. forces in Iraq during the height of that conflict.

MBITR: AN/PRC-148 Multiband Inter/Intra Team Radio. A handheld multiband, tactical software-defined radio, commonly used by special operations forces to communicate during operations.

MIL DOT: A reticle-based system used for range estimation and long-range shooting, based on the milliradian unit of measurement.

MK 186: An intelligent two-way radio system designed to initiate explosive devices, including claymore mines.

Mk 23: A massive .45-caliber handgun adopted by SOCOM and produced by Heckler & Koch that epitomizes wasteful bureaucratic spending.

Mk 24 MOD 0: A .45-caliber handgun made by Heckler & Koch, used by SEALs. This handgun is often equipped with a sound suppressor or "silencer."

Mk 48 MOD I: A belt-fed 7.62x51mm light machine gun designed for use by special operations forces. Weighing 18 pounds unloaded, the Mk-48 can fire 730 rounds per minute to an effective range of 800 meters and beyond.

NCIS: Naval Criminal Investigative Service. A federal law enforcement agency whose jurisdiction includes the U.S. Navy and Marine Corps. Also a popular television program with at least two spin-offs.

NOD: Night observation device. Commonly referred to as "night vision goggles," these devices amplify ambient light, allowing the user to see in low-light environments. Special operations forces often operate at night to take full advantage of such technology.

NSW: Naval Special Warfare. The Navy's special operations force, includes SEAL teams.

OH-58D: A now-obsolete helicopter, nicknamed the "Kiowa," used by the U.S. Army for observation, utility, armed reconnaissance, and fire support operations.

OODA Loop: Observe/Orient/Decide/Act. A

decision cycle theory developed by Colonel John Boyd of the U.S. Air Force.

P226: 9mm handgun made by SIG Sauer, the standard-issue sidearm for SEALs.

P229: A compact handgun made by SIG Sauer, often used by federal law enforcement officers, chambered in 9mm as well as other cartridges.

Pakistani Taliban: An Islamic terrorist group comprised of various Sunni Islamist militant groups based in the northwestern Federally Administered Tribal Areas along the Afghan border in Pakistan.

PETN: *PE*ntaerythritol *T*etra*N*itrate. An explosive compound used in blasting caps to initiate larger explosive charges.

PLF: Parachute landing fall. A technique taught to military parachutists to prevent injury when making contact with the earth. Round canopy parachutes used by airborne forces fall at faster velocities than other parachutes and require a specific landing sequence. More often than not ends up as feet-ass-head.

PTSD: Post-traumatic stress disorder. A mental condition that develops in association with shocking or traumatic events. Commonly associated with combat veterans.

PVS-15: Also known as the M953, a purpose-built ground operations binocular night observation device currently issued to members of U.S. Special Operations Command.

PVS-18: A night observation device that can be used as a handheld pocket scope, eye-mounted monocular, or weapon sight when mounted in conjunction with a laser or night-vision-compatible primary optic.

QRF: Quick Reaction Force, a contingency force on standby to assist operations in progress.

RHIB/RIB: Rigid Hull Inflatable Boat/Rigid Inflatable Boat. A lightweight but high-performance boat constructed with a solid fiberglass or composite hull and flexible tubes at the gunwale (sides).

ROE: Rules of engagement. Rules or directives that determine what level of force can be applied against an enemy in a particular situation or area.

SAP: Special Access Program. Security protocols that provide highly classified information with safeguards and access restrictions that exceed those for regular classified information. Really secret stuff.

SCI: Sensitive compartmented information. Classified information concerning or derived from sensitive intelligence sources, methods, or analytical processes. Often found on private basement servers in upstate New York or bathroom closet servers in Denver.

Scouts and Raiders: A joint Army-Navy maritime commando unit created after Pearl Harbor and distinguished through actions in the North African, European, and Pacific Theaters of World

War II. Direct forefathers of today's SEALs.

SEAL: *SE*a *A*ir and *L*and. The three environments in which SEALs operate. The U.S. Navy's special operations force.

SERE: Survival, Evasion, Resistance, Escape. A military training program that includes realistic role-playing as a prisoner of war. SERE students are subjected to highly stressful procedures, sometimes including waterboarding, as part of the course curriculum.

SIGINT: Signals intelligence. Intelligence derived from electronic signals and systems used by foreign targets, such as communications systems, radars, and weapons systems.

SMU: Special Mission Unit. Elite special operations units that fall under the command of JSOC. If we told you any more, we'd have to kill you.

SOCOM: United States Special Operations Command. The Unified Combatant Command charged with overseeing the various Special Operations Component Commands of the U.S. Army, Marine Corps, Navy, and Air Force. Headquartered at MacDill Air Force Base in Tampa, Florida.

Special Reconnaissance Team: NSW teams that conduct special activities, ISR, and provide intelligence support to the SEAL Teams.

SSE: Sensitive site exploitation. A term used to describe collecting information, material, and persons from a designated location and analyzing them to answer information requirements, facilitate subsequent operations, or support criminal prosecution. Basically, grabbing everything that looks important for later use.

S-Vest: Suicide vest. An explosive-packed garment worn on the body that turns a human into a deadly area weapon. A tactic employed frequently by insurgent and terrorist groups.

SWAT: *S*pecial *W*eapons *A*nd *T*actics. Paramilitary law enforcement teams trained and equipped to respond to special incidents. Can vary wildly in terms of capability and effectiveness. Dog owners beware.

Taliban: An Islamic fundamentalist political movement and terrorist group in Afghanistan. U.S. and coalition forces have been at war with members of the Taliban since late 2001.

TDFD: Time Delay Firing Device. An explosive initiator that allows for detonation at a determined period of time. A fancy version of a really long fuse.

TIC: Troops In Contact. A firefight involving U.S. or friendly forces.

TOC: Tactical Operations Center. A command post for military operations. A TOC usually includes a small group of personnel who guide members of an active tactical element during a mission from a secured area.

TOR Network: A computer network designed

to conceal a user's identity and location. TOR allows for anonymous communication.

TS: Top secret. Information the unauthorized disclosure of which reasonably could be expected to cause exceptionally grave damage to national security that the original classification authority is able to identify or describe. Can also describe an individual's level of security clearance.

TST: Time-sensitive target. A target requiring immediate response because it is highly lucrative, a fleeting target of opportunity, or it poses (or will soon pose) a danger to friendly forces.

UAV: Unmanned aerial vehicle. A fancy acronym for drones, which have become the staple of aerial imagery for law enforcement and military surveillance activities both inside the United States and abroad. UAVs can range vastly in both size and capability.

UCMJ: Uniform Code of Military Justice. Disciplinary and criminal code that applies to members of the U.S. military.

VPN: Virtual private network. A private network that enables users to send and receive data across shared or public networks using an encrypted tunnel to increase privacy and security.

WARCOM / NAVSPECWARCOM: United States Naval Special Warfare Command. The U.S. Navy's special operations force and the maritime component of United States Special Operations Command. Headquartered in Coronado, California,

WARCOM is the administrative command for subordinate NSW groups comprising eight SEAL teams, one SEAL Delivery Vehicle (SDV) team, three Special Boat teams, and two Special Reconnaissance teams.

ACKNOWLEDGMENTS

No book can be written in a bubble, and that is certainly the case here. There are many people to thank for helping make this novel a reality, some of whom can be named, and some of whom cannot, because they are still working in the shadows.

First and foremost, this book would still be sitting on my nightstand, or in a folder on my computer, if not for **Brad Thor**. To say I have no words to express how thankful I am for your advice, your counsel, and for taking a risk on me would be an understatement. Brad, thank you for making this lifelong dream come true. You gave me a piece of advice that I will never forget when we first spoke. You said, "the only difference between a published author and an unpublished author is that the published author never quit." You would have made an exceptional Team Guy.

And, to the amazing **Emily Bestler**. It is never good for an author to be at a loss for words, but our every interaction has left me speechless. A better mentor, editor, publisher and friend is not to be found. Thank you for reading the manuscript and seeing its potential. What started over a long coffee in Manhattan that I never wanted to end has turned into the fulfillment of a lifelong dream. Thank you for everything.

The engine of this speeding train is our agent, **Alexandra Machinist**. Your aggressive and energetic spirit is contagious. Thank you for making this such an incredible experience.

To the entire team at **Emily Bestler Books**. Thank you for your support and guidance. A special thank you to **Lara Jones**, for ensuring everything stayed on track, and to our publicist, **David Brown**, for pulling me, albeit reluctantly, into the unfamiliar world of "tweets," "likes," and "friends." Nobody does it better. And, to **Ann Pryor**, a master of marketing, for leading the charge into that uncharted territory.

To **Vince Flynn**, for your leadership in blazing the path for a new generation of thriller writers. A true master of the craft, you live on and continue to influence through your remarkable work. You are missed.

To **Lee Child**, who welcomed me into the club of scribes and made me feel like I belonged before I even finished the novel. Thank you for your encouragement on the title and for your advice. As you can see, I took it.

To **Stephen Hunter**, for crafting a fictional former scout/sniper that has inspired more than a few to seek the Hog's Tooth. Thank you for sharing your gift with the world and for your kindness to me. I eagerly await your next novel.

To **David Morrell**, for creating one of the most iconic characters to ever grace the page and screen, and for being one of the first to mention SEALs in a thriller back in 1984 before many people knew what they were. Thank you for connecting me with ITW and for your sage counsel.

To **Brad Taylor**, for mentoring me through the unique pitfalls associated with the transition from special operations to publishing. Thank you for taking the time to guide me around the land mines.

To **Terry Flynn**, my oldest friend, going back to the preschool playground, who was also the first person to read and review the manuscript—your initial critique made this a better book.

To **Christian Sommer**, for parting with his 1985 Navy SEAL edition of *Gung-Ho* magazine back in the sixth grade. It had quite the influence, and I still treasure it today.

To **Chris and Courtney Cox**, for your example of strength and courage in the face of unimaginable adversity. Your grace and poise under pressure, becoming the very definition of resolve is a lesson to us all.

To **David Lehman**, who read a first copy on a well-deserved vacation in Turks and Caicos while trying to keep the pages from blowing down the beach. I'll have it bound next time.

To **Graham Hill**, for your thoughtful comments and insistence that your law review skills would catch all our poor grammar.

To **Dave Kilcullen**, for your influence on an entire generation of warfighters. Our nation is in your debt.

To **Jeff Rotherham**, for reading the demolition-centric sections of the book and ensuring they were close to the way a terrorist would do it while making sure we left out enough key details to keep this out of the how-to section.

To **Brent Bogart** at **Tradewind Technologies**, for guiding me through the world of covert communications in a way even I could understand. I know it's not perfect, but I didn't want to give away all your secrets.

Thank you to **"Goat,"** for your mentorship during some interesting times in Iraq and for your service to the country.

To **Justin Henderson**, a man of integrity, loyalty, and wisdom beyond his years; thank you—you know what for. Someday I might even write a book about it.

To **Mike Atkinson**, for your continued mentorship and support, and for standing with me when it counted.

To **Wayne Gregory**, for everything you do for our service members. It does not go unnoticed.

To **Katie Pavlich**, for being there when I needed you. I'll never be able to thank you enough.

To **Jason Salata**, for your patience, humor, and support.

To **Lacey Biles**, for your friendship and all you do for freedom.

To **Biss**. Thank you for inviting me to that Reds game and follow-on King Ranch trip. It changed the course of my life.

To **Larry Sheakley** and **Lou Lauch**, for bidding on that auction item, and to Ric Kayne, for inviting me to lunch on your yacht. It turned into so much more.

To **Larry Vickers**, for your friendship, wisdom, unprecedented knowledge of firearms, and service to the nation.

To **Tom Davin**, one of the best business leaders of this generation. Thank you for always having time for me and never making it seem like a burden. You exemplify the warrior-guardian.

To **George Kollitides**, for your energy and enthusiasm in all that you do.

To **Trig French**, for inviting me to **Camp Fire Club of America**. It's an honor to know you.

To **Hoby Darling**, a great leader and a better friend. Thank you for welcoming us into our new home and for your inspiration on the workout front. You are a machine!

To **Andrew Kline**, for not just reading the book but for all you do for my family. I am humbled beyond words. The difference you make in the lives of people you touch is astounding.

To **Darren LaSorte**, for an incredible omelet and unwavering loyalty. I think I'll keep you around.

To **Kevin O'Malley**, **Jimmy Klein**, and **Frank Lecrone**, the best collection of friends a guy could ever have. We have more adventures to come!

To the **Brothers of the Mystic Lodge**, for your unwavering support. A better band of pirates would be impossible to find.

To **Dom Raso**, patriot, founder of **Dynamis Alliance** and the personification of brotherhood.

To **Alec Wolf**, **Andrew Arrabito**, and **John Devine**, for always being there.

To **Eric Frohardt** and **Jeff Houston**, warriors.

To **Sean Haberberger**, for being a great Teammate, in our platoons and out.

To **Jon Dubin**, my brother in arms. Thank you for what you do at the FBI and for including me in Lanai. Amazing!

To **Pat McNamara**, for your service, drive, energy, and expertise.

To **Jocko Willink**, for two incredible pre-deployment unit level training cycles.

To **Josh and Audrey Waldron**, for your early book review, great feedback, and friendship.

To **Daniel and Karen Winkler**, for your kindness, exceptional craftsmanship, and dedication to those at the tip of the spear. Your influence goes far beyond the blades.

To **Angus McQueen**, **Revan McQueen**, **Katie McQueen**, **Tony Makris**, **Melanie Hill**, **Lacey Duffy**, **Carl Warner**, **Eric Van Horn**, and

Hayley Holmes. It has been an eventful year. Thank you for your support.

To **Keith Walawender**, **Mike Biller**, **Matt Coufalik**, **Wally McLallen**, and **Nick Pontikes** at **Tomahawk Strategic Solutions**. You have put together an incredible team!

To **Dr. Rob Bray**, surgeon extraordinaire, mentor, friend, and patriot. The country owes you a debt of gratitude, though I doubt your contributions will ever be declassified. Thank you for your guidance and support throughout the transition from Naval service. We think about your generosity every day—and thank you for a steady hand during my spine surgery.

To **Rick and Esther Rosenfield**, words can't describe my feelings for you both—thank you for adopting me and my entire family—we couldn't do this without you.

To **Nick and Tina Cousoulis**, for your love story.

To **Clint and Heidi Smith** at **Thunder Ranch**, for your support in all aspects of life and for always saying yes even before you know the question.

To **James Jarrett**, for teaching me to think logically while staying devoted to my principles, a debt I will never be able to repay. Thank you for your service and sacrifice to the country in the jungles of Vietnam and for paving the way for the current generation of special operations warriors. I am humbled and honored by your continued mentorship and guidance.

To **Jim and Nancy Demetriades**, for your brilliance, example, and kindness.

To **Ross Perot**, for what you do without recognition behind the scenes for our military and their families, and for what you did for mine.

To **Wayne LaPierre**, for your steadfast leadership in the face of unimaginable pressures. Thank you for standing strong and fighting for all of us. And to **Pete Brownell**, **Richard Childress**, **Woody Phillips**, **Millie Hallow**, **Wayne Sheets**, **Scott Christman**, **Andrew Arulanandam**, **Joe Debergalis**, **Doug Hamlin**, **Jim Kohlmeyer**, **Amy Hunter**, **Chris Dewitt**, **Lisa Supernaugh**, **Deb Sargol**, and everyone at the **NRA** for standing the line and for the tireless work you do in behalf of all Americans day in and day out. Thank you for fighting for our rights, and for giving those who fought for it a free country to come home to.

To **Josh Powell**, for your vision and determination.

To **James Yeager**, for your attitude, and for your early and enthusiastic support.

To **Shane Mahoney**, for your eloquence and passion in defense of wild places and the animals that inhabit them.

To **Jeff Crane**, **Phil Hoon**, **PJ Carleton**, and

the staff at the **Congressional Sportsman's Foundation**, for always including me—it's my turn to help now.

To **Hugh Wiley, Larry Keane**, and everyone at the **National Shooting Sports Foundation**, for your leadership and for putting on SHOT Show, an event with no equal.

To **Mac Minard** at **Montana Guides and Outfitters Association Big Hearts Under the Big Sky** program, for all you do for veterans and their families.

To the staff at the **Department of Defense Office of Prepublication and Review**— you have a thankless task but your efforts are appreciated.

To **Larry Ellison**, for your inspiration, for showing us what is possible, always making us feel welcome and for reintroducing us to tennis and sailing—I still think George Marshall is the most influential General of the twentieth century, by the way.

To the Chicago Crew of **Jimmy and Pam Linn, Danny Wolff**, and **Shelly Sorosky**—I am looking forward to our next linkup.

To **Jimmy Spithill**, for reading an early version of the book and going through the sailing chapter—I hope I didn't butcher it too bad.

To **Jonny Sanchez**, for sitting next to Brad at that fundraiser.

To **Scott Grimes**, for your example and

friendship—my next book just might have that real estate protagonist.

To **Greg Garrison**, for loaning me your car . . . for a year.

To the **Coronado Book and Beer Club**, we may have finally found a book everyone will read.

To **Becky Stein**, for your early read of the prologue and for wanting to read more.

To **D'Arcy Echols**, for taking the time to read the book—you make one heck of a rifle.

To **Roman Tsunder** and **Terry Hardy**—thank you for **PTTOW**! You have created something truly special.

To **Ben Bosanac**, for your insights and support.

To **Jon Hart**, not many people can say they changed an industry. Well done, my friend. And to **John Barklow** at **Sitka Gear**. Thank you for your time in uniform and for spending all those years on Kodiak refining your skills and passing them on to the next generation of Frogmen. There are few, if any, better in the woods.

To **Tim Fallon**, **Chip Beaman**, **Doug Prichard**, **Dave Knesek**, and the instructors at **FTW Ranch**—I wish I'd had your levels of skill when I was behind the glass in Iraq.

To **Craig Flynn**, even though I am not sure you actually read the book. Thank you for your unwavering support and loyalty.

To **Razor and Sylvia Dobbs**, for opening your home and hearts to our family.

To everyone who read early copies of the manuscript and provided valuable feedback: **Billy Birdzell, Spencer Bray, Mike Schoby, Ryan Rich, Jed Davis, Ross Seyfried, Ron Jensen, Brian Rosen, Melissa Petro, Alan Must**, and both **Jeff Johnstons**. To **Christopher Ball**, for your aviation expertise. To **Dr. Montoya, Dr. Bucolo**, and **Dr. Smalley**, for helping us unravel the intricacies of beta-blockers and brain tumors. To **Will Searcy**, for your expertise in all things postmortem.

To **Steve Magennis**, for your extremely helpful update on Afghanistan and to all those that provided expertise in aviation, seamanship, communications, explosives, and ballistics. All errors are mine alone.

To **Derek Anderson** and **Pete Osyf** at **Winston and Strawn** for shepherding me through the DOD review process, and **Brad Bondi, Brock Bosson, Michael Wheatley**, and **Danny Stemp** at **Cahill Gordon and Reindel**, for your support on the business side of things.

To **Evan West, Sean Parnell**, and the **Branding Freedom** team for your creativity and expertise in what was completely uncharted territory. Thank you.

To **Michael Davidson, Adnan Kifayat**, and the entire **Gen Next** team, you are doing amazing things for the future of our country—count me in! Your leadership and expertise in countering violent extremism is inspiring. Big problems require bold leadership and innovative solutions, so I encourage readers to learn more about the Gen Next Foundation. Their global security portfolio includes the Against Violent Extremism network—the first and only network of former violent extremists to thwart recruitment and radicalization—and the Redirect Method—an anti-extremist advertising campaign that redirects individuals to compelling counter-narrative content. Together, they are the only private sector led solutions to combat the ideology of violent extremism. I support the organization and encourage others to get involved as well, because our security depends on innovation and leadership.

To those at the **SEAL Family Foundation**, **Special Forces Charitable Trust**, **All Eagles Oscar**, **The National Ability Center**, **Special Operations Warrior Foundation**, **The Honor Foundation**, and all organizations working tirelessly in support of our warriors and their families. To **The Brain Treatment Center**, for their commitment and assistance treating war fighters struggling with Posttraumatic Stress Disorder after serving in the longest sustained combat operations in our nation's history. And to those at **Valor for Life** and **DISC Sport and Spine Center**, for providing veterans with no-cost surgical spine care and best practices in the treatment of PTSD.

To **David** and **Nancy**, for raising such an amazing daughter.

To my mom, **Caroline**, for reading what I know is not "her type of book" but suffering through it and providing incredible feedback—thank you for introducing me to a lifelong love of reading—your days of correcting my papers apparently did not end when I left for college. To my dad, **George**, for reading what is most definitely "his kind of book" and guiding me through the waters around Fishers. To my brother, **Roger**, a professor of music composition, for helping with the music selection, and my sister, **Emily**, and her husband, **Scott**, for their encouragement after reading an early version of the prologue.

To **Brigadier General and Mrs. Kenneth Strong**, in whose **Hill House** this book was written and to whom I will always be indebted.

To **Emily Wood**, for putting up with this venture and opening your home to me. Thank you.

Most of all, for my beautiful wife, **Faith**—thank you for believing in me. I am more in awe of you each and every day. And to our three children—thank you for showing me what is truly important.

And finally, to the other half of this writing

team, **Keith Wood**—without you I'd still be pecking away at the keyboard, trying to figure out how to start the book. Your skill with the written word brought this story to life. I hope I carried my share of the ruck. Here's to many more.

Center Point Large Print
600 Brooks Road / PO Box 1
Thorndike, ME 04986-0001 USA

(207) 568-3717

US & Canada:
1 800 929-9108
www.centerpointlargeprint.com